THE HOUSE OF TRYSTS

LUCY WHITE

'Oh what a tangled web we weave, when first we practice to deceive'
Sir Walter Scott.

1

To my husband Steve for his love and support.

Acknowledgements

Thank you to Nicola Mohan for her editorial skills and helping me find the character of Laura.
Thank you to Samuel Clerk, my grandson, for helping me get the text ready for publication.

CHAPTER 1

She was determined to get him into bed after dinner. It had become an overwhelming need to return to the intimacy they once had but first she had to persuade the client, a pernickety Italian woman, to accept the interior design lay-out she had put many hours into getting right.

Twice before she had failed to entice him. The first time they had been interrupted by a work phone call. He had then left immediately to return to the office. The second time he couldn't get it up. She was determined to make this time, 'third time lucky.'

Laura furtively glanced at her watch as the wretched woman changed her mind yet again and said she would have to consult her friend Paolo, an Italian designer with international experience who had great taste. Laura hated him immediately. She resisted swiping Signora Pernickety's imperfectly botoxed face with the upholstery swatch book and sighed audibly, covering the obvious annoyance with a cough. They wrapped up their meeting without conclusion. Some clients gave her the pip and this type of woman, with her over-blinged fingers and gold fob chain round her scrawny neck, was the worst. On the drive home she fantasized about grabbing that chain and throttling the bitch. Oops- Watch it Laura –You just ran a red.

Laura needed a drink – Perhaps two or four. Drinks – She knew she should cut back, but why when the pleasures in life were slowly diminishing? Life seemed so much more bearable through the bottom of a wine glass. It made her stroppy – the drink. On more than one occasion she had berated her husband in front of friends. It was as if the alcohol plus company gave her permission to let rip over her husband's irritating habits.

Last time it had been something quite trivial – The way he always re-stacked the dishwasher after she had filled it.

She made a mental note to watch her alcoholic intake tonight but that didn't stop her filling a glass, the smallest wine glass, of her favorite New Zealand Sauvignon as she raced upstairs to change. After chucking a pile of rejects in the corner she chose a short black skirt and low-cut cream silk blouse. She wished Jules was here to give an opinion. Juliet: - her daughter, just turned sixteen and now away at boarding school.

This was the night that David would succumb to her charms and make passionate love to her. David, her husband of eighteen years.

They had met at a party in Bristol where she was at Art School and he was in his final year of an engineering degree at Bristol University and learning on the job at his father's building company. He had come into the room with a willowy Indian girl with shiny black hair that fell half way down her back. Laura noticed him straight away. He stood tall and rangy with thick fair hair that stood up on end. Laura was aware that he kept trying to tame it by sweeping it back away from his face. When they were introduced, his amused grey eyes had held her gaze for a little longer than necessary and as he took her small hand in his large one, her eyes travelled to his wide sensual mouth, and noted his lopsided smile. She was smitten. She thought about him a lot during the month after they met and then he had rung up out of the blue and asked her to a student dance. Fancy dress. Tarts and Vicars.

Later that night the tart and vicar had become one. They were inseparable after that and got married after Laura had finished her degree.

Their love life had been fantastic in the early years of their marriage, but after Juliet was born, two years after they were married, they had tried for over seven years for another baby. She had miscarried once then nothing. Juliet was now away at boarding school. Early on Laura had tried to talk to David about seeing a specialist - they had a blazing row about it - but he firmly said 'no' to that. She had been thoroughly checked out and had passed all the tests. She had also suggested counselling to talk through possibilities of in vitro fertilization but David seeing himself as a virile type reckoned they should be able to succeed through the normal channel. Every time she brought the subject up he had switched off and left her seething in frustration.

She had been tempted to have an affair a few years back. An older guy with 'come to bed' eyes had come on to her at a work function – a landscape architect with a good body and a balding head. They had met twice at a discreet bar and the second time had engaged in a teenage fumble in the back of his Peugeot. She got cold feet at the critical moment, yanked up her knickers and bailed out.

In the last year she and David had got it on only once. His desire for her had cruelly diminished. Nothing was said but the distancing had begun. She felt ugly and a complete failure. She couldn't bear to think about the possibility of failing again. She knew also there was a still a small possibility of getting pregnant at 39 but she decided to keep any baby hopes very much to herself. The unbearable yearning that overcame her when watching a young mother cradle her baby, tenderly adjusting the soft blanket and kissing the little pink cheek, had receded into a dull ache. If only ….

They decided to go to the gastro pub just outside Kingbridge for the Friday night dinner. They both enjoyed the upbeat atmosphere and quality food at a reasonable price. David had just landed a prestigious and lucrative renovation job on the large London home of a wealthy Indian entrepreneur. The Manning Renovation Company was on its way up. The company was run by David and his brother Peter, with Peter's wife Cindy manning the phones and running the office. Along with Laura's interior design ability they made a formidable team.

Even though they were enjoying a delicious bottle of French Merlot with their Boeuf Bourguignon, Laura kept an eye on the number of glasses consumed. She told him about Signora Pernickety and he told her not to worry – The stupid woman wasn't worth it. They spent a lot of time laughing over stories relating to past customers of The Manning Renovation Company.

"Do you remember the cat lady?" Laura said.

"Gawd yes. Cats from pillar to post, getting under our feet and the smell."

"..And she told you not to make too much noise as loud noises upset them and they would go bonkers".
David gave a hearty laugh. "And she was already bonkers".

David reached across the table and took her hand, his grey eyes focusing intently on her blue ones and he said how lovely she looked and then followed on,

"Thank you".
She gave him a quizzical look but he had not been forthcoming as to what the 'thank you' had meant.

After the meal they had coffee to finish and Laura went to refresh her lipstick. She unbuttoned the top of her silk blouse and returned for her jacket. Arm in arm they left the pub, Laura over-balancing slightly on her nude heels. David put an arm round her waist and she leant into him inhaling his lemony cologne. They had entered the house through the garage and Laura had kicked off her shoes. She took his hand and drew him into the sitting room and throwing her arms round his neck,

"Thank you darling for a lovely dinner..." And whispering in his ear,

"I want you to fuck me right here and now".

Then she kissed him full on the mouth. She could feel him pull away from her and disengaging her arms he put his hands on her shoulders. He spoke softly.

"Sweetheart I've got to finish the paperwork for Mr. Gupta. We have a meeting tomorrow morning. Now you go on up...I've got about an hour's work."

He hugged her and kissed her chastely on the cheek. Giving her a fleeting glance he quickly turned on his heel and went into the study closing the door behind him.

Laura stared at the study door for some time, her arms hanging limply at her sides as she let her bag drop to the floor. She knew then that the moment was lost. It had been going so well. Had she said something to change the mood? She began to think the unthinkable that he was seeing someone else; that must be the reason he had rejected her yet again. Perhaps he was texting her now or sending an email telling said lover about the dinner. Oh God, was there someone else to whom he was giving intimate details of their marriage? Who was she? A work colleague? Cindy would have alerted her to that. Someone he had met on the internet? Yes that would be more likely. So many desperate women out there looking for love. Her mind snapped to attention. Jesus!

8

That's me.

At that moment Laura decided to have it out with him. She took a deep breath and in one movement flung open the study door. David was head down over the computer. He looked up quickly when she came in and with one hand promptly shut down the web page he was looking at while the other hand appeared to brush away something in his lap.

Laura was distraught and so intent on challenging him that she did not take in the clues set before her.

"There's someone else isn't there."

For a moment he just stared at her, then, "What?"

Laura raised her voice. "You've got another woman".

"What are you talking about?"

"You're having an affair, aren't you?"

She had begun to shake with rage and the tears were about to fall.

"Of course I'm not. What on earth made you say that?"

Laura spat out the words. "If you're not fucking me then who the hell are you fucking?"

After what seemed like an eternity, "Go to bed Laura".

Laura exploded and grabbed the nearest object which happened to be a gilt framed photo of David in cricket whites and hurled it at David's head. He ducked quickly and the photo hit the desk and shattered in pieces. In two strides he was holding her to him. She struggled against him pummeling his chest in the process all the while screaming with frustration. He tried to calm her down.

"Darling …please...I'm sorry about tonight. Please calm down".

He whispered in her ear, "There isn't anyone else. Only you".

As she slumped against him, he pushed the hair back from her tearful face, kissed her mouth gently. "You're exhausted. Go to bed and we will talk in the morning".

Defeated she dropped her head and without looking at him left the room. She dragged her feet up the stairs and sat on their bed for what seemed an age, her eyes staring at her lap. She undressed and throwing her clothes in a corner, she looked at her naked body in the full length mirror. Did her body disgust him that much? She ran her hands over the smooth skin on her rounded breasts and over her flat belly. She twisted round to look at her backside and ran her palms over her buttocks. Was her arse too big? She touched her face and placed her fingers on the corners of her eyes. Yes there were some tiny wrinkles. Perhaps he saw these and thought she was too old. Did he think she was too old for sex? She put on her night T shirt and lay rigid in the marital bed. She was determined to stay awake and wait for him to get in to bed next to her so they could discuss what had happened, or in her case not happened, but around midnight she couldn't keep her eyes open any longer and fell into a fitful sleep.

In the early hours of the morning Laura found herself hugging her pillow and silently weeping while David snored gently alongside her. He arose an hour earlier than usual and went to work without saying a word. Later when she was having a soothing cup of tea and trying to alleviate a headache, she received a text from her daughter Juliet away at boarding school.

> *Hi Mum, Hope you had a good dinner with Dad. Good News I came top in my Math test and I am thru to the final! of the inter-house tennis singles comp. Not sure date of final but will let you and dad know asap. See you soon. Luv you heaps. Juliet. xx*

Hugging the phone to her chest, she bowed her head,

her long fair hair covering her face as the tears fell anew.

Later in the kitchen while chewing a piece of toast and looking out at the garden, she could see that the runner beans in the little vegetable garden along the border fence were covered in red flowers heralding a good crop of green beans and the spinach plot was coming along nicely. She tried to focus her mind on the garden and what needed doing there but her thoughts kept turning to the debacle of the night before.

In the past when she fretted over work problems, walking and running had helped calm her down. She fought the idea of opening a bottle of wine and glugging it back under the bed covers. What happened last night was a major setback and it was going to take more than healthy exercise to sort out her mental state, but for the moment getting her body moving seemed like good start. She tried not to dwell on the humiliation she was feeling. In fact it was more than humiliation, it was grief that his desire for her had died. She felt totally worthless. She forced herself to dress and go out.

Laura put on her running shoes and set off at a brisk pace round the village. It was early summer in Kingbridge and a favorite time of year for Laura. Running round the village she loved to see the cottage gardens beginning to burst into bloom, the oak trees round the village green were budding beautifully and the apple trees were a mass of pink and white flowers. The wisteria along the vicarage wall was covered in drooping lilac colored flowers, their aroma pervading the soft air.

Laura had set up her painting studio in the small room off the kitchen. It doubled as a spare bedroom for extra guests but most of the time was used as Laura's lair. Facing south east, the room had good light and a pleasant outlook. It looked out onto the back garden of their nineteenth century cottage that she and David had

11

renovated many years back. While she was painting she could enjoy watching the birds having their daily bath in the ceramic pedestal birdbath that she had placed in the back garden. She was working on an abstract painting in sea colors to entice a possible buyer for the latest Manning Company's renovation.

She and David had seen the cottage on one of their country outings away from the pokey London flat that they rented in South London. It had been a rare English summer that year; very hot, days of cerulean skies and temperatures soaring into the 80's. Fed up with stuffy London and fighting the tourist crowds, they were both longing for the open countryside. On Sundays they enjoyed traveling along the winding country roads looking out at the high flowering hedges and meandering through picturesque villages occasionally stopping to check out a village church. It was their dream to buy a cottage in a village not too far from London. On one of their trips into Surrey, they decided to take a detour off the main road and found by chance the village of Kingbridge. Immediately taken with the quaint village green they had stopped for a drink at the local pub- The Bell- and then strolled round the village lanes. Passing the Old Vicarage, they had turned a corner and there it was - Pippin Cottage - built of old rosy bricks with a pleasing symmetrical front and surrounded by an overgrown lawn. The flower beds by the front entrance were infested with weeds although Laura to her delight noted some old roses peeping through.

There was a prominent 'For Sale' sign in front of the house. It was love at first sight. They went immediately to the Estate Agent's office and set up a time to view. They both knew it was exactly what they were looking for. They put in an offer and were accepted. The Mannings learned that an elderly gentleman had lived there for most of his life but as he was no longer able to care for himself, his daughter had moved him to a rest home nearby. She had no interest in keeping the cottage and had put it on the market. The name 'Pippin' came from the old apple tree in the overgrown back garden.

As the old man had not done anything to the interior in 25 years except half-heartedly mend the odd window frame and patch the roof, the new purchase needed a complete face-lift inside and out. Afterwards David thought that perhaps they had been too hasty in buying the property without checking the damp course and the timbers for dry rot but his hunch that this house was meant to be for them proved to be without any major setback and with his engineering experience and his brother Peter's expertise as a jack of all trades, the cottage came under the wing of The Manning Renovation company.

David and his younger brother Peter had formed their renovation company eight years back to take advantage of the opportunities in run-down areas round London.

Peter had the practical building experience, learnt from their father and David took care of the engineering work and also ran the business, buying and selling property as well as the marketing side. Peter's wife Cindy was employed to run the office and help with the accounts. Laura was in charge of the interior design and sourcing materials for the interiors. Having had an Art School training she also designed and created paintings which were used to dress and sell each property. She made a modest profit from the occasional sale of her paintings. Although the renovation business was ticking along nicely, Peter was constantly trying to reign in David's quest for "The Big Deal". The new client, an Indian entrepreneur Mr. Ravi Gupta, was a huge coup for the company.

Cindy, Laura's 33 year old sister-in-law, was an energetic upbeat friend to Laura and her well-organized positive manner kept the Manning clients on an even keel. Cindy was envious of Laura's slim build and was forever struggling to lose some weight. In contrast, the men loved Cindy's buxom figure, green eyes and dark auburn hair and she had been propositioned more than once. Peter far from being jealous was proud of his lovely wife and showed his love for her openly in public. Laura envied Peter and Cindy's passionate relationship. They were constantly affectionate toward one another, so much so that David had said,

"Leave it out guys. Too much P.D A. We've got work to do".

When Cindy told her what David had said, Laura had resolved to put into place her strategy for the date night.

Laura waved to Mr. Pelham, the pub landlord as she passed The Bell. He was taking a delivery of soft drinks and gave her a salute. Her mind was churning over. There must be someone else; what other explanation was there?

She thought of telling Cindy about her row with David. They were good mates. She would have loved to have confided in Cindy and spilled the beans on their barren sex life but Cindy was a terrible tell-tale and her sister-in-law's sex life, or more pointedly 'lack of' would be all round the village in no time. Cindy never seemed to be fazed by any disaster. With her bubbly personality she was blissfully happy in all aspects of her life. She adored Peter and he was besotted with her. She confided in Laura that she and Peter were trying for a baby and seemed surprised when Laura's response did not elicit the same level of excitement that Cindy was experiencing.

Cindy had a kind heart and felt compelled to help

14

others. She was always dashing about assisting some old lady with her shopping, babysitting a neighbor's baby or driving someone to a doctor's appointment. In Cindy's eyes, Laura would need to be helped and she would be the one to sort out the problem. Laura envisioned Cindy at her computer doing all kinds of internet research on how to seduce your man, even to the point of putting information in front of David. Laura dismissed this excruciatingly embarrassing scene in her mind's eye and wisely re-affirmed to herself to keep silent on the sex issue.

The new client Mr. Ravi Gupta who, although based in Mumbai, travelled frequently to London for business interests. He owned property all around the world and his London pad- a three story Regency house, was in London's Belgravia.

The Manning Renovation Company was just about to start on the job, the quote having been accepted much to Peter's astonishment as David had inflated the costs even more than usual. In fact they had had a heated discussion about it.

Peter had come storming in to the office.

"I've just seen the figures...What are you doing David? You can't possibly justify charging this client these kind of fees. This is a huge job. He's no fool either...we'll lose him to someone else."

David had retorted. "Look at his portfolio...the guy's almost as wealthy as Donald Trump. He'll pay."

"God David are you mental? He chose us for 3 reasons. We have a good name which I would like to retain, our standard of workmanship is exceptional, we make every effort to finish the work on time AND we do not charge like a wounded bull...."

In the end David had agreed to revise the figures just a little and Peter had held his breath until the green light

15

was given in the form of an acceptance letter and deposit.

The corpulent Mr. Ravi Gupta liked people and he absolutely loved to give parties so just as the job was about to start and before the inside of his property was demolished, his entertainment secretary had sent The Manning Renovation Company a fancy printed invitation edged in gold leaf inviting all Manning management and staff to a cocktail party. Dress Formal. Music and entertainment. He had invited all the people concerned with the upcoming refurbishment of his London pad as well as a black book full of business associates and a few names from the film and television industry. For good measure, he had added a stable full of models and escorts to spice up the proceedings. Mr. Gupta was a man of many appetites and he especially like girls with auburn hair and fuller figures.

Laura and Cindy agonized over what to wear and decided to go up to London to see if they could find something in one of the sales in Oxford Street. They found success at Selfridges. Laura bought a sale price short black designer dress in lace and Cindy, getting into the Indian theme, bought a deep cobalt blue flowing Salwar Kameez with a sequined top and matching trousers which she was delighted to see covered a multitude of lumps.
Laura approved.

"Color's lovely with your auburn locks".

Cindy then said, "Now we've got to have some new heels to go with our outfits."

The girls wandered around the shoe shops giggling as they tried on ridiculous "fuck me" style shoes. In the end they both purchased elegant strappy sandals, gold for Cindy and black with a diamante trim for Laura.

"You've got great legs Laura. Not like mine. Cankles

never did look good in anything but trousers or a Burqa!"

The Manning quartet had decided to drive up to London and leave the car somewhere away from strict parking regulations and take a taxi to the event. David's hope was to network, meeting and greeting Mr. Gupta's well-heeled friends and business acquaintances and he planned to give his business cards discreetly to some of the more wealthy people at the party.

It was decided that Cindy would be the sober driver on the journey home. She was a light drinker at the best of times and having calculated her ovarian cycle, knew she had a good chance of getting pregnant that night. She made a mental note to keep an eye Peter's alcoholic intake in order to avert any possibility of brewer's droop later in the proceedings.

Mr. Gupta's mansion was ablaze with lights; they could hear laughter and jazz coming from the open windows. The front door was open and a young Indian man in a crisp white uniform bowed to greet them and took the girls' coats. He then ushered them into an enormous entrance hall from which a majestic staircase rose up to the mezzanine floor where a minstrels' gallery was in evidence. Perched high above the arriving guests, a jazz quartet was playing. The girls noted the shabby paintwork and stained ceiling but the Persian carpets and French gilded furniture impressed. Laura pointed out to Cindy the beautiful gilded Indian chandeliers and bronze statues and expensive wall hangings. David and Peter having seen the house before, marveled at the architecture and mentally rubbed their hands together at the thought of getting it restored to its former glory. They helped themselves to a glass of Krug from an attendant and as they turned to join the throng, an accented voice was heard.

"Mr. Manning...David..."

They all turned to the staircase to witness a short rotund Indian gentleman with his arm raised, his ringed fingers glittering in the light. He was dressed in a traditional Kurta, the black silk straining a little round his well-filled stomach.

"Welcome...Welcome...Mr. Ravi Gupta at your service", and he gave a little bow.

"Please call me Rav".

Laura estimated him to be in his forties.

David introduced Laura and Peter and then turned to Cindy.

Mr. Gupta was already holding Cindy's hand and gazing with deep intention into her startled green eyes. Having no concept of personal space, he had stepped in and being a few centimeters shorter than Cindy, had his nose a millimeter away from the top of Cindy's ample breasts. She stepped backwards and still holding her hand, Rav kissed the back of it.

"My dear. It is an absolute pleasure to make your acquaintance. What is your name?"

Peter quickly responded, underlining the words "my wife":

"This is my wife, Cindy".

"A beautiful name and how lovely you look in our traditional costume" .

Ignoring the trio, he took the arm of astonished Cindy.

"Come, I must show you the house".

With a wave of his ringed hand he swept Cindy away, leaving the Manning trio, with open mouths, wondering what had just happened.

David laughed. "Looks like Cindy has made a conquest. Do you think we will ever see her again?"

Peter was staring after them. "What on earth do you

18

mean?"

"Just kidding. It's great that Mr. Gupta fancies Cindy. It'll make our job easier. He won't query all the accounts we send him".

"Don't you be so sure. Indian people never pay full price for anything. They're always after a deal. Not to be trusted either. I'd better follow them and see where Mr. Ravi Gupta is taking my wife."

In the past Peter would have been pleased with regard to the attention paid to Cindy but this Indian guy had emphatically swept her away. Peter saw them go up to the next floor. Where on earth were they going? He said a few words to Laura and set off upstairs. David laughed.

"Hope Pete gets there before Rav has her spread-eagled on the master bed...Anyway I'm off to meet and greet."

Without a word to Laura, David turned on his heel and pushed his way into the crowd. Doesn't want to take me with him she though; she was dismissed. Well she was not going to be a droopy wallflower. She refilled her champagne glass and began to do a tour of the reception rooms all the while looking around for a friendly face to engage with.

Cindy frantically looking back for Peter tried hard to free herself from Rav's grasp as he continued his impassioned upstairs tour. He had taken her almost immediately into his own private suite of rooms which included a sitting room full of Persian carpets and a bathroom which he said that The Manning company were going to do up in Italian marble. Then he took great pride in showing her his bedroom with wall to wall cupboards. He drew her over to the super king bed complete with sumptuous jade and cream silk covers and a clutch of ornate cushions.

"Shall we sit?" He said, trying to move her close to the bed.

Thinking quickly of a way of escaping from the situation, she said incomprehensibly,

"Oh No...No I can't...I'm allergic to cushions...I mean feathers. I'll sneeze the house down!"

He laughed. "How delightful you are Cindy, come let us continue."

The tour took them to five more bedrooms and Rav, still holding her tightly, enthused volubly, pointing out all the improvements he was going to make. Cindy's mind was in turmoil. How was she going to escape his clutches? Interrupting his flow of words,

"Your wife must be thrilled to be involved with such a beautiful house and I am sure she must have some great ideas about redecorating".

"My wife?" He laughed.

Pulling her a little closer so that she could smell his garlic breath upon her neck, he whispered,

"Which one?"

Then looking at her shocked reaction, "I'm joking Cindy. My wife is in Mumbai with her mother". And he rolled his eyes heavenwards.

His response told her that this escape route was blocked.

"Now come and look at these lovely guest quarters. Every bedroom will have its own ensuite, my dear. Perhaps you would like to help me make some decisions with regard to female needs...in the bathroom?"

He looked at her pointedly.

Cindy trying frantically to think of a way to remove herself without punching him in the stomach or somewhere more intimate heard the words' female needs and bathroom' and blurted out,

"Rav, thank you so much. I must go to the toilet...

NOW".

She wrenched her arm away and raced off down the corridor. Peter came careering round the upper landing and they cannoned into each other.

"Cindy! Are you alright?"

Out of breath she nodded. "I need a drink. Take me to a champagne station".

Arm and arm they descended the stairs, Peter occasionally laughing as Cindy told him all about Rav's campaign to lure her into his love nest. They reached the hallway and Peter became serious,

"If he so much as touches you again I'll punch him so hard that he'll be spraying those gold teeth all over his fucking Persian carpets".

Cindy cuddled up to him. She felt sure that tonight was the night they were going to make a baby.

David had introduced himself to two or three possible business contacts and then handed out his card to them. They seemed interested but he knew that in the main people would tuck the card away and forget about it. He hoped that Mr. Gupta would throw another party after the completion of the renovation so that his work could be displayed and he could take full advantage of a job well done. He felt sure that enquiries would flood in. He wandered over to refill his drink and suddenly realized he was alongside a willowy Indian girl with a model's figure. She gave him a doe-eyed look and smiled sweetly. She was almost as tall as David with long wavy hair and warm brown eyes. She was dressed in a mid-thigh gold sequined sheath dress, low cut over her boobs and adhering like a limpet to her perfectly curved rear. She stood alongside David on impossibly high heels and his eyes fixated on the neckline of her dress. She said "Hello".

Taken aback by this vision of Asian loveliness he

staggered slightly against the drinks table and toppled a glass of champagne. God what an idiot.

"Oh …er...well… hello".

During their conversation he fought the urge to run his finger along the tops of the beautiful caramel colored breasts in front of him. He learnt that she was a friend of Rav's. She was a model but worked occasionally at a "Private House" in Chelsea. David did not immediately comprehend what she was telling him and chattered on inanely about the business, his wife and then blurted out,

"Do you like cricket?"

She laughed and gave him a beaming smile but was then ushered away to meet some other people. He mentally kicked himself for being so gauche and he hadn't even found out her name.

Laura and Cindy were deep in conversation. Cindy was having a restorative glass of champagne and was regaling Laura about her escapade upstairs.

"Honestly Laura, the guy practically forced me onto his bed and then I told him I was allergic to cushions".

Laura laughed. "What?"

"Feathers… in the cushions. But he would not take 'no' for an answer and dragged me through another eight bedrooms. What a nightmare. I nearly kneed him in the balls but I thought that might turn the Manning company contract into a train wreck".

"Poor Cindy. Let's get you out of here. I'll round up the men."

Cindy laid a hand on Laura's arm ."Do you think he was like that because I'm ovulating? Perhaps he could smell me!"

"Smell you? …Jesus …you're not a mare in heat."

"Well I want Pete to be the stallion tonight. Wouldn't it have been awful if Rav had got in there first? He practically raped me!"

"A lucky escape."

The guests started to leave. The Manning quartet looked around for their host but he was not in evidence. In light of what had happened to Cindy they agreed to slip away.

David caught the Indian beauty's eye, she smiled and gave an imperceptible sideways nod toward the terrace. David turned to the others.

"I'd better just find Rav to say goodbye. See you outside".

He extracted himself and went out through the sliding door to the terrace. The girl was standing with her back to him and as he approached, she turned and in one movement slid past him, brushing her breast against his jacket, she slipped a white card into his jacket pocket.

Cindy drove sedately on the way home and would not stop talking about her grapple with Rav. Peter became annoyed and told her to pipe down and in any case, if anything should ever happen again, he would give Rav a bunch of fives.

David said that it might be a good idea to leave any punching until after Rav had paid his final bill.

Alone in his study later that night David took out the card and read-

Casa Blanca where dreams become reality.
Let us serve you discreetly.
Your fantasy is our command.

A phone number was written underneath.

He tucked the card between two building manuals and turned on his computer and went to his favorite website. "Sultry Sex Goddesses from India – How to get the best from The Kama Sutra". He scrolled through to lesson five- The Double Decker Bus.

CHAPTER 2

A few days later it was Laura's day to travel to London to source materials for the company and art products and for her painting business. Cindy phoned in the morning brimming with excitement.

"After the party, Peter was like a man possessed".

"You mean Ravi turned the enraged Peter into a rutting stag?"

"He ravaged me all night. It was fantastic. This is it Laura. I must be pregnant".

Laura laughed. She hoped the ravaging was successful and she said she would keep her fingers crossed for some good news. She then cut short the conversation by pleading lack of time to chat. Laura hung up. She contemplated the word 'ravage'. It was a good description of a vigorous fuck and an activity that she hadn't experienced in a long time. So long in fact that she felt sure spiders were spinning an impenetrable web across her tunnel of love.

She decided to go via Fulham and then to the Chelsea Design Centre at Imperial Wharf. She spent a design filled day there and managed to collect some good ideas and samples. Laden with material swatches she jumped on the tube at Imperial wharf and headed up to Sloane Square where she wanted to check out The Chelsea Artefact Wholesalers in Kings Road before heading home. A successful half hour visit later and now laden with more packages she started walking quickly back towards the tube stop. Ahead of her she could see an older lady walking a large belligerent looking dog. As they approached each other, the dog turned suddenly let out a loud bark and twisting the lead round his owner's ankles set off at a lumbering pace in pursuit of a cat. The lady's legs ankles locked together and still gripping the dog's lead she fell sideways onto the pavement in front of Laura. The lady let out a bellow,

"Fuck! Dandi you bastard. You'll be the death of me".

Laura rushed over to her. "Oh dear are you alright? Let me help you up. Oh you've gashed your leg. Come and sit over here".

Dumping her parcels, she helped the lady to sit on the front step of the nearest terraced house.

"Thank you so much my dear. I don't usually swear…you understand...but Dandelion…or Dandi as I call him can be a confounded nuisance…and a liability where cats are concerned".

Dandi was sitting quietly next to his owner with a detached look on his face as if nothing had happened and certainly nothing to do with him. Laura glanced at him nervously and thinking what an ugly brute,

"He seems quite calm now. He's a British Bull dog isn't he?"

The lady nodded and holding her wrist,

"Look what the litle bugger has done to my stockings. Shredded!"

Blood was starting to ooze from a long graze on the lady's leg. Laura took a tissue from her bag and mopped the wound then concerned for her welfare,

"Are you in pain? Have you broken anything? Your wrist?"

"No I don't think so, just a sore wrist and gashed leg".

"Do you live nearby? Perhaps I could help you home and get you cleaned up".

"That's very kind. I do feel a bit shaky and I live just round the corner…32 Davenport Gardens. My house is called Casa Blanca."

25

Putting out her hand to Laura, she continued,

"My name is Lady Pamela Spencer-Brown …You must come in and have a cup of tea. What's your name dear? ".

Laura introduced herself and helped the lady up then firmly clutching Dandelion's lead the trio hobbled slowly to Lady Pamela's front door. They ascended the front steps and Lady Pamela said,

"Just ring the buzzer, Tanice will answer".

She pointed to the name "Casa Blanca" on the intercom.

Laura pressed the buzzer and an accented voice answered,

"What is password?"

Laura looked enquiringly at Lady Pamela. Lady Pamela leaned in

"It's me Tanice. I've had an accident."

The voice replied, "Is dat you MadamPam?"

"Yes I have just said it's me"

"Might be someone who is pretendin'. I need password. I not allowed to let anyone in wid out password".

Lady Pamela leant into the intercom camera and bellowed,

"You can see me! For Christ's sake Tanice let me in. I've had a fall".

There was a pause and then a small voice said, "Password please".

Laura turned away in amusement. Lady Pamela screeched into the intercom.

"For fuck's sake....No I know that is not the password. It's ….Christ I can't remember... we changed it to....Humphrey Bergman".

The door clicked and Lady Pamela turned to Laura and softening her tone,

"Sorry about that but she has been taught to be extra security conscious".

The voice turned out to belong to a buxom middle-aged West Indian woman with a gap-toothed smile called Tanice. When she saw the damaged leg and heard what Dandi had done she rolled her eyes skywards,

"Lord save us. Dat dog goin' to be the death of you MadamPam".

"Thank you Tanice, we'll have tea in the main parlour please and some of those orange cupcakes."

She turned to Laura. "Come through dear. If you'll excuse me I'll just go and take off these damned stockings and clean myself up a bit. Dandi you are a disgrace. Go and sit in your basket and don't move."

Dandi with head down went and plopped down on his bed.

While Lady Pamela was out of the room, Laura had a chance to glance round at her luxurious surroundings. A titled lady no less with the most exquisite taste. She noticed the elegant Georgian Tall Boy, antique chairs, probably French and the delicately patterned silk drapes. She was admiring some 19th century miniatures when Tanice entered with the tea tray.

Laura smiled at her and noted how Tanice's dark skin contrasted strikingly with her pristine white shirt and apron.

Tanice gave Laura a gap-toothed smile and thought what a pretty young lady but far too thin. "I pour your tea. Mad...Miss?"

"Thank you. Perhaps I'll wait for Lady Pamela".

At that moment there was a loud guffaw which seemed to come from above her head and then she heard a clatter of high heels and more laughter. Tanice looked up and said wildly,

"Um...er...Visitors...Watching TV..." And she shot

27

out of the room toward the kitchen as Lady Pamela entered from a side door. Laura took a good look at her hostess and noted a tall elegant woman in her seventies with a strong chin and wide set dark eyes. Her thick hair was steel grey and bobbed to chin level. Laura hid her chewed nails as she noted the perfectly manicured hands of her hostess. She had changed into a sleek pair of dark pants and an emerald green silk blouse. She seemed younger now that she had tidied herself up and Laura could see there was no major harm done to her by the disgraced Dandi.

Lady Pamela poured them both some tea, offered Laura an orange cupcake and started to talk. It was if a talk tap had been opened, the words flowed out of her. Laura mused that the lonely old dear must have no-one to talk to. Even though she longed to get home and put her feet up, Laura settled in and nodded encouragement.

Lady Pamela was delighted to have an intelligent listening ear and she told Laura that she had been educated at Cheltenham Ladies College, a very prestigious establishment.

"Of course after that I was finished…"

Laura looked concerned. "Oh I'm sorry to hear that...what happened?"

Lady Pamela laughed. "You misunderstand me Laura. I went to Finishing School in Switzerland. That's what all well-bred young ladies did in the late fifties. We studied everything that might fit us for a union with a Peer of the realm. I was quite clever, well actually I was top of my class in French and Italian and I did well in European History and political studies. We also studied Literature, art history, bookkeeping, cordon bleu cookery and the art of decor and estate management...in case we landed a castle or two".

She laughed at the memory. "My mother was hoping

28

that I would land a Duke or at least a Knight preferably with pots of money and a huge estate. I'm afraid to say I disappointed her."

"Oh what happened?"

"I did a dreadful thing and went on the stage. My parents had me all lined up to do the London Season and felt sure I'd snare a foreign Prince. Instead I became a chorus girl for a risqué revue in Soho. They were horrified. My mother said I had disgraced the family and she wouldn't speak to me for a year, and not only that, all those well-bred young people I was mixing with dropped me like a hot scone."

"What a terrible mistake".

"Oh No dear. I had the time of my life. I was bored out of my tree with stuffy aristos and had a much better time mixing with the theatre set. Of course Les Kitty Kats, as we were called, attracted a lot of attention - we were scantily clad you understand - from all sorts of interesting people. Actually,"

She leant forward and glancing slyly at her guest spoke under her breath.

"It was there I discovered two of the best "C's" in the world. – Caviar and cunnilingus".

And as Laura's eyes widened at this crude revelation, her hostess threw back her head and roared with laughter. Unperturbed at Laura's shocked expression, she was unstoppable.

"I got three offers of marriage from three delightful but totally unsuitable men and the presents…My dear you should have seen the jewelry…I have a wonderful collection..."

At that moment there was a light knock on the door and Lady Pamela said,

"Come"

The door opened and a tall Indian girl with model

29

features and figure popped her head round the door. Seeing Laura she smiled and paused a moment,

"Just finished Lady P. I'll see you tomorrow"

"Thank you Nef".

Lady Pamela did not enlighten Laura as to who the Indian girl was and continued on with tales of her youth. In the end she did please her parents by marrying Sir Greville Spencer-Brown and bore him one son, Giles. Sadly Sir Greville was killed in a shooting accident when Giles was 19.

"It was a terrible time for Giles. He took it hard. On the positive side Greville did leave us both a fortune in his will. I'll say that for him. He was good for something in the end".

Laura deduced from that remark that she had not been deliriously happy with Sir Greville. Lady Pamela continued her life history. When her son was attending a theatre production management course in New York she went over to visit him and met an American steel magnate and married him within six months. It was a major mistake. What she hadn't bargained for were his two poisonous teenage daughters who made her life a misery.

"The less said about them the better...Lord I have been prattling on and I do want to thank you so much for assisting me and more to the point, hear about you. Are you married?"

"Yes...to David. We have one daughter who is 16 and away at Boarding School."

"And do you have any other children?"

Laura paused and then said quietly that she and David had just the one child. Lady Pamela noticed the hesitation, even a sort of sad resignation and veering her conversation away from children, she asked Laura about work.

"Do you work in London?"

"Just on the edge, near Twickenham. I help out at David's house renovation company and I'm in charge of the interior design aspects."

"How interesting. Did you have to do a training for that?"

"Yes I went to Art School initially and then I learnt on the job. I do paint from time to time, mainly abstracts that are used to dress our house renovations".

As Laura was telling Lady Pamela about Art School in Bristol and how she met David at University where he was training to be an engineer, her hostess noted her nibbled fingers and deduced that her guest was of a nervous disposition and should be treated carefully. Lady Pamela prided herself on her sensitivity. Laura continued and said that they had both graduated in their different fields of study, married and moved to the country. She added,

"Compared to your life, mine seems rather insipid".

"Insipid could be rather calming I feel".

Lady Pamela smiled and followed on, "Do you have any brothers and sisters?"

"Just one brother and he lives in New Zealand with his wife and two sons".

"And your parents dear, are they still going strong?"

"Well they got divorced when I was 30. My mother passed away two years ago from cancer and my Dad lives in Devon so I don't see him much".

Lady Pamela commiserated with her and then added, "I was extremely relieved when my mother died".

"Was she terribly ill?"

"Oh Lord No. I couldn't stand the woman and to spite me she lived 'til she was 97".

Lady Pamela was extremely frank and forthright about her past and even though Laura was not aware of it

31

at the time Lady Pamela's manner was helping her open up and share her personal history. As Laura was telling Lady Pamela about herself she realized how nice it was to talk to someone who actually listened and was interested in her story. Laura couldn't help but enjoy the old lady's company and was intrigued with her extraordinary tales of theatrical exploits. How bold to defy her parents and take to the stage. Laura wished she had the guts to do something out of the ordinary. Lady Pamela then came out with another surprising remark that Laura looked very like the poor deceased Princess Diana.

"Surely people have mentioned this to you before? You have her eyes you know and her lovely legs".

Laura felt awkward at this comparison and dismissed the comment. Lady Pamela could see that Laura was embarrassed at being given a compliment. She obviously wasn't used to receiving flattering attention and perhaps, being a diffident type of personality, she had faded into the background of her own life. Lady Pamela probed a bit more and then said,

"Are you happy Laura?"

Laura paused before replying. She took a deep breath, "Ner...NO".

Laura could feel the tears welling up and was powerless to stop them and she started to blurt out all the intimate details of her marriage. Lady Pamela became concerned and reached into her handbag for a tissue as Laura sobbed her heart out. She couldn't seem to stop herself.

In between gasps, Laura said,

"Oh dear I'm s...sorry. It's just that...I...don't...know what ...to...do. I've been so lonely and I couldn't tell anyone".

Lady Pamela moved nearer to her and took her hand.

"My dear, I'm so sorry to hear about this. Please tell me all about it, from the beginning. In fact, even though you don't know me, I feel I am your very good friend already".

Laura started to weep anew but after a little while she collected herself and told her new friend the whole sorry saga. After Laura unburdened herself, she continued,

"What you must think of me...blurting out all this stuff".

Lady Pamela took both Laura's hands and looked at her kindly.

"We all have to blurt from time to time. There is nothing to be ashamed of and let me assure you that I am exactly the right person to talk to on these matters."

Laura suddenly thought about the ramifications of what she had said and how much further the information could go.

"Please, you won't tell anyone about this will you?"

"No, of course not. I am the soul of discretion. What goes on in Casa Blanca, stays in Casa Blanca".

After Laura collected herself she glanced at her watch and was startled to see that time had flown. David would be wondering where she was. Or would he? Laura rose to leave.

"Thank you so much Lady Pamela...for everything".

They stood together and Lady Pamela put her arms round Laura and embraced her warmly.

"Now I do insist on seeing you again Laura. Let's have lunch soon. I'll ring you my dear".

Lady Pamela took a gilded business card out of her handbag and handed it to Laura.

"Here is my personal number. Now please write down your details for me "

Laura did so and then said her farewells. She reiterated her thanks as Tanice escorted her to the front door.

After she shut the door, Tanice mused to herself that she hoped MadamPam was not embarking on one of her little schemes.

"Dat young lady should not be forced into doin' someting she don' want to do".

CHAPTER 3

A week later Laura got a call from Lady Pamela asking Laura to join her for lunch the following week at an upmarket restaurant in Chelsea. Lady Pamela said that she had some interesting people whom she would like Laura to meet. She told Laura to dress up as the place was very smart and then she said,

"This is my treat Laura".

What a kind offer thought Laura, she need not have gone out of her way to organize a special lunch, and who were these people Lady Pamela wanted her to meet? Probably a couple of her ancient buddies and no doubt one or more would be deaf. Laura decided to go along with the offer but not to pursue any more contact with Lady Pamela. The big question now was what should she wear? Laura flicked through her summer dresses-she only had 3 as she was used to dressing in a practical style in trousers and tops. She took out the little black lace number from the sale. Perhaps it's a bit formal but maybe if she put her cream linen jacket with it and her mother's emerald pendant - that might work. She tried on the outfit added her new black heels and was pleased with the result.

The following week, early on the day Of Laura's lunch outing, David was pre-occupied with organizing his paper work for an important meeting at the bank. While he checked his mobile Laura, in her dressing gown, announced,

"I'm going up to London to check out some fabrics and I may drop into a friend's for lunch".

Texting, he made no response and dashed off without a word.

Her thoughts returned yet again to the date disaster. David, as usual, had said not a word and she didn't feel strong enough to confront him. She would bide her time.

Having worked on a new abstract, she tidied up the art studio and changed out of her paint spattered jeans. After a long hot shower she dressed carefully and put on her makeup. She could not decide whether to put her fair hair up or down and decided down with an elaborate comb at the side. She buckled on her new shoes, sprayed a little perfume all over and thought -For God's sake, you are not dressing for a lover, just an old lady and her ancient friends. Laughing at herself she left the house.

Lady Pamela wearing her favorite pink Chanel vintage suit was carefully made up. Her thick grey bobbed hair was sleekly styled, and her hands immaculately manicured and painted, small drop diamonds adorned her ears. She stepped out of the taxi outside her favorite French restaurant 'Le Petit Jardin'.

She had found the place quite by accident on one of her afternoon walks along Chelsea's back streets with Dandelion. Dandelion had become quite stubborn, had sat down firmly outside the restaurant's front door and had refused to move. She had tried treats, talking in his ear and eventually pulling on his lead with brute force but the wretched animal had glared mutely at her and sat firm. She had glanced up and noticed that through the restaurant window the wait staff were peering out over the bright window boxes and laughing at her discomfort. So embarrassing. At that precise moment, the Maitre D, a whippet thin Frenchman with fluttery hands, remonstrated with his staff and came rushing down the front steps.

"Madame...Can I 'elp you? Quel chien magnifique...J'adore le Bulldog. Il a soif peut-etre-Thirsty or maybe hungry?"

Georges, as that was his name, took control of the situation. He signaled to one of the waiters to bring out a steel bowl filled with water and then personally went to collect some meat scraps from the kitchen. Dandelion was in seventh heaven. He wolfed the lot, drank the water, happily stretched and giving Georges a look of love trotted away alongside his mistress.

Ever since that incident Lady Pamela had vowed never to go back to that street with Dandelion but she resolved to return, alone, or with friends to take lunch on a regular basis. She and Georges had become firm friends and he always made sure that her favorite champagne and seafood was readily available. He also asked about Dandelion 'le beau chien' without fail.

Georges greeted her effusively.

"My lady Pamela. Comment allez-vous? It iz very good to see you again. Your usual table...it iz all ready for you."

"Thank you Georges"

"Thank You my lady!"

Georges ushered her to a table by the window and assisted her to sit. He opened the white damask napkin and laid it on her lap with a flourish.

"Are you well Madame et le beau Dandeleon?"

"Nous sommes tres bien. Thank you Georges. I have The Colonel coming to join me along with an American gentleman and a young lady friend"

"Of course my lady. I will personally attend to them".

He bowed and then gestured to a waiter to bring iced water to the table.

The Colonel, with a ramrod back and an imposing six foot three inch frame, stood by the restaurant entrance. He was formally attired in a dark suit. He waved to Lady Pamela from the entrance area. He was accompanied by a silver-haired man in his forties wearing a dark blue blazer. Georges ushered them over.

"My dear Pamela. Looking lovely as ever. Of course

37

you remember James Jefferson Kirkpatrick ...."

Lady Pamela proffered her hand. "Yes of course. James Jefferson Kirkpatrick ...the third·
Is that right? What happened to the other two?"

James started giving an explanation when the Colonel cut in,

"Pamela darling, don't intimidate the poor man...She's joking James ".

Lady Pamela and Colonel Henry Dunwoodie DSO retired had been lovers many moons ago. They had met at a country house party somewhere in Norfolk in the late fifties. He had arrived late still in his Lieutenant's uniform and was having some supper when she came across him in the kitchen. Unable to sleep and thinking that a cup of hot chocolate might help her settle, she had donned her pink silk peignoir and entered the kitchen bare-footed, her dark hair loose around her shoulders.
As she entered the room he had stood to attention. They had stared at each other transfixed; she remembered nearly fainting with shock at the beauty of the man. He too fell hopelessly in love and their affair could have started there and then. In reality, due to a sense of decorum in relation to the circumstances they were in, they had to control their feelings. A week later she had been well and truly ravished at The Savoy Hotel in London.

Lady Pamela had left finishing school in Switzerland in her 19th year after coming top in her class. Tall and willowy and blessed with perfect legs and pert rounded breasts, this dark haired beauty very soon became the center of attention at all the aristocratic events in London.

Earls and Viscounts began vying for her attention. Spurning many offers of marriage she threw everything away to go on the stage:- Not some turgid dramatic role but as a scantily dressed chorus girl in a naughty revue in Soho. Her parents were aghast and ceased all communication with her for over a year.

The gossip had circulated like a contagion round the upper class set and in the men's eyes at least Pamela became even more desirable. She was regarded as only good for one thing –A good lay.

The women in the main avoided contact and froze her out of their conversation. Behind her back they were vicious. The words 'Whore… tart… slut… in the gutter' were spoken with venom. One or two of the girls secretly admired her pluck and wished they had the balls to deviate from the path of upper class marriage as set out by their parents who believed that making a good match was paramount to a girl's happiness in the 50's.

After a few months at Johnny's Revue Bar in Soho, in a peep show called "Ooo La La", she was noticed by the heir to a huge estate in Norfolk –The Honorable Greville Spencer-Brown- and she was invited up to Norfolk to join the house party to celebrate his 21st. birthday. Lieutenant Henry Dunwoodie, an old Etonian friend of Greville's was also invited. When Henry and Pamela clapped eyes on each other nothing else mattered. The fact that she was being courted by The Honorable Greville, a steady if unremarkable suitor, had not deterred their passion in any way. Henry's friendship with his school friend ended abruptly.

Their affair had lasted almost a year. Then Henry was posted overseas and other men had begun to catch her eye or more to the point she made sure that the most handsome men noticed her. Eventually The Hon Greville regained her attention and quickly made her his wife before she could skitter off on another of her adventures. She settled into her role as Lady of the manor and bore Sir Greville one son, Giles.

Over a period of 50 years Pamela and Henry had a tacit agreement to keep in touch. He had married twice and fathered two sons. The ex-lovers, now in their seventies and unencumbered with other halves, came chastely together for Sunday bridge, cocktails at The Ritz, occasional lunches and theatre outings.

Lady Pamela smiled broadly at the Colonel and remarked to herself how handsome he still was. Tall and craggy with his army bearing and always impeccably turned out. The dark suit, white shirt and club tie set off his excellent physique.

She turned her attention to James Jefferson Kirkpatrick the 3rd. How odd the Americans were with their first second and third. It seemed so unoriginal to keep calling the first son of each generation the same Christian name as well as being so confusing for telephone callers, letter writers and restaurant bookings. Lady Pamela remembered the American from his two or three visits to her establishment. The Colonel had introduced him and the girls had commented on his beautiful hair and perfect manners. They had called him Gentleman Jim. She inspected his silver swept back hair, his crisp button down shirt, yellow and blue tie, and navy blazer. Yes you'll do ...You'll do very well.

"Do I pass muster Colonel?"

James was fingering his tie nervously.

"Next time ditch the tie. Bit gaudy... and a haircut would not go amiss old boy".

James saluted the colonel. "Yes sir".

Lady Pamela took Henry to task.

"Still a stickler for army haircuts Henry? Not everyone is marching on parade you know"

"Do 'em a damn lot of good I reckon".

Lady Pamela laughed. "Now let's not start on the current generation."

The waiter appeared carrying a silver ice bucket in which was placed a bottle of Dom Perignon Rose champagne 2003. He gave the bottle to Lady Pamela.

"Ah excellent… the 2003-such a beautiful color and served at the wedding of Prince Charles and Lady Diana…"

She glanced at James Jefferson Kirkpatrick and smiled. The Princess Diana look-a-like was definitely his type. To the waiter she said. "You may serve".

The waiter opened the bottle with a satisfying pop and poured three glasses and gesturing to the fourth glass, he was given the nod to pour. He carefully placed the bottle in the ice bucket and folded a pristine white napkin over the side of the bucket.

After the waiter left the table, Lady Pamela lent forward and spoke in a stage whisper,

"Gentlemen, the young lady joining us today has no idea what sort of establishment I am running. I require you to be discreet and not frighten her off with any lurid details-"

The colonel broke in -"Surely you know me better than that. I am the soul of discretion".

"This is mainly for the benefit of Gentleman Jim."

James Kirkpatrick reacted inquiringly to her comment.

"That is what the girls call you. You are a favorite of theirs. Now I spoke to The Colonel on the phone about this meeting and he thought you James would be the perfect person to introduce to this lovely but sad English rose, Laura. As you know I very much enjoy doing little favors for people especially pretty young ladies who need some joy and-"

The Colonel mouthed the word '-s e x'.

"-excitement in their drab lives. Colonel, let us not coarsen the tone."

The Colonel hid a wolfish smile.

"Laura is a beautiful young wife in her thirties. She lives a simple life in the country pursuing her interest in art and design. Her daughter aged 16 is away at boarding school. Her husband is over-involved with his renovation business and has been neglecting his bedroom duties".

The colonel could not resist a "tut tut".

Annoyed, Lady Pamela said crisply,

"Thank you Henry. In fact, and I tell you both this in strictest confidence, Laura and her husband have not made love in over a year. She is desperately lonely and even though she does not realize this herself, she is seeking a lover..."

"...and you are going to help her find one". Henry cut in and then he smiled at James,

"Are you up for it old boy?"

"Can't wait".

Lady Pamela continued, "She is definitely your type James. A blonde English rose with great legs. Now before she arrives, I just need to confirm the business side of things. I have had to increase my introduction fee, and there will also be the usual rate for the room. I have re-done the Venetian room, it was looking very shabby... and it is now decorated in Chinese style...lots of red and gold very opulent...so..."

Lady Pamela totted up some figures in her notebook.

"The total comes to 2,500 pounds... in cash of course".

Henry joined in. "We don't want to worry the taxman... Poor chap has enough on his plate what with all money laundering that is going on these days; the world is full of shysters and scoundrels."

Without a murmur James pulled a wallet full of notes out of his jacket pocket. Horrified, Lady Pamela put her

42

hand up to stop him.

"No. No… Not here...Please... Have you no sense of decorum? Firstly you meet her and then you can tell me if she is suitable...and softly softly with this one James. If she is, Henry will deal with the transaction. Henry takes care of all my business dealings".

Laura decided to park the car at Twickenham station and go by tube to Chelsea. Lady Pamela had asked her to be at the restaurant at 1pm, so factoring in a visit to the fabric wholesalers and a nearby carpet warehouse, she left the house at around 10-00am. She noted as she locked the front door that the weeds were beginning to creep back in the flower beds either side of the garden path. Percy her black and white cat was luxuriating himself on the sunny front path and he gave a little mew as she passed him.

"Bye Percy. Be good".

In keeping with the cottage Laura had planted some summer annuals in the front beds; bright pink and white Petunias, Sweet William and multi colored Snap Dragons along with some trailing bright blue Lobelia. She also had some herbs outside the kitchen window and on a summer afternoon she would open the window, lean out and pick a sprig of rosemary. She would crush between her fingers and inhale the pungent aroma. Her domain was to keep the weeds at bay and tend to the flower borders while David reluctantly mowed the lawn and only when prompted. When they moved in, the garden at the back of the property, a level half an acre, was mostly lawn with some old-fashioned roses on a broken trellis, an old lilac tree and an Orange Pippin apple tree that became laden with fruit every year. Laura had pushed hard to put in a flower border and David had agreed only as long as she did all the work. David had a wonderful eye and interest in house renovation but gardening was at the bottom of his hobby list.

She dug out the new flower bed and prepared the soil, feeding in some topsoil and blood and bone nutrients. She then planted old fashioned Roses, Delphiniums, Lupins, Stocks and Canterbury bells along with some pretty white edging plants. The border looked a picture during the summer months.

Having parked her trusty SUV in the station car park, Laura glanced at her watch and realizing she only had two minutes to spare, raced onto the platform and checked the noticeboard. The train Laura was planning to catch was delayed by twenty minutes putting her already frayed nerves further on edge. She turned up the collar of her cream jacket and paced up and down the platform, checking her watch regularly, garnering curious looks from an elderly Chinese gentleman and his wife quietly seated on a platform bench. When the train eventually arrived she stepped on board and found a window seat. Two teenagers crashed through the carriage door and sat opposite her and spent the whole journey giggling either into their iPhones or looking at Laura and giggling some more.

Watching the passing urban sprawl Laura kept thinking what an idiot she had been blurting out all that detail about David and their sex life. Lady Pamela had been very kind and had promised not to say anything but you never knew. What if these friends of hers did know and all the time would be laughing at her behind their hands. Well she was committed now and would have to stick it out. Afraid she was going to be late, Laura decided to flag the carpet warehouse and making a mental note to buy cheaper groceries for the next week, she dismissed the cost and took a cab to the 'Le Petit Jardin'. Laura avoided looking at the meter and just as the cab entered the Kings Road, she grappled for the mirror in her fake Versace hand bag and re-applied her lipstick. She was checking her hair when the cab rolled to a halt. In her haste to pay and get out of the taxi, she left her handbag half open and her lipstick rolled out into the gutter. Laura hoped Lady Pamela and her guests couldn't see her scrabbling around on the pavement. Flinging everything back in the bag, she tugged down her black dress, smoothed her hair and checked the clasp. As she opened the restaurant door she noticed her hands were shaking.

"Bonjour Mademoiselle. Welcome to Le Petit Jardin"

"Oh...mm... I am meeting with Lady Pamela-"

The Frenchman on the door interrupted, "-Of course. Please follow me".

He took Laura over to a window table; she prayed that no-one could hear her knees knocking and with a flourish he said,

"Voila! Here she is".

Lady Pamela rose and kissed Laura on the cheek. Alongside her were two gentlemen, one a similar age to Lady Pamela and the other around forty five with the bluest eyes she'd ever seen. They stood up and Blue Eyes gave an obvious sweeping look from Laura's feet to her breasts. She could feel her cheeks redden. Lady Pamela handled the introductions.

"May introduce Colonel Henry Dunwoodie DSO. Retired"

The Colonel straightened his six foot three inch frame, took Laura's hand and a made a little bow. "Laura...At your service".

Laura took note of his military bearing and estimated him to be in his late seventies. A very distinguished retired army man. Lady Pamela continued,

"And this is James Jefferson KirkPatrick the 3rd."

Blue eyes took her hand and gently kissed it while

45

holding her gaze and unable to bear his intimacy, she focused on his thick silver hair which was smoothed back from his face and curled slightly over his collar. Was he… Canadian? No American.

"Your eyes –beautiful- and just like hers".

Laura pulled back slightly in embarrassment and almost found herself blurting out 'and so are yours'. She mentally kicked herself for stuttering:

"S….so....sorry?"

Lady Pamela came to her rescue.

" Laura, my dear, you really are so like Princess Diana – now you must have a glass of this pink heaven". She gestured to the empty chair next to Blue Eyes.

"Talking of Champagne, I must tell you this extraordinary story about the dear Queen Mother. At age 97 and lying in her private room in hospital after a medical procedure, she managed to smuggle a case of Krug D'ambonnay- the 96 no less, into her hospital room under the noses of all the nurses and doctors."

The Colonel was unbelieving. "Surely her Body Guards would have known about it?"

"Of course they did and they all enjoyed a bloody good party at her expense".

Lady Pamela had laid on an expensive spread of oysters, and caviar, followed by salmon in a prawn and champagne sauce. Conversation sparkled between Lady Pamela and the men. The Colonel and Lady Pamela were reminiscing about the old days when the upper set gave country house parties which usually included a concert or dance party and everyone was dragged out of bed to walk the estate the following day at an early hour, but not too early as everyone had to allow time to get back to their own bedroom. The Colonel added,

"At 5am the upper floors turned into King's cross station with everyone scurrying back to their legitimate beds".

Lady Pamela was surreptitiously gauging Laura's reaction to this talk and was pleased to see that she was beginning to relax and enjoy herself. She was amused to note that Laura was now forgetting to hide her nibbled nails. What lovely skin, now rosy from the champagne. Oh to be young again. Lady Pamela glanced down at the liver spots on her hands and thought too late for me but not for pretty Laura. Would she grab the opportunity offered?

Laura couldn't believe how much fun she was having. The rakish Colonel was a delight and Lady Pamela, beautiful in her day, with a very racy past. The champagne was excellent; how long was it since she had enjoyed top quality food and company? She was acutely aware of the good looking blue-eyed man on her right. As Lady Pamela and The Colonel discussed their memories, Blue Eyes began to tell her about himself. She learnt that he lived in coastal Connecticut, owned 3 beachfront homes and two luxury apartments in New York; all either inherited or bought with family money. He travelled a great deal and being an Anglophile enjoyed visiting England on a regular basis. He and The Colonel had met at an exclusive club in London. While he was talking she found herself having trouble concentrating on the information he was giving her. His warm smile was drawing her in. She kept looking at his tanned handsome face and became transfixed on his smooth grey hair. She couldn't deny that she was longing to touch it. James began to probe Laura gently for information.

"So you're an artist. Have you exhibited at all?"

"Well not really. I did have a show in the village where I live, in Kingbridge, but I mainly work as an interior designer for The Manning Renovation

Company. My husband's company".

How she hated saying that but there was no point in denying the fact that she was married. Anyway why not tell him about David, at least inform him of the basics of their life together. He had not mentioned a wife but she felt certain he was married with a string of accomplished blonde offspring. He was bound to be married and why on earth should that matter anyway, she was probably not going to see him again. The word 'probably' hung in her mind.

He asked her about children and she told him about Juliet away at boarding school.

"Do you have any other children?"

"Er...No…just the one".

She did not qualify her statement as the date disaster was still raw in her mind and she certainly didn't want to burst into tears in front of this gorgeous man. So astonished was she at being in such prestigious company, she did not notice the imperceptible glance and nod of the head that passed between Blue Eyes and Lady Pamela.

At a certain point, just after the plates had been cleared away, Lady Pamela gave the Colonel a surreptitious look and they both rose together.

"My dear, the Colonel and I have some business to attend to. I am leaving you in the capable hands of Mr. Kirkpatrick. I'll call you in a few days.

Laura looked concerned.

"Don't worry… and enjoy the rest of the afternoon".

Laura mumbled a 'thank you'. Lady Pamela took the Colonel's arm, and as they walked toward the exit, she whispered something in his ear. He laughed.

Laura turned to James. "I should get back too. I have to drop some samples into a client".

James said, "Can I get you some strawberries, they're

chocolate covered. Fattening I guess but let's be decadent." He grinned at her.

"Decadent? Well why not? It's certainly a while since I've been decadent".

And she smiled into his intense eyes.

"And coffee?"

"Yes please".

He hailed the waiter and made the order.

She loved the sound of his rolling American accent, and she came to the conclusion that it would be very easy to be more than decadent with him. He was definitely a vaginal opportunity. She suddenly had to know about his marital state. Was he married?

"James, I hope you don't mind me asking but are you married?"

He gave her a knowing look and then said disconcertingly, "Would that make a difference?"

"Sorry? I didn't mean to pry".

She knew of course to what he was alluding.

He laughed, "Yes I have been married."

Then he took her hand and looked closely at her.

"But as to my present state. Let's just say I'm separated."

Laura looked away in embarrassment and panicking slightly said,

"If you'll excuse me a moment I have to go to the…"
She waved her hand in the general direction of The Ladies.

He held and stroked her hand lightly and then released it and she somewhat unsteadily skirted her way around the table to the far end of the restaurant. Once safely inside the toilet cubicle, she silently screamed. What was she thinking to even contemplate having sex with this guy? But he was so gorgeous and separated so therefore available. The salient fact of the matter was, she was not. She swore softly.

"Bugger bugger".

Life was so bloody unfair. Tidying herself up she resolved to thank him kindly for his company and quietly extract herself as soon as politely possible before she did something totally crazy like kissing him passionately in front of the whole restaurant.

The coffee and strawberries had arrived on her return.

While he was telling her about MOMA in New York, one of the best known museums of modern art in the world and that he had acted as a sponsor for a recent exhibition, she couldn't helping feeling enormous regret that this meeting was about to come to an end. If only she had the guts to ask him out to lunch, just the two of them.

They left the restaurant and as he was hailing a passing cab he asked if she would like to have another lunch with him.

"But this time just the two of us."

Laura masked her delight and pretending to be unsure frowned a little for effect. He added.

"Lady Pamela can be our Go-Between".

"Lady Pamela?"

Did he envisage Lady Pamela as her chaperone? Laura couldn't imagine Lady Pamela playing the gooseberry. Why had he mentioned her?

"Don't look so worried Laura. Here is my cell number".

He fished a card out his pocket and gave it to Laura. He then took her in a warm embrace, and kissed her on the cheek.

"Goodbye beautiful Laura-don't forget me. Please call".

He helped her into the taxi and as the cab drew away from the kerb she turned to look back. He blew her a kiss.

She collected the car from the station and drove back to the village in an alcoholic daze, just stopping in time at a pedestrian crossing where two old ladies were arm in arm assisting each other across the road. One of the ladies angrily waved her stick at the car. Laura smiled and waved back and taken by the extraordinary experience of her lunch meeting burst out laughing. She realized that this was the first time she had felt ineffable joy in a very long time. She sped home, her mind full of James-his eyes, his smile, his mouth.

CHAPTER 4

It was mid-morning at Casa Blanca a few days later. Lady Pamela, dressed in her elegant black work trousers and cream silk shirt, was sitting on her French chaise longue readying herself to lead the weekly staff meeting. At her feet Dandelion lay sprawled on his own personal bed made from a Persian rug. He was snoring loudly. A battered one-eyed teddy bear lay abandoned next to him. She was checking her large desk diary and was making a note, when there was a knock at the door. Lady Pamela nudged Dandelion, he snorted and looked up confused.

"Come".

The door opened and Swati, a tall Indian model with dark hair almost to her waist slipped through the door closely followed by a six foot curvaceous woman in her late thirties with shoulder length strawberry blonde curly hair. Her shoulders were hunched and she was pulling her cable knit cardigan over her voluminous breasts. She sniffed, dragged a hankie out of her cardigan pocket and blew her nose loudly. Dandelion on bandy legs staggered over to smell the girls' ankles. He took a shine to Swati and pressed against her leg. She tried surreptitiously to shove him out of the way. Undaunted he stayed close. Lady Pamela addressed the cardigan-clad employee.

"Tracy...What on earth is the matter with you?"

"Sorry Lady P – All stuffed up. Ethan brought a cold home from school-"

"-And you caught it… You have two important clients coming in today- Dear God I'll have to put them off 'til tomorrow. And I've told you before ...Take off that disgusting cardigan. Have you not learnt anything under my tutelage?"

She tutted loudly to herself. Seeing Dandelion was

making a nuisance of himself, she called to him. "Dandi! Come away from there".

He took no notice and gazed adoringly at Swati.

"Just remember that in this house we have to keep up appearances at all times. As soon as you enter through the front door you are on the stage. Tracy becomes Pandora, a six foot booted leather-clad Amazon with magnificent breasts, a whip and spurs that would scare the shit out of the Prince of Wales".

Swati was getting the giggles and snorted loudly.

"And you Swati… You are Nefertiti…Queen of the Nile...not some giggling Indian girl with a dreadful name...Swati.... Oh dear...Sweaty Swati-Quite repulsive".

Swati reacted to this by lifting her head and uncoiling her spine to her full height of five foot ten inches. She flung her long dark hair away from her face and gave Lady Pamela a mutinous stare. Lady Pamela returned the stare and looked her up and down.

"Aha- Now you become a perfect Nefertiti...a beautiful imperious princess with smoldering eyes…and a body so stunning that men swoon at the sight of you…even Dandi here is smitten. Girls. This is a serious business. You have to take control of the audience. When I say audience I mean the men who wish to lose themselves with you in their own fantasy world. Not only do you have to make them believe in you…You have to be mysterious, alluring, sometimes cruel sometimes kind...Your work at this level is a form of artistry and that is why you are very well paid. You will keep your standards high at all times. Do I make myself clear..?"

The girls answered in unison. "Yes Lady P".

"Pandora, you may now go home and get rid of that cold…Blow it out and be back here tomorrow – 11am sharp. I need you to try on the new French maid's costume. Nefertiti- go and change and then come and see me… I want to make sure you are properly attired for your one o'clock appointment. Remember… you are Queen of the Nile."

Lady Pamela turned away and busied herself with her appointment diary. Pandora gave Nefertiti a meaningful look and stifling giggles, they disappeared into the hallway, clutching each other in silent mirth.

Dandelion, disappointed that his Indian love had gone, wandered over to where his battered Teddy was lying, picked it up and placed it on his Persian bed. Teddy's one eye glittered with disgust as Dandelion gave him a good humping. Hearing Dandi's grunts, Lady Pamela spun round,

"Stop that Dandi you randy devil-Dear God –Do all male creatures have a one-track mind?" She picked up Teddy and chucked him into a corner of the room.

Tanice, taking a break from the morning's chores and knowing Lady Pamela was occupied with her morning meeting, was sitting at the kitchen table with a large exercise book open in front of her. She rolled her ample thighs back and forth on the kitchen chair, her face a mask of concentration, tongue tip slightly protruding as she carefully wrote in her neat hand, complete with crossings out, the key to her fortune and fame.-

A Bonk Buster to eclipse all Bonk Busters. The minor problems of spelling and grammar were not going to get in her way.

Lady Delphine dressed in no ting but a slinky red nitey/neglijay paced de floor like a bitch/tiger on heat. Her long dark hair fell in ringlits over her tanned shoulders. Droplits of swet/perspiration gathered between her bosoms and tinkled down onto

54

her flat brown belly. Why doesn't he come to her?
Renching open the terris door, she ran out onto
de/the veranda and breeved in deeply. The sent of
the gardenea flowers made her head explode/reel.
"Rastus" She shouted, her voice horse with desire.

A braying voice interrupted her thoughts."Tanice".

Tanice stood quickly, shut her exercise book and placed it to one side.

"Yes MadamPam?"

"The Colonel is coming to dinner tonight. Please make sure you buy his favorite sirloin steak when you go shopping today."

Tanice, silent, her mind focused on putting the concept of lust onto the page, stared blankly at Lady Pamela.

"Is anything the matter?"

"Noo No. Everyting jus' fine"

"And add toilet paper to your shopping list there".

Lady Pamela gestured with a manicured nail at Tanice's exercise book.

"Oh yes we need some more cock covers. All sizes, flavors and colors...God knows how we get through so many...I'll have to talk to the girls about economizing. Have you got that?"

"Yes MadamPam, I writin' it all down."

Tanice opened the exercise book. Lady Pamela sighed with annoyance.

"I am writing..with a g... it all down"

"NOO... I writin' Madame ....Condoms-"

"-Don't ever say that word in my house. Only street girls use that common term...."

Lady Pamela swirled out and Tanice, scowling at her retreating back, started writing in large capitals at the bottom of the page:

55

'CONDOMS. S.M.L XL.ALL colours' and underneath 'Serloin'.

Laura had thought a great deal in the following days about Blue Eyes. She had three or four times taken out his card from its hiding place under a paint pot in her studio and it now had a blue thumb print in one corner. She was determined to resolve her relationship with David and had no intention of calling James but why, she wondered, was she still hanging on to the card? She was waking often in the night and had started to fantasize about Blue Eyes, indulging in romantic scenarios which alarmingly led to him removing all her clothes. She imagined what his skin would feel like and his mouth caressing her breasts. While David was deep in sleep she relieved her sexual arousal by a slow masturbation, clamping her lips together to stem any escaping orgasmic moan that might awaken her husband. After these night exploits, she awoke refreshed but with a hint of guilt.

It was Friday morning. David and Laura were about to start their trip to Juliet's school to see her play in the inter-house tennis finals match. Juliet also had permission to have dinner with them after the match and had asked to go to her favorite place, an Italian restaurant ,"La Primavera" in the local town.

They had taken great care to find somewhere for Juliet that firstly was not too far away and also had smaller classes. Both Laura and David agreed that as Juliet was an 'only', it would be best for her to be with other girls her age and due to her extrovert personality, they felt she would thrive in a boarding school environment. Springcourt School seemed to fit the bill. It was a Victorian pile set in eight acres of grounds and had top class hockey pitches and tennis courts. She had started there at twelve and despite a shaky start with a bout of home sickness, she had settled well and made some nice friends.   She was like her father to look at with his physique and thick unruly hair. She had inherited his ability in Math and his prowess on the sports field. From Laura she had inherited blue eyes and drawing skills. In the last year she had turned from a gangly giggly fifteen year old into a beautiful sixteen year old on the brink of womanhood. She had two more years at Springcourt to complete her final exams and then she planned to study architecture at University.

"David. Are you ready? We really should be going".

There was a muffled answer from the study. It was nearly ten am and David had been on the phone from early morning sorting out suppliers and subcontractors. With Mr. Gupta's job about to start there was a lot to do.

Laura knew the journey would take them around three hours and they had decided to allow time for a lunch at a cafe on the river.

The main tennis final started at 3pm so they would have plenty of time to enjoy a cosy tete a tete. Laura couldn't decide whether to broach the subject of their sex life while they were driving or wait until they were having lunch together.   Starting the conversation was not going to be easy but at least she would have his undivided attention and in any case she felt he owed her an explanation. She was desperate for him to open up to her and for them to discuss calmly and rationally the state of their marriage.

Laura opened the study door, "I'm going to the car."

David, on the cell phone, nodded and gave her an irritated wave. She began to think that perhaps the drive down would not be a good time to open up as to what was on her mind. David was busy and distracted with all his work details.

At last they were on the road; David's phone kept signaling with texts coming through and while driving he was furtively looking at the phone.

"Connect into Hands Free Mode David. It's so dangerous constantly checking texts."

"Thank you Nanny for pointing that out. You don't seem to realize that I have a lot going on at the moment."

With ferocity he connected up the Hands Free and pressed down hard on the accelerator as they entered the Motorway system. Laura turned to look out of the side window all the while thinking he's speeding with annoyance. We're off to a bad start. I'll have to wait until lunch now and start the conversation after he's had a calming glass of beer.

They talked very little on the way to Springcourt and David turned on the radio for most of the journey. They arrived in good time at the cafe by the river and were able to secure a table on the terrace overlooking the water.

Her heart sank when he took a call at the beginning of the meal but when the food arrived Laura was relieved to see him turning the phone off and put it in his pocket. David ordered Fish and Chips and a beer and Laura, a Chicken Salad and her favorite lunch drink, a glass of New Zealand Sauvignon Blanc.

Now was the time to give the elephant in the room a big shove.

"David "

"Mmm?"

"We haven't talked".

He knew very well what she meant but he was not going to make it easy for her especially in light of the fact that he was going to have to tell her that he did not want her, in that way. He tried stalling at first. "Talked? About what?"

"Please David…Why are you making this hard for me… for us?"

"I'm not sure what you want to talk about Laura?"

Laura took a deep breath and said, "We have not made love in almost a year".

He tried playing the innocent party. "Is it really that long?"

"You know it is. The other night I lost it because I was so frustrated with the situation, by the way, I am not apologizing for breaking that cricket photo, what I'm trying to say is…are we ever going to get back to the way we were?"

David tried to steer the conversation toward what they did have together.

"We have a comfortable life don't we… with plenty of money to support us? I provide for you and you have freedom within the business to organize the interior designs as you wish. We have created a lovely home together-"

"-Stop! That is not what I meant and you know it. You obviously don't want to talk about it but let me ask you this. Is our sex life well and truly deceased? Or to put it more succinctly. Am I to remain un-fucked by you for the rest of our married life?"

Laura had raised her voice to such a level that the families alongside their table were throwing them alarmed glances. One woman took her young daughter out of earshot.

David noticed.

"Laura, pipe down, people are listening in".

"I don't bloody care. Would you like me to shout out loud that I have not been fucked by MY HUSBAND for over a year"?

And she made as if to stand up to make the announcement.

"Laura. Sit Down."

She sat and leaning toward him said quietly, "Well fuck you!"

David abruptly got up from the table and disappeared inside. Laura gulped her drink and looked away from the curious onlookers. She grabbed a tissue out of her bag and pretended to blow her nose as she carefully wiped a tear from the corner of her eye. Well that went well she thought. The elephant had been loaded with explosives and blew up in her face. Nothing was said for the rest of the journey until just before the turn toward Springcourt. David turned to her and said coolly,

"I think we should maintain a united front where Juliet is concerned".

Laura nodded mutely. United front indeed; it sounded to her like a political party. She had been mulling over an important decision on the journey from the cafe and had been debating with herself a course of action which she knew might change her life forever.

They arrived a little early at the school and took a turn round the playing fields. They walked apart for a while and then David came alongside Laura and said,

"It's not the end of the world is it?"

She decided not to dignify the question with an answer and quickened her pace to get ahead of him. How dare he say that. It underlined the fact that he wasn't planning a bedroom onslaught on her any time soon. He must have taken up with someone else. Well if he can do that then so can I.

They had five minutes with Juliet before she went on court. She gave them both a big hug. Dressed in her whites with the school crest emblazoned on the pocket of her shirt and her baseball style cap in the school's colors, she looked invincible. Laura remarked that she felt Juliet had grown another inch. She now towered over Laura. David gave Juliet a quick kiss on the cheek,

"Sock it to her Sweetheart and don't forget what I said to you".

"Dad I know… Keep moving my feet. Oh by the way I've had some coaching on my serve and I can place it a whole lot better"

Laura gave her daughter a big hug,

"You'll be victorious darling."

Juliet raced off and David and Laura took their seats in the stand. The match wasn't a straight forward victory for Juliet. The opposing finalist was a petite dark girl with flying feet who came at Juliet like a ferocious little terrier and took the first set six games to four. At the break Juliet looked across at David and Laura. David, sitting, raised his leg slightly and pointed to his foot. Juliet nodded and with a determined look on her face took to the court. Laura whispered.

"Come on Jules you can do it".

Juliet then pushed herself into another gear and serving very strongly, over-powered her opponent in the second set. The third set was a battle royal and went to six all with Juliet just managing to get two points ahead to win the tie-breaker nine points to seven. A huge cheer went up from the Leamington House supporters and everyone got to their feet and gave Juliet a standing ovation. David turned to Laura and gave her a big hug. Then he said,

"Our daughter is bloody amazing".

Laura thought ruefully that at least we got that right.

After Prize Giving Juliet went to change and then came racing out of her boarding house and flew into David's arms. They both congratulated her. In the car on the way to "La Primavera" Juliet was full of chat about the match, her friend Holly who got to the doubles final and lost, Miss Evershed the Head Mistress who was thrilled with her success and the number of points she was going to get for her Boarding House. David and Laura let her rattle on happily.

They were seated close to a window which overlooked a pretty vegetable and herb garden edged with wild flowers. The Italian restaurant, La Primavera, was renowned for its fresh variety of vegetables and herbs. Juliet announced she was hungry as a hunter and almost immediately decided on her favorite veal dish, Saltimbocca, some pesto pasta with extra pine nuts and a side of vegetables. Laura ran her eyes down the menu, the early tiff had taken her appetite; she ordered a Caprese salad.

David commented. "Have some pasta Laura."

Laura shook her head.

"We'll at least have some wine. What do you think Jules? Some champagne to celebrate your win?"

"Oh Lovely Dad. Yes please"

David laughed. "And we won't tell Matron".

David and Juliet chatted on during the meal. Laura added a few comments but watching them banter away together she felt strangely detached from the proceedings. Juliet noticed.

"Mum, you're very quiet. Are you alright?"

"I'm fine darling...perhaps a little tired. I've been a bit busy lately what with one thing and another."

She avoided looking at David then she smiled at Juliet and said,

"You did brilliantly today Jules. I am so proud of you and I know I don't say this as much as I should. I love you very much".

Juliet said softly. "And I love you too Mum....and Dad".

To compose herself and to stop herself crying in front of her daughter, Laura went to find the Ladies.

62

After coffee Juliet looked at her watch and said that she had to get back to school. She also mentioned that end of year exams were looming and she had a stack of revision to get started on. They dropped her off at school and started on the journey home. Half way there Laura suddenly stated.

"Well that's it I suppose".

David, with eyes on the road, said, "Maybe not".

He glanced across at her and smiled. Nothing more was said.

On their arrival at the house Laura went inside and as she bent over to take off her shoes, David flung his arms around her waist and pressed against her backside. She pushed back against him raised her arms and twisted round. His mouth found hers and kissing passionately, their hands started desperately to undress each other. Laura quickly removed her shirt and bra, flinging them to one side. They half fell onto the sofa. With trousers at half mast, David had his hand between Laura's legs. He pulled her pants down and was working his fingers around her clitoris. She gasping with pleasure had her hand firmly on his cock. His tongue was winding itself around her nipple. Within a moment she was on the edge of coming and when he hitched up her skirt and thrust himself inside her, she cried out.

They came quickly together and then overbalancing, they both fell laughing onto the floor. They lay in each other's embrace for a while, he then kissed her gently on the neck and gathering the fallen clothes disappeared upstairs.

Laura smiled got up and shaking her head with disbelief collected her belongings together. Her thoughts tumbled over each other. I certainly didn't expect that and a forceful rogering to boot. Fantastic…Let's hope this is only the beginning.

Later awake while David was snoring lightly beside her, she mulled over the events of the day. Something was niggling at her in relation to the complete turnaround in David's behavior. Had he done it to shut her up? Was it, Heaven forbid, the last fuck he would ever give her? A sort of 'goodbye thrust'? She knew how pleased he was with Juliet's win, so perhaps he felt Laura deserved a gift of sex and at the same time his actions would stop her nagging and keep her happy for a while. He used to say he loved her after sex but this time he hadn't said it. Stop! I cannot go on thinking like this. As she turned over away from David she noticed the light of dawn starting to creep through the curtains.

In the morning he was all smiles and brought her a cup of tea in bed, something he hadn't done in years. He chatted on about what was happening at the office. Mr. Gupta was due in to approve the first lot of alterations and to pay an instalment. Cindy, behind the front desk, will be thrilled said Laura.

Cindy had stated to David that he needed to be there when Mr. Gupta came in as he had already almost given her a heart attack when she was alone in the office by coming up behind her unexpectedly when she was bending over the filing cabinet. She had felt a pudgy hand brush her arse. David had laughed heartily when Cindy had relayed this but Peter was fuming.

"Dirty bastard. We should never have taken him as a client".

David then asked Laura what she was up to and she reminded him that she had a client meeting to discuss paint colors and finishes in the afternoon. He kissed her goodbye and whistling happily ran down the stairs. At the bottom he said,

"Can you check on the study computer to see if the bank has sent through those papers and if they've arrived please print them for me. Thanks."

After a hearty breakfast of bacon and eggs and a large black coffee Laura went into the study to check the emails. She found the bank documents and printed them out. She remembered a 'How to' art website that she wanted to check and keyed into google. Finding what she was looking for, she checked the content and printed out the instructions. Sipping on her coffee she was mulling over the thought that David spent a lot of time in here working on the computer, coming up to bed late and even in the early hours of the morning. She had crept down the stairs a few times and noticed the study light under the closed door. Idly spotting the website history icon she pressed the key and taking a random timeline, keyed in one week ago. She looked and gave a gasp. Twenty different porn sites came up. She tried going back further and the same thing happened. Her fingers trembling slightly, she checked out "Hot black bitches teach you the Kama Sutra". Yelping as she opened up the website to see both Indian and Black girls in such explicit positions as Fantastic Rocking Horse, the Catherine Wheel and the Double Decker Bus. She quickly shut down the computer and sat back stunned. So this is what he had been up to. There was no 'other' woman as such just lots of them mainly of the darker variety with their pudenda and arses smiling at the camera. Their lack of a sex life became abundantly clear and last night was probably done just to keep her happy for a while. She certainly could never compete with what she had just seen.

After the shocking revelations on the computer, Laura poured herself a large brandy and going out into the garden sat down in one of the chairs. Now what? Another confrontation over this latest exposure? No she couldn't face that at present. She finished the brandy in

65

one gulp and closed her eyes to the soft morning sun. She could feel a light wind blowing her hair. It would be best to keep busy at present and as she was under pressure to finish two paintings for the latest renovation, Laura went into the studio. Her cat Percy was perched happily and sunning himself on a box of paints by the window. He jumped down when she appeared and rubbed himself against her legs. She murmured.

"Percy, petal, at least you are true to me".

She stroked his black and white fur. He purred away happily.

The client having seen Laura's portfolio on the Manning website definitely wanted to buy something and needed two large square soft color palette art works to go with the modern white interior that Laura had designed. Laura had finished one; it had been a pig to get right: - All soft greys with a hint of pink and apricot. She started to gesso the other canvas and when she had done two coats she made herself a cup of coffee and began to wonder. How on earth had she not realized? All those nights hunkered down in front of the computer. What an idiot not to have known. She suddenly was transported back to their first meeting. David had come to the party with a beautiful Indian model. She now realized the significance of this. He didn't fancy blonde girls, but he had married one. He must have been wanking off in front of some black cunt for years.

Laura banged her coffee cup down and swore "Shit, shit shit!"

She retrieved Blue Eyes card from its hiding place under an old paint pot. She stared at it for some time and then picking up her cell phone she began to press his number. She quickly hung up half way through. A text would be better; talking to him or even leaving a message could be awkward.

Her text read,

*Hi James..*She nearly put *Blue Eyes*
but felt this was too personal. Chewing her nail she then put-

How are you?...
Innocuous enough, now what.

It was nice meeting you the other day. I will be coming up to London next week on Wednesday. Perhaps we could meet for a coffee? I will be in the Chelsea area if that suits you.

Or should she put *area to suit you'.*

He might be miles away in Hampstead or USA for all she knew. She decided to leave the area as Chelsea. He probably hasn't remembered who I am anyway she thought. She took a breath and pressed the 'send' button.

A few moments later the phone buzzed and she read,

Hi Laura so pleased you contacted me. I'd love to buy you lunch. Let's meet at Hong Kong Harry's in Sloane Square. They do some excellent duck dishes. It's almost next door to the Little Chelsea Hotel. See you at 12 midday. Very much looking forward to seeing you lovely Laura. James.KP 3rd.

Laura stared at the message for some time. She went into the kitchen to wash up and glanced unseeing out of the window; her thoughts in a turmoil. Lunch? Next door to a hotel? Wasn't that just a bit too convenient? She smiled to herself as she made some more coffee and taking the mug back to the studio, she picked up the phone and texted back,

Lunch would be lovely. Thank You. See you at 12. L

And to herself she said, "Well that's done it".

CHAPTER 5

The Casa Blanca staff were gathered together in Lady Pamela's sitting room for the weekly meeting. Lady Pamela was about to introduce a new young lady to the team. Pandora and Nefertiti were sitting alongside each other on Lady Pamela's cream damask patterned sofa and they glanced curiously across at the new girl seated alongside on the mahogany dining chair. She was of Chinese origin, petite, with doll-like features; her thick blue black hair fell down to breast level and her deep set eyes with lustrous false lashes were gazing at her tiny hands clasped in her lap. She was seated with her legs pressed tightly together; her minute feet, in jeweled heels, were perfectly aligned. Mindful of the sort of job she was about to start, she had given herself the name Jezebel.

Lady Pamela took off her slim gold reading glasses, collected her papers together, cleared her throat and addressed the girls.

"First of all I'd like to introduce you to our new member of staff. She, of course, will be occupying the Chinese room. This is Wilma Wong."

Pandora bit her lip and turned away to suppress a laugh. Nefertiti nodded hello and smiled at her secretly pinching Pandora's thigh. Wilma raised her head to reveal heavy lidded deep brown eyes with a guarded expression. She smiled tightly at the assembled company then slowly put her hand up.

"Yes Wilma?"

A sharp high pitched voice emerged from Wilma's perfect rosebud lips.

68

"I have different name. Prease Madam my name is Jez...ee...bel".

Lady Pamela cringed in disbelief at Wilma's speaking voice.

Pandora seeing how uncomfortable Wilma was, spoke enthusiastically.

"Jezebel…What a great name. Nice to meet you. I'm Pandora and this is Nefertiti."

"Nefertitty?"

"Close enough...We all call her Nef...I'll show you around. We are all good friends here…like a family ...You'll love it here, Lady P-"

"---Pandora that is enough prattling from you. Now Jez…Wilma, I have decided that the name you have chosen for yourself is not in character with the sort of service you will be providing here. You are to be called Cherry Blossom."

Wilma turned her head slowly to look at Lady P. Her face betrayed no emotion.

"Chelly Brossom? I don't like".

"It's not a question of whether you like the name or not…That is what you are to be called. You will also be starting elocution lessons with me tomorrow morning".

Wilma stared at the floor.

Lady P checked her capacious leather bound office diary.

"Come at 10-30 am tomorrow. We have to wrestle into submission not only your voice but also your accent. The gentlemen who come here may want you to recite poetry..."

The newly named Cherry Blossom looked up bewildered. Nef coughed to cover a giggle.

Lady Pamela ploughed on, "Your voice needs to be lower and softer. At the moment you sound like cross between a strangled chicken and a braying donkey".

Nefertiti pressed her lips together and took a deep breath through her nose barely holding back a snort.

It was obvious to Pandora that Cherry Blossom was at a loss and understood very little of what was being discussed.

Pandora touched her arm and said slowly, "I'll help you Cherry…Wilma. Don't worry. May I give Cherry the tour Lady P? Fill her in on all the rules?"

Lady Pamela nodded. "Make sure she comes in tomorrow at 10-30am sharp."

She checked her agenda.

"Today I'm going to talk to you about a hygiene problem…It concerns the gentlemen…"

The girls nodded in agreement.

"Smoking cigarettes, cannabis and especially cigars is absolutely forbidden. Tell your clients, forcefully but in a charming manner,-ABSOLUTELY NO SMOKING!"

The girls jumped to attention at the increased volume of her voice.

"If the clients want to do a Bill Clinton, then that is quite acceptable but smoking the cigar afterwards is strictly forbidden".

Pandora and Nefertiti raised eyebrows at each other while Cherry Blossom stared blankly at Lady P.

"Smoke gets into all the silk draperies and bedlinen not to mention causing a possible fire hazard. Let us not forget the arsonist client who set alight a girl's negligee while she was still wearing it. An ex-fireman I believe".

The girls exchanged horrified looks.

"Smoke also yellows all my beautiful ceilings…oh yes and talking of yellow, there is something else I want to mention. I've had a complaint from Tanice. Male genitalia when used for Le PeePee and in her words: *Dey…THEY is… ARE swishin' like a donkey's tail* ..so before and after the event please ask them to be mindful of direction".

Pandora was longing to laugh but knew she would be reprimanded. She brought her palm to her mouth and bit the side of her hand. Cherry Blossom sat in a fog of incomprehension. She raised her hand slowly.

"Yes Cherry blossom?"

"Solly Lady P. I not sure. What is Bill Clinton?"

"Fill her in please Pandora....Later. Now off you go. Nefertiti you have your first client at two pm. make sure your Turkish Belly dancer costume is in good order".

Pandora, Lady Pamela's dominatrix employee was a tall well-built no-nonsense woman in her late thirties with an impressive forty six inch double D cup, long muscular legs and a great sense of humor. She was blessed with long curly strawberry blonde hair and limpid dark blue eyes. She had been with Lady P for five years; a long time in the escort business but as she was a solo mother with one school age child and an aged mother to support she needed to earn substantially in order to clothe and feed her family. She lived with her mother Dot, a former escort, in a two bedroom council flat in Battersea. Dot was Pandora's best friend and confidante and was able to help out with Ethan at night and during the school holidays. Pandora's position with Lady Pamela was extremely well paid and the conditions were far superior to her previous place of employment: - a seedy dive in Soho. She enjoyed a good relationship with Nefertiti and was always very welcoming to any new girls in Lady P's stable. She had a sneaking admiration for the old lady and was amazed that Casa Blanca appeared to function very efficiently without any of the neighbors being aware of what was going on. Occasionally she had been looked at curiously by a passer-by but that was probably she was wearing her spike heeled boots and had her treasured sable coat pulled up round her ears to ward off the winter chill. Pandora was a very beautiful woman but she was not the sort of person who would trade on her looks out of escort hours and was naturally a very down-to-earth warm person.

Later that day Lady Pamela received a phone call from The Colonel. The Colonel's deep voice sounded pleased.

"She's taken the bait".

"Who? Oh you mean Laura".

"She took a little while to decide but they are having lunch together next week at Hong Kong Harry's".

Lady Pamela smiled. "That place is so convenient isn't it being almost next door to where James stays. I must say I am very pleased. She has come to the right decision"

"And you won't have to refund any of the money".

The Colonel rumbled happily.

"Colonel that is not the point. All I want is for Laura to be transported-"

The Colonel broke in. "-To the land of orgasmic pleasures".

"Henry please. All I meant was that I want Laura to be happy and fulfilled".

"Of course my dear and another piece of business executed in your impeccable style. By the by I'll check Edward is around for bridge on Sunday. Toodlepip Old Girl".

Lady Pamela put the phone down and mulled over the fact that The Colonel was never going to understand her motives for helping those in need. He didn't have her sensitivity. She felt in a small way she was helping women like Laura to find their true selves but for him it was all in the deal, in other words, how much could they could make out of sexual liaisons.

Lady Pamela never tired of saying to anyone who would listen or even if they were not listening that she was in the business of helping people. Pandora and Nef who came from very ordinary backgrounds were being helped to better themselves by brushing up against men of influence, well perhaps a little more than 'brushing up' but they were very well paid and their part-time jobs fitted perfectly with their domestic arrangements. The men who came to Casa Blanca could go home to their marital beds, refreshed and renewed. Tanice again very well paid was being exposed to a beautiful house and surroundings which must improve her education. Lady Pamela voiced a sudden thought.

"I must approach Tanice about her literacy."

As Tanice was at the end of her working day and possibly might not react favorably to MadamPam's suggestion of helping her with reading and writing, Lady Pamela decided to speak to her later in the week.

In the kitchen Tanice was busy on her life's work. Her exercise book lay open in front of her on the kitchen table. She re-read the words complete with crossings out that she had written a few days before.

> *Lady Delphine,she lay on her back along the ege of the pool, her long shaved/smooth leg trayled in the cooling blue water. The warmth of the late sun entered her sex/body and filed her head with wiked things/thorts. Rastus, Rastus she wispered, then Moneing/groneing a little she skooped up some water and poured it onto her belly and thiyes. It trinkled down between her legs.*

Tanice let out a low whistle and muttered,
"Delphine you is getting me hot".

73

Lady Pamela's bell rang in the distance. Tanice slammed shut the exercise book.

"But I can't do no more 'cos Madam want her tea and biscuits".

Tanice was told on her first day in no uncertain terms to use only loose tea leaves. MadamPam had firmly pronounced, 'Those bags are an abomination'.

She prepared a tray with an embroidered cloth. On it she placed a fine Wedgewood china cup and saucer and a matching plate. Opening an antique biscuit tin with a picture of The Queen on the lid she took out two home-baked shortbread biscuits and placed them on the plate. Having warmed an ornate silver tea pot she put in two heaped teaspoons of green tea leaves, MadamPam's special mix and added boiling water. Alongside the teapot she placed a dish of two lemon slices and a silver tea strainer. A snow white linen napkin completed the picture.

Carefully balancing the tray with one hand she opened the kitchen door and went into Lady Pamela's sitting room. Dandi looked up expectantly. He raised himself on bandy legs and ambled over to Tanice as she placed the tray on Madame's footstool.

"Ah Tanice. Pandora has just finished for the day. Make sure the lavatory is properly cleaned and change those sheets please."

"Yes MadamPam. Can I leave after doing de cleaning please? It's My Victor's birthday tomorrow an' I want to bake a cake tonight."

"That will be fine. Is my supper tray ready?"

"Yes MadamPam. I prepared de prawn, spinach and avocado salad like you ask me".

Lady Pamela nodded her assent.

Tanice noticed that Dandi was sitting very close to the biscuits and was loudly sniffing. Tanice glared at the dog.

Dandi eyed the biscuits. Lady Pamela admonished him.

"Dandi. Go to your basket!"

Dandi looked crest-fallen. Lady Pamela consoled him with baby talk.

"Aar, poor baby, is Mummy being mean to you? Mummy give you an ickle treat later".

Tanice took a breath and stiffened her posture. She supressed the urge to growl. Giving his mistress a doleful look, Dandi wandered away to his bed.

"Thank you Tanice. That will be all".

Tanice turned on her heel and clumped out, shutting the door forcefully behind her. Lady Pamela winced. Back in the kitchen Tanice banged her hand on the table.

"Dat dog don't know what's coming to him. De only ting Dandelions are fit for is weed killer!"

After she sent the text to Blue Eyes, Laura experienced a mixture of excitement and guilt. One part of her was thinking what have I done and I shouldn't be doing this and the other part was thinking I can't wait to see him. Excitement seemed to overcome her guilty feelings and she was counting the days. In the meantime she was observing David and looking at him with completely new eyes. David had been upbeat and chatty after the forceful fuck, which initially made her feel that perhaps she had been too hasty in contacting James, but in light of the porn discovery she reckoned she owed herself a treat and tit for tat anyway. In David's case, more tit than tat. She wondered whether she should confront David about the porn websites but decided that she might leave that discovery until a later date. His predilection could possibly be used to her advantage in the future.

75

Wednesday morning arrived and even though Laura had not had a good night's sleep she felt uplifted at the thought of seeing Blue Eyes. David had rushed off early to talk to the subcontractors so Laura had the morning to get through before heading up to London on the train. To pass the time and to stop her from pacing the floor, she decided to clean the oven.

She left the house in plenty of time even though she had changed out of her outfit of designer jeans and denim jacket at the last minute. Deciding that the outfit was 'too pubby' and not 'flash lunch place with new man', she put on a navy and white silk shift dress with a designer cardigan and wound her long blonde hair into a topknot. Donning some heels and a pair of pearl earrings she set off for the station. Her stomach turned somersaults on the train; she wondered if she would actually be able to swallow a morsel of food and became even more knotted when David sent a text,

> *What's for dinner? Shall I get some steak on the way home?*

She texted back.

> *Lovely. Thanks.*

She found Hong Kong Harry's quite easily and as she was ten minutes early decided to take a walk around Sloane Square. She passed the Little Chelsea Hotel that Blue Eyes had mentioned. As there was a small park almost opposite she crossed the road and went to sit on one of the benches overlooking the central grassy area. A young mother and her two young children were sitting on the grass have a picnic lunch. How happy they looked. She checked her watch and seeing that it was a minute to twelve, she set off back to the restaurant. Blue Eyes was waiting for her outside. Her heart did a flip when she saw him.

"Laura, you look lovely. How are you?"

He gave her a warm kiss on the cheek. How delicious his aftershave smelled.

"And it's ...it's nice to see you too"

She cleared her constricted throat and smiled into those wonderful eyes.

"Shall we?" And he took her arm and escorted her in the restaurant.

Hong Kong Harry's was half full although she noticed that all the other tables had reserved signs placed on them. Blue Eyes led her over to a table in a secluded corner and in gentlemanly fashion pulled out the chair for her to sit. He looked exactly as she remembered him and was dressed in an open necked long sleeved navy striped shirt which contrasted beautifully with his silver hair. As he looked across at her, she could feel her face pinking up. Just keep it together she thought. It's just a lunch. The waiter appeared and handed them some menus.

"First of all what would you like to drink Laura. Some wine?"

"Um…er perhaps I could just have a glass of sparkling water?"

As the waiter was writing this down, Blue Eyes gave Laura a searching look.

"Are you sure? Perhaps a glass of Champagne to go with it?"

She laughed. "Oh alright then".

Blue Eyes ordered a bottle of Dom Perignon.

For Laura the lunch seemed to pass in a blur. Ascertaining that she liked duck, he ordered Peking Duck plus a couple of side dishes. The food arriving promptly was exquisite and the champagne even better. He asked her what she had been up to. Laura told him how busy she was with The Manning Company, especially now they had a lucrative contract with an

Indian multi-millionaire Mr. Gupta. James said that he had heard the name and had read about him in the business news.

"Be a little careful there. He's not too reliable where paying is concerned…and I've got a feeling he was embroiled, not too long ago, in a sexual harassment case".

Her eyes flew open. "Really?"

And thinking Cindy will be very interested in that piece of information. Blue Eyes did not ask about David and she was not inclined to mention him either.

He chatted on about his travels. He had been back to The States since they first met ostensibly to check on his property portfolio and organize some work to be done on two of the seaside homes.

"Actually I'd like your opinion on the interiors. I'm thinking of a radical change".

"I'd love to but with my life the way it is I don't see how I can help you".

He smiled at her and said, "I'm sure we'll find a way".

At the end of the meal he asked her if she would like to take coffee at another place down the road. Whispering across the table,

"Chinese don't know how to make coffee".

"That would be nice".

Laura rose from the table and went to find the Ladies. When she returned he had paid the bill and tucking her arm through his, he walked her down the steps onto the pavement. They turned right out of Harry's and began to walk where Laura had killed some time. They came to the entrance of The Little Chelsea Hotel and James swept her up into the entrance hall. Feeling rather disorientated from the champagne and realization that perhaps more than coffee was on offer, she stuttered,

"A Ho...Hotel? For coffee?"

"Actually I'm staying here at present. They have a very good barista here" and he gave her sly look.

"Oh I see."

Laura paused and as she looked at him he came alongside her and put an arm around her waist and kissed her gently on the back of her neck. Laura closed her eyes and half aware of her surroundings, she was led gently to the lift. The lift arrived and two business women in their fifties, arguing loudly, got out and harangued each other across to the reception desk. Laura and James entered the lift and after James had pressed floor number eight, he put his arms around her and began to kiss her passionately. Laura with no hesitation lifted her arms to encircle his neck and hungry for him pressed her mouth and body against his. The lift doors flung themselves open and James, almost bodily lifting a laughing Laura past an elderly Japanese couple who babbled incomprehensibly at this surprising sight, swept Laura into his room and kicking the door shut behind him he lifted Laura onto the bed.

Laughing she kicked off her shoes, pulled the clasp from her hair and let her blonde locks fall around her shoulders. Without a word he stripped off his shirt, trousers, and shoes and pressed himself against her, his cock straining against his jockeys. He started to kiss her neck, her ears, her eyes and then her willing mouth.

"Sit up a little" he said softly.

She complied and he carefully removed her dress and lacy bra. He traced his hands gently all over her breasts and then cupping one to his mouth he teased the nipple with his tongue. Laura could feel the dampness grow between her legs and she writhed with arousal. She started to try to remove her pants but he stopped her and said,

"Not yet".

79

And parting her legs he kissed her thighs and started to rub his cock over her black lace panties. Laura knew that this action would result in her coming. She couldn't help herself. As the pressure of this action began to bring her to orgasm, her mouth opened and she gave an audible sigh.

He growled in her ear.

"I'm going to eat you alive" and then said, "Turn over".

She turned onto her stomach and flung her arms above her head.

He stood quickly and stripped off. He then pressed himself into from behind, pushing against the black lace; leaning in, he began to pull the lace down. He buried his face in her arse and then ran his mouth over the smooth skin of her backside, occasionally gently biting gently while Laura let out little yelps of pleasure. In one movement her pants came off and flipping her on her back, she gasped as he stood before her in all his glory. She closed her eyes for a second to savor the moment. He was coming to get her. She couldn't wait. He entered her slowly lifting himself slightly to ensure a delicious friction on her clitoris and then as she writhed under him lifting her hips to meet him, he increased his speed and brought them both to a shattering climax. When they had lain together for a little while he started stroking her all over again ending with his tongue fluttering across her clitoris. She came again for the second time.

They lay together not speaking for what seemed only a few minutes but when she opened her eyes she realized she had fallen asleep and thirty minutes had passed. She heard the shower running. Frantically looking at her watch she saw the time was after four. She'd have to take a later train. James came out of the bathroom with a towel round his waist.

"I didn't want to wake you, my love. You looked so beautiful lying there".

"James. James".

She put her arms up to him and they embraced.

On the train back to Kingbridge she couldn't stop smiling. Everything had been perfect. A sudden thought assailed her. They had used no protection. So immersed was she in his physicality and the wonderful feeling of being caressed with such passion that any thought of protection had been driven clean out of her head. A tiny doubt formed in her mind but it was dismissed when she made a quick monthly calculation. She mused on David's secretive hobby and reassured herself that taking her pleasure where she could was perfectly acceptable. There was certainly no need to feel guilty. She knew that her relationship with Blue Eyes would continue. He had underlined the fact that it was up to her to contact him and they had parted knowing that another meeting would be arranged.

On her arrival home, she noted that David had started preparing the dinner, something he rarely did. He greeted her with a kiss,

"You're back late".

"Bumped into someone I met at a design course a few months back".

"Who was that?"

"Oh no-one you'd know. We had a cup of tea together".

As David was making a salad, Laura said,

"Been marching around London all day, I'll just go and take a shower".

It seems quite easy to lie she thought. I think I'll do it again.

CHAPTER 6

Lady Pamela was seated in her usual chair and while waiting for the girls to join her for their meeting she was mending Dandelion's Teddy. A new one, number eight, had been bought to replace number seven and had already been through the wars and lost a leg. Even though Lady Pamela would regularly splash out on the most expensive food and champagne, she baulked at paying out anything for Dandi's entertainment. Using cat gut to sew on teddy's limb, the irony of which was not lost on her, she muttered to herself,

"Bloody dog gets through more teddies than the clients get through cock covers."

She finished the last stitch and threw number eight across the room hitting Dandi on the nose. He grabbed the missile and placing it beside him subsided into his usual torpid slumber.

Lady Pamela put her sewing basket away and checked the large mahogany casket placed on her footstool. A notice was taped to the top of the box. It read-

For Cell phones, iPads, iPods, lap tops, PCs and any other paraphernalia that beeps.

When she had first introduced this holding pen for the girls' electronic devices, they had baulked at allowing their precious appendages to be severed from their bodies but Lady P had been adamant. In retaliation, Pandora mischievously decided to give the old dear a shock by secretly putting a clattering vibrator among the cell phones. Lady P was not amused.

There was a soft knock on the door and the girls trooped in and draped themselves about the sitting room.

Cherry Blossom, still a little scared of Lady Pamela, sat the furthest away. Dandi, sniffing Nefertiti, ambled over and sat on her shoe.

"Pandora, please take Dandi to the kitchen and ask Tanice to give him a treat and keep him there 'til we have finished our meeting".

Pandora took the reluctant dog by the collar and pulled him over to the adjoining kitchen door. She pushed him through and without saying anything to Tanice, shut the door firmly and sat down.

Tanice was in the middle of trying to decide on the title for her book when Dandi was shoved through the door. They glared at each other and Dandi started sniffing. Tanice had just put a meat loaf, a house favorite, in the oven. Now this damned dog was going to ruin her concentration.

Ignoring Dandi, she opened her exercise book and got to work. She had mulled over all sorts of titles:-

'Lady Delphine was no lady'

'Hot and Wet in Paradise'

'The lady and de/the veg boy'

But the right title had not yet come to mind.

The knotty problem of describing Rastus' desire for Delphine in written form did not come easily to her.

> *Rastus was working in the garden cleering the weeds from round the corjet plants. The swet was trinkerling down his crack/back to his buttoks and catchin on the hare on his chest. He wiped de swet off his face with the pretty wite kercheef she give him. His nose smelled her smell/perfewm-My Lady-Soon we be lying together he thort. He picked a large corget and stroked it. A funny look came on his face and he felt his cocky stifen up under his coton shorts.*

83

> *Delphine my lady she like it big and hard. I go stuff it in her tonite.*

Tanice shook her head and crossed through the last sentence and wrote:

> *I go and fill her tremblin trumpet flower*

Dandi slumped on the floor looked between her and the stove drooling all the while.

Lady Pamela, glancing around at her staff, began.

"Today we are going to talk about security. As you know I have a horror of any security breaches with regard to our clients and as we have all seen in the media, electronic equipment can be easily tapped or hacked. Discretion is paramount and I have to rest easy in my bed knowing I can trust you all implicitly. If I find you have secreted a second cell phone about your person....I will find out Pandora! You will be fined twenty pounds and the offending device will be confiscated. Now please turn off all of your devices and place them in this box."

Pandora and Nefertiti fished out their cell phones and Nefertiti took her iPad out of her bag. They dropped all the items into the box. Cherry Blossom clutched her iPhone to her chest and was reluctant to part with it. Looking warily at Lady Pamela, she said,

"I need it for emergency".

"Cherry Blossom, if a client causes trouble all you have to do is press the panic button under your bed and the fire alarm goes off. It's so loud it could wake the dead. The clients will be out of here like scalded cats with or without their trousers. In fact the alarm has been used only once so while you are here you are quite safe. Do you understand?"

"I no like". And clutching her phone closely, she shook her head.

Lady Pamela put on her stern voice. "If you cannot

84

part with your device while you are on these premises then your contract is terminated forthwith."

"Solly Madame I don't under-...?"

Nefertiti lent across-

"You're sacked".

Cherry Blossom tearfully collected her things and made for the door. Flicking her hair back in defiance she eyeballed Lady Pamela and in her familiar donkey bray spat out some choice Chinese insults.

"他妈的你的母狗!" ..

She slammed the door behind her.

"Thank goodness. I've been having complaints and I was actually planning to terminate her employment... and quite frankly she's N Q O K D."

Nefertiti looked inquiringly at Pandora. Pandora enunciated in a cut glass accent.

"Not Quite Our Kind Dear".

Poor little Wilma. She would be much happier in a Chinese brothel on the other side of town.

"Now there is one more thing on my list. Tanice has brought it to my attention. It concerns chocolate".

Nefertiti dropped her head and tried to give Pandora a sly glance.

"Yes Nef. It does concern you. I know there is a certain gentleman who likes to lick chocolate off ...well I don't have to tell you where...BUT in future he will not be doing any licking in the bedroom. Poor Tanice has had a devil of job removing melted chocolate off the sheets...next time get into the bath tub…both of you and clean up after yourselves. Have you got that Nef?"

"Yes Lady P".

The meeting concluded after Lady Pamela had discussed the question of updating the girls' photographs.

"We need some new ones of you Pandora, as pretty

nursey Spankybot".

She laughed as Pandora made a face. "And Nefertiti has to be photographed in her new Turkish costume".

Dates were discussed and organized and then Lady Pamela dismissed the team with the promise of another theme party in the next few weeks.

"And Pandora I need you to man, or should I say woman the phone this afternoon from 2 pm…In your best telephone voice".

"Righto Lady P".

Lady Pamela had two landlines at Casa Blanca - one for the business and one for her private use. Even though she was very strict on staff cell phones that did not deter her from having a cell phone of her own. She had resisted the technology for some time until The Colonel eventually persuaded her by saying,

"You might need it for an emergency".

She smiled at the irony of the phrase 'Do as I say not do as I do'.

As customers had requested a Chinese girl she decided to redecorate the Venetian room in Chinese style. The gondola scene along the Grand Canal had become marked and the golden draperies were badly torn in one area where one of the gentleman in a fit of passion had tried to wrap his naked consort in the golden silk before ravishing her on the four poster. Lady Pamela was not amused.

After the girls left the room Lady Pamela ran her hand along the middle shelf of her mahogany book shelf and removed a large leather bound copy of the Encyclopedia Britannica, volume six. She opened the cover and retrieved her personal iPhone from the space cut into the center of the book. She had chosen the William Tell overture as her ringtone but still had trouble hearing the phone so had turned the volume onto high. Peering at the phone she had trouble finding the "on" button. She muttered.

"Can't see or hear the damn thing".

She put on her reading glasses and taking the phone to the light. A message came up. It was from the Colonel. She stabbed a nail on the message icon.

> *Confirming bridge on Sunday @ 4pm. Both Tony and Edward are able to come.*

Lady Pamela had met Tony Fredericks a few years back. She had come across his book shop on one of her outings with Dandi. She had noticed a beautiful Italian interior decorating hardback in the window and felt it would be a great help in assisting her in her choice of design for Casa Blanca. She had tied Dandi to the railing outside the shop and the nice young man with dark brown eyes and thoughtful expression had come out from behind the counter and said she was quite welcome to bring Dandi inside, out of the sun's glare. She had told him that Dandi had a propensity for paperbacks and needed to stay outside. The young man had looked inquiringly at her and she continued,

"He likes to chew them in small pieces...A naughty habit...I think he likes the taste of the paper and the crunch of the cardboard. This shop would be a chewer's heaven to him."

The man had laughed and introduced himself as the owner of the shop:

"Tony Fredericks....At your service".

Lady Pamela was delighted to meet someone who shared her love of the written word. He collected rare antique books as well as stocking the shelves with modern and literary novels and special interest books as well as second hand titles. They discovered that they both had an abhorrence of Kindle and she was pleased to find someone of the younger generation-she estimated to

87

him to be around forty- with whom she could have a good grouse from time to time about the technological age. They came to be across the bridge table from one another when Lady Pamela had asked him if he would mind putting up a notice in his window. He had read it and then said,

"Bridge partner? Well I learnt a while ago but because the shop keeps me busy I haven't had the time to play in recent times."

Lady Pamela had pressed him to join her regular Sunday game.

"Do Come ...it's just the Colonel and I and a young friend of ours, Edward Hanbury...he'd be around your age. We start at 4pm and finish around 6-30pm. The colonel and I often go to The Ritz for a cocktail afterwards. You are very welcome to join us".

As Tony was looking a little wary, she continued,

" ...and we don't bite".

"Well I shut the shop at 4pm usually but I could close a little earlier....if you are sure? I'm a bit rusty".

And so it was arranged. Tony Fredericks became their fourth player at the bridge table.

Lady Pamela had firmly said to Henry that their new bridge friend had no inkling of what really took place in the house and must not be made aware. Before Tony's first visit Lady Pamela had telephoned Edward and said,

"There will be no lewd conversations or recounting of Pandora's exploits with the latest peer of the realm. Do I make myself clear....Edward?"

"Crystal Auntie P".

Lady Pamela was particularly fond of Edward, Henry's nephew, the son of Henry's sister. Edward Hanbury was a good if flashy player and made an effort to turn up most Sundays if he was in town. Edward knowing he was her favorite surrogate nephew was

88

hoping for a substantial windfall when the old lady kicked the bucket. He felt that as her only son Giles was out of the picture living in The States, this could give him the perfect opportunity to stake a claim on the old girl's will. He made a point of ingratiating himself and flattering the old duck. A handsome old Etonian in his mid-thirties with perfect manners, Edward was always a charming and amusing guest. She had overlooked Henry's comments about Edward's drinking problem and dismissed Henry's disapproval with regard to Edward's current occupation - a fashion model.

"Needs a proper job and a boot camp for character building would not go amiss".

The Colonel had said.

"At least he gets to travel frequently and gets paid handsomely for what he does".

The Colonel grumbled on about the sort of people Edward was mixing with, getting into a bad set with a load of gamblers, drunks and coke-snorting wannabees. Too much money and not enough sense.

"The army would sort him out double quick".

Lady Pamela smiled and wrote a note to remind herself to order the Black Forest Gateau that Edward was so fond of.

In the course of a month of Sundays Lady Pamela had learnt that Tony was divorced. He had suffered a 'coup de foudre' at twenty two and as a passionate love-struck fool married his Norwegian girlfriend only to discover that she suffered from a bi-polar disorder and was either swinging from the chandeliers or in bed with the duvet pulled up over her head. She had tried to control her moods with medication but she put on weight and became even more depressed. They had struggled on for a few years and he had even tried living in Norway teaching English Literature but in the end he made a break and returned to London. The week before he met Lady Pamela he and his long-term French girlfriend Francine had decided to part.

Even though Sundays could have been quite lucrative for Casa Blanca, Lady Pamela believed that Sundays should be kept for rest and recreation. The girls had been sent home to be with their families and Tanice was tending to her husband and children. MadamPam used to quote words from that famous song.

"Never on a Sunday for that's my day of rest".

To that end Tony Fredericks while bidding three No Trumps was completely unaware of what was hidden at the heart of 32 Davenport Gardens. He loved looking around at Lady Pamela's elegantly furnished sitting room, glancing from the beautiful cream damask sofas to her extensive collection of hard back books, her French porcelain collection and the charming carriage clock on the mantelpiece. He thought that he spotted a Barbara Hepworth sculpture and wasn't that an original Hockney drawing?

To him Lady Pamela and her companion the Colonel seemed to be a charming well-heeled couple who were enjoying the sunset of their lives, with gentle walks, games of bridge and cocktails at The Ritz. He was cautious where Edward was concerned. He'd met that handsome popular type at public school and had learnt to be wary of their flashy ways and smooth clever repartee.

Even though no business was transacted on Sunday, Lady Pamela had to answer the phone to prospective punters. Edward's ears were always a-flap and latterly Tony had overheard some interesting titbits. Lady Pamela always took calls on the kitchen extension but often left the door open allowing the group to overhear. Tony was intrigued by such comments as -

"Yes you may come in by the back door" and "Three

to a room is quite possible".

The Colonel headed Tony away from the truth.

"She has lodgers you know. Pays the gas bill and being a kind landlady, she allows them to share a room".

Edward cackled loudly at this and Tony gave him a raised eyebrow.

Dandelion tolerated Lady Pamela's bridge afternoons-just.

He made friends with Tony almost straight away as Tony showed him respect and noting that Tony had a pleasant odor, he had presented no threat. The Colonel being an old friend of Lady Pamela's had been introduced to him as a pup so the Colonel's musty familiarity was perfectly acceptable. Edward Hanbury was another kettle of bones. As soon as Edward turned into Davenport Gardens in his silver Porsche, Dandi stiffened his posture; his hackles rose and lifting his head, he started a low growl baring his ill-arranged teeth in the process. After Dandi had taken a piece out of Edward's expensive trousers leaving tooth marks on his lower calf, the Colonel had immediately insisted on taking Edward to the doctor for a clean-up and a tetanus shot. The Colonel had mentioned to Edward that perhaps the liberal use of after-shave lotion was troubling Dandi and the smell could have possibly enraged him. In any event Dandi had been banished to the kitchen for the duration of all further bridge games. Lady Pamela horrified at Dandi's behavior had said,

"I can't understand it. He's usually quite friendly. There's only one other person he doesn't like and that's the dustbin man".

Dandelion knew what sort of person Edward was; a piece of garbage where Dandi was concerned. Edward was more upset at being lumped together with the dustbin man as Dandi's 'most hated' than he was at being bitten.

The last time the foursome had got together Lady Pamela and her partner Tony had held excellent cards and crowed about their win while The Colonel, a grumpy player at the best of times, had muttered to himself about the fickleness of fate in delivering him a constant stream of poor cards.

"Not even something I could defend with….."

Then to Edward who saw himself as a player with flair but in reality was maddeningly slapdash.

"For God's sake pay attention Edward. I signaled my lead. We could have taken them down a trick".

Edward had brushed off the mistake and excused himself as Lady Pamela went into the kitchen to organize the afternoon cuppa and cake. Dandi had come bounding out and growled as Edward side-stepped nimbly and then slipped out into the hall before Dandi could nip his ankle, shutting the door quickly behind him.

Edward, earlier in the day, had decided that he needed to avail himself of something to provide funds for a little cocaine party he was planning and more pressingly to pay back the debt of several thousand that he had organized through a loan shark. The shark had made a menacing phone call the day before.

"Yer got three days pretty boy, pay up or we'll turn yer face into strawberry jam".

There was only one thing for it and that was to obtain by fair means or foul cash to get him out of the jam.

Edward had moved quickly and quietly up the stairs and had gone directly into Lady Pamela's bedroom situated at the top of the stairs. It was a large double windowed room overlooking the sprawling garden with its own ensuite bathroom and separate dressing room. Lady Pamela had chosen soft beige carpet and curtains to go with the off white walls. On the double bed lay a pristine white bedcover. The whole effect was calm and relaxing, exactly what she wanted after a day at the coal face of Casa Blanca.

Edward had already cased the joint a few weeks before so knew exactly where to look and what to look for. In the bottom drawer of her mahogany wardrobe under a silk Chinese throw was an ornate silver jewelry box. For some reason Lady Pamela had left it unlocked. She had lost the key at one time and had to have it opened by a locksmith and even though a new lock had been fitted, she preferred not to experience the stress of possibly losing the new key and so the box remained free for anyone to open.

Edward had listened and checked the landing and then quickly opened the wardrobe drawer. He uplifted the box and inspecting the contents took out a heavy gold bracelet studied with emeralds, a silver and sapphire necklace and a pair of sapphire and diamond drop earrings. Deciding on the earrings, his experience at Aspreys having helped him to evaluate their worth, he had pocketed them. He had carefully replaced the other pieces before tucking the box back under the Chinese throw.

The Colonel had tried very hard to persuade Lady Pamela to put all the valuables of which she had a considerable collection in a safety deposit box at the bank but she would have none of that.

"Two reasons Henry. One, I do like to wear my jewelry from time to time and two, it could get stolen".
The Colonel had assured her that it would take a dynamited tank to break open the bank vault. She had argued her point.

"What about that case where they tunneled into the bank vault through the basement of the shop next door and in any case, how do you know that all the bank staff are trustworthy? You can't trust anyone these days. If there is something to be had especially cash or jewelry a dishonest employee will always find a way".

She had not factored into her calculations that charming Edward who was almost like a son to her was boldly lifting her prize possessions right under her nose. The old duck won't even notice he had thought. On leaving the bedroom he had heard a familiar bray coming up the stairs.

"Edwaard…Hurry up we're having tea. Would you like a whisky? The Colonel's pouring".
Edward took a sharp look around the bedroom and exited saying,

"Just coming. Still fighting the curry from last night" And he ran down the stairs two at a time, the earrings jingling in his pocket.

Just as Lady Pamela was going through to the kitchen to collect Dandi and talk to Tanice about her cleaning duties for the day, she received another text from The Colonel.

JJK3 -Mission accomplished. Explosive result!

She smiled and nodded to herself knowing that she had been right about Laura all along. She was very pleased that Laura was taking this possibility. The only nagging thought was that knowing James this liaison might not last more than six months. Notwithstanding it was lovely to help people, something she knew she was good at. Anyway it was over to them now to make it work. She dismissed the thought that the result of this matching could possibly be unpredictable in the long run. She made a mental note to remind James that as he had paid for the Chinese Room, there was no need to spend extra dollars on a hotel room. She must remind him though to book in advance. She opened the kitchen door.

Tanice was standing with her back against the kitchen counter glaring at Dandi. He had his mouth open and a pool of spittle covered the floor as he gazed at the meat loaf that she had just been removed from the oven.

"Well there you are Dandi. Naughty boy dribbling over Tanice's delicious looking meat loaf. Off you go". And she shooed him back into the sitting room while Tanice looked away and scowled.

"It's that time again Tanice".

"Yes MadamPam".

She sighed audibly and she shut the exercise book in front of her.

Tanice knew what was coming as MadamPam was a stickler for cleanliness and there was one task that MadamPam insisted Tanice carry out on a regular basis. It was time for Spring Cleaning. A task Tanice dreaded and the worst job of all was scrubbing out Pandora's basement and dealing with that hideous storage container, Pandora's Box, a large mahogany chest covered in Chinese dragons and hieroglyphics that MadamPam had picked up in Shanghai. This ghastly box contained an array of leather whips, paddles, clamps, ropes, chains, hoods, handcuffs and various sizes of what looked like giant nut crackers. Tanice shuddered every time she handled these and did not want to speculate on what they might be used for.

Early on she had found a wooden rolling pin and it looked suspiciously like the one she used to roll out pastry for MadamPam's Quiche Lorraine. She checked and sure enough it had been purloined for nefarious purposes. She immediately went out and bought a replacement.

MadamPam insisted that Tanice wash all the

equipment by hand in hot soapy water to which she must add a cupful of bleach.

"We don't want any of our clients to become infected".

Tanice mused that any client who came in for a good whipping from Pandora might quite enjoy being infected as it would add to the level of pain that they obviously got off on. Anyway her view didn't count and as MadamPam paid her handsomely not only for keeping Casa Blanca ship-shape but also for keeping her mouth shut, she did as she was told and got to work. While the weapons dried she scrubbed out the inside of the chest. MadamPam had emphasized,

"Make sure the inside is properly dried out. I don't want any mold in evidence".

Head down and arse up at the bottom of the chest, Tanice had a sudden brain wave. Rastus and Delphine could start experimenting ....just a light spanking to start with and then....

Tanice, with renewed vigor, finished cleaning the chest and then set to work on the room itself. Pandora's basement had once been the old kitchen at Casa Blanca and in keeping with the times a dumb waiter had been installed in the far corner. This contraption ran on an ancient pulley system and was used to ferry food and crockery up and down between the kitchen and the dining room above; a saving grace for the poor kitchen maid's well worked legs. Before Lady Pamela had been bequeathed the property, the kitchen had been re-instated on the ground floor and so the old kitchen in the basement had become Pandora's lair. The dumb waiter had been turned from an innocent work horse into a sinister cell reminiscent of Nazi concentration camps where Pandora made her trussed victims crouch in the dark. Tanice shuddered as she cleaned it out. She then

96

polished up the gym horse that MadamPam had bought cheaply from a defunct girls' boarding school and washed down the wooden stools. She cringed as she stripped the cover off the single iron bed, revealing its thin ancient rubber mattress probably purloined by MadamPam from a prison refurbishment. The wall hooks had to be washed, dried and then polished until they shone. She then scrubbed the floor and checking the chest was completely dry put back all the equipment. Then smiling to herself, she extracted a notebook from her apron and jotted down the words 'Rastus gets spanked' and then suddenly remembering the comment her neighbor had said about her cat and the flap it used to enter the kitchen, she wrote down 'pussy door', for that is what it had been called by Ribena her Indian neighbor. Why on earth had she been called after a blackcurrant drink? Tanice dismissed this thought but 'Pussy Door' could be put to good use.

Later in the kitchen while she was enjoying a well-earned cup of coffee, she jotted down a few ideas.

> *'Lady Delphine tremblin with exsitement, removed her dress and slid into a pare of high heeled black lether boots. She kept on her black lacy bra and frilly nickers/panties. Round her waste she tide a silver chane.She loosed her long dark hair and put a fansy mask over her glistery eyes. As she was putting on the long blak lace gloves,she heard a nock on the bedroom window. Rastus,my big boy. He in for a big surprise, she thort. Grabbing the riding wip...'*

"Tanice...Tanice...I have been standing here for the last couple of minutes. What is it that you are so assiduously writing in that notebook?"

"Oh…er...MadamPam...sorry. I ...um… have to write a story for my English writing class"

97

"Oh I see. Excellent. Good that you are keeping up with your studies... By the way...the chocolate business is sorted. "

Tanice sighed with relief.

"I tort they was mud wrestlin'...it disgustin'… Chocolate goes on de cake not on de titties".

"Quite. They'll be in the bath doing …whatever they do…from now on...much easier to clean up".

Tanice breathed out deeply as she left the room and then having second thoughts,

MadamPam re-entered.

"I would be most willing to help you…with your story…with spelling perhaps?"

"Thank You MadamPam. I am tryin' to do it by myself"

"Very commendable Tanice. If you need someone to check it when you've finished?"

Tanice nodded glumly and resolved to be more careful in future. The last thing she wanted was for MadamPam to discover the real reason for the notebook.

CHAPTER 7

Back at Kingbridge Laura was being kept busy with client work. She was thinking about Blue Eyes frequently and was planning when she could see him again She had sent him a quick text following their liaison saying how much she had enjoyed his company and their 'coffee!' time together. Being of a cautious nature where cell phones were concerned she did not spell out in detail that she would be very happy to accept a return match in the sheets.

Mr. Gupta had seen her portfolio and commissioned a very large opulent abstract design in black, golds, reds and jade for his entrance hall. She hesitated in starting the work as she was afraid that his standard would be extremely high and she was worried that she might not be able to reach it. He had underlined to her that he would be willing to accept her choice of design but to ensure this she had drawn up and painted a mock-up of what she had in mind.

David was pleased with progress on the renovation job and even though Mr. Gupta had been over a week late with his first payment, the work was going according to plan. Peter made sure someone was present when Mr. Gupta came into the office and on the occasions Cindy was alone with him, she always kept the front desk between herself and the Indian. She was polite and business like in her dealings with him. Laura decided not tell Cindy about the sexual harassment case as she knew this news would increase Cindy's anxiety. He came into the office once or twice a week when he was in the country, sometimes for no reason at all, and tried hard to get Cindy to drop her professional front while staring at her breasts.

Cindy had phoned Laura the day before and said Mr. Gupta was keen to see the template for the painting and could Laura come in that week, possibly in the afternoon of the following day. They had agreed a time and then Cindy said,

"Honestly Laura he's a nightmare. Keeps trying to get me out of the office for coffee and God knows what else. If Pete is in and Mr. Gupta is talking to David, Pete roams around the office like a caged tiger. I keep thinking he's going to rear up and take a bite out Gupta's neck."

Laura laughed and Cindy continued, "The only good thing about being pursued by a short arse Indian is that Pete is all over me in the sack. Indirectly Mr. Gupta may be responsible for getting me pregnant....if you see what I mean".

After the conversation with Cindy, Laura thought yet again about Blue Eyes. She decided to send him a text.

> *Dear James. Still thinking about our tryst. How are you?   Next week would be good for me. Same place? and time? Let me know which day would suit...if you can make it.*

A few moments later Blue Eyes texted back.

> *My lovely Laura.. In US at present but back on Monday. Can you make Wed? Same time and place. Can't wait to see u.xx JJK3*

Cindy was head down over the computer doing some accounts when she heard a familiar voice.

"Hello my dear. I'm a little early for my appointment with Laura."

Cindy's head flew up, "Good Morning Mr. Gupta".

"My dear Cindy, please call me Rav. Mr. Gupta is so formal especially as we have become the best of friends".

Cindy smiled tightly and gritting her teeth, "Laura

100

will be in shortly to see you about the art work. Please take a seat".

Rav gave her a toothy smile and with a soft wheedle in his voice,

"Perhaps you would like to have a little coffee with me after the meeting?"

At that moment Peter popped his head round the door, "Hi Rav. Have you got a moment before Laura gets here to discuss some details on the architect's plan?"

Cindy caught Peter's eye as Rav got up from his chair and as he went into Peter's office she stuck her tongue out at his retreating back.

That evening back at Pippin Cottage Laura had cooked David's favorite meal of steak and tomatoes with roast potatoes and courgettes from her vegetable patch. Now both with secret lives, they chatted companionably at the kitchen table and shared a bottle of Beaujolais and then as usual David had upped and gone into his study to do some paperwork. Laura left him to the delights of his Indian whores and decided as the light was still good she would continue to work on her commissioned work for Mr. Gupta. The meeting had gone well although he had been distracted when Cindy brought in their coffees. She now felt more confident in commencing the design.

David did an hour's work and then extracted from its hiding place the gold edged card that the beautiful Indian model had given him at Mr. Gupta's party. He stared at it for a while and re-read.

Casa Blanca where dreams become reality.
Let us serve you discreetly.
Your fantasy is our command.

David keyed into google and typed in 'Casa Blanca'.

Websites for the film starring Humphrey Bogart and also travel sites came up. He tried putting 'Casa Blanca Escorts London' for he recognized the South London phone number. Various restaurants popped up. He scrolled down a few pages but nothing an appeared on the screen. There appeared to be no website and therefore no pictures or detail about pricing.

He listened for Laura and then called the land line number and after a few seconds a posh female voice answered.

"Good Evening. How may I be of assistance?"

David stuttered his question. "Um...er… is that…Casa Blanca?"

"Yes Sir. Could I please ask if you were recommended to call?"

"I was given your card by an Indian model at a party. I'm sorry I didn't catch her name".

"That's perfectly alright sir. Now what kind of young lady would you like to assist you? We can offer a full service with all our young ladies. Perhaps you would like to tell me your fantasy sir?"

"Fantasy? ...Just wondering if the lovely Indian girl is available".

"That would be Nefertiti. She is indeed sir. When would you like to come in?"

David grabbed his desk diary and had a quick look for the following week. He could see a window of opportunity over lunchtime on Tuesday and asked if Nefertiti - was that really her name? - was available.

"Yes sir. She could see you at 1pm. A one hour appointment sir?"

David answered in the affirmative.

The voice continued. "Now sir, as you are a new client we do have some formalities to attend to. First of all please give me a nom de plume if you know what I mean, a false name, just one."

David thought frantically and blurted out, "Santa".

Lady Pamela gritted her teeth and thought how stupid

men could be. She replied in clipped tones.

"I'm afraid that has already been used sir."

"Sorry ...I'm a bit nervous…um....Darcy".

Lady Pamela rolled her eyes and thought oh so predictable.

"That will be perfectly acceptable sir. You will be known as Mr. Darcy".

David smiled. This was going to be even more fun than he anticipated.

"Now one other matter and I am telling you this in strictest confidence, we have a password system here. Our current one is "Cactus Flower". Please remember this and speak it into the intercom when you arrive. We do insist on clients being on time preferably a few minutes early so that Nefertiti can ascertain your desire sir. Will that be alright?"

"Perfectly".

He was then given the address. David felt as if he was entering a James Bond movie.

"And one last thing sir, payment is strictly in cash. Our base hourly rate is two hundred pounds, any extras such as going by the back door, golden showers, threesomes, sex during a period or any form of sado-masochism all have to be paid for in advance."

David gave an audible gasp.

At that moment Laura came into the study and said,

"That BBC drama, the sexy one, is starting. Do you want to watch it?"

David spoke quickly into the phone. "Yes. Thank you. I do understand. I'd like to confirm that appointment. Goodbye".

Then to Laura who was looking at him enquiringly. "Yes. just coming".

Every few months Lady Pamela liked to have what she

called 'one of my little soirees'. She would invite the most popular clients, all the girls would be in attendance and one or two of her closest friends. She had recounted to Tanice, repeating herself many times as Tanice had noted, stories of the old days when people used to dress for dinner or even come in fancy dress; music and dancing would be part of the entertainment and people would leave their cares at the door. She was fond of telling Tanice how friendly she was with the upper class set and how she had rubbed shoulders with men of influence in her heyday. She mentioned yet again how popular she was with two high class actors.

"Shakespearian actors. Very accomplished in their careers but of course if I told you who they were, I'd have to kill you".

She laughed as Tanice remained underwhelmed. Tanice couldn't have cared less, but thought that bearing in mind MadamPam's racy past and her present occupation, she must have rubbed more than just shoulders with men of influence.

MadamPam was keen on theme dinners and Tanice was constantly challenged to create exotic menus to accompany Madam's chosen theme. The most difficult catering task had been assembling a large bullring out of sponge cake complete with an edible matador and charging bull for the Spanish theme night. MadamPam had worn her Flamenco cabaret costume. A scarlet figure-hugging floor length silk dress with a ruffled skirt. Unwisely, after a few drinks, she had insisted on dancing The Flamenco. The Colonel had tried to dissuade her but she was adamant.

"At Johnny's revue bar I was renowned for my Flamenco…Even the Spanish Ambassador said he had not seen a better performance".

The Colonel had underlined the fact that she was

twenty two at the time and possibly a little lighter and lither than she was now.

Lady Pamela, incensed, had retorted,

"My figure is exactly the same as it was at twenty two and as for being lithe...I'll have you know I can still do the splits...but not in this dress."

She had leapt to her feet signaled to the Spanish guitarist and flourishing her castanets had taken to the floor. Two twirls later, she found herself flat on her back, with her head resting on one of the Colonel's black patent shoes, and an ankle badly twisted. She had to suffer the embarrassment of clumping around in a moon boot for weeks.

MadamPam was discussing her latest idea with Tanice.

"I think we should have a Caribbean evening. The food will be easy for you to prepare. I'm sure you must know some delicious Caribbean delicacies...and we must have Caribbean music…A steel band...Do you have any musical contacts Tanice?"

"Me Dad played the spoons Madam...but he dead now."

"Well he's not going to be much use then..."

"...But me Trinidad cousin… he play de pan"

"Pan? Frying pan perhaps?"

"Nooo...He in a steel band group here in London".

"Excellent...get in touch with him and ask him what he charges".

Tanice made a mental note to ask him and to double the figure quoted.

"Next job is to fix a date...Oh yes we'll need your daughter to help".

Tanice's daughter Darnelle a twenty year old dance student thoroughly enjoyed waiting table at MadamPam's events and marveled at the dresses and

105

entertainment provided for the guests. Tanice had put her in the picture with regard to Casa Blanca's secret and told her to keep her mouth shut. MadamPam was always very generous with a cash payment for Darnelle's services and she often collected the added bonus of generous tips. Even though Darnelle had been told not to fraternize with the guests, her mother kept a close eye and constantly checked the gentlemen's' intentions toward her attractive extrovert daughter. She had firmly stated,

"I not havin' no daughter of mine turned into a skally".

While Tanice was writing down some recipe ideas, MadamPam was burbling on about what sort of costume she should wear.

"Well, it's got to be tropical, something flowery, hibiscus maybe or perhaps I should go for a Hollywood tropical look...sort of Carmen Miranda with a fruity headdress. What do you think Tanice?"

Tanice was busy trying to decide between Callaloo soup and savoury stuffed crab backs for the entree course.

"Madam?"

"Carmen Miranda with large earrings and a pineapple headdress?"

"Too heavy Madam".

Tanice raised her shoulders to emphasize how the weight of the pineapple would make Madam's neck disappear.

"Pineapple much better in de dessert...I have nice recipe. It have rum...very sweet".

"How sensible you are. The trouble is I am so creative. We creative types can easily get so carried away with all the marvelous ideas that stream through our brains. Now I must ring my dressmaker. "

As Lady Pamela busied herself with her own arrangements, Tanice wryly observed,

"Only one person in dis house with a brain and dat is me".

After Lady Pamela had talked to her long-suffering dressmaker, she started to write down a guest list. All the girls would be there and their favorite clients would be asked. The clients would of course be charged for the evening, the rooms and the big breakfast the following day.

Lady Pamela had a black book full of men who enjoyed her soirees; she invited the ones whom she knew would be more than happy to pay the fee. She made a note to call Fortnum and Mason and order from their breakfast takeaway menu. Kippers were always popular and a regular item on the breakfast table. She had used Fortnum's services many times before and had been one of their VIP customers for years. She added some more names to the list - The Colonel, James Jefferson Kirkpatrick the 3rd, Edward Hanbury, if he was in the country, a wealthy farmer, 2 merchant bankers who were irrepressible and Adela Johansen, an ex-employee who was always good fun and still looked amazing at fifty. Her husband was wheel-chair bound so she might enjoy some R and R. She added Ravi Gupta a regular and frequent client then she paused a moment. There was something distasteful about him; the girls had confirmed this. She decided that he would not be welcome and crossed his name out. Then of course there was Laura. Lady Pamela had thought quite a bit about Laura and she was so pleased that she had decided to take the plunge with James. As The Colonel had commented James was the perfect man to break her in so to speak. Lady Pamela did not hold with The Colonel's viewpoint that Laura would join the Casa Blanca's stable of fillies. The Colonel could be extremely crass and insensitive and was really only interested in how much money The House could make for them both. In light of her association with James and their future trysts at Casa Blanca, Lady Pamela felt it was time to let Laura into her confidence. An invitation to the West Indian party would be a perfect way to introduce Laura to the employees of Casa Blanca especially as James Jefferson Kirkpatrick the 3rd would be in attendance. She added Laura's name to her list.

In point of fact Lady Pamela was longing to confide in Laura and saw her as a friend she could trust and even, to some extent, a surrogate daughter. Lately she had been feeling her years and even though The Colonel was a great friend and support to her, he didn't understand the emotional life of women. He quoted Professor Higgins on a regular basis.

"Why can't a woman be more like a man?"

She had given up trying to argue her case.

Her oldest female friend Margarita who knew all her secrets was slowly but sadly going round the bend. Margarita had been part of the bridge four until she was certain that the King of Spades was her dear dead husband Donald. A short while after that she was carted off to The Home for The Bewildered. That will be me in the not too distant future, mused Lady Pamela.

Lady Pamela, now in her mid-seventies although she always maintained she looked a lot younger, was becoming painfully aware of her lack of close family. Her son Giles was happy in The States with his boyfriend Bobby and doing very well in his theatrical endeavors. He did occasionally call and email but showed no intention of coming back to see his old mother anytime soon. Only now did she wish she had a daughter; a daughter to confide in, to laugh with and to nurture.

She was fond of Edward but she knew, despite his solicitous ways, he was a bit of gold digger and therefore more interested in her dead than alive. Notwithstanding she enjoyed his charming ways and good manners. On the other hand The Colonel she felt was sometimes too hard on him. Lady Pamela had conveniently forgotten the incident when Edward, drunk out of his skull, had punched his girlfriend in the face and had been up for assault a few years back.

She realized that Casa Blanca, its employees and all it stood for, had become her family by default. She felt uneasy at this revelation and ruefully pondered the undeniable fact that she was the Head of an Illegal Enterprise and could still be hauled up in front of The Beak and sent to prison before kicking the bucket. On the strength of these disturbing thoughts she poured herself a double brandy and soda and busied herself with party preparations.

The girls were all gathered for their Monday talk from Lady Pamela and she had just introduced the replacement for Wilma Wong; a beautiful petite Malaysian girl who had the tiniest waist Pandora had ever seen. She was to be the new Cherry Blossom. Her English spoken with a soft lilting accent was excellent. This pleased Lady Pamela and she delighted in recounting that Cherry Blossom spoke three languages and had trained as a specialist seamstress in designer fashion back in Singapore. She had some experience in the escort business but as she wanted to improve her English and have a better understanding of British customs and etiquette, she had applied for a position at Casa Blanca. Secretly she hoped to snare a wealthy English husband.

"Now girls... some good news...I've taken delivery of

the new underwear from the Parisian Emporium…and I have made sure that they have adhered strictly to your measurements. Please try all items labelled with your name…I've taken Pandora's advice and ordered a variety of panties, feathered, lacy and sequined, lacy suspenders and G strings and crotch-less knickers in varying colors and they all come with matching bras so enjoy your new work uniforms and let me know if there is anything that does not fit you. There are also some boned bustiers and a new stock of black stockings plain and lacy".

The girls exchanged delighted glances.

Lady Pamela began to explain to Cherry Blossom the policy with regard to cell phones.

"You do understand that having a cell phone while you are working increases our security risk. Pictures can be taken and people compromised. Exposure is-".

Suddenly she was interrupted by the strains of The William Tell Overture ringing from somewhere behind the girls' heads.

Pandora spoke up. "The bookcase is ringing Lady P".

And she shot a grin at Nefertiti. "I think there's a book that needs answering".

While the girls were tittering together, Lady Pamela sprang to her feet and scrabbling for the wretched Encyclopedia Britannica, flung open the cover and grappled for the 'off' button on her iPhone.

"Yes I know Pandora. It's do as I say not as I do.

If it's any consolation I hate the thing. Now down to business. First of all we have a date for the next party."

She gave a date a month away.

"Please diarize immediately and decide which gentleman you would like to ask. Our theme this time will be Caribbean. I'll discuss costumes and entertainment with you at a later date".

The girls gave each other excited glances. They all knew that Lady P made a point of pushing the boat out party-wise and no money was spared on food, grog and entertainment. It was done as a marketing ploy and to keep the customers coming back to Casa Blanca. Even though she insisted on payment for the evening and use of the bedrooms in advance, the clients kept returning to Casa Blanca. The service she provided was five star.

"Now item two on the agenda. Cherry blossom has a new client, a top civil servant and quite the gentleman..."

Lady Pamela indiscreetly informed..."who is interested in receiving your special tea ceremony. Cherry. Do you have everything you need?"

Cherry Blossom nodded. Lady Pamela turned to Nefertiti.

"Nefertiti. You have a new client on Tuesday...a Mr. Darcy. And you are to be his dusky Elizabeth Bennett".

She laughed at her little joke. "He said you had given him our card at a party? As I must keep reminding you girls handing out our cards willy nilly is not what this agency is about-."

"-But Lady P it was Mr. Gupta's party".

"Mr. Gupta, one of our regulars? Oh well that's alright then."

Nefertiti remembered the tall muscled torso of the fair man at the party who had asked her about cricket. She smiled. A good looking client; that will be a nice change and so much more fun than the sweaty pot-bellied business men she had serviced of late.

Lady Pamela continued, "Now Pandora, your usual 3pm Saturday has asked for an extra half hour. He wants the 'slow torture' routine so unleash your box of tricks and remember everyone, discretion above all. Enjoy!"

Mr. 3pm Saturday was the only client whose sessions made Pandora a little uneasy; she wasn't exactly afraid

111

of him as he adhered strictly to the role playing rules of their time together but there was something about him that made her wonder if he might one day suddenly lose control. He was known officially by the agency as Mr. Big as he was, in every respect. Mr. Big was a well-spoken gent with immaculate manners, no doubt instilled by the cane at Public School. He was a fine figure to look at with dark good looks and stood six foot in his socks; aged in his early forties, Pandora marveled at his gym-honed body, all rippling muscle with not an excessive inch of fat and she wryly observed that his penis, when extended, was the largest she'd ever seen.

As he was a switch, their sessions together alternated between him being submissive and she dominant and then vice versa. It was at these times of her being submissive that she had to be super-vigilant. Pandora had a panic button in her domain which she had only pressed once before when a client, obviously high, had tried to smash the place apart. Lady Pamela had yelled for Tanice, shouting "Code Red!" - their signal for trouble - and Tanice had taken the baseball bat from the pantry cupboard and galloped down to the basement. One look at a formidable black woman brandishing a bat in his face resulted in the client taking to his heels, never to return.

Mr. Big was a perfect submissive and lay compliant on his stomach as Pandora to put her back into tying him extremely tightly by his wrists and ankles to the prison bed. She, wearing nothing but a thong and heeled boots, would firstly walk on his back and then straddle him and whisper menacing abuse in his ear using the filthiest language she could muster. She would then take to his bare buttocks with the riding whip. He could take a lot of pain which worried her and led her to believe that he had been badly abused at home and at school. After his submissive session where no sex act took place, he would thank her formerly, dress quickly and leave.

The following session usually a couple of weeks later would focus on him being the dominator and would involve full service. He asked that she dress as Mathilda his kitchen maid so she waited for him in plain flat shoes, crisp white shirt and a long black skirt under which was a pair of plain white knickers as requested. She tidied her long curly locks into a neat bun. They would then play the classic game of Master and Servant. He made her kneel in front of him and look him in the eye while he verbally abused her. He then made her take off her shirt so he could inspect her for purloining some of the family jewelry and yanking off her bra, he brushed his hands all over her breasts. She would then have to beg him for mercy and he would say that she had to be punished. He dragged her to her feet and tied her hands in front of her. He then bent her body over the weapons' chest. He pushed up her skirt and ripped off her knickers and exposed her cheeks to the flat of his hand followed by the paddle. It had been agreed beforehand that the paddle would be used lightly as part of their role playing contract and this was adhered to. His initial smacks elicited yelps from her. She would then act out her reaction to much harder blows by screaming. After six paddles of the best, he would stop, loose her hair so it fell forward over her hands and say huskily,

"I'm not finished with you yet Mathilda".

He then yanked off her skirt, lifted her off the chest and onto one of the rubber floor mats. Undoing his belt with a flourish, he stripped off his trousers and his cock rose majestically to the occasion. He stood with eyes glittering while she pretended to cower away from him. He would then remove a condom from his pocket and make her put it on while she, pretending to shake with

113

fear, encased his magnificence with trembling fingers all the while begging for mercy and saying she was an innocent.

"A virgin Sir...Don't take my maidenhood Sir, I beg you".

He then promptly did, with vigor. To her it felt like he was filling the place between her vagina and her throat with a long rod of steel.

After the session he would untie her, lift her to her feet and tenderly place her dressing gown round her shoulders. Nothing more was said. He would dress quickly and say a polite 'thank you' and leave.

It was quite common for clients to do the business and leave without any small talk before and after but due to Mr. Big's singular requests for both submission and domination, Pandora deduced that his past had badly damaged him and could possibly make him lose control in his role as Master. In their contract it was agreed that if one or other of them wanted to stop they would say the safe words,

"Stop the bus".

She had tested him in the early stages and he had stopped immediately and was unusually sensitive to her needs. He had made quite sure she was alright before leaving Casa Blanca that day. None-the-less Pandora knew human nature in all its forms and kept her wits about her at all times.

As the girls were leaving the room after Lady P's little talk, Pandora intrigued to learn the significance of the special service Cherry was going to provide came alongside her and asked,

"Tell me Cherry, about the special tea ceremony."

"We start very formal. We bow...then he sits and I, dressed in my high necked long cheongsam, pour him his first little cup. I kneel before him and take off his

114

shoes and socks…it's a bit smelly sometimes".

Pandora made a face.

"I then wash his feet in warm tea and dry them and massage them with perfumed oil. Then he takes off my slippers and he does the same...you see?"

"I do".

"In end I wash his dick in tea and suck him off".

Pandora's eyes rolled heavenwards. "O charming! I shall never look at another teapot again without thinking of what you've just told me."

Cherry Blossom looked inquiringly at Pandora.

"And you? You are the pain lady?"

"I take the men who get their rocks off exposing their lily white bottoms to a good spanking. Madam Lash that's me".

And she slapped her hand on her rump as Cherry Blossom giggled delightfully.

"And when I'm not caning the daylights out of them I am either playing pretty nursey no knickers or nanny feeds the baby routine"

And Pandora cupped her breast in explanation.

Cherry smiled and nodded. She spoke softly "I have one man who brings his train set".

Pandora's eyes flew open. "Train set?"

"Yes he brings track and places the track between my legs and then he says 'choo choo train going through the tunnel'.

Pandora looked horrified. "Please don't tell me he puts the train in the tunnel".

And she mimed with a hand between her legs.

"Oh No. He says that the signal says stop…it is red… so train not going. It stops outside".

"Thank heaven for that."

"Then he checks the tunnel is all clear with finger and-"

115

"-Yup got the picture. Men are such babies aren't they. Some of them want to be breastfed and some of them want to be beaten and the rest of them want to play with their train sets.   Welcome to the mad house. I'm going to call you CB...If that's OK?"

Pandora gave the surprised CB a warm hug and they parted company as comrades in arms.

CHAPTER 8

Cindy and Laura were taking a break and enjoying a cup of morning coffee together at the Manning Renovation office on the following Tuesday. Cindy was full of excitement and was bursting to tell Laura her news.

"I'm late Laura".

"What for?"

"You know."

"Oh Cindy...Do you think?"

Cindy was nodding her head madly.

"That's wonderful news".

Cindy whispered. "Don't say anything to anybody will you?"

Laura shook her head.

"You know me, regular as clockwork but I'm 5 days overdue. I have been feeling sick in the mornings. Pete has no idea and I am going to wait to tell him after I've had a proper test at the doctors. I'm going tomorrow."

"You could get a test from the chemist".

"No I want it to be officially confirmed".

As she was saying those words Peter appeared in the doorway. "Officially confirmed? What's that my darling?"

Cindy stuttered slightly. "Noth...Nothing...well just a client of Laura's who has commissioned her to paint...Isn't that right Laura?"

Cindy stared intently at Laura as she said,

"Yes that's right...It's someone I met at …um…at that design seminar I went to a few months back".

"Great, well done. How is Mr. Gupta's artwork coming along?"

"Fine thanks".

117

Peter began to grumble about Mr. Gupta's habit of querying every expense and once the bill instalment for payment had been sent to him, his exasperating habit of coming into the office to argue items already covered in a previous telephone call. Cindy bristled.

"The less said about him the better."

Peter bid them farewell and went out to the car park.

"How am I going to cope with the groping Gupta when we've only just started on his job? It'll be weeks of him coming in and trying to pin me either to the wall, or trying to bend me over the desk. I am at my wits' end".

"Well, indirectly, you should perhaps thank him for your condition?"

"Ha ha...very funny".

Laura went in to see David to discuss timelines for one of their client's interior design brief. After their meeting she suddenly noticed he had on one of his best long sleeved shirts, his designer-style jeans and polished-God forbid- shoes; not at all like his usual work wear of T shirt, battered jeans and ancient trainers.

He had left before she was up in the morning so she hadn't noticed this change of attire.

"Off somewhere nice David? You look very smart".

"Got to have lunch with some possible financial contacts".

Laura gave him a searching look.

"David, we're not in any financial trouble are we?"

"No...No. of course not. We have more work than we can handle"

"And Mr. Gupta? Has he paid his latest instalment?"

"It'll come through this week"

"You mean he hasn't paid yet... so he's late again"

"Look .. I'd better finish this accounting work."

He looked at his watch. "I'm due in town for lunch".

"Won't keep you then". She gave him a little wave and

118

left the premises.

David watched her jump in the car and drive away. He checked his watch, grabbed his jacket and making sure the Casa Blanca card was in his coat pocket, closed down the computer and went into the reception area. Cindy was busy on the computer and she was humming away to herself happily.

"Just off Cindy. Tell clients that I won't be back 'til around 4pm."

"Fine. Have a nice lunch". She beamed at him. Happy little soul he thought.

As he approached the door of 32 Davenport Gardens, David began to sweat. He took off his jacket and opened another button on his shirt. Surreptitiously he sniffed his armpits and taking out a breath freshener from his jacket pocket he sprayed his mouth. He had thought about having a bite to eat on the way to Casa Blanca but his stomach was in knots and he didn't want to belch or fart or worse vomit in front of the stunning Nefertiti. What a name he thought. No idea what was in store except the obvious, he resolved to play the whole afternoon by ear, well an ear attached to his cock at least. He kept saying the password over and over in his mind and he must remember to be "Mr. Darcy" for the whole afternoon. Acting was not one of David's strong suits and even though he looked impressive on the stage as Jack Worthing in the university production of 'The Importance of Being Ernest', an unkind reviewer compared his performance to a fence post and said the play should be re-titled "The Importance of Being Wooden". Luckily these thoughts were not anywhere near David's mind when he rang Casa Blanca's bell.

An accented voice spoke through the intercom.

"Your name please sir."

"It's Da...Sorry it's Mr Darcy"

119

"Please give de password"

He suddenly had the mad thought that he was about to enter a den of drug dealers. That voice sounded like it belonged to a colored person.

"Yes it's Cactus Flower".

"Come in sir and wait in de reception hall".

The buzzer sounded and he entered the premises.

Inside David could see that this was the home and it certainly looked like a private residence of Georgian origin with all the unique period features intact. It was also the property of someone with excellent taste in furniture and furnishings. A colored woman, around 50, asked him to sit and she would tell "MadamPam" that he had arrived. He perched warily on an antique Heppelwhite chair.

Lady Pamela came sweeping in and holding out her hand gave David's a firm handshake. Computing in his mind he assessed the woman in front of him as being in her 70's.

"Welcome Welcome Mr. Darcy. How lovely to meet you. Please call me Lady P".

Amused by this introduction David suppressed a smile. Lady Pamela speedily checking him out knew Nefertiti would be very pleased with her new client.

"Please come through to my study and we can dispense with the formalities ASAP".

In her usual professional way she first of all took 200 pounds in cash, then asked him what Nefertiti could do for him. She then said,

"As I mentioned on the phone any other erotic services will be extra and have to be paid for in advance".

David paused and stuck for words eventually said, "Just the usual, thank you."

He was already smarting at the fee. Lady Pamela gave

him a coy little smile. She was always hoping for something more exotic that she could stick on the bill, perhaps he'd like a threesome.

"Don't be shy. You can tell me. What goes on in Casa Blanca stays in Casa Blanca. Discretion is our watchword".

He cleared his throat. "No extras, thank you".

She looked at him and knew he could be persuaded into something more than the missionary position, it would just take a little time.

"Perfect Mr. Darcy. Now there is one other matter pertaining to security. We do not allow cell phones or cameras in the rooms. Discretion is our watch word so I have to ask you to   hand over any electrical device you may be carrying".

"Yes...um...I'll turn it off."

"And give to me please".

"Oh I see".

David reluctantly took his cell phone from his pocket, turned it off and handed over to Lady P.
She placed it in her desk drawer and then rang a little bell on her desk. The West Indian woman appeared.

"Tanice this is Mr Darcy".

Tanice gave a tight little smile and nodded.

"Please take him to the Egyptian room, thank you"

Without a word Tanice left the room and David followed meekly. They climbed the stairs to the first floor and began to walk along the corridor. Various doors on either side were in evidence. At the end of the landing she stopped at the last door on the right, knocked and then opened the door for him and after he had entered she closed the door quietly behind him. He was alone.

The bedroom was large and airy with an elaborate cornice and decorative plaster ceiling rose. It was painted in a pale apricot with matching drapes. The antique gilt lamps gave a soft light and the mood was further enhanced by a dozen candles dotted around the room. Fresh flowers were placed in a crystal vase on an antique chest o' drawers. He looked around and admired the Georgian sash windows. One wall was covered with a painted version of the pyramids at sunset complete with camels in the distance. A Sphinx-like sculpture sat at the end of the King-size bed and was draped with fluffy white towels. He sat on the champagne colored silk bed cover and counted ten opulent cushions. To one side, on an antique oak tea table, two glasses of Champagne on a silver salver were waiting in expectation.

There was a soft knock on the inner door to the bathroom and Nefertiti entered. Throwing him a seductive glance from under her long dark lashes, she loosed her long dark locks around her face and posed barefooted against the door post with one hand above her head and the other running down her thigh. She was just as he remembered her, but with a little less on.

"Hello Mr. Darcy. Would you like me to dance for you?"

He gazed at her nut brown breasts enfolded in a red jeweled bustier and nodded. She pressed a switch alongside the window and some soft Eastern music started playing. She began to pirouette slowly, showing her perfect curves through the sequined veils tied around her waist. She twisted and turned and then parting the veils and revealing her red satin G string, she bent forward and gyrated her hips. This gave him a front row view of her magnificent backside and long shapely legs.

Seductively she said, "Would you like to touch me Mr. Darcy?"

David, transfixed by this erotic beauty, was stuck like

122

a limpet to the bed; suddenly he leapt forward and grasped her round the waist. She turned slowly, put her arms round his neck and ran her tongue over his mouth. He started to kiss her fervently. She pushed him back onto the mound of cushions as the old fella stood to attention.

"Steady Tiger". She murmured, thinking what a change from the tiny wieners she often had to deal with.

"Remember we have plenty of time. Now please undress leaving your jockeys on."

He obeyed speedily. Nefertiti knew this encounter would only take a few minutes to reach its conclusion which meant there would be plenty of time in between erections for her to be fully aroused and guide him towards pleasuring her in the way she enjoyed, namely putting his tongue on her secret place.

She pushed him down onto his back on the bed and straddled him rubbing her pudenda against his straining cock. At the same time she loosened the zip of her bustier and threw it to one side. Her perfect soft round breasts brushed against his face and he took a dark nipple in his mouth and gently sucked.

Time passed extremely quickly after this; David was able to receive his pleasure twice and then after they had soaped together in the bathroom he asked those magic words,

"And what would you like me to do to you?"

Nefertiti told him what she liked and lay back on the bed, her legs apart. David had never seen such a beautiful sight as she raised her hips slightly to meet his eager mouth. He ran his tongue along the inside of her exquisite mahogany colored legs and came to rest at the entry to her vagina. She groaned with pleasure as he began a slow lapping over her clitoris. As she came she cried out and ran her fingers through his thick blond hair. Not only was he loving pleasuring this gorgeous dark-skinned girl, but being with a woman who was in control excited him just as much.

He realized after he dressed that very little had been said, polite conversation having been completely dispensed with; He knew nothing about her. He kissed her goodbye and said:

"Thank you Divine Nefertiti. Can we meet again...soon?"

She smiled sweetly, kissed him back and told him to talk Lady Pamela on the way out.

After he had retrieved his cell phone from Lady Pamela he asked to make another appointment with Nefertiti. Assessing him with the view to becoming a regular, Lady Pamela told him about the special rate available.

"If you would like to book nine one hour sessions we are able to let you have the tenth session free. We have a card system here and every time you come in we stamp your card. You can ring and book these sessions at any time. We do require payment in advance. Now please don't be shy about telling us what other services you would like."

David decided to book for one session but he was sorely tempted to take the special on offer. He told Lady Pamela he would let her know.

"No problem Mr. Darcy. It was a pleasure serving you".

Laura and David continued their parallel lives unhindered. Both observed that their other halves seemed more relaxed and at ease with each other than they had been in a long time. David, in the dark with regard to Laura's affair, was delighted that she appeared to accept their bedroom situation and was relieved that she did not raise the subject of sex over the intervening weeks since Juliet's tennis success.

Laura thinking David was happily relieving himself in front of the computer decided to continue her satisfying encounters with Blue Eyes. The second time they made love at The Little Chelsea Hotel, events were deliciously slow-paced and seductive.

They had undressed each other in a measured way. After he had massaged her shoulders and back he had run his tongue all over her skin, circling her nipples and making her shiver with anticipation. Wet with desire she had taken his cock in her mouth, something she had done in the early days with David, and under his guidance had brought him to climax. As he writhed and moaned under her, her mouth filled with oyster tasting juice and she spat out his cum onto her knickers lying conveniently on the floor at the side of the bed. She said,

"Well that's buggered my pants".

He roared with laughter and hugged her 'til she squealed.

"You'll have to go home with a bare ass Laura".

And they laughed some more.

Then he started to kiss her, using his tongue tenderly, he ran kisses down her belly into her cleft. Her clitoris practically rose to attention. He ran his tongue in a circle round the bud until she was begging for him to suck her. As he gently took her clitoris in his mouth, she could feel the exquisite rising of her fire until she exploded with an orgasmic cry of pleasure. They held each other silently for some minutes and overcome with emotion she tried to hold back the tears but they were intent on falling.

He gently brushed them away with his hand and said,

"Honey…What's the matter? Are you OK?"

"Yes. Yes… It was wonderful. You are

wonderful...I'm a bit...overcome".

She didn't elaborate further and he did not press her. They parted reluctantly.

"New place next time Laura and come bare assed. I'll wait for your call".

She laughed and kissed him.

She knew it was going to become harder to leave Blue Eyes as time went by and in the not too distant future she would have to confront David over his porn habit. Could their relationship continue in light of all that had happened?

David had returned from his meeting with the financiers in a good mood and she asked him about the details. David was vague and evasive which led her to believe that he was hiding something.

"Is everything alright?"

"All sorted. There is nothing to worry about".

Even though his confident manner should have put any money anxieties to rest she felt that there was something he was withholding from her. Yet another thing perhaps, but who was she to ponder when she had secrets of her own. He was in a very good mood and suggested they go out for another dinner, just the two of them, the following week.

Laura thought about Cindy and wondered if perhaps that dinner could include Cindy and Peter in light of the probability of Cindy being pregnant.

Two days later just as they were finishing the Shepherd's Pie she had made, the phone rang. David answered it and there was a loud scream the other end. David held the phone away from his ear for a moment and gave Laura a wry look.

"It's Cindy.....screaming".

Laura took the phone from him and Cindy's voice screeched in her ear.

"I'mpregnant,I'mpregnant.I'vejusttoldpeteandheisoverth
emoonit'ssoexcitingthetestresultcamethroughthisafterno
onanditwaspositiveIjustknewitsdueinMarch-"

"-Ok OK. Fantastic. That's wonderful news. Say 'Hi'
to Pete and many congratulations to both of you. We
should all go out for a celebration....and we could ask
Mr. Gupta, couldn't we Cindy?"

There was a loud guffaw the other end of the line and
then Peter came on the phone. David said how pleased
he was for both of them and then after he congratulated
Pete, he put the phone down and said to Laura that he
knew Cindy and Pete would make terrific parents and he
was sure they would have a large tribe in the future.
Laura noted that he must have forgotten the heartache
over trying for another baby sister or brother for Juliet.
He seemed totally unaware of the painful emotion she
was now experiencing as she couldn't help but recall the
shattering disappointment month after month when her
period kept coming back with monotonous regularity.
She realized that he had well and truly let go of that
period in their lives.

Even though David was very busy with Gupta's job
and two other properties, he was determined to make
time to see Nefertiti the following week. He mulled over
the venue Casa Blanca and felt on entering this domain
that he been catapulted into the middle of a BBC
costume drama. The owner or should she be called
'Madam', an extraordinary aristocratic old lady, could
have stepped out of The Tatler Magazine like some posh
totty's granny and the maid Tanice from an Ernest
Hemingway novel. Nefertiti presumably a stage name
was stunning and her performance was all he could have
wished for. With her sultry looks she appeared to be of
Indian nationality, perfect in every way bar the slight

127

difficulty she had in hiding her Cockney accent. He couldn't wait for the next assignation and was planning to use part of his hour to find out all about her before burying his head in her caramel breasts and sucking on her perfect deep brown nipples.

CHAPTER 9

Saturday was always a very busy day at Casa Blanca. Pandora had two regular clients for her punishment services and in between became Pretty Nursey Spankybot, examining and administrating to a patient's tackle. Cherry's expertise with the teapot had spread to the extent that she had gained three new clients for her special tea ceremony. Nefertiti was in demand for her belly dancing routine and occasionally was asked to make up a threesome with Pandora. In the early days the two of them spent the whole hour trying not to giggle but now, as the action became predictable, they just thought of the extra money they were to be paid. On Saturday evenings in between clients Lady Pamela always made time to feed the girls and furnish them with some much needed alcohol. They were able to have two drinks of their choice and Tanice usually made a substantial meal to keep up their stamina. Roast lamb and mint sauce followed by apple and blackcurrant crumble with a big dollop of ice cream was always much appreciated.

Tanice left at 9pm on Saturdays and Lady Pamela turned in around 1am after the last client left so she was deep in sleep when her cell phone rang at 7am on Sunday. Wearing her eyeshades, she sat up quickly and nearly fell out of bed while grappling for the wretched device in the bedside cupboard. She swore loudly and startled Dandi sat to attention on his bed in the corner of the room. She stabbed at the 'on' button and said.

"Fuck who is this? Christ, Henry, Do you know what the time is? This better be important."

129

The Colonel said he'd been up all night at the police station as Edward had got drunk at a party and driven some girl at speed through a picket fence and into someone's garden and hit a child's wooden climbing frame at 2 am.

"Climbing Frame? God No. Are they alright? Is Edward hurt?"

"Cracked rib, bruising and cuts and the girl's got a broken arm. Bloody idiot. Climbing frame's in bits and the car's a right off."

"What'll happen to Edward?"

"He'll be disqualified for sure. Not sure how long for but there will be a huge fine too. I'm organizing a lawyer as we speak. He could go to prison".

Lady Pamela put her hand to her head. "Dear God when will he ever learn. Oh by the way. How are his finances?"

"Don't ask. He's already tapped me for a grand two weeks ago and now I'll have to stump up probably around five thousand pounds for the fine".

"Let me take care of that."

"Thanks old girl. I'm off to bed. Pooped. No bridge today I'm afraid".

Lady Pamela turned the phone off and pondered on young Edward. Such a promising start as a young man and he had been excellent at rowing and cricket at Eton. Not blessed with a huge brain but had the breeding and good looks instead. Then at twenty he had got into the wrong set and seemed to do nothing but party. He'd had a spell at Aspreys, a job The Colonel had sorted for him, but too many hangovers had put paid to that. He'd been tapped on the shoulder by a model scout in Regent Street and for the last decade had sporadic modelling work, some of which had taken him to exotic locations. The problem was the drink and latterly, as The Colonel had pointed out to her, he was dabbling in the hard stuff. The Colonel had whispered,

"Cocaine. He said he takes it as an appetite suppressant. Total cock of course. He'll be dead at 45. Bloody Fool".

She mused on this and thought about the Black Forest gateau in the pantry that Edward had happily scoffed on a regular basis. She had read somewhere that it was called "The Munchies". People with an addiction got huge food cravings in between drug hits. What could she do to aid Edward and help him get out of this dreadful downward spiral? He needed to meet someone who could act as a steadying influence. Well no bridge today and she had a pantry full of cake, the girls would enjoy it. As she was giving Dandi his breakfast she suddenly thought about Laura and the fact that she was going to ask Laura to the Caribbean evening. Thinking of a long Sunday afternoon with no distractions she decided to text Laura and ask her to come and have tea. Tony might like to drop by too. She spent a long time sending Laura a text and swore loudly every time the wretched device put up a word that was nowhere near the one she wanted or when her fingers would not work nimbly enough to press the right letter keys. Eventually she sent through.

> *Good Morning Laura. How are you? It was loved to meet up with you for lynch the other day. James ESPECIALlY enjoyed your company. Would you care to take tea with me today? Please execute poor text. Fingers very poor. Come at 4. LP*

As Lady Pamela was drinking her morning coffee, her cell phone pinged and she read,

> *Thank you for the invitation .I would love to pop into see you. Would 4-30pm be alright? I have appointment with a client not far from u before*

that. Laura

Lady Pamela rang Tony Fredericks and told him about Edward and the bridge cancellation and asked him to drop by anyway. He accepted the offer and she felt pleased that she would be enjoying the company of these two young people and not spending a depressing afternoon worrying over Edward.

It was raining in Kingbridge and Laura was looking gloomily out of the studio window when she received Lady Pamela's text. David had gone to sort a leaky tarpaulin problem at one of Manning's smaller property renovations and Laura was wondering how she could fill her time between the present and early afternoon when she had to leave for her client meeting. She was pleased to receive the text and felt it would be an opportunity to thank Lady Pamela properly for her generous lunch and possibly find out a bit more about Blue Eyes. At least Lady Pamela would be lively company. She replied to the text in the affirmative. Her thoughts strayed to Blue Eyes. She was sure that he would not have told the old lady about their trysts or would he have done? The Colonel was more likely to know as they seemed to be old friends. A sense of unease began to form. Would Blue Eyes have betrayed her trust and told anyone? She put the thought out of her mind and resolved to question Lady Pamela discreetly. Laura told herself that Blue Eyes would have kept their affair to himself.

Tony Fredericks had been stock-taking at the shop when the call came through. Edward in deep shit. Well he wasn't at all surprised. Edward had already tapped him for money.

"Just a few quid .I'm a bit short this week".

Tony had handed over a twenty and resolved not to do so again. He was no pushover and knew that Edward would be back for more. It was only a matter of time. It amused Tony to note that Lady Pamela thought the sun shone out of Edward's arse but in Tony's eyes Edward was well on the way to skid row. Anyway it would be nice to have a cuppa with the old dear and find out more about her past.

Laura rang the bell at Casa Blanca at precisely 4-30pm and was buzzed in straight away. As she was dropping her jacket on the hall chair, she could hear a man's voice chatting to Lady Pamela. The voice did not belong to The Colonel whose deep sonorous tones she remembered from the lunch. Was it Blue Eyes she thought wildly? No-The voice was English so who was it? She pushed open the sitting room door and beheld a chunky dark haired man around her age. He turned as Lady Pamela greeted her,

"Laura. How lovely to see you. Do come in and meet Tony."

They shook hands and Laura noted his firm grip while observing his warm brown eyes on a level with hers, wavy hair and crinkly smile.

Lady Pamela, later recalling the events of the day, came to the realization that first impressions, physical and emotional, were nearly always accurate except in cases of clever con men.

Laura and Tony gave the impression of liking one another immediately. Laura after the initial stiffness of introductions relaxed and chatted happily about her life in Kingbridge, David and the business and Tony responded by telling her all about the book business. Lady Pamela who was hoping to off-load some of her worries and also tell them both about the upcoming Caribbean soiree but she did not get much of chance to put in her conversational oar. Knowing that these two decent young people were enjoying each other's company, she sat back and listened. Used to holding

133

forth and being the center of attention she was not a listener. Allowing the conversation to be out of her control did not come naturally.

Laura mentioned her cottage garden and Tony was just in the middle of telling Laura about his allotment when Lady Pamela, fidgety and bored by gardening chat and unable to suppress a yawn, made a long sigh. They realized they had been nattering on for far too long without including her in the conversation and to their horror not asking about Edward.

Tony jumped in quickly.

"Lady P. Apologies for forgetting to ask about Edward What on earth happened?"

Laura, not realizing what had occurred, said, "Edward?"

"Yes. The Colonel's nephew. Ran his car through a fence and into a climbing frame in the middle of the night injuring his female passenger and cracking his rib. He was drunk. The Colonel spent the whole night at the police station sorting him out and getting a lawyer organized".

Laura felt genuine sympathy. "I'm so sorry. What a worry for you?"

"And an expense my dear. The Colonel said the fine could be as much as five thousand pounds. Edward might even go to jail. He'll be disqualified for God knows how long".

Tony was not surprised by this news. He glanced at Laura and could see that she was genuinely concerned. What a lovely girl and great legs. Such a pity she was married.

Lady Pamela began to tell them about the Caribbean evening she was planning complete with steel band and Caribbean food. They listened intently occasionally catching each other's eyes as she rattled on. She gave them a date two weeks hence and then,

"Now I really do insist that you both attend. Laura?"

"Well um...Is David invited?"

Lady Pamela dropped her voice and looked at Laura like a conspirator.

"I thought you might like a break from your husband Laura, and come alone?"

Laura, realizing her intent, "Oh I see. Um Yes. I'll just check the date".

She consulted her cell phone diary. "That would be lovely. Thank you".

And all the while thinking what on earth was she going to say to David.

Pleased that Laura had said 'yes', Tony accepted with alacrity and said he had never heard a steel band playing live so he would be looking forward to it. In fact it was Laura- without her husband- he was looking forward to seeing again.

Lady Pamela chatted on about the dress code; something Caribbean was requested for attendees and then began to tell them about the outfit she was concocting with her dressmaker.

"It involves a parrot but that is all I am prepared to reveal at present".

Laura laughed and said it all sounded great fun and as she hadn't had any excitement lately, she was looking forward to the party. Lady Pamela gave her a quick glance under lowered lids and thought about James Jefferson KirkPatrick the 3rd. How smoothly Laura had massaged the truth about her life. She was learning fast. Lady Pamela then added,

"If you would like some help Laura, with your outfit, I can fit you with something of mine. We look to be similar sizes. I have a wardrobe full of designer ball gowns, some exotically patterned which I had made for my trips on cruise ships round the Med and the West Indies".

"That's very kind...I'm not sure-"

"-I insist ...If you could come a little earlier on the night...say an hour before people arrive I am sure we can find a glamorous little something for you".

Laura realizing the old lady was not going to take 'No' for an answer acquiesced and Tony, enjoying the proceedings hugely, gave her a big grin. Feeling the effects of the early phone call and exhausted by all the rising excitement for the party, Lady Pamela gave a large yawn.

"Sorry my dears, I think I'll have to throw you out and take to my bed for a little nap".

Both Laura and Tony got up to leave. They thanked Lady Pamela profusely and then Tony said, "Great meeting you Laura. See you at the party. I might come as a pirate or Captain Hook perhaps."

On her way home Laura noted that while engrossed in the conversation with Tony and then Lady Pamela's extraordinary invitation to the costume party, she had completely forgotten to ask Lady Pamela about Blue Eyes.

Later that evening after dinner Laura received a text.

> *Can you meet up next wed for lunch at Le petit jardin. 12-30 OK? I have somewhere special to take you for coffee!! Miss you.x JKP3.*

She and David were watching the end of a film as she checked the text and she smiled to herself. David noticed this.

"Good news?"

"Just some fabric I wanted. It's arrived".

Then a few moments later another ping on her cell phone.

"Busy night".

136

Laura read the text.

Hi Mum. Nearly the end of term. Can't wait to see u and dad. Exams nearly over. Have 1 science paper and then that's it.

English paper was a pig-Probably failed. We r all going to a NT country house for a tour and concert and then picnic. Should be cool. How are u? Not heard recently. Love you heaps. Julietxx

"It's Juliet. All good there. Nearly finished her exams and looking forward to the last day of term".

David smiled and said that it would be good to have her back home and then went back to watching the film.

She was struck by a sudden thought. Juliet's homecoming could possibly be before The Caribbean party which would mean that she could not attend. She quickly checked the diary and was relieved to see that Juliet was due home the following week.

They watched the end of the movie and then David said,

"Work to finish Laura. You go up. I'll be awhile. Just leave the night light on. I'll find my way".

Laura looked at his retreating back and thought we are both beginning to lose our way in this marriage. As he closed the sitting room door she replied to Blue Eyes and then re-reading what she had written, laughed and thought 'Laura you're turning into a right trollop and it's so much fun'.

Her text read.

Wednesday confirmed. I'll be dressed up but minus one article of clothing! xL

She added a smiley face.

137

CHAPTER 10

Once a month on Tuesdays it was Lady Pamela's day to take poor dear mad Margarita out to lunch. She had said to Tanice.

"So sad, you know. She's in some dingy asylum at the bottom of Kings Road. The lunches consist of pieces of brown meat, could be horse, watery gravy, boiled cabbage and sludge and custard for pudding. I owe it to her to take her out somewhere nice for a decent lunch. Poor darling doesn't have a clue who I am but knows me as her favorite Aunt Netty who used to take her out when she was a child. We have to take a minder with us as she can suddenly up and run for it and I'm well past rugby tackling her on my own."

Tanice looked forward to MadamPam's outings with Margarita as she could rest up and continue her masterpiece and even though she was meant to be minding Dandelion, she made sure the dratted dog was carefully locked in MadamPam's bedroom with all his toys, water bowl and some treats. She would have liked to have kept him quiet by drugging him for a couple of hours.

"See you later Tanice.... oh yes... and if that whispering man rings AGAIN about his prostate check from pretty nursey, tell him to sod off in the nicest way".

Tanice was also on appointment duty over this period and had mastered her posh voice for answering the telephone with MadamPam's elocution tuition. MadamPam had given her a script to follow. She always hated asking if the clients would like extras but MadamPam insisted on this, as extras were charged out at one hundred pounds an item and were good for business. Tanice had to grit her teeth after saying 'we do provide a full service' and then recite, as quickly and as clearly as possible, the Extras List. Occasionally some pea-brain punter or possibly an aging deaf dunderhead asked her to repeat the items and then generally didn't want to take any of them anyway which pissed her off no end.

Tanice made herself a sandwich and strong cup of coffee and prayed the phone would not interrupt her as she got to work. The book was now titled "Copulation Capers in the Caribbean". She had seen this title in a newspaper and having looked up 'copulation' in the dictionary and decided she liked the way the words ran together; this was to be her title. She felt she had made some excellent headway with the plot but she was a little concerned about the latest turn of events as it seemed the bonk buster was taking on a life of its own. She reviewed her latest paragraphs.

> *Rastus was hiding on de ege of the vegetebel pach behind the large avacado tree. He crouching down and pressing hisself against the tree trunk. Dat Delphine has gorn crazy in the head,he thort.She turning into a mad cow with a padle.She wanting to beat the livin daylites out of me. he could here her calling.*
>
> *'Ra..a...astus.Raaaastus. It's time for yor punishment'.*
>
> *He told her last time.*
>
> *'I had enuf Delphine. I black and blue. look at my arse'*
>
> *She said his arse very nice and raised de padle again.*
>
> *He could not understand why she turn into a violent vixen.She always so soft and sexy wid*

139

him and now she like someting on de murder channel. He shaking in his size 12 feet. He wood have to overpower her and give her a taste of the padle hiself but first he gotta catch her. Risin up to his full hight he flex his ripplin mussels and he aks hiself.

'Am I a man or a bat? I no bat. I gotta be a man'

Delphine girl you gotta be tort a lesson.

Tanice congratulated Rastus on this about turn and reviewed the early events in her mind. The spanking started very well and she was enjoying describing Delphine's role as The Dominatrix. Delphine ordered Rastus to strip and bend over the back of an old leather chair. She tied some rope round his wrists and ankles and then she stood and abused him gently.

you done bad tings rastus. rastus is a norty boy

Delphine had especially enjoyed the sight of Rastus' beautiful backside:-Two brown well-rounded cheeks exposed for her delight. She tickled him with the whip to start with and he giggled and wriggled. He loved to have her standing in her high-heeled boots in front of his bowed head with her legs apart and as she started to increase the lashes he could put his nose round the edge of the black lace panties and bury it deep into her crotch. Before she lost all concentration she clambered on his back and rode him like a stallion and whipped his backside. He grabbed her and threw her onto the floor where they fucked merrily away until they were spent.

But something sinister was beginning to happen to Delphine. Tanice was alarmed to discover that Delphine was starting to steer the course of the action by herself. The result was not very pretty. Her character was entering the dark side. Tanice tried remonstrating with Delphine.

140

"You not real girl. I invented you so you gotta do as I say".

She could hear Delphine in her mind say like a defiant child,

"Not going to".

But Tanice knew that Rastus was a man on a mission and she couldn't wait to describe the taming of the tigress.

> Rastus strode out from behind the tree,beat his chest and roared,
>
> 'Come here girlie.I got someting for you.'
>
> Delphine strutted toward him, flicking her wip and shouted,
>
> 'On yor knees brown boy' and she poynted with her wip to the grownd in front of her. While her head was bowed he lept forward and lifted her in the air. She screemed and her boots started to pedle in cercles.
>
> 'Let me go you beast'. Rastus swung Delphine over his showlder like a fireman and started to smack her bumsie.

Tanice, warming to her theme, stripped off her cardigan and thumped the table. The phone rang and Dandelion started to bark.

"Bugger".

Tanice wrenched the phone from its cradle and taking a deep breath said in her best rendition of Lady Pamela's upper class bray.

"Good afternoooon. Yew have reached the premisees of Carsa Blarnca. Yew are speaking with Tanice. How may I help yew?"

There was a pause as she listened to the request. She grimaced and then said,

"Ehm afraid that pretty nursey has had to go back to

141

Oarrstraliah. Her koalas have run amok epparently and are savaging the emus on her farm. No ehm afraid there is no-one else heaar who performs thet funckshun.

Thenk you for calling. Goodbye."

Dandelion was now howling to be let out so Tanice was unable to continue Rastus' revenge sequence without Dandi barking to be let out for a dump. Sighing loudly she went to fetch two plastic bags and Dandi's scoop.

On Wednesday morning Laura was putting the finishing touches to Mr. Gupta's commission. She had used a mixed media technique, scraping back and then adding another glaze. She had to wait painstakingly for each layer to dry before applying another color. The effort had paid off and she was pleased with the result. The only problem was that Mr. Gupta had turned into a tortoise where paying was concerned and was three weeks behind with the latest payment on his renovations. Peter was tearing his hair out over their cash flow and David had sunk into one of his cold and distant moods with everyone.

Peter had fixed up a crisis meeting with Mr. Gupta. The atmosphere in the office was very tense. David went into the gents for a quick wee and wash of the nether regions and as he was passing reception, Peter came out of his office.

"Ready?"

"Sorry Pete. Something's come up at one of the sites."

Peter was furious. "David. I need you there. Fuck it. This guy could be a major problem."

"You can handle it. This is an emergency".

As David strode out to the car park, Peter shouted,

"What do you think this is?"

Instead of going to the crisis meeting, David decided

he needed a quick trip to Casa Blanca to relieve his tension over the Gupta problem and managed to forget all his money worries in the arms of Nefertiti.

This time she was dressed as a belly dancer complete with jeweled belly button, cantilevered pink lace bra and very little else. After shaking the little bells on her fingers and gyrating her booty and hips in front of his nose, she knelt and removed his underwear and began a soft moist patrol of his penis with her tongue. He groaned in ecstasy and begged for her mouth. She expertly placed a strawberry flavored condom over him and her mouth began a delicious slow pull up and down the shaft. Her tongue flickered over his slit. He began to dribble a little. Then she lay with legs wide apart and her tiny pubic triangle of hair rose up to meet him. He fell on her breasts, tongued her erect nipples and thrust himself inside her. Even though the rubber came between them he orgasmed within seconds. She removed the condom gracefully and went into the bathroom and when she returned her breath smelled of mint leaves.

He whispered, "Could we do it without protection next time?"

"We'll see". I have to be able to trust you".

He asked her, "Now would you like me to do what I did last time?"

How delightful those words were to her ears. So few clients bothered with her needs that she knew she would have to make sure this lovely man came back to Casa Blanca on a regular basis. She said she would like to take a shower with him and he readily agreed. He soaped her tenderly all over, massaging gently her breasts and between her legs and rubbed his soapy body against her back. He then laid towels on the bed and lifted her onto her back and gently dried her all over. As he ran his hands all over her perfect body he felt his cock stiffening again. She whispered.

"Lick me Lick me".

He grinned down at her and placed himself between her bent knees and ran his tongue along the inside of her thigh and then placed it deep inside her vagina. She cried out as he began to suck on her clitoris. She came and in her heightened orgasmic state said,

"Fuck me. Fuck me."

A second later he was naked inside her and they were writhing together in perfect harmony. As he was dressing she said,

"Thank you Mr. Darcy. It was wonderful. Clients are only interested in their own pleasure but you, you are different."

She came and put her arms around him and kissed him. He stood and held her in his arms.

"And you are sensational. What is your real name?"

"Shouldn't tell you really but its Swati. In Hindi it means the third brightest star in the sky".

"To me you are the first star. I can't pronounce Nefertiti,

I'm going to call you Star…beautiful Star".

"And what is your Christian name Mr. Darcy?"

Forgetting himself for a moment, he said: "It's Dav....Peter. Peter Darcy."

"Peter".

She whispered, "Perfect Peter. Would you like to come to a party here at Casa Blanca? It's a Caribbean evening that Lady Pamela is organizing for VIP clients. It's a dress-up party. There will be great food and Caribbean music. Do say you'll come and stay over too".

"Stay over? I'm not sure I can. When is it?"

Nefertiti gave him the date and he checked his cell phone and saw that he was free that night. He had flouted the house rule with regard to cell phones by telling Lady Pamela that he had left his in the car. What could he say to Laura? An evening out would be fine; he'd often been to get-togethers for people in the building industry but overnight? Perhaps he could say that he was going to a conference, not in London, but in some distant city or maybe because of a late work dinner engagement and the amount of wine he would consume he would not be safe to drive home. Just as he was giving Nefertiti a long kiss goodbye, his cell phoned trilled. It was Peter. As he moved away from Nefertiti, Peter shouted in his ear,

"Where the fuck are you David? No support as per bloody usual.   Get the fuck back here ASAP. The financial picture is looking like crap".

David said as calmly as possible that he was sorry about the situation and would be right back.

"Did Gupta cough up ?"

"Half. Like getting shit out of a brick and he wanted a fucking discount. The man's a nightmare. If you'd been here we could have worked on him together and got the whole lot. If this goes on we are in deep shit".

David said he would be back directly.

Nefertiti then warned him. "Don't let Lady P catch you with that phone. If she finds out you won't be allowed back to Casa Blanca."

David made a face and laughed and then kissed his beloved Star a swift farewell. He said he would let her know about the party. On the way home as he was mulling over what to do about the Gupta job, he suddenly realized that he had used his brother's name as an alias with the beautiful Star. At least he hadn't blurted out his surname too. He reprimanded himself and vowed to be more careful in future.

Peter and David had a huge row in the office

145

following David's return and Cindy, thinking they were about to come to blows, burst in and was told in no uncertain terms by David to 'fuck off'. She quickly retreated and rang Laura.

"They're having a huge barney...over Gupta. Slimy Indian toad. He is holding back payments and asking for discounts. Peter is at his wits' end."

"And David's buried his head as usual I suppose?"

Laura heard a door slam.

"Who's walked out? David?"

"Yep. I better go".

Laura told her to look after her precious cargo and to try not to get involved. Laura knew Cindy loved Pete dearly and would be worrying for him even more than he was worrying for the situation.

Laura tried asking David what was going on that evening but he said he would sort the problem and for her to keep out of it.

The following morning David, who had hardly spoken to her since the volatile meeting, said he was going out for the day and would be back late that evening. Snail's pulling his head in, thought Laura. As it was her day for the meeting with Blue Eyes she felt relieved that she would not have to be worrying about the business for a few hours.

She smiled to herself as she remembered what he had requested with regard to dress code. She put on a short pink linen-mix shift dress and her nude heels and underneath decided on a plain white g string which she intended to remove at a convenient moment in The Ladies. She had tried wandering around a few days before with no knickers under her skirt and had even gone for a short drive but had felt very vulnerable and unprotected somehow. Even though she had travelled home from her assignation with Blue Eyes, intoxicated, bare-arsed and on Cloud Nine, she had the ridiculous notion that on the way to see Blue Eyes she might be involved in a traffic accident and need to be taken to hospital. God forbid that anyone, the doctor especially, could take a gander at her privates without underwear.

Blue Eyes was standing waiting for her at "Le Petit Jardin" casually elegant and looking as handsome as ever in a sky blue shirt and khaki pants.

Georges greeted them like long lost friends and ushered them to a discreet table away from the windows. The meal came quickly. They both ordered sea bass with new potatoes and Laura decided to have her favorite tipple of Cloudy Bay New Zealand Sauvignon Blanc. Under the table Blue Eyes put a hand just above her knee and gently stroked the warm flesh.

"Have you?"

She grinned, "I don't know what you're talking about."

"Shall I explore and find out?"

Laura clamped her knees together. "People will see".

"Let them".

His fingers began to go a little higher. "James. Don't...Not yet anyway".

She laughed, tugged her dress down and moved out of reach.

"Guess I'll have to wait then."

They continued sharing information about themselves all the while eyeing each other like a pair of hungry coyotes. Laura told Blue Eyes about Mr. Gupta and the problems of the company finances and the fact that David was distancing himself from her and telling her not to be concerned. She also told him about David's appetite for porn especially Indian porn and the fact she had seen some disgusting pictures on the web. Surprisingly Blue Eyes did not seem at all concerned.

147

He touched her cheek.

"We all have our little secrets Laura".

She smiled and said, "And what are yours pray?"

"If I tell you..."

Laura joined in"....I'll have to kill you".

Soon after this Laura repaired to The Ladies and removed her G String. She took a quick look at her backside in the wash room mirror and decided she was reasonably well covered by her dress. Refreshing her pale pink lip gloss, she ran a comb through her blonde locks and went back to the table. Blue Eyes had ordered some coffee and as they sipped their expressos alongside each other, Blue Eyes put his hand on her knee and began to push under her dress, up the thigh, toward her crotch while looking vacantly out toward the front of the restaurant. Laura tensed and then lifted her white napkin from the table and placed it over his wandering hand. The waiter arrived with the bill, averted his eyes and waited politely while Blue Eyes gave his signature. Laura smile inanely at the waiter and he smiled back as Blue Eyes' fingers began to tease at her trimmed pubic hair. When the waiter left, Blue Eyes turned and kissed her cheek.

"Oh Laura, Laura, Look at me".

And he indicated with his eyes at the bulge in his trousers.

Then he said, "Let's get out of here now".

And they did.

Clutching each other, Blue Eyes hailed a cab and gave an address to the cabby, inaudible to Laura who was trying to clamber in a not-so-lady-like fashion into the back of the cab. The cab did a few lefts and rights and then ended up in Davenport Gardens. Laura saw the name plaque as they entered the street.

"James?" She said in alarm "We're not going to Casa

Blanca are we?"

"It's the perfect place Laura"

"But Lady Pamela will see us. I couldn't bear her knowing what we are getting up to. So embarrassing."

"All arranged sweetheart. She was delighted to help"

"Help? What do you mean ....she knows?"

James helped Laura out of the taxi, paid the cabbie giving a generous tip and before Laura could run away he rang Casa Blanca's bell. Laura cringed away from the camera when she heard Tanice's voice.

"Password please".

Laura tried to back away but James clasped her to him.

"Cactus Flower." And then to Laura,

"Don't worry Honey. Nobody will see us. We'll be let in and then I know exactly where to go. Just trust me".

They were buzzed in and Laura knowing that she couldn't escape shot through the front door and made for the stairs clutching her bag to her face as though expecting the paparazzi to snap flash photos in front of her. As James steered her along the upper landing the Indian model she had met during her first encounter with Lady Pamela came out of one of the other rooms and nearly cannoned into Laura's bent head.

"Oops sorry."

Laura did not see the smile that passed between James and Nefertiti. James opened a door to her left and she ran in and threw her bag on the bed. She sat on the bed and hugged herself in alarm.

"I can't do it...knowing she knows. It's like having sex next door to your maiden aunt".

"Honey, Lady Pamela is so far from being a maiden aunt. She's a wonderful woman and very experienced in the ways of the world. She knows how unhappy you've been and is letting us use her place out of the kindness of

149

her heart".

Laura sat uncomfortably and thought back to the conversation she had had with the old lady. After spewing her heart out about David, she remembered Lady Pamela saying something along the lines of 'I am exactly the right person to talk to'. She was beginning to understand why.

As Blue Eyes offered her a cleansing glass of Champagne, all ready for them on the mahogany table, she suddenly realized that Blue Eyes had been introduced to her for the express purpose of bringing some much needed love and excitement into her life.

She said quietly, "So she told you about me."

"She did and in glowing terms."

"It was a set up then...Our meeting"

"She wanted to help you Laura and she thought I might be the man to do it",

And then he added, "The Old lady has had a rip roaring life and she loves nothing better than to bring two people together with matching needs and see them happy as a result. Darling Laura, you have made me so deliriously happy".

And he took Laura by the hand and embraced her as she stood before him. He kissed her tenderly.

"Now my Honey Bee. Will you do something for me?"

Laura smiled and put her head on one side, "I might".

He then instructed her to take off her heels and go and sit on the high backed chair in the corner.

"Keep your knees together please".

Laura did as she was told and sat primly, dress down as far as it would go, knees together on the antique chair. While waiting for Blue Eyes to return from the bathroom, she cast her eyes about the room and realized it was done or more like over-done in a faux Chinese style complete with a red canopied tasseled bedcover over a four poster bed hung with deep red silk curtains. Dragons were climbing up the wallpaper. Golden lanterns hung from the ceiling. Lady Pamela was turning into somebody completely different in Laura's eyes - a woman of gaudy opulent tastes.

Blue Eyes returned with just a towel round his middle and knelt at her feet. He began to massage her feet and then started to suck her toes one by one. Laura giggled and said she was very ticklish.

"And where else are you ticklish Laura?"

He ran his hands over the smooth skin on her legs and then gently prizing her knees apart began a slow exploration with his hands of her upper thighs under the linen dress. Gradually the dress rode up above her hips and he could gaze lasciviously at her exposed pubic cleft with its neat landing strip ready for his tender care. Laura began to breathe deeply. His caressing finger found her the entrance to her vagina and fluttered over her clitoris. When he put his head between her thighs, she lifted her knees and clutched his silver hair as he flicked his tongue on and off her sensitive point until she could feel the waves engulf her and panting she begged for more. He sucked her to orgasm. Immediately after this he raised her up and laid her face down on the bed, placing a pillow under her hips. Her dress was bunched at her waist. He then took her forcefully from behind and bit her shoulder as he came.

"Ow!"

"Sorry Honey. Kinda got carried away".

They lay in each other arms for a short while and as just she was about to ask him some more questions about his life, he got up and went into the bathroom. She heard the shower running. While relaying to herself the recent events, she realized that yet again they had had sex

151

without protection. Why wasn't she scared shitless at the possibility of becoming pregnant to her secret lover? Her satiated being had become defiant and reckless. The feeling of "I don't care" came over her. She rapidly started to calculate her cycle. Her calculations told her that she had finished a period around 2 weeks before so would definitely have entered the 'danger zone'. She concluded that the decision, if it should come to pass, would be either choosing baby or husband. She certainly couldn't pass off James' baby as David's or could she? Feeling a kind of madness over what the future could hold she was so pre-occupied that she could hardly say goodbye to Blue Eyes.

He kissed her gently and noticing her worried frown. "Is everything alright Honey?"

"Oh. Yes Fine. I'm just a bit concerned about the business".

He said he was sure there was nothing to worry about and then told her that he was off to The States for a couple of weeks and would see her on his return.

On her way back to Kingbridge, when she had calmed down, she decided to be sensible over a possible pregnancy and made a quick stop at a chemist shop a few miles from Kingbridge. She sidled up to the counter and asked the elderly iron-faced woman behind the counter for the "morning after" pill. She paid quickly and skipped out knowing that two cold grey eyes were boring into her back.

Reading the instructions she was just about to swallow the pill with some water that she carried in the car when she thought better of this plan and decided to wait until she was back at The Cottage. The business with David and having another baby came cannoning back to her. In light of her circumstances she couldn't possibly have another baby with another man; yes, she said to herself, she must take the Emergency contraceptive pill. If she did not take the pill and became pregnant, how on earth was she going to explain the situation to David? Immaculate Conception? Not at all likely unless an alien being had landed on their roof and ravished her one night. She reprimanded herself for being so silly. But what if she and Blue Eyes could be together? She already felt as though she was falling in love with him. He was so tender and loving with her. Perhaps he felt something for her? Did he love her too? He adored her body but would he be willing to enter into a relationship? Could they possibly bc together? The unanswered questions whirled round in her mind as she tossed and turned next to David in bed that night. In the early hours she began to answer those questions herself. Firstly she knew very little about James except for the fact that he was very wealthy and owned God knew what in The States. He had been married but was he now? He had told her he was separated but that could mean he was just away from his wife not necessarily permanently separated. The more she stewed on this, the more she became sure he had a wife hidden away somewhere in the US.

In the early hours of the morning, as David snored beside her, she came to the realization that her longing for another baby had never gone away and this yearning was now stronger than her relationship with David. In fact in light of what she had discovered about David she was seriously beginning to examine the possibility of ending their marriage. The big question was assuming her affair with Blue Eyes would come to an obvious conclusion - she had a chilled feeling that this would be the case in light of any pregnancy - and if David was out of the picture, could she raise a child on her own? A daunting task, but she was 39 years old and soon the window of baby opportunity would clang shut. She either had to take the pill now or leave the outcome to fate.

Downstairs The EC pill sat quietly waiting in her handbag.

The following morning she noted that David was looking very pale and sat with his head bowed over his morning coffee.

"David. What's the matter? Are you ill?"

"Gupta is proving to be a late payer par excellence. Peter is furious with me for not being at the meeting. I've got a meeting with the bank this morning which I am not looking forward to. Also our suppliers and subbies at Gupta's place all need paying...it's a fucking nightmare".

Laura patted his shoulder and thought to herself this was not the time to talk about their marriage. He gave her a quick kiss on the cheek and disappeared out of the door. Her conscience said that she should support her husband despite his porn habit over this difficult work period but her mind was teaming with other possibilities. She was just finishing her coffee when the phone rang. It was Cindy.

"Hi. Don't know what to do. Pete is rampaging about like a wounded bull. Furious with everyone including me. Is David coming in?"

"Yes. He's pale as a ghost and looks like he might be sick at any moment. He's gone to the bank this morning. Bloody Gupta".

Cindy continued, "Peter guessed he'd be trouble when the first payment was late. It's such a huge job and involves so many people. Pete hates letting people down. We've got to do something Laura."

Laura knew Cindy hated a problem that could not be solved. She was a 'solver' par excellence. Laura suddenly had a radical idea. She knew Cindy would be totally against what Laura was about to say but it was worth a shot.

"I think the only way to get Gupta to cough up the full payment owing is for you to talk to him, preferably wearing a low cut top".

"How could you? I'd be prostituting myself. He's a pervert. It would be awful."

"Listen…"

Laura was warming to her theme. "We'll make sure Pete is out at one of the sites, David can position himself in the carpark near the front office and watch the windows and I'll be in Pete's office with the door shut so if he gets up to any funny business we can stop him before he starts on you".

"Oh Charming. –"

"-When Gupta comes in, I'll come in and chat and then disappear into Pete's office to check the computer. I'll help you butter him up before you press him for payment".

"Laura, you're mad! And all the while I'm pressing what's he pressing? My boobs or my arse?"

They both started laughing at this crazy idea. Cindy then said,

"Pete won't allow it".

"Pete won't know."

"But what if I have to go for coffee with our fat friend and Pete finds out?"

"You'll have to play that part by ear."

"You're turning me into bait...and…and I'm pregnant."

"Flirting with Gupta is not going to hurt the baby Cindy. Do you want to help Pete and David out of this nasty financial mess?"

"Yes but not...Oh God...I don't know".

155

"I think it's worth a shot and if he starts touching you up, David will race in and rescue you."

"And that will be the end of The Manning Renovation Company. It's hugely risky but I have to admit pretending to be a loose woman", Cindy paused for effect, "I am warming to the idea. I just wish he was better looking."

Laura laughed. "Good girl. Let's have a meeting with David in the office later. Let me know when Pete is going out to the site."

Laura hung up and pondered uneasily on the fact that she had omitted to tell Cindy about Mr. Gupta's previous form as a sexual harasser. It was probably best that Cindy was not made aware of this while the honey trap was being set.

Cindy sat and chewed her nails over their mad idea but something had to be done and it was looking like she was going to be the one to do it.

Laura's commission for Mr. Gupta was complete and it was decided to unveil the work of art in The Manning Office a few days later. At the same time Cindy would work her busty charms on the lascivious Indian. Cindy was agonizing over what to wear and decided on some bum fitting black trousers and a white bra she had not worn as it made her breasts look two sizes bigger. Over her cantilevered chest she wore a sky blue low cut lace top that left little to the imagination. She cringed as she checked her appearance. Cindy had managed to find out when Peter was going to be out at one of the sites and knew she would have a window of around forty five minutes to work her magic. Laura had told David about the plan and he looked at her in astonishment and then laughed.

"You devious pair of hussies but what a brilliant idea."

"Wait in one of the trucks in front of the reception room window. From there you can keep an eye on Gupta. After I have presented the painting, I'll disappear into Peter's office and keep out of sight. If, by any chance, Peter returns earlier than expected you'll have to head him off at the pass".

"Roger that" then he added, "We'd better synchronize watches like they do in the movies".

Laura inspected him closely. "This is not a game David. Do you want that bill of Gupta's paid?"

"Of course".

"Then you must be alert to what is going on. Gupta is a slimy creep. It's horrible for Cindy   to have to manipulate him into paying but she is willing to try".

'She's a trouper...and yes I will be eagle eyes".

As Cindy and Peter travelled in together in the mornings and Cindy did not want Pete to see her exposed breasts, she put on a voluminous jacket to cover her revealing top. Peter as usual had a stack of emails and phone calls to get through and in the end he left the office a little later than planned. He said 'Hi' to Laura who after a sleepless night had come in early to support Cindy. Peter commented on her art work then he said,

"He won't pay you know…Bastard!"

Laura smiled and wished him well for the day. Just as Peter was jumping into his pickup, Gupta's new Mercedes came careering into the car park. He just missed Peter's tail light as he swung into the prime spot outside the front door. Peter was about to get out and have another conversation with Gupta about the money owing when he saw David driving in and parking. Peter decided that it was about time David pulled his weight with Gupta and he said to himself,

'Let him sort the bastard out. I'm out of here'.

He put his foot down and roared away.

Gupta was thrilled with the painting and even though Cindy was revealed to him in all her glory, he couldn't stop enthusing about Laura's work.

"My dear, you must come and see it hung in my entrance hall".

"So pleased you like it".

Laura was just about to take her leave, when Gupta surprised the girls by extracting a wad of 100 pound notes.

"Now let me see. The painting is how much dear? And the amount owing to the company?"

He then turned to look at Cindy properly as she came out behind the desk to greet him. She simpered at him and as Laura turned away to suppress a giggle, his eyes widened and he said hoarsely,

"Cindy! What a vision of loveliness you are today. I insist you come out for some lunch today...please. I insist".

His nose stood a centimeter away from her heaving bosom as he gazed with adoration into her limpid green eyes. He lifted her hand and put it to his lips, kissing the palm. As Cindy stood her ground and gazed provocatively at his sweaty forehead, Laura mumbled something, stumbled past them and shot into The Ladies.

When Laura returned, Gupta was seated next to Cindy on the two seater couch and in front of her on the coffee table was a very large stack of cash. Gupta was holding Cindy's hand and stroking it. Cindy silently handed the cash to Laura and gave her a triumphant grin. Laura clutching the cash with one hand turned to the reception room window and put her other hand on the glass.

"Rav has asked me to lunch today. Can you man the phones please?"

"Yes. Of course. Where are you going?"

"To the little Italian place round the corner".

"Lovely".

Laura made a note to tell David.

Someone would have to rescue Cindy after an hour. While observing them both she couldn't believe how easy it had been to extract payment from Gupta. Gupta had handed over wads of cash to Cindy but not without asking,

"A little discount, my dear, for cash? Shall we say 10 per cent?"

Cindy was having none of that. Doing a rapid calculation, she thrust her bosom a little closer to him and batting her eyelids, "I think 2 percent is a little fairer Rav. We are already passing on very good prices to you from our suppliers for the materials".

Mr Gupta laughed and gave the positive opinion that she was a tough negotiator and then he looked her in the eyes,

"I agree to the discount Cindy with the proviso that you have lunch with me today. I will not take 'no' for an answer."

Cindy with lips clenched, smiled and nodded.

After Cindy had been swept away on the arm of Mr. Gupta, Peter returned to the office and was startled to see the wad of cash that David was waving under his nose.

"He coughed. We beat him down to a 2 percent discount for cash"

Peter said in disbelief, "In cash? The whole lot? You don't think he's a money launderer, do you?"

"Let us not look a gift horse in the mouth, Pete".

Peter was amazed and congratulated David on his cash extraction technique. Knowing Peter was to be kept in the dark as to the method of extraction, David basked in the glory of success and then took his leave and went straight round to the bank, saying as he was leaving,

"Oh By the way. Cindy's out at lunch with Gupta.

159

Round the corner at the Italian place."

Without a word Peter rushed out of the office and roared off in the direction of Cafe Firenze.

CHAPTER 11

The three Casa Blanca girls were enjoying a well-earned coffee break and chatting in the kitchen. Tanice was in the middle of making a Caribbean chicken curry and was listening in and hoping to glean some more ideas for the bonk buster.

The girls were talking about the upcoming Caribbean evening and asking each other about the invitees. Pandora would have liked to have asked Mr. Big but knew he was too high profile to be seen in company so she decided to ask an undemanding public servant who enjoyed a gentle spanking and then was happy to bury his head in her boobs and tell her about his 'Mummy' fantasies. Cherry Blossom put her head on one side and asked,

"Does he like to be wrapped up in bandages?"

Pandora laughed uproariously. "No...No.   Not an Egyptian Mummy. He likes to be the baby on the mother's breast then I just have to pull his tool a little and he comes all over his nappy".

Cherry Blossom giggled and then asked Nefertiti, "Who are you asking?"

"I've just met a new client. Very handsome and he's happy to do mostly what I want. It's a nice change. His name's Mr Darcy".

Pandora chuckled. "Oh very Pride and Prejudicey then. Lucky you Nef."

Cherry Blossom said she was bringing a young Malaysian student who was studying English and Business Studies.

"Is he a client? "Asked Pandora

"Er…Well...Sort of".

"He's your boyfriend?"

A look passed between Nef and Pandora.

"Don't let Lady P know, she'll have a fit. She'll think he's a foreign reporter and Casa Blanca will be splashed all over The Chinese Daily Express. Are you sure he can be trusted?"

"I met him at my sister's. He's very nice."

"Does he know what you do...here? "Asked Nef.

"He thinks I am hostess at a tea house in the West End.When I not work here I mind my sister's children".

Nefertiti jumped in, "Be careful. Firstly don't fall in love with him, for if you do and he finds out what your secret occupation really is he'll run a mile...Is he staying the night?...After Lady P's parties, all our clients do".

"Oh No… Not proper for him to stay. He from good Malaysian family".

Pandora and Nef laughed at this and Pandora said, "...And you… A cheeky Cherry...with your trusty teapot, rinsing a gentleman's tackle before sucking the dregs".

Tanice's eyes shot open and she expelled some air in astonishment as Pandora continued,

"...dear dear…If your boyfriend finds out he'll run a mile."

Tanice was astounded at this information and thought to herself how extraordinary it was that these bright beautiful girls were quite happy to let men do execrable things to them, or vice versa and that Pandora shoved her trussed up clients into the dumb waiter and then paddled them for a living. Still, she was in the perfect place to mine their experiences for her book. She made a mental note with regard to Cherry's tea ceremony.

Nef asked her a question, "What's on the menu ? Smells divine whatever it is".

"I just cookin' up a chicken curry for de party. I think

162

we goin' to have 50 people and den I gotta cook for de band-"

Pandora broke in, "-Band? Do you mean a live band?"

"Yes MadamPam booked me cousin's steel band".

"Wow-That will be fun. I hope the neighbors don't complain".

At that moment Lady Pamela put her head round the door.

"Back to work girls. Pandora your 3 o'clock will be here in fifteen minutes. Go and get into your nurse's uniform please. It's time for Nurse Spankybot to administer a bed bath".

Pandora turned away from Lady P and made a face. The girls trooped out and Lady Pamela turned to Tanice, "Party's on Saturday. Are we all sorted for the menu?"

"Yes MadamPam. I cookin' up de Chicken curry."

"Just run through the items please".

Tanice picked up a piece of paper and read from the list.

"For de entree we are havin' stuffed crab backs wid sweet chilli and lemon sauce, de mains are de chicken curry with all de trimmins. I making some Roti bread to go wid it. We also havin' garlic pork with hot pepper sauce-"

MadamPam interrupted, "- on the side please. Some of us have delicate stomachs".

"I also servin' fried plantain, green banana salad with tomato salsa, rice and peas, mixed salad greens, and macaroni pie".

"Macaroni pie? Is that really necessary? Seems an odd choice."

"-Very traditional MadamPam. De English Mummies in de Caribbean got de cooks to serve it to der children".

"Oh I see. Well the clients who like to be nannied will

lap that up".

Then she said, "Well done Tanice. It sounds like a feast. I'll organize some seafood platters from Fortnum's to have with drinks and order some tropical fruits for an exotic salad. Can you make up some nice ice cream?"

"Yes MadamPam. Coconut and mango. It very nice. I also make de pineapple party cake with rum. It goin' to have a Caribbean decoration."

"Well done". Then she added like an army captain, "Keep up the good work".

After MadamPam left the room Tanice sat down to rest her weary feet. Darnelle was all teed up to give her a hand and was already talking about her Trini Carnival costume that she was going to wear. Tanice had said,

"Listen girl. You not a guest. You helpin' me in de kitchen. You need sensible shoes".

But she knew Darnelle would want to wear her highest heels, a tarty pink sequined outfit with a short frou frou skirt and a black feathered headdress. Tanice knew she would have to wrench away that dreadful feathered headdress from Darnelle's head. She was not going to have a daughter of hers fannying around in front of horny gentleman looking like a tart. She made a note to remind herself to pack secretly Darnelle's trainers and decided to enlist MadamPam's help in getting Darnelle to wear these shoes for waiting table. It was going to be a long night. Tanice sighed deeply and opened her recipe book to check the ingredients for the Pineapple and Orange Caribbean Gateau she was planning to make.

Lady Pamela was just finishing her telephone conversation with The Colonel. He said that Edward had had his license removed and that the fine paid was indeed five thousand pounds. Lady Pamela then assured The Colonel that she would take care of the damage.

She followed on, "I just wish we could fix Edward".

"Well there's no more money coming from me. If he gets into trouble again he'll have to stew."

"What's happened to that nice girlfriend of his?"

"Which one? There are several and one with a broken arm. She's buggered off. Not surprising".

The Colonel then added, "He's coming to the party and did ask to bring someone but I declined on your behalf. With him, security is too much of a risk".

"Is James Jefferson KP3 coming?" Asked Lady Pamela.

"Not sure. He's in The States at present trying to sort out his matrimonial problems. Wife number two is taking him for all she can", then he asked, "Laura?"

"Yes she's coming and also Tony. The girls have put forward their favorite clients and we have a couple of ex-employees, some of our wealthy regulars and of course a party would not be a party without two or three Chelsea pensioners."

"I heard that dear old Bob kicked the bucket a few months back. God it will be us next old girl. Oops-the bathroom calls and if I don't get there in time there will be trouble. Toodle pip".

Lady Pamela hung up the phone and ruminated on getting old. She'd read somewhere recently that 'getting old was not for sissies'. How true that saying was. She went back to her list of attendees and rang the bell for her afternoon cuppa. Dandelion looked up expectantly and stayed riveted to the door into the kitchen. His tail thumped on the carpet. Those biscuits were on their way.

In light of the fact that Gupta had coughed, David decided that the team could do with congratulating and bought a couple of bottles of Moet. Cindy declined the champagne and unable to tell Peter of her success with groping Gupta sat sipping an orange juice and smiling to herself as Peter enthused about David's negotiating skills. She suppressed the niggling feeling that the Gupta problem was not entirely sorted:-The lunch had been tortuous; she felt Rav's pudgy hand squeeze her thigh twice and then he left his sweaty paw playing on her knee. She disappeared off to The Ladies to gather her wits and on returning sat away from him on another chair. He tried to ply her with wine even though she told him she was pregnant. Luckily Pete appeared just as they were finishing their pasta dishes and gave Cindy a big kiss 'hello'. Rav took the hint and formalizing his behavior started to talk to Pete about the project.

Later that evening David and Laura stopped for a fish and chip takeaway and as they were driving home both were silently mulling over possible alibis for the night of Lady Pamela's party. Laura spoke first as soon as they were inside the front door of Pippin Cottage.

"Oh by the way" she said lightly "I am staying up in Putney on Saturday. My old design friend, who I bumped into the other day, has asked me to have dinner and stay the night".

David smiled and said, "That'll be a nice catch-up for you. Actually I've got a cricket club dinner in North London that night and knowing how much booze those buggers drink I may well lay my head somewhere. I certainly won't be in any condition to drive."

They both nodded and smiled at each other while independently thinking how easy and straight forward it was to spin a crooked tale as to their future plans. David, looking forward to laying his head between Star's breasts, went into the study and promptly shut the door.

Laura dropped her things and greeted Percy who was meowing loudly for a snack. She fed him some cat biscuits and stroked his soft black and white fur smiling

166

to herself in anticipation of a wonderful evening in the company of Blue Eyes. Even though she was apprehensive about meeting Lady Pamela again, in light of the fact that the old lady knew about her dalliance with James, Laura was secretly excited about not only wearing one of Lady Pamela's designer gowns but also kicking up her heels in the company of exotic strangers. What a sly old bird Lady Pamela was turning out to be. No doubt she would be dressed in something extraordinary. Laura suddenly remembered that the nice guy she had met at tea would also be there. What was his name? It was Tony and he had said that he was coming as a pirate. She made a mental note to look out some sexy underwear and to buy some more of her favorite perfume. Her heart lifted at the thought of seeing Blue Eyes.

David, in the privacy of the study in front of his favorite porn site, took out his tool and began stroking it while envisaging Star's face on one of the writhing Indian females in front of him.

Over the last few days Laura thought about her decision to leave the Emergency Pill in her handbag. Even though she had come to the conclusion that having James' child by mistake would be a completely idiotic idea, she couldn't quite bring herself to swallow the solution. She chastised herself for having the foolhardy notion of leaving fate to decide the course of her life. She knew so very little about James. He was in The States but where and for how long? He had been evasive about his marital status, but so drenched in desire was she that she had lost all sense of reason and any caution had disappeared out of the window during the height of their passion.

Laura's period was due on the Sunday or possibly Monday. On the one hand she was praying for it to

167

arrive on time as usual and allay any fears of being pregnant and on the other hand for it not to come early on Saturday the night of the party when she was expecting to spend a whole night with Blue Eyes, unencumbered.

The longing for another child was still at the back of her mind and she knew it would never entirely disappear. Practically she had to sort out her marriage and reign in her lust. Before Blue Eyes came on the scene, she had wandered through a barren desert of desire over the last year and knowing there would many more years to come, it would be very hard to give up her affair with Blue Eyes and why should she? David was getting his internet jollies which seemed to Laura such a soulless way to experience passion. She began to ponder on what his activity could lead to; visits to prostitutes or possibly an Indian lover? She banished this idea from her mind and concentrated on trying to sort out her feelings in relation to everything that was happening in her life. On Saturday she resolved to find out all about James Jefferson Kirkpatrick 3rd and while Lady Pamela was helping her choose a designer gown from her collection, Laura decided to ask the old lady outright about Blue Eyes.

Meanwhile she said a little prayer to The Lord above for blood to flow.

MadamPam's regular Cockney maintenance man, 'call me 'Arry' had been busy the day before the party shifting the large pieces of furniture to create a dance floor. A wiry short-arsed guy who had had the success of coming third in the Hackney Strong Man Champs circa 2005 had been her Man Friday for over 15 years. She paid him well and they had an understanding that he would keep his 'norf and souf', or in everyman's

168

parlance, 'mouth' shut with regard to the comings and goings of the people at No 32 Davenport Gardens. Down the pub after a few jars he was heard to make ribald remarks about the caliber of her ladyship's female companions with special mention of the well-endowed Pandora.

"Talk about Bristol cities. You could make a nest in them titties".

He had checked all the electric plugs as per her ladyship's instructions and repeated yet again to her ladyship,

"Yer plugs are feather plucked yer ladyship".

Lady Pamela had looked quizzical. "Plucked rhymes with....?"

He nodded vigorously and continued, "In a word... brown bread".

Pedantically she pointed out, "That's two words actually...so you mean they're dead?"

"Good as, yer ladyship. Fire 'azard, that's wot they are. By rights I should report this to 'ealth and safety'.

"Now 'arry, I mean Harry, you're not going to do that because I'm going to make it worth your while not to. How would you like an invitation to the Caribbean party tomorrow?"

'Arry rubbed his hands with glee. "Rather."

Needs must thought Lady Pamela and she decided to seat him next to the Chelsea Pensioner mob.

"Please wear something appropriate Harry. It is a fancy dress party so if you've got a clean tropical shirt or something".

She had trailed off wondering if he had understood that she wanted him to get out of the dirty denims he usually wore.

"Don't you worry yer ladyship. I scrub up bright and shiny. I'll wear me fancy waistcoat and me sexy Lionel

169

Blairs"

She looked at him enquiringly.

"Me flairs. They're velvet."

He grinned and continued, "ta muchly too" and went back to sorting the dodgy wiring.

When he had finished that job, Lady Pamela called him into the study and said she would like him to come in early the following day as she was expecting a large order of tropical pot plants from Harrods and she needed him to lift them into place.

"Righto yer ladyship".

Whistling happily, his thoughts turned to the possibility that he might get laid on the morrow; now that was something to look forward to.

On Saturday Tanice started her day at The House at 8am, two hours earlier than normal as she knew MadamPam would have her on cleaning and polishing duty in the morning and what with greeting the regular day clients and organizing the catering there was a great deal to do.

Ten exotic orchids in white pots along with brightly colored hibiscus and half a dozen waving palms duly arrived just before lunch. Casa Blanca began to resemble the hot house at Kew Gardens. 'Arry was instructed to place the plants in strategic positions round the house. He muttered about 'aving a sore back but lady Pamela retorted.

"Just put your back into it Harry and you won't feel a thing".

At one point when Lady Pamela changed her mind yet again about the placement of some of the palms, he was heard to utter,

"Make up yer bleedin' mind yer ladyship".

The girls had discussed their fashion choices for the party a couple of weeks before and after looking at West

Indian Carnival websites had mainly gone for the Hollywood meets Caribbean choice of evening dress. Lady Pamela always funded her girls into their new costumes as she knew they could be used again for the delectation of the clients. Pandora, who knew Lady P's preferences, had said,

"Figure hugging. Lots of tits and arse and not much dress but over the top you must wear a bolero, jacket or shawl to cover up the merchandise so that you can reveal your charms on the dance floor. I'm wearing a strapless black and pink number with a long detachable skirt, heeled boots and a pink ostrich feather cropped jacket. I just hope it doesn't molt all over the place"

Nefertiti had chosen a be-jeweled bustier and scarf and a tight front-split jeweled long skirt, all in matching royal purple diaphanous, or in the girls' parlance 'difanious', material. Underneath she was planning to wear her favorite deep blue lace sequined panties. Cherry decided to go flowery in a red hibiscus adorned cream silk negligee and matching peignoir.

Lady Pamela had told them that she had organized some fancy masks and headdresses 'A La Carnivale'.

"And I've tied a bit of tinsel to my whip..." Pandora quipped.

Lady Pamela asked the girls to come in an hour earlier than usual on Saturday. There was much to be done for the Caribbean Soiree. The girls all mucked in on these occasions and were paid a handsome bonus for their help. Lady Pamela had them sorting flowers into arrangements, folding napkins into fancy designs, setting up fairy lighting and making sure their respective rooms were immaculate. Being a hard task master, although she always thought of herself as scrupulously fair, Lady Pamela did not allow them to slacken in their sexual duties with their regular day-time clients. They were

171

allowed to stop work two hours before the party started to enable them to get showered and changed into their respective finery. She always organized a hairdresser to assist with any elaborate hairstyles. Lady Pamela then required all of them to parade in front of her 15 minutes before the first guests were due to arrive and as she was a stickler for the immaculate appearance, she closely inspected them for any discrepancies in their chosen outfits and makeup. Pandora was an old hand at these events and made sure that Cherry Blossom, who she had taken under her wing, had just the right color lipstick and heel of shoe.

The question of Dandelion and of what could be done with him during the party preparations and for the party itself was a vexatious one for Lady Pamela. On one hand she would have liked him to join in, decked out in a doggy pirate costume, but on the other hand she knew he would only make a nuisance of himself and probably howl when the music started. She had occasionally left him in the tender care of Monsieur Georges at Le Petit Jardin restaurant but never for a whole day and night. In the end she had one of the girls take him over to Monsieur Georges for the day and had instructed the Doggy Night Care people to collect him from there in the evening and put him up for the night in their kennel area. Dandi, not knowing what was coming, was delighted to find himself on the end of the lead with his beloved Nefertiti and smiled sweetly up at her as they trotted down to the restaurant. Lady Pamela knew he would fall into a doggy sulk when those kennel people arrived and would not enjoy an uncomfortable night in one of their kennels surrounded by riff raff from all over London. But needs must and off he went in the reluctant hands of Nefertiti. Monsieur Georges felt himself privileged to be looking after 'Le beau Dandeleon', so in

172

return he gave Nefertiti a box of sweet French Pastries to be served as part of the evening's dessert. Lady Pamela was delighted to receive them and any leftovers could be served at breakfast.

Lady Pamela bustled into the kitchen where Tanice was knee deep in stuffing for the crab back starter.

"Tanice, we have an extra guest tonight, I have had to ask Harry. Don't ask me why".

Tanice gave her a searching look. "We have plenty food MadamPam."

Privately, she was thinking what on earth has that Cockney monkey got over MadamPam and if he had got an invite, why hadn't she? She didn't trust 'Arry ever since he had pushed up against her while supposedly mending the dishwasher. Bloody men:-All they want to do is get up a ladies' bumsie. Her brow furrowed as she thought of Darnelle, her troublesome daughter who could so easily get way out of control. With 'Arry on the loose anything could happen. She had managed to steal Darnelle's trainers from the bottom of her wardrobe cupboard and stuffed them in the bottom of a shopping bag but had not been able to 'lose' the dreaded black feathered headdress. She knew that Darnelle had hidden it away from her mother's prying eyes. They had an argument over Darnelle's outfit and Darnelle had won much to Tanice's annoyance. Her daughter would be parading around in a low cut sparkly number with a frou frou skirt. MadamPam had said she would speak to Darnelle about the 'fuck me' style shoes she was planning to wear. Tanice was beginning to feel exhausted and it was only 11 am. A long afternoon stretched before her.

CHAPTER 12

Saturday morning was spent mainly in domestic tasks for Laura and David. Mowing the lawns and washing the car for David while Laura was head down weeding the vegetable garden and tidying her flower borders. Juliet had rung the day before and sounded very excited about coming home at the end of term. She asked if they were both coming to fetch her and not to forget that Prize Giving was starting at 12 midday. She mentioned that the school orchestra would be giving a short concert and then said,

"Not short enough. They're terrible".

She continued happily, "I am getting the top tennis prize and I might get the Math Prize for my year too so please don't be late and then you can sit near the front".

Laura had assured her that they would both be there, on time.

Happily occupied with their own daydreams, Laura and David came together for a cup of coffee mid-morning and discussed such mundane issues such as ordering in coal and wood for the winter fires while their minds were pre-occupied with plans for the evening's events. While Laura was deciding whether or not to take two or three different bra styles with her to cover all possible dress designs that Lady Pamela might fit her with for the party, David was thinking about asking his Star if she would engage with him in the wheelbarrow position. With their minds elsewhere, David's cell phone trilled. He checked the number and answered.

Bill? How are you? The meeting? Did we have one? Oh it's today. Sorry I had forgotten. No. No. Of course I appreciate you're off to France tomorrow. 6-30pm? Any possibility we could make it 5-30pm? Oh I see. 6-30pm it is then. Yes. Yes that's fine.

He put the phone down and silently swore. He would now not be able to get to Casa Blanca until around 8-30pm: - An hour and a half late for the party.

He relayed his annoyance to Laura about the forgotten meeting with Bill, an old school friend, who was renovating his third country cottage and while Laura was nodding in sympathy over David having to arrive late for his special Cricketer's bash, she was calculating that she would have to pack her bag surreptitiously and leave her hair and makeup 'au naturel' until she arrived at Lady Pamela's. As she was planning to leave the house around five o'clock to allow plenty of time for travel, preparation and titivating, she had already told David the time of her departure to Putney to see her old design friend, so now with the added complication of David's meeting, it was natural for him to say,

"I'll run you to the station Laura and I'm sure Cindy could pick you up tomorrow. I'd do it but I'll probably have a humungous hangover and not be fit for anything before the afternoon".

In fact he was hoping to be well and truly pussy whipped, not only into the morrow, but into next week.

Laura, assessing that it would seem odd if she refused his offer, accepted and they both went back to their respective tasks.

Percy joined Laura in the garden and enjoyed pouncing on the pile of weeds that he was certain

175

contained imaginary prey. At one point Laura arose to stretch her back, stroked his soft fur and said quietly,

"What am I doing Percy, what am I doing?"

Percy rubbed his head against her hand and purred softly in approval. While Laura was communing with Percy, David went into the study and phoned Casa Blanca. Lady Pamela's response was polite but icy. She did not like anyone disrupting her timetable. She told him that dinner would be served at 8.15pm and could he please make a concerted effort to be there before 8.30pm. He assured her he would try.

After laboring in the garden, Laura showered and washed her hair and left it loose to dry. She changed into her best jeans and a white cotton shirt. While David was on the phone in the study, she quickly packed her little wheelie case with three different bras, an extra T shirt, some sexy undies, her wash bag and make-up and the pair of diamante heels she had bought for Gupta's party. In the event of a see-through choice of dress, she packed her long nude petticoat, she then unearthed her ancient electric hair roller set that had been given to her on her 21st birthday and stuffed it into the case; she hoped the rollers would still be safe to use:-Heaven forbid that they should set Casa Blanca alight. She sat on the groaning case and pulled shut the protesting zip.

They were both quiet on the way to the station. David hummed 'My Girl' to himself and tapped the steering wheel and Laura stared out of the window at the surrounding countryside. It was a still soft summer's evening with the smell of newly cut meadow grass on the air. A nostalgic aroma for Laura who was reminded of summer evenings in the past when family life was secure and happy and her father had mown the grass at her family home in Devon as the light was beginning to fall.

At the local station David touched her hand, said a quick goodbye and then turned the Peugeot round and sped away. Laura stood for a moment watching the dust from the back wheels; he turned the corner and was gone. At the very point he disappeared from view, Laura felt an overwhelming realization that she was at a crossroads in her life and it was up to her to choose a new path. The cliché 'parting of the ways' came to mind and imprinted itself stubbornly in her consciousness.

On the train up to Waterloo, she shared her carriage with a bird-like elderly lady. They smiled at each other and the little old lady went back to knitting a baby's jumper in pale blue, her fingers flying over the needles. Laura watched the passing countryside and started to go through the major events in her life starting with a happy childhood in Devon; playing with her younger brother Chris on the sands of the Devon coast, racing, what seemed like half a mile, to see who could get to the sea first as the wind swirled around their chilled bodies; her mother unpacking the picnic basket, cold chicken and cheese and chutney sandwiches; her father erecting the compulsory windbreak; the house and garden of her youth, parties and barbecues that her parents had organized. She remembered the home-made barbecue her father had made for her sixteenth birthday party:- Half a metal drum filled to the brim with wood and coal .It had got so hot that it had exploded the sausages all over the lawn and then promptly died. She laughed at the memory. She drew a veil over boarding school as that experience had not been a happy one and yet David had insisted that Juliet, being an only child and in need of companions, should go away to school. She had been in two minds about the decision and in the first term, Laura had missed her as much as Juliet had wanted to come home. Juliet has turned out so well, thought Laura. She

177

loved her daughter dearly and could not at present envisage telling her that she and her father were ending their marriage. Her mind moved quickly to University days, meeting David and their subsequent life together. How happy she had been; buying Pippin Cottage, doing it up, having Juliet and all the excitement and exhaustion of a new baby and the triumphant moment when she slept through the night; Juliet's first day at the local primary and then Laura's re-commencement of her art endeavors which led to working eventually for The Manning Renovation Company. People looking in would have said a charmed life, but outsiders are never fully aware of what goes on behind closed doors.

As she was cataloguing the past, she arrived at a shocking parallel. It was to do with something she had read recently; that supposedly a person very near death has their life played out in front of their mind; this, she realized, was happening to her; either this meant that the train was going to crash and end her life, or that her marriage to David was well and truly train-wrecked. She concluded it was the latter. Their relationship had run its course. She was now ready to admit to herself that she had fallen out of love with him. Coupled with the strange feeling of arriving at the crossroads and her growing awareness of choosing to be true to herself, she knew it was time to assert her independence and let the consequences be damned. On the fifty minute journey to Waterloo, many concerns paraded through her mind. When should she confront David? How would Juliet react to the news of their breakup and the biggest hurdle of all how would she support herself?

Financially she could survive for a while. She had a small legacy from her mother's estate and she had put aside some funds from the sales of her art work ostensibly in case The Manning Company ran into difficulties. They would have to sell the house eventually and she had a cold feeling that David, bearing in mind she would be the one to split, would dig his toes in and try and stay put. Even though Pippin Cottage was in both their names, she had no idea whether or not as matrimonial property they could spilt the proceeds fifty-fifty and in any case, there was no way she could put up the cash to pay David out. She was sure he would refuse to pay her out. Should she when the time came take her half of the joint account? She needed legal advice and she needed it fast. She had deliberately not mentioned any of this to Cindy as Cindy would immediately try to do some mending. Laura did not want her marriage to be mended, she wanted it, pure and simple, ended.

The whole issue suddenly seemed so daunting. What she needed, she realized, was someone with whom she could talk things through; someone she could trust. Blue Eyes was a possibility but for some reason she felt uncomfortable about that idea. As his dear laughing eyes appeared in her mind she started to yearn for him; she knew it would be easy to fall hopelessly in love but she was savvy enough to know she was in lust with him but not in love as yet; he had ignited a fire which she was unwilling to put out and that had led to a careless moment; she was still kicking herself for letting herself go, but how sweet it was to be abandoned in his arms.

With regard to a possible pregnancy she was relieved to note that on exiting the shower that afternoon she had begun to feel the familiar tender breasts and stomach ache that heralded her monthly flow. At least that would be one problem sorted thought Laura ruefully; a desperate thought assailed her; had she packed any sanitary protection? So concerned was she with outfits and shoes, could she have forgotten to pack the obvious? There certainly wouldn't be any protection in Lady

179

Pamela's bathroom. Her mind went through the contents of her case and she was relieved to remember that she had thrown some protection in at the last minute.

Unbeknown to her, James Jefferson KirkPatrick the 3rd had gone under the knife for a vasectomy after his fourth child. 2 girls by his first wife and 2 boys by the second seemed more than plenty. He also had a stepson.

Laura sighed and gathered her possessions as the train slowed into Waterloo and ground to a halt. She helped the little old lady with her suitcase and as the lady turned to thank her she touched Laura's arm.

"Please don't worry so much. I'm sure it will never happen".

Laura smiled and wished her a nice evening and exited the train. As she hurried along the platform she knew that there was only one person in whom she could confide and that was Lady Pamela. Laura resolved to ask her advice after the party was over.

In her efficiency Laura realized she was a little early for Casa Blanca so she decided to do a short detour passed the pretty garden in the square adjacent to The Little Chelsea Hotel. She felt a keen anticipation for the evening ahead and wondered what Lady Pamela had in store for her to wear. She trundled her case through the wrought iron gates and sat down on one of the park benches. The summer air was cooling down but the temperature was still pleasant in the early 70's. She observed the bright flower beds filled with petunias, salvias and ageratum and noticed alongside a small herb garden filled with aromatic thyme, rosemary and mint. Somebody obviously liked to use fresh herbs in cooking. The grass was short-cut and bright green after the showers of rain the week before. She breathed the air and felt restored. She had been brought up in the country. It would be difficult to make the transition from

180

Pippin Cottage, into which she had put so much love and attention, to a dubious flat in a cheap area in London.

After a while she left the city garden and walked along opposite The Little Chelsea Hotel. She smiled as she remembered the afternoon of hot passion with Blue Eyes and as she was about to go past, her eye caught two figures coming down the hotel steps. One of them, a man in a blue shirt with familiar silver hair and the other, a slim blonde girl of about 25 in heels and a short skirt. They were laughing together and he had his arm round her waist. They stopped at the bottom of the steps and the man encircled the girl with his arms, stroked her backside and kissed her passionately. Then talking animatedly they began walking in the opposite direction to Laura. Stabbed by the truth, she stopped and clutched her stomach. Blue Eyes was with someone else. He had moved on to pastures new. The realization left her devastated. She went back to the garden and slumped down on the bench, the wheelie case dumped beside her. How could he? They had hardly even got to know each other and now she had been usurped by a younger model. Bastard! There was no way she could go to the party knowing that while he was smiling at her he had been sleeping with another woman, a few hours before. She resolved to call Lady Pamela and cancel.

Struggling through tears of frustration and anger she wrenched her cell phone from her handbag and stabbed in the private number of Lady Pamela. A familiar upper class bray greeted her sharply,

"Hello. Who is it? We're very busy you know, make it short please".

There followed a long tearful conversation as Laura relayed the bitter truth. Lady Pamela was consoling and then said that he did have the reputation for being a bit of a player. This news just increased Laura's tears until she said,

"I'm s... s… sorry. I...can't…face him tonight".

"But Laura dear, he's not coming...something about sorting out his divorce settlement. He said he would be in The States for a while...Oh…but he's not is he?"

Laura broke into a fresh round of tears. After more protestations from Laura and declining the party repeatedly, Lady Pamela eventually managed to persuade her to come anyway. She also felt it might cheer Laura up especially in light of her husband being out for the night which would mean a bleak empty house to go back to. For one thing Lady Pamela did not want anyone to muck up her table seating. She laid on the fact that someone would take care of Laura's hair and she could choose something beautiful to wear. She then added,

"I have some lovely sapphires, a necklace and some earrings I would like to lend you for the evening. Do come and we can have a good talk in the morning after the party."

These comforting words made Laura decide to attend the party. In any case she felt even less like going back to empty Pippin Cottage where she knew she would make herself even more miserable checking on David's porn history while quietly getting drunk.

After Lady Pamela rang off, Laura trudged the streets to Davenport Gardens all the more feeling like a volcano deep in her gut was about to explode. Bloody men. How could she have been so stupid as to look at Blue Eyes not only as a long-time lover but also a suitable candidate for another round of happy families? What a bloody idiot. She climbed the steps to Casa Blanca and stabbed the bell. Lady Pamela answered,

"Password please".

There was a pause as Laura took a deep breath and

shouted into the intercom.

"I don't fucking know what the fucking password is...."

Then more quietly. "Sorry".

Lady Pamela said softly,

"Come in dear and I'll pour you a drink".

A bedraggled Laura entered the hall and was greeted by the open arms of Lady Pamela. She fell into them and started sobbing anew.

"Darling Laura. What a dreadful revelation. Men are the end aren't they? Now go upstairs and put all your things in my bedroom and I'll be up with a brandy in a minute".

As she climbed the stairs she noticed on the top step an Amazonian woman with a head full of rollers, in an amazing pink and black dress complete with high heeled boots and an elaborate feather jacket. The figure waved.

"Hello, I'm Pandora, are you looking for Lady P?"

Laura indicated that she had been sent to wait in Lady P's bedroom. Pandora pointed out the room and with a wave said, "See you later at the party".

Laura sat on a chintz chair in Lady Pamela's bedroom and felt immediately soothed looking at the plush beige decor and wonderful French antiques. All around her the noises of Casa Blanca and its occupants made her feel she was about to be part of something special. The female voices of the other guests, for she supposed they were guests, rose and fell in the rooms adjacent with an occasional shriek of laughter. It appeared that there were quite a number of overnighters all preparing for the big event. She could hear some music coming from downstairs; someone was tuning a steel drum and another person was running a hand over a keyboard.

Lady Pamela, bearing a brandy, breezed in and immediately took charge. She insisted Laura have the restorative beverage to settle her nerves.

"First of all we will put James Jefferson KirkPatrick the 3rd out of her heads. Banished! Now let's get you out of those clothes and into a dress that's going to knock'em dead. Firstly I'm going to run you a bath and then we will choose something to wear. When you are ready, come into the bedroom and take a look at my choices. You look to be a UK size 10?"

Laura nodded and began to say something but her words were batted away like flies.

"When we have dressed you I'll have Michelle come in and do your hair and makeup. You have lovely hair and you should wear it down. I'm just going to run you a bubble bath".

Lady Pamela swept off to run the bath and check her collection of evening wear in the wardrobe.

Laura stripped off and stepped into the welcome warm water, her tension easing as she covered herself with watery bubbles. As Lady Pamela entered, Laura said quietly,

"Thank you so much".

"It's going to be fun. I promise you".

Then she added, "Now if you'll excuse me I've got the menu to sort."

Downstairs in the kitchen, Lady Pamela was going over the dinner arrangements with Tanice. Darnelle, looking bright eyed and frilly tailed in her party outfit was grinning madly and nodding enthusiastically while teetering about on her ridiculous shoes. Tanice listened to Lady Pamela's instructions, the second time that day that she had heard them and then tried to alert MadamPam to the problem of Darnelle's unsuitable footwear by staring hard at her employer and then surreptitiously pointing at Darnelle's feet. MadamPam then said obviously,

184

"No, I haven't forgotten".

She gave Darnelle the once-over. "I love your costume".

Darnelle simpered happily.

"But and it's a big one, you will not be allowed to wear those shoes".

Darnelle's face fell and before the sparkly creation could utter a protest, MadamPam continued, "For waiting table you need some flat shoes. It is dangerous to carry glasses and plates in shoes that could create an accident; in fact if you fell with a tray load of dishes someone could be maimed, or possibly stabbed by a falling knife..."

Darnelle had been trying to break in during this but as she was a little afraid of MadamPam she hung her head and began to scowl.

Lady Pamela continued, "Now I know your mother has brought some trainers".

At this point Darnelle's eyes flew to Tanice and she let out an audible 'humph' and crossed her arms round her middle.

"So please put them on and we can all get started."

Lady Pamela turned to Tanice, "Usual terms Tanice but there will be a substantial bonus to both of you for all the hard work".

With that she turned on her heel and went to attend to Laura.

When Laura, refreshed, stepped out of the bathroom wrapped in one of the old lady's fluffy white towels and came into the bedroom, she was delighted to see that there were four long colorful gowns laid out on the bed for her delectation. Lady Pamela returned and watched as Laura began to choose something to her liking. The red chiffon ruffle dress was lovely but Laura felt she might be overwhelmed wearing that color. She liked the simple pink silk off-the-shoulder number but Lady Pamela felt it wasn't dressy enough. Laura tried on the turquoise backless shift with silver trim and they both agreed that the color suited her beautifully.

"But do try the cream crepe. It was one of my favorites. I was encased in that when I met The Maharaja",

She closed her eyes and reminisced. "Yes...a very lucky dress".

Laura was eventually persuaded to wear the beautiful cream strapless crepe dress trimmed with shimmering crystal beads. It hugged her boobs and waist and then skimmed straight down passed her hips. On one side, from floor to mid-thigh it had an alarming side split. Laura, uneasy at this exposure, said she looked like a Hollywood bride.

Pandora was brought in to allay her fears and agreed with Lady Pamela that the color and style was very Caribbean and not bridal at all. Lady Pamela gave her a matching crystal beaded scarf to wear and then said,

"And now I have something special to lend you dear". She went to the drawer in the bottom of the wardrobe and took out the ornate silver jewelry box from under the Chinese throw. Sifting through the contents she brought out an elegant necklace of diamonds and sapphires and as Laura gasped at the magnificence of such a valuable piece of jewelry, Lady Pamela placed it around her neck and told her to look in the mirror.

She looked and saw herself transformed from bedraggled housewife into a beautiful movie star.

"Oh...Goodness...It's stunning...Are you sure..?"

She trailed off as lady Pamela interrupted. "Laura, you look wonderful. It could have been made for you."

Pandora watching these proceedings ruefully remembered that Lady P had said exactly the same

186

words to her a few years back, but being a good sport she said,

"Super. You look terrific".

Lady Pamela then rummaged through the contents of the box, muttering to herself.

"They must be in here somewhere...those matching diamond and sapphire earrings. Pandora can you look please. My eyesight is not what it was".

It was determined, after Pandora had checked the contents, that the earrings were nowhere to be found. Similar to the squirrel that she said she was like, the old lady could not think where they had been secreted. Instead Laura was given some simple diamond drops to wear.

Michelle the lively Irish hairdresser and makeup artist was then summoned and worked her magic on Laura's blonde locks, curling them seductively round her shoulders. She complimented Laura on her fine skin and made a professional job of leaving Laura's complexion as natural as possible while giving her eyes and lips extra sparkle.

And so it was that Laura was prepared to meet a new and extraordinary group of revelers while still being completely in the dark with regard to Lady Pamela's business within the walls of Casa Blanca.

After Laura was introduced to the other girls and Lady Pamela had done her inspection, she disappeared upstairs to change. The girls were to entertain the first guests who turned out to be, to Laura's amazement, three elderly gentlemen in the uniform of Chelsea Pensioners. Had they come to the wrong address? Pandora stepped in and gave them all a big kiss after which they beamed happily and the smallest of them crept up to Laura, his mouth close to Laura 's breast and said slyly,

"You're new aren't you and what services can you

provide? "And he winked lasciviously.

Laura jumped away alarmed and went to find herself something to drink.

Lady Pamela would never call herself a show-off but she did like to make an entrance at her little soirees. Her dressmaker had created an extraordinary costume which was a cross between glamorous female pirate and musical hall dame and she wanted everyone to be transfixed when she stood at the top of the stairs.

The dress was a slim fitting black and red sheath dress with a black fishtail net skirt. Lady Pamela, in her mid-seventies, was very proud of her slim figure and worked hard on her yoga and flexibility exercises daily to keep in trim. Her long-suffering dress maker had tried to persuade Lady Pamela that perhaps female pirates needed to have freedom of movement and some culottes might be more suitable but Lady Pamela would have none of that. She wanted to look as glamorous as possible. For safety reasons she decided on sensible shoes:-Black pumps with a Cuban heel. She did not want a repeat of the Flamenco solo at the Spanish soiree, in front of the Spanish ambassador no less, when in high heels she had slid in an unladylike fashion and landed half under the table.

Lady Pamela's outfit was complimented by some long black kid gloves and a sexy eye patch that she had decorated with rhinestones. She dispensed with a tricorn hat as it would have messed up her hair but instead put on some large glittering gold hoop earrings to complete the outfit. The piece de resistance was to be buttoned to her shoulder by its feet and that was a drunk-looking wired parrot made of red and green material complete with flying tail feathers. The parrot proved a little difficult to button into place. Just as she had him balanced he would annoyingly fall forward and land

188

bum over beak. Eventually she got him buttoned into position and turned his wired head to face her ear as though he was about to alert her to a marauding enemy. As she moved he nodded sagely to himself. His name, she decided, was to be Bonny after the infamous 18th Century British pirate, Anne Bonny, on whom she had based her costume. She had managed to procure a toy musket although she wished it was a real gun so that she could fire a shot over the heads of her guests and frighten the daylights out of them, but she didn't fancy the anti-terror squad and God knows who else storming the premises. After Michelle had teased her hair and tidied her makeup, she appraised herself in the mirror and pronounced herself ready to meet her public.

She strode to the top of the stairs and stood looking down, one hand on her hip and the other brandishing the musket aloft.

"Heh Ho m'hearties, let the rum flow and the party begin."

All mouths below fell open, then after a second or two, led by The Colonel, all the guests started clapping. Pandora caught Nef's eye and they both burst into fits of giggles. Lady Pamela looked down and was greeted by a sea of pirates, bare tummy beach goers, tropical cocktail dresses, a few castaways and who was that person in a frightful afro wig, and dark red balding velvet flares? She caught his eye and he raised his glass. It was 'Arry' in his Lionel Blairs. She descended the stairs, Bonny nodding on her shoulder as the steel band started to play 'yellow bird'. Tanice, resting her back against the kitchen door-frame, raised her eyes to the ceiling. MadamPam had outdone herself and 'what de blazes is dat ting on her shoulder.'

189

CHAPTER 13

While Lady Pamela was surrounded by admirers Laura, feeling awkward, was standing at the back and watching the spectacle unfold. Alongside her someone suddenly approached and touched her arm. Startled she turned and beheld a tall pirate with chiseled features and an aquiline nose wearing a ruffled white shirt split to the navel and a bejeweled dagger stuffed in his belted jeans. A gold medallion glittered on his chest. She couldn't help noticing the contrast of the gold chain against his dark chest hair. He gave her an obvious appraisal, smiled rakishly and held her gaze with deep green eyes. He held out his hand.

"Hello, I'm Edward Hanbury and you fair princess of the Caribbean Sea, are?"

"Oh I'm Laura"

"And does beautiful Laura have another name or is she in disguise perhaps?"

"Just Laura is fine"

"Then I'll call you Laura princess."

He then lent forward and she caught a whiff of Force 10 aftershave. He whispered in her ear. "Are you one of the new fillies in Aunty P's stable?"

She pulled away alarmed. This was the second time she'd been asked a leading question.   Fillies in a stable? All very puzzling.

"Oh No. I met Lady Pamela on the street".

Edward's dark eyebrow shot up in amusement; Laura, realizing the confusion, continued,

"No No...Not... um not like that...I...helped her up when she got tangled in her dog's lead and she brought me in for a cup of tea."

Edward laughed and then suddenly surprised her by putting his hand up and touching the diamond and sapphire necklace.

"My, that's a fine piece of jewelry, very beautiful".

"Lady Pamela lent it to me".

"Oh really... she has an amazing collection of jewelry... Apparently paid for in kind".

He lent in and said quietly in her ear. "It is said that she fucked her way through The House of Lords and has been rewarded handsomely for her favors".

Laura was shocked and reacted by pulling away and clutching her necklace. Edward smiled and took her arm gently, "Come and have a drink. Champagne? "

While they were chatting, at least Edward was giving her his life history and telling all about his exploits as a model as well as the fact that he knew many film stars and society gals and boys, Tony across the room in his Captain Hook's outfit was trying to get her attention. Tony had not managed to find a suitable black coat to fit his chunky frame and his unruly dark curls flew out from under his pirate's hat. He had fashioned a hook for one arm out of a small garden fork which had bent to form a claw and lashed with gaffer tape to his forearm but as the sleeves of the coat were too long the menacing claw kept getting hidden and he was disappointed it did not have the effect he wanted. Also the party had only just begun and he was already far too hot. Underneath the coat he had a cleanish white shirt and round his waist he had wrapped a red wool scarf which was already making him itch horribly. To add insult to injury he noticed Laura had already been commandeered by Dickhead Edward. He needed a cleansing ale to get started.

Lady Pamela breezed over to Edward and Laura.

"Ah you've met. Laura this is The Colonel's nephew, Edward".

191

She pointed to the parrot, "And this is Bonny. He doesn't say much but he has his eye on everyone...so no funny business Edward" and she gave her horsey whinny and sashayed off to chat to the Chelsea Pensioners.

Just as Tony was about to go over and say 'hello' to Laura and Edward, the band struck up an energetic boogie and Laura was whisked onto the dance floor by the 'don't I know it' handsome pirate while poor Captain Hook in his ill-fitting outfit was forced to stand and watch. He glanced around and realized there were a lot of very beautiful girls in the room dressed in the most revealing of costumes. Perhaps the evening would turn out alright. He turned to the vision in purple standing next to him, tapping her feet to the music.

Brandishing his hook in front of this gorgeous dark-skinned girl, he asked her to dance. She shied away from him in alarm. He realized that his hook was going to hamper his chances of a close encounter and more to the point either tear delicate dresses to shreds or inflict dreadful scratches on bare shoulders and backs. Tony kicked himself for not foreseeing this unfortunate consequence. He might as well lie down like some half-man half-beast and howl at the moon. There was only one thing for it and that was to divest himself of hook, coat and scarf and turn himself into a lowly pirate deck scrubber but before that he was determined to make contact with Laura. He watched her dance with Edward the Dickhead and became transfixed at how absolutely stunning she was.

Tanice, in the kitchen, was on fire, perspiration trickling down her back as she prepared the first course. Darnelle, resigned to the trainers, was dancing in and out of the kitchen on tiptoe and hoping people would not notice her embarrassing footwear. To deflect their eyes from her feet she was waggling her frou frou bumsie.

She was helping the two drink waiters, provided by Monsieur Georges at no cost to Lady Pamela, by carrying the trays of hors d'oeuvres provided by Fortnums; every now and then she would do a little pirouette, bumsie wagging and tray aloft to gain some attention. One of the waiters was heard to remark,

"Regardez La Creole...thinks she iz la prima ballerina. She 'ave mousse de salmon on the 'eads and down ze corsage...aye ..aye.."and he went over to remonstrate with her.

Darnelle, cross at being told off by a Frenchman, stumped back to the kitchen and complained to her mother who gave her another telling off and shoved her back into the fray with a new tray of appetizers.

'Arry poked his head into the kitchen. "Ow are ya luv?"

Tanice turned and did a double-take. The Cockney Monkey looked as though he had a dead poodle on his head and as she looked him up and down she was alarmed to note that the ancient zipper on his balding velvet trousers looked about to explode under the strain of an obviously padded up cock. She turned back without acknowledging him; he continued,

"Eh, your daughter's a bit of tutti fruity. Very tasty".

Tanice turned quickly and eyeballed him. She snapped, "And you can keep your midget digits off her Khyber Pass".

He laughed and raised both hands in supplication. "'Ere no offense luv. She gotta lovely arse but no touchee, promise".

With that he scuttled off in search of a nubile body to dance with.

Laura and Edward had finished dancing and Edward went in search of a drink. Tony came racing over before she could be swept away by The Colonel who was hovering nearby.

Laura greeted him warmly. "Tony. How lovely to see you". She landed a smacker on his cheek. He colored a little and showed her his home-made hook and said,

"Trouble is, it's dangerous... could inflict an injury".

Laura, with a hand over her mouth, was creasing with laughter. She spluttered, "Captain Hook? Oh it's a garden fork" She burst into further laughter.

Edward, holding two glasses of champagne, approached and said,

"What have we here? Looks like a poor cousin of Captain Hook to me. Tony, sorry you couldn't afford a proper costume mate."

Laura seeing Tony's embarrassment took charge of the situation.

"Come on, let's sort something more comfortable for you". And she swept him away.

Edward, with raised eyebrows, was left holding the two drinks. Watching them go, he held both drinks aloft and slurped from both glasses at once.

Laura and Tony repaired to the hall and he took off his pirate coat and scarf. Laura unstuck the gaffer tape from his forearm and placed the bendy fork on the hall table. He bemoaned the fact that he had buggered his best garden fork and they laughed anew. She inspected the rest of him leaving his pirate hat crammed over his curls. Laura needed some pirate loot to put round his neck; something to detract from the fact that his shirt was somewhat grubby. She had an audacious idea.

"Come upstairs to Lady Pamela's room. I'm staying there tonight".

He gave her sideways glance. "Is that an invitation? So to speak?"

She grinned, "Tony...we're just going to get some loot".

194

Laura peered back into the main room and could see Lady Pamela actively engaged with a bald elderly gentleman on the dance floor; everyone else was either slurping drinks, chatting or dancing. The two loot finders ran up the stairs and practically fell into Lady Pamela's bedroom. Laughing, they clutched each other and Tony unable to help himself put his arm around her waist and drew her to him, his brown eyes on a line with her blue ones.

Laura tried to pull away and then said softly, "Tony....we...."

Her words were halted by the soft touch of his lips on hers; a gentle kiss followed by the touch of his hand on her hair and his lips again on her neck. They stood holding each other, not saying anything but savoring each other's aroma and touch for, what seemed to Laura, a long minute. With her heart pounding and her skin flushed, Laura pulled away.

"Oh Tony".

He held onto her hand. "Oh Laura".

She gently extracted her hand and said in a shaky voice. "Er...now I think we should find you some loot".

She had noticed on getting into the crepe dress that Lady Pamela had some colorful beads draped over one of the wall sconces; these would do admirably to party up Captain No-Hook. As she was draping two different ropes of beads round his neck, his eyes darted from her cleavage to the layout of the room. He asked,

"Are you and Lady P going to cuddle up in the double bed tonight? I wouldn't fancy it. She'll probably fart all night".

She laughed and said, "No. I'm going to be in the single". And she pointed to a door next to the bathroom. "In the dressing room".

Laura, thinking he needed a cummerbund of some

195

kind, went into the dressing room and checked in her case where she thought she had thrown a long dark blue and pink silk scarf at the last minute. Just as she was tying this round Tony's waist and giggling while he put a hand under her chin and was trying to kiss her again, voices and footsteps were heard outside the door; Tony jumped like a startled rabbit and Laura with not a second to spare pushed him into the bathroom. As she was closing the door, the bedroom door opened and a familiar voice said,

"Who's here? Oh it's you Laura? Are you alright dear? You look a little flushed."

Laura mumbled something about going to the toilet. Lady Pamela then informed Laura that she had come in to collect her pills and explained that she had to take them with dinner. Much to Laura's consternation, she began to walk toward the bathroom door and then suddenly stopped.

"Silly me. I keep them in my bedside cabinet. Don't be long Laura. Dinner will be served shortly".

She retrieved the pills and at the bedroom door, she turned and made a cryptic comment.

"Very strange you know, I found an odd looking garden fork, all twisted up on the hall table…don't know anything about that do you?"

She gave Laura a conspiratorial look, pursing her lips amusingly and swept out before Laura could answer.

As soon as the bedroom door clicked shut Laura let Tony out of the bathroom and they both clutched each other laughing. Laura, spluttered, "She f...found your f...fork. I'm sure she knew someone was in the bathroom".

Tony held onto her and twirled her round until they over-balanced onto Lady Pamela's luxury Queen Size bed. Laura hurled a couple of cream frilled cushions at

196

her attacker. He pinned her down and brushing her messed up hair away from her eyes and planted a passionate kiss on her laughing mouth. She tried to push him away but his strength held her down; she thrashed weakly and then lay compliant and gave way to his warm sensuous mouth.

Eventually breathless she said, "Tony, please, we have to go down to dinner".

He released her and she went to tidy herself in the bathroom. Looking in the mirror she beheld a smudge-faced hussy with hair like a bird's nest. The expensive necklace had slewed sideways. She grinned at her reflection, adjusted the necklace and repaired her messy face. She was relieved to see that the cream dress had not suffered any damage as she hitched the half-mast bodice over her semi-exposed breasts. Checking her silhouette, she gave herself a tick of approval.

Tony, Captain No Hook, tucked his shirt into his trousers, checked his fly, adjusted the beads and crammed the pirate hat back on his unruly curls. They smoothed down the crumpled bedcover and replaced the cushions then Tony took Laura's hand as they exited the bedroom. They walked demurely one behind the other down the stairs. The sounds that greeted them led them to believe that the rum punch was proving to be very popular. The Steel Band was playing the Caribbean hit song 'Jean and Dinah' and Lady Pamela was sighted in full swing on the arm of Pirate Edward with Bonny bouncing on her shoulder.

Laura and Tony stepped into the paneled dining room adjacent to the main sitting room and had a close look at the table settings. Two long tables had been covered with thick white linen cloths. The silver settings and candlesticks, polished by Tanice the day before, gleamed under the play of the glass chandeliers. The girls had organized posies of bright red geraniums interspersed with lines of exotic shells scattered between the posies. Lady Pamela had chosen deep blue glass goblets and matching water glasses to complete the Caribbean theme. A white bird-shaped linen napkin, made by Cherry for each place, enhanced the table settings. In front of each place was a name written in Lady Pamela's neat script.

Tony, quite prepared to change the names so that he could sit next to Laura, was pleased to note that her name was placed between his and Edward's. Tony lent in and swiftly removed Edward's name. He replaced it with someone called Mr. Darcy from the other table.

"No idea who this Mr. Darcy is but anyone is better than that Dickhead Edward."

They slipped back into the throng although not unnoticed by their eagle eyed hostess and went to find a cleansing glass of champagne.

Back at the kitchen coalface Tanice glanced at the clock and noted that it was time for the dinner to be plated up. MadamPam had said twice, in her usual precise way, that dinner was to be served at 8.15pm. Perspiring heavily Tanice took a tray of piping hot crab backs filled with seafood mixture out of the oven. Their brown parmesan toppings sizzled as she balanced them on top of the hob. Darnelle, waiting alongside but still dancing on the spot was barked at by her mother.

"STAN'STILL...You not on de stage. These are very hot".

She took some fresh chopped dill and parsley and dusted the shells. She then grabbed Darnelle by the arm and eyeballing her said,

"CAREFUL. If der is an accident...you gonna pay and no bonus".

She instructed Darnelle to take the shells and place

198

them on the white plates in the dining room. Darnelle took heed and placed the shells on their individual plates with a flourish. The waiters were busying themselves opening wines while The Colonel, who had sourced and paid for all the grog, kept a weather eye on the proceedings.

Lady Pamela broke off the dance and went to alert the band. The bass pan player made a rolling beat and Lady Pamela announced that dinner would be served directly and would everyone please take their seats.

"Quiet please everyone. Just a matter of housekeeping. If you have a mobile device please turn it off NOW. I do not allow any photos to be taken in Casa Blanca for reasons of security. Is that clear?"

There was a shuffling and clicking as her guests did as they were told.

The girls, on the arms of their chosen guests, made their way through to the dining room and everyone exclaimed how attractive the tables looked. Pandora led her client, a pale-faced bean pole with a receding hairline, to his place. He was dressed as a missionary. He had eyes only for her and thoughts for more than just the missionary position later in the evening.

 Cherry's partner was chattering away with excitement and Nefertiti, with still no sign of Mr. Darcy, took one of the Chelsea Pensioners by the hand and led him to his place. He sat down creakily and she gently patted him on the head. Edward was delighted to see that he was seated next to beautiful Nef and he held her chair with a charming smile. He looked across to Laura and observed that she and Tony had suddenly become very friendly. Nef looked around puzzled as she had checked the place names previously and had made sure that Mr. Darcy would be seated next to her. She noticed that there was an empty place on the other side of Laura. As Edward sat down and gave her a wolfish grin, she said,

"I think there's been a mix-up. Your place is next to the lady in cream. Mr. Darcy, my client, should be seated here, but he must be running late". And she indicated Edward's place.

Edward sat tight.

"Well, that's his loss and my gain…Now let's get you something to drink. What'll it be?"

Nef knew there was no point in protesting and as Lady P had her eagle eye on proceedings she would have to acquiesce to the seating arrangements. She hope Mr Darcy would arrive soon. Lady Pamela noting the empty place next to Laura looked across at Nef and raised her eyebrow. Nef shrugged her shoulders. Lady Pamela abhorred lateness and she pursed her lips in annoyance but the show must go on. Forks clattered as the guests tucked into the crab backs and Tanice watching in the wings was pleased to note that everyone appeared to be enjoying their entree. The waiters bustled about pouring wines and Darnelle was dispatched to get The Colonel a large whisky and soda.

"Easy on the soda and no ice." And as an afterthought "Wine gives me a belly ache".

Darnelle danced away to fulfil the task.

Laura was deep in conversation with Tony; they were discussing home grown vegetables so she did not hear the front door bell chime. Lady Pamela did and she beckoned Darnelle over and asked her to answer the door. Mr. Darcy had arrived and not before time; she did so despise the trait of lateness. Darnelle skittered away to fulfil the task and as Laura had her back to the hall she was unaware of the identity of the last guest. As he entered the room there was a slight lull in the conversation and he was heard to say,

"So sorry, everyone. So sorry to keep everyone

200

waiting."

Laura froze; her upper body became rigid and she gripped Tony's arm. She gabbled quickly in his ear, "Christ, its David. Fuck! Oh Jesus, I've gotta get out of here."

Tony, alarmed, said, "Who?"

She hissed back, "My husband".

Luckily Mr. Darcy who for some strange reason that only Laura would have appreciated was dressed as a vicar complete with dog collar, black frock coat and tricorn hat was making his abject apologies to his hostess on the other table and not looking in Laura's direction. Just as she was pointing out his place next to 'the lovely girl in cream', Laura threw herself under the long white table cloth. Tony pretending he had no idea what was happening glanced under the cloth and had a fine view of Laura's cream backside as she negotiated her way between swinging legs and feet. He smiled awkwardly at his questioning dining companions and blurted out,

"Medical emergency". And then as someone began to punch his cell phone for an ambulance, "NO...NO...Not an emergency. She's feeling sick...needs some air".

Some wag retorted. "Well she's not going to get it under the table!"

As Mr. Darcy was taking his seat, Tony took the initiative and moved swiftly to Laura's seat pocketing her name card in the process. Full of bonhomie, he said,

"Well Mr. Darcy at last, we thought you were a 'no show.' Very nice to meet you. I'm Tony". He pumped David's hand.

He wittered on frantically about how terrible the traffic was in and around London as Laura peered out from under the cloth and saw a door almost in front of her. Praying it wasn't locked, she had to make a move

201

and fast. She made a quick dash for the door almost overturning someone's wine glass and wrenched it open. She practically fell inside, quickly closing the door behind.

Mr Darcy was vaguely aware of some sort of commotion but Tony managed to block a full view of the fleeing guest. Inside the room Laura, panting heavily, could see she was in some kind of storeroom with stairs leading down to a lower level. It was filled with catering boxes, planters, old chairs and shelves of china and glass. She had stumbled into The Butler's Pantry. In one corner was a small sink with an ancient tap. Still feeling frantic she checked the door and seeing it had a key she quickly turned it and locked the door. She sat on one of the boxes and burst into tears.

On the other side the guests were discussing their concerns for the runaway. Pandora began to get up.

"Someone should go and see if she's alright"

Tony, out of the corner of his eye, saw Pandora stand and he shouted across at her,

"NO ...No. She said no need. Feeling a bit faint. She'll be back in a moment".

Pandora, used to subterfuge, gave him a searching look and sat down again.

Lady Pamela did not fully understand what had happened. Where had Laura disappeared to and why? Tony was chatting madly to Mr. Darcy all the while sizing him up; the cogs in his mind whirring crazily as he deduced the reason for Mr. Darcy's invitation to the evening's entertainment. Nef came over and gave Mr. Darcy a big kiss; a cog found its place in Tony's mind as he realized that Nef, definitely a lover, had invited him. Tony moved across to his own seat to allow them to canoodle together. He saw Lady Pamela beckon him over.

"Tony dear what is going on? Laura's disappeared like a puff of smoke. Where is she?"

Tony said she was feeling ill and had gone to get some air. The old lady seemed placated by this and told him to go and search her out and make sure she was alright. Edward, a few guests along, grabbed Tony by the sleeve.

"Trouble at mill?" And then "What gives?"

Tony hissed back, "None of your business".

He wrenched his arm away from the inquisitor.

Laura in her Butler's Pantry prison looked around tearfully; how on earth was she going to get out of this mess. David, here; what a dreadful scenario and Mr. Darcy, how the fuck had he come up with that name? Obviously he needed to be incognito, so he could fuck whom? He was staying the night, that she knew; she realized with a mental thud he was here to be with her; the Indian princess, Nefertiti; but what the fuck did Lady Pamela have to do with all of this? Had she introduced them, like Laura had been introduced to Blue Eyes; was she a sort of sexual fixer?

The whole scene was doing her head in, but first things first; she had to get out of this place, get out of Casa Blanca. She ran the tap in the old basin and slurped some cold water, splashing some on her tear-stained face. Suddenly there was a discreet knock on the door and a Cockney voice said,

"Ere, are yew awright Miss?"

The door knob was tried. Who the hell?....She gathered her wits and said in a throttled high voice,

"I'm fine thanks. I'll be out in a minute"

"Okay".

She held her breath but no more was heard. She looked around desperately. How on earth could she escape? Spying the stairs she peered down them and

203

wondered if they led to a basement, and if there was a basement, perhaps there would be a door out into the garden or street. There was a light switch near the top; she switched it on and descended slowly below. She came out into a small tiled hall and ahead of her was another door. She hesitated a moment and then opened the door. It creaked ominously. The room ahead was like a large dim lit cavern with a stone flag floor and high barred windows on one side. Feeling around for the light switch she bumped into what appeared to be a large free-standing chest. Moving to the other side of the doorway, she could make out a strange floor to ceiling wall rack on which hung thick ropes and weird leather straps. She found the light and switched it on. The room came rushing toward her in all its ghastly barbarity. Laura gasped; it was a torture chamber. She took in all the grisly equipment; a horrifying assortment of paddles, whips and handcuffs lay strewn in front of her; an old gym horse stood in sinister half-light. Over in one corner was an ancient iron bed with a rubber mattress. What in God's name went on here? Where people held here against their will? Was Lady Pamela, God forbid, a white slaver? In essence The Devil's Handmaiden? Laura's mind turned somersaults as she clutched her arms about her body and began to shiver; perhaps she would be next, enslaved and sold to the highest bidder. She had to get out now.

She shut the door on the Chamber of Horrors and returned to the hallway. There must be a door out onto the street. Examining the walls, she could find no exit. She would have to go back into THAT ROOM and see if there was a means of escape. Laura steeled herself and re-opened the creaking door; she put on the light and cautiously looked about her. At the far end of the room was a large cupboard-like contraption and to the right of that a curtained area. She hurried across a couple of rubber mats and shuddered as her shoes stuck slightly to the surface. Lifting the curtain gingerly, she was relieved to see a door, solidly bolted and chained. With difficulty she pulled back the bolts at the top and bottom and removed the safety chain. She prayed the main door was not locked for there was no key. Turning the battered knob she pulled the heavy door open and the cool night air rushed in to greet her.

CHAPTER 14

Tanice, having served the main courses – the chicken curry had been very popular - was now desperate for a breather.

Peering into the dining room, she could see that everyone was happily engaged in their meal except for one place where the chair was empty. Who was missing? Too hot to be concerned, she took a cold beer from the fridge and planned to sit quietly on the front steps. She said to Darnelle.

"You in charge now. Don't cock up".

She slipped out through the front door.

Enjoying the night air, she sipped her beer and congratulated herself on a successful evening's work. Musing on her culinary success, she became aware of a slight noise against the dustbins at the bottom of the basement stairs. It was probably next door's scatty cats. She got up and leaned over the railings.

"Oi, scat, shooo, bloody cats. Get outta here".

The noise stopped and a small voice said,

"Tanice, it's me".

"Who's there?"

Tanice was shocked to see a slim white bedraggled figure emerge and start slowly to climb the steps.

"Is that you Miss Laura? Lordy… Lordy… What the devil happened to you?"

Tanice put her arms out and Laura grabbed her hand and slumped against her.

"Oh Tanice...What a nightmare. I've got to get out of here right now"

"You not well Miss?"

"Not really. Could you help me? Get my clothes, my

case in Lady Pamela's room?"

"Yes I do that. What happened Miss?"

"Long Story...Just say I met my husband unexpectedly… in there" And she pointed to the house. Tanice consoled her and then Laura reached behind her neck and unclasped the necklace. She said, "This belongs to Lady Pamela. Can you return it to her?"

She handed the necklace to Tanice who put it into her apron pocket.

Laura continued, "I'll leave the dress in that Chamber of Horrors down there". She pointed to the basement. "What on earth goes on in there?"

"Oh it's Pandora's dungeon. She entertains clients...she dominatrix".

Laura looked incredulous. "Dominatrix? Clients?"

Then as the terrible realization dawned she said quietly,

"Please don't tell me that Casa Blanca is a knocking...a brothel".

Tanice nodded and then said, "Lady Pamela...she de...Madam...MadamPam"

Laura swore under her breath and then,

"Christ. She can't be a…a… MADAM? God, I've got to go...Can you hurry with my things? I'll wait down there".

They parted company. Laura disappeared down the steps and stood waiting by the basement door. Lady Pamela was a High Class MADAM, and Casa Blanca was a BROTHEL? Unbelievable. This was turning into a total nightmare and she had stumbled through the gates of Hell. She couldn't bring herself to re-enter The Chamber of Horrors so she hugged the wall next to the old dustbins with no care for any marks that might ruin her cream dress. In any case the night, for her, was completely ruined. As she waited more sordid details

207

began to fall into place. David must have contacted Casa Blanca and made an assignation with the Indian girl, but how? He must have got her name from someone. The irony of the situation was not lost on her and she began to laugh; what a fucking nightmare! A sobering thought struck her; in true Hollywood style, she could end this marriage with the most public humiliation possible. She could stride in and make a speech about all of David's inadequacies and then point the finger at the other woman; this could be the bloodiest end of a marriage yet. She was in a prime position to do this with no obvious partner at the party but inwardly she knew she could not do this. The time to confront David was in private, in the light of day, when she had a clear head. Revenge is a dish best served cold.

Tony had been eyeing Laura's exit route from the dining room for some time. He was waiting for an opportune moment to go and help her out of this sticky situation. He would have to wait until after dinner when everyone was up and dancing. He didn't see Tanice moving quickly across the hall and up the stairs.

Tanice went into her employer's bedroom and through to the dressing room. She found Laura's case and handbag and re-packed her belongings and then went into the bathroom to retrieve any makeup left behind. There came a soft click from the bedroom and she heard someone open the bedroom door. Quickly she pushed the bathroom door to conceal herself and waited. Someone was rummaging in the wardrobe; she heard the drawer being wrenched open. She put her eye to the crack in the door and spied Edward sifting through MadamPam's jewelry box. He took out a few things, inspected them and pocketed what looked like MadamPam's favorite pearl encrusted 18 carat gold bracelet. Incensed, Tanice was about to fling open the

208

door but then thought better of it and decided to mention Edward's thievery to The Colonel. He would be able to confront him and deal with Edward's deceit. She muttered to herself,

"Dandi knew. Dat dog sniffed him out".

She felt a grudging admiration for Dandi's sniffing abilities. That Edward was not what he seemed. Edward, having taken the loot, shut the bedroom door. Tanice, case in hand, came out of the bathroom. She waited a moment and then cautiously opened the bedroom door. The coast was clear. Quickly carrying the wheelie case, she descended the stairs and was about to cross the hall to the front door when Tony appeared in front of her.

"Making a run for it?"

"Er...No...I just puttin' dis case...into storage".

"And why are you doing that?" And then more forcefully, "You have to tell me where Laura is. You know don't you?"

He grabbed her arm to stop her getting away.

"Please… you hurting. She outside".

Just at that moment a few of the guests decided it was time for a smoke and as they were coming out of the dining room, Tony hurried Tanice through the front door to the outside. The guests followed, laughing and chatting. They were unaware that two people had shimmied down the back steps, one of whom had clapped his hand over the mouth of a third person and they were all cramming themselves through the basement door and into The Chamber of Horrors.

Tony looked around and exclaimed, "My God! Is this what I think it is?"

Tanice nodded, "is de Dominatrix cave and der is Pandora's Box".

And she pointed to the old chest that Laura had bumped into on entry.

"Shall we look inside?" Whispered Tony.

Laura gave a little cry, "Please...Pleeease...don't".

He put his arm around her,

"Perhaps better not. We might unleash The Devil himself".

He made a strange gurgling noise and Tanice giggled. Laura tried to put a stop to their antics.

"It's not funny. You do realize that Casa Blanca is a place...where... It's a brothel Tony."

He raised his eyebrows, "Well, well, I did have my suspicions. Naughty Lady Pamela, outwardly the doyen of respectability, running an illegal operation in the middle of Chelsea. What would the neighbors say?" And he gave an expression of mock horror.

Tanice, wanting to put her oar in, said importantly,

"She..de Madam...MadamPam".

While Tony and Tanice were comparing notes on Lady Pamela's operation, Laura went behind the curtain and took off the cream dress. She called out to Tanice who gave her the wheelie case. A few minutes later she re-emerged in jeans and her shirt and gave the dress to Tanice. As she handed it over, she stated fiercely,

"Madam up there said this dress was lucky; she met a Maharaja wearing it. I think it's the unluckiest dress ever."

Tony tried to placate her, "But Laura, it isn't... because we met...and we..."

He tailed off and then added, "I need your cell number ...please"

They exchanged numbers and then sending Tanice outside to make sure the coast was clear, Tony embraced Laura and they kissed softly. They vowed to meet again in less troubled times. She declined Tony's idea of a taxi and said she wanted to walk to clear her head. With that Laura ran up the steps, dragging the case behind her and

210

with a determined stride made off towards the nearest Tube station. She did not look back.

Tony and Tanice were left to repair the damage done and he offered to inform MadamPam of what had transpired. He was not looking forward to that conversation but she had to know the truth of what had happened. His mind was full of Laura; such a gorgeous girl and she must not get away from him.

Back in the kitchen, Tanice could see that Darnelle was at long last earning her keep. She was bossing the waiters around and making sure all the dirty plates had been cleared away; she had enjoyed organizing food for the band during their 'chinks' break and had them amused by the story of the Chelsea Pensioner 'a little old bloke in a red coat' who had placed his arthritic hand on her frou frou bumsie.

"Dirty old geezer!"

Previously, while the guests were enjoying their main courses, Tanice and Darnelle had laid out all the desserts on MadamPam's Victorian mahogany sideboard. The three desert island style rum-soaked sponge cakes had turned out triumphantly. Tanice had filled them with whipped cream and fresh pineapple and had outdone herself in creating a desert island on each one with different colored icing. Sand colored butter cream for the sides and in a circle in the center to denote the island. She had then made blue colored sugar icing for the surrounding butter cream island. She was particularly proud of the plastic palm trees placed on the island and the fancy cocktail umbrellas stuck into the sides of the cake. She carefully cut out some little banana boats made of melon to place on the sea. She had also made some coconut and mango ice cream to go with the exotic fruit salad. Monsieur Georges' sweet pastries had been placed alongside. Crystal glass bowls of cream and rum

211

sauce completed the picture.

As the band began to tune up for the next set, people were milling about and starting to help themselves to dessert. A flustered Lady Pamela came rushing into the kitchen.

"Where have you been Tanice? You are in charge here. You can't just disappear like that and where..."

Darnelle interrupted, "I got it all under control MadamLady...er…MadamPam"

"That's as maybe but your mother is the one in charge. "And with a harried expression she added, "But where is Laura or Tony for that matter?"

At that moment Tony appeared and came to Tanice's rescue.

"Lady P, could I have a word...privately?"

With that she took his arm and led him into her study and shut the door.

While Mr. Darcy and Nef were feeding each other dessert and giggling as they wiped the cream off one another's faces, Tony was pouring out the whole sorry saga to Lady P. She became quite upset on learning that Mr. Darcy was Laura's husband and was mortified that they should have cannoned into each other under her roof; she who was usually so careful over identity and a stickler for security. How dreadful that this should have happened. She did blame herself; something that did not come easily to her. She then began to worry over poor Laura's state of mind. Tony re-assured her that Laura was a trooper, a word to which he knew she would react favorably and despite the initial panic, she had recovered, changed and gone home. Lady P reacted to this,

"Gone home? Oh poor darling. The person who should have been sent packing was that bloody Mr. Darcy ". She was spoiling for a fight.

212

Tony persuaded her not to say anything to dastardly Darcy as this would surely ruin the party. He did not mention that Laura had found the Chamber of Horrors and that both he and Laura were fully cognizant of the fact that Casa Blanca was a House of Ill Repute. He then explained that Tanice had the cream dress in her safe keeping; she wondered about the necklace but felt sure Laura would keep it safe; the idea of gifting it to Laura as some sort of recompense for the disastrous events came to mind.

As they were leaving, she looked at him and said, "Nice beads by the way, they suit you".

And her mouth twitched in amusement. They suddenly came upon Edward lurking by the door.

"Everything alright Auntie P?"

"Laura's not well and has gone home".

Edward gave Tony a wolfish grin. "Bad luck old chap. Perhaps she didn't fancy you after all".

Tony would have liked to have landed a smack on that curled lip but instead gave a tight smile and squired Lady P onto the dance floor. Madam or no Madam, they had to keep up appearances.

Tanice, back in the kitchen carefully put the cream dress on a hook behind the pantry door.
Darnelle saw her do this and asked,

"The lady's naked then?" And giggled.

"De lady in question has changed and gone home. Now get back out there girl and clear de dessert plates".

Darnelle, summarily dispatched, did not see her mother put a hand in the apron pocket and pull out MadamPam's valuable necklace. She had forgotten to replace it in the bedroom. The necklace reminded her that she had to speak to The Colonel about Edward's thieving ways. She made a quick glance at the dance floor and saw that The Colonel was deeply involved in a slow shuffle with Lorraine, an ex-employee of Casa Blanca; he seemed pre-occupied with the lady's bumsie. His large hands were cupped over her pert cheeks. This was not an opportune moment to spill the beans on Edward. That would have to wait. She felt the necklace in her pocket and decided to leave it in a safe place in MadamPam's study.

As she crossed the main room to the hall, Edward lounging by the bar noticed her disappearing figure and followed. She entered the study and shut the door. Edward loitered a few moments by the toilet area and then strode in after her as though on a mission for his aunt. Even though he knew that Laura had gone home there must be more to her sudden escape and he was sure Tanice could fill him in on all the information. What he wasn't prepared for was the sight of Tanice holding Auntie P's diamond and sapphire necklace.

He took control and in a commanding voice said, "Tanice, I think you should give that to me." She jumped in alarm .He then added, "Lady P has asked me to take care of it",

Tanice knew for a fact that this was a downright lie.

"No...It much safer in de locked drawer".

She took the key from its hiding place at the bottom of the antique sewing box and opened the desk drawer. Edward, with an eye for the main chance, took all this in and nodded sagely.

"Yes…you're right…a much safer place".

The necklace was carefully placed in the drawer. Tanice turned the key and replaced it in its obvious hiding place. A moment later she realized the consequence of revealing the key placement to a jewel thief.

"Mr Edward, I tink MadamPam wanted to tell you someting. Someting important…to do with Miss Laura."

Edward perked up and promptly left. He deduced that he could come back and take the loot at a later date when all was quiet. He planned to take the necklace and place the blame squarely on Tanice.

He was already rehearsing the conversation with Lady P. "I saw her…in here holding the necklace…She was pocketing it when I came in."

Tanice, thinking to herself 'he goin' to jail', took the key from the sewing box and put it in her apron pocket and neatly thwarted Edward's little plan. Also he had no idea that she was about to shop him to The Colonel for stealing the gold bracelet which she knew was somewhere secreted about his person. He was about to be exposed as a common jewel thief to all and sundry.

Laura was sitting in a half empty tube carriage on her way back to Waterloo station. She ran over the events of the day and was still stunned to think that she had risen in the morning with such high expectations for the night ahead and here she was in the middle of the same night escaping from all manner of horrors and embarrassment. There was so much to take in. Not only had she been smacked in the head by David's deception, there was the unbelievable truth about Lady Pamela and Casa Blanca. A brothel in Chelsea run by a posh old lady and her doting Colonel along with compliant servants; it did not bear thinking about. Blue Eyes' betrayal seemed insignificant in comparison to the degenerate tangled web that she had discovered tonight. The fact that she was also a deceiver had not yet touched her conscience; and then there was Tony, her friendly pirate rescuer. She thought fondly of him and realized that he was the one saving grace in the whole sorry mess. She fished out her phone and sent him a text.

Hi No Hook! Thanks for everything. On train

215

> *Will contact again after showdown with D.*
> *Marriage busted. What a fuck-awful night! Love*
> *L xx*

As she was peering out into the dimly lit tunnel approaching Waterloo, she could feel yet another unfortunate event on the horizon. As the train pulled into the station, her monthly period was arriving simultaneously.

For once Laura was pleased she was not pregnant especially to an American philanderer.

Later on the journey home, she received a text from Blue Eyes. Hearing the cell ping she was hoping for a goodnight response from Tony, so with excitement she read,

> *Luscious Laura. How is the party going? Sorry I*
> *couldn't get there. Business held me up in US.*
> *Next week? Text with time. Let's lunch at Hong*
> *Kong Harry's. JJK3*

She scowled, chucked the phone into her bag with disgust and mouthed 'Fuck you'.

Back at the party, the dance floor was in full swing. The band were playing 'Brown girl in the ring' and Nef having removed her skirt was doing her cabaret number in sparkly panties, swinging her hips and making suggestive gestures at Mr. Darcy. He was grinning wildly and clapping her on. Darnelle having ditched the trainers was watching and dancing on the spot at the kitchen door; she could not resist a moment longer and dashed out to join Nef. Together they took the floor by storm and the guests all pulled back to allow them some more space. Someone began clapping and another guest, who had somehow procured a dildo, was waving it madly and singing along. Tanice looked on horrified. Pandora, also minus her skirt, was tapping her high-

216

heeled boot and swinging her tinseled whip along with the music. Her meek escort was watching her with obvious adoration on his face.

Both Edward and 'Arry were propping up the bar. With no lady to ensnare in an embrace they resorted to getting rat-arsed or in Cockney parlance 'Brahms and Liszt'. They had ordered beer with whisky chaser follow-ups and were competing with one another so it would be no time at all until one of them fell in the line of drinking.

Lady Pamela was taking a breather on one of the sofas lining the party room. Bonny was tipped forward drunkenly on her shoulder, with his bedraggled tailed butt stuck up in the air while Dicky, her favorite old pensioner sitting beside her, snored gently. They had been chatting and then he had suddenly dropped off, his head coming to rest on her shoulder. She was still distressed over the business with Laura and needed to work out what to do about this dreadful faux pas. She glared at that Darcy person and resolved never to allow him back into Casa Blanca. Tanice, seeing that Lady Pamela was alone, went over and asked to have a word.

"Yes? Sorry I'm not myself Tanice. A bit tired".

"MadamPam. Here is the key to the desk drawer". And she handed it over.

MadamPam looked puzzled. "Well can you put it back...you know where".

"Noo...Can't do dat...I put de pretty necklace in de drawer and Edward came in an' saw me do dat and then he saw me put de key back in de sewing box"

Lady Pamela felt a tired grouch coming. She snapped. "So? Go now Tanice and put it back IMMEDIATELY".

"Nooo. I got to tell you sometink".

Lady Pamela sighed in annoyance.

217

"Well get on with it then".

Tanice then poured out the details of fetching Laura's belongings from the bedroom so she could change and make her escape and while doing that she had spied Edward coming into the bedroom and rifling through MadamPam's jewelry box.

Lady Pamela eyes widened and she urged Tanice to continue. Tanice then told her about the theft of her favorite gold and pearl bracelet,

"It in Mr Edward's pocket. I saw him put it there".

Lady Pamela screeched at this news. She leapt from the sofa, practically knocking poor Dickie to the floor and said in a commanding voice,

"Colonel...COLONEL. Will someone fetch the Colonel please? Where the FUCK has he gone?"

One of the guests pointed out that The Colonel had slipped away and taken his lady love Lorraine upstairs. Lady Pamela guessed he was probably undressing her this very minute in the Chinese Bedroom. He would have ascertained that with James Jefferson KirkPatrick the 3rd being a no show, the room would be empty all night and in any case being first in meant no other client could get in before him. The Colonel planned to make a night of it.

She swore loudly ."Bugger Bugger Bugger".
Everyone turned and a snigger began to run round the room, then she screeched,

"TONY ...TANICE GET TONY"

Tanice did not need to as Tony galloped over to Lady Pamela's aid and stood waiting instructions.

'Arry and his drinking companion were completely oblivious to all of this and were toasting each other loudly and then shouting out obscenities related to the female anatomy while roaring with laughter. The rest of the guests waited quietly and were excitedly anticipating what would happen next. Something major was foot. She said something quietly to Tony who then strode over to the bar and said to Edward,

"Games up. You're nicked, dickhead".

"Wha..did you...call ..me..you lille shit". And he took a mis-aimed swing at Tony's head and belched loudly.

"You have stolen Lady Pamela's bracelet. Hand over."

Edward cackled wildly as 'Arry egged him on. "You're a fuuucking wanker No Hook".

And he took another swing but staggered and half fell to the floor.

Tony put a fist to his jaw and he collapsed in a heap at Tony's feet. The guests stood around agog as Tony rifled Edward's pockets and eventually came upon the bracelet in the inner pocket of his jacket. He held it up triumphantly. Edward was hauled away to a discreet corner to sober up and the party resumed with everyone saying that this was one of the best 'dos' they'd ever been too.

Lady Pamela now had to decide what to do next; she needed to consult the Colonel; Tony was dispatched upstairs to the Chinese room. Lady P shuddered at what sort of reception Tony would get but this was an emergency and the Colonel had always said,

"You can call on me old girl, anytime, day or night".

Tony rapped on the door of the Chinese room and then put his ear to the door and heard muffled sounds within. After a moment he rapped again and inside the sound, starting like a growl then turning into an almighty lion's roar as the door was flung open and The Colonel, dressed in only a shirt, yelled in Tony's face.

"FUCK OFF YOU MORON". And slammed the door shut.

Lady Pamela realizing that Tony would not be able to

219

lever The Colonel from his comfy hole had followed him up and now banged loudly on the door.

She shouted through the keyhole. "Colonel. It's an emergency. It's Edward. He's been caught stealing."

After a while the door opened and The Colonel came out with his trousers on. He pushed Tony aside and padded down the stairs behind the Old Girl.

They went over to the corner where the comatose Edward lay sprawled on his back. Bending over The Colonel got creakily onto his knees and shouted in Edward's ear.

"GET UP YOU DRUNKEN LOUT".

Edward made no response. A group of guests began to gather.

Lady Pamela yelled for Tanice. "GET SOME COLD WATER AND ICE".

Everyone waited expectantly while this was organized.

Darnelle brought a saucepan of water and a small bag of ice and gave it to The Colonel. He threw the water over Edward's face and rammed the ice down his shirt front. There was a gurgled response from Edward who burbled tipsily,

"No...No it wasn't me Mummy. Honest".

The crowd tittered.

It was decided that Edward should be dragged out into the open air and given a bucket of coffee. Once that had been done The Colonel pushed hard for a visit to the local police station to reinforce the error of his ways. Lady Pamela, although admitting that Edward had committed an offence and should be punished for it, strongly resisted the police being involved.

"Henry, what are you thinking? We can't have Mr Plod and his minions crawling all over Casa Blanca interviewing the guests. Are you mad?"

"Trust me old girl. Edward does not know, at this stage, that we won't press charges. He needs a good talking to by someone in authority. Police will not be snooping round here. I'll make sure of that."

"I don't like it Henry but if you think this is the best plan of action then I trust you".

And so, an hour later, a protesting Edward was pushed into a taxi with The Colonel alongside and taken down to the local Nick. A few hours later, when all was quiet at Casa Blanca and everyone had gone home save the overnighters, Lady Pamela was laid out on the sofa in her dressing gown, enjoying a cup of herbal tea and surveying the party wreckage around her. She heard the front door open and The Colonel appeared in what appeared to be a mighty grump. He saw her resting and said,

"Don't ask. Lorraine gone I s'pose?"

The Old Girl nodded and he gave a soft growl and expleted, "Shit…Evening ruined".

He stumped off up the stairs to the Lorraine-less Chinese room. Lady Pamela called out after him but he had gone. A few moments later he came barreling down the stairs and bellowed,

"There's a Chinese tart in my room with one of the Chelseas-I think its Dickie but I can't be sure. A bald-headed little bugger anyway".

Lady Pamela managed to calm him down and then fed him a large whisky. It was agreed that he would spend the night in her dressing room on the single bed and so it was. Lady Pamela tossed and turned for the rest of the night as a cacophonous snore erupted through the door, at regular intervals, from the dressing room.

CHAPTER 15

Laura had got home in the early hours of the morning and just as she was getting out of the shower she received a text from Tony.

> *My Lovely-Are u home safe? Huge drama here…Edward busted. He stole Lady P's favorite bracelet. He's at the nick with The Col. Knew he was a Dickhead!   Miss you double time. Be strong when the bastard returns…Kisses from Capt No H.xxxx*

She texted back.

> *Home safe. Edward a thief??   Dreading tomorrow. I'll call you when it's done. xx*

Laura lay on the marital bed and stared all night at the ceiling. She got up at eight o'clock feeling like a wet dish rag. Making a cup of coffee with a shaky hand she decided to fill in the morning in the garden. The beans and courgettes had got away and needed picking and freezing and the roses needed dead-heading along with a general tidy up. Around eleven she decided to text Mr Darcy to find out his estimated arrival time. With her jaw tight with tension and her hand trembling, she wrote,

> *What time u home? We need to talk.*

She pressed the 'send' button and sat back and closed her eyes.

She had no idea what his reaction would be when she confronted him. There was only one thing for it and that was to tell him that she knew everything from the porn to the prostitute to the party where they had almost collided. She wavered over the reason for her being at the party but decided that as she had been invited by Lady Pamela he didn't have to know about Blue Eyes. She planned on telling him about Lady Pamela's

223

accident and that the old lady had not only taken her to lunch but also invited her to the Caribbean evening. His rejection of her was still running deep and even though she should probably tell him about Blue Eyes she could see there was no need. There was no way to predict what would happen next. Her cell pinged and she read,

> *Back 2 ish. Great to catch up with all the Cricket crowd. Good bash... Bit worse for wear. Stayed at Adrian's...*

She said aloud 'Lying bastard' and threw the phone on the floor.

She still couldn't get her head round the brothel business; totally illegal. The old lady obviously had shed loads of money and didn't need the cash from the business. Laura felt sure that Lady Pamela had plenty of private money at her disposal; perhaps the old girl did it for kicks; that seemed to be the most likely outcome; it was clear she liked to be surrounded by a young crowd; perhaps she was addicted to dangerous pursuits and running a brothel was as close as she could get to being arrested and thrown in jail. The whole risky enterprise beggared belief.

It seemed to Laura that Lady Pamela was at heart a fantasist and a risk taker. She had lived a sexy racy life and now wanted to experience the adrenaline rush of living close to the edge while facilitating other people's carnal desires. In her mind The Colonel now took on a sinister air. So charming at lunch initially but had he been sizing her up? A new filly to join the stable? In light of all this new information, Blue Eyes took on a predatory role; she had slept with him twice and then he had moved on. In other words he had used her for sex just like a common tart.

Dear God. Casa Blanca was an evil infestation of vice. She resolved never to return to Casa Blanca and if Lady

224

Pamela contacted her she would not speak or text her ever again.

The following day, breakfast was served late in the dining room of Casa Blanca to a very quiet gathering.

Fortnum's, delivering at ten o'clock, had come up trumps with two huge hampers of hot breakfast food and thermoses of tea and coffee. Mr. Darcy, much to Lady Pamela's annoyance, tucked into double bacon and eggs followed by a kipper chaser; she had thought of confronting him this morning and exposing the ghastly truth but decided Laura needed to tackle him herself and in her own time. The others guests downed copious coffees, croissants and pastries before thanking her profusely for her fantastic hospitality and disappearing out the door.

Lady Pamela had sent Tanice home at 1am as she could see that the poor maid was dead on her feet. Tanice was given a wad of cash and told to put her feet up and have a good Sunday rest. Darnelle wearing her 'fuck me' style shoes and having tippled copiously on left-over drinks, was protesting loudly. As she was being dragged along behind Tanice, she was heard to yell,

"I wanna stay. Party not finished yet...I wanna daaance".

Tony had told Lady P that he would be back the following morning to have some breakfast and help clear up. He also felt she would need support after finding out about Edward and so it was that he found himself in the kitchen sorting out the hampers, serving and then washing up. He was very keen to hear what had happened to Dickhead Edward and wondered if DE was, at this very moment, languishing in a police cell with a potty for company. Looking out and seeing that The Colonel had a thunderous face, he knew it was not the

225

time to ask for information. He noticed that Lady P looked exhausted but was as usual keeping up appearances; she was chatting to Dickie who had his hand on Cherry's knee. She smiled and thought how nice it was to give the oldies a good time. At one point The Butler's Pantry door opened and a strange creature with what looked like a curly red poodle on its head emerged, ashen-faced and blinking sleepily in the light. The creature croaked,

"'allo… 'allo… Mornin' All. Wot a great 'ale and 'earty yer ladyship. Tirrific party. .Got a bit Brahms and Liszt so I tucked m'self up nice and comfy like in yer butler's bantry bay. .sorry, I did a barf in the Butler's basin.. All cleaned up now".

Without drawing breath he added, "'Eh. .I'd kill the ol' bill for a cup of the black stuff"

He made a bee-line for the kitchen where he slurped on a black coffee and hoovered up the left-overs.

Throughout this The Colonel sat silently consuming his bacon and eggs with a kipper on the side, while observing the proceedings with a beady eye and growling intermittently.

After everyone had left, Lady Pamela lay on the sofa and dozed as 'Arry and Tony set to and cleaned the whole place from top to bottom. The Colonel plonked himself on an easy chair and perused The Sunday Papers while dropping off from time to time. Occasionally the Old Girl raised herself up and said weakly,

"Thank you Tony dear, but do leave the rest for Tanice tomorrow."

She gave a simpering grimace at 'Arry who said cheerily,

"S'alright yer ladyship. You rest yer Khyber Pass. We'll have yer place in fine fettle and clean as a whistlin' kettle in no time".

226

Eventually after 'Arry had gone home - Lady Pamela had to grudgingly acknowledge that he had done a good job - Tony was able to sit down and ask them both about Edward. The Colonel gave him a gimlet eye,

"My nephew is a bad egg. Firstly thank you for your help in apprehending him. Taking him down the police station proved fruitless. He denied all knowledge and then said he wasn't even at the party. I have decided to take alternative measures."

Tony then asked Lady Pamela if she was going to press charges and before she could answer, The Colonel jumped in.

"No...Let us now drop the subject". And he went back to his paper.

Tony gave Lady P a look of support and then draining his coffee, took his leave. She got up and embraced him.

"Thank you Tony...for everything. Do be in touch won't you?"

He said his goodbyes. The Colonel gave him a curt nod, and he left.

Just as he was leaving, the Doggie Night Care people were delivering Dandelion back to his owner. He came bounding through the door, and practically threw himself at his mistress, his stump wagging madly. She hugged him to her and kissed his head,

"Darling Dandi...Mummy is so pleased to see you...and you are so pleased to see me too...and here's The Colonel to say hello". And she took Dandi's paw and waved it at Henry. The Colonel harrumphed and raised his hand without any enthusiasm.

Dandelion then rushed all over the house yelping with excitement and came back into the sitting room bearing a gift for his mistress. She looked down and was met with the sight of Dandi holding a long pink dildo in his mouth. He dropped it at her feet and panted expectantly.

She kicked the battered article to one side and clutching the beloved dog to her bosom took him upstairs. As she was climbing the stairs, she was whispering in his ear.

"I've got so much to tell you Dandi...Edward, yes I know you don't like him and it turns out you were right. He stole ...."And her voice trailed off as she entered her bedroom and shut the door.

The Colonel, gazing between the dildo and the stairs and back again, shook his head and muttered to the obscene object,

"I can see you got more action than my old fella".

He then took a glass from the cabinet and gave himself a super-size snort of whisky from the decanter and lay down on the sofa, the glass beside him on the floor.

Later, after The Colonel had gone home, Lady Pamela made herself a plate of left-overs and poured a cold glass of Pinot Grigio. She took a tray into the sitting room and dined with Dandi at her feet. She put on her favorite CD of Mozart piano concertos and began to mull over the events that had brought her to Casa Blanca. The old lady cast her mind back to the very beginning; to the event that led her to commence her operation at 32 Davenport Gardens. She hated to say the word 'illegal' in the same breath as 'operation' as she felt the business was more a community service; helping people on both sides of the blanket so to speak.

32 Davenport Gardens had belonged to a dear friend and lover. While she moldered away in the country miles away from London and endured a difficult marriage to Sir Greville, Giles was away at Boarding School. She was bored and lonely. She decided to uplift her life and rekindle the romance with Marcus De Lyle, an old boyfriend in London and now divorced.

Marcus' wife Oona, no longer on the scene, had been

an eccentric character with wild curly black hair and bright blue eyes who had dressed as a hippy in long flowery skirts and red stockings. Thin as a reed, she was descended from Irish aristocracy and many people had thought she was somewhat 'touched' as a result. They had all rocketed around the London party scene back in the early 60's. Having married Marcus de Lyle and moved to the Chelsea townhouse, Oona had begun to collect stray cats around Chelsea and had set up a cattery in the basement of Number 32, much to Marcus' displeasure. Following this theme, her animal enthusiasms had led her to collect a menagerie of birds which she housed in rickety cages attached to the garden fences of the neighboring properties at the back of Number 32. Terrible rows ensued, not only between the cats and birds. Eventually Oona had abandoned Marcus, every animal and bird in her care and had gone off to join a religious community in Scotland.

Marcus, relieved at her departure, had rid himself of the smelly cats and raucous birds and filed for divorce.

Lady Pamela remembered how attentive Marcus had been in her youthful hoofing days. They had enjoyed many tete a tete dinners and more besides. He had been thrilled to hear from her and it had been wonderful to slip back into their easy relationship. Marcus had been left a fortune due to his connection with a well-known sugar and related product company and even though he was not in the business, he had invested wisely and his work at a stock brokerage made him a pretty penny.

Oona had been unable to have children so there he was, all alone in a beautiful London house, ready for the picking.

Lady Pamela smiled as she remembered the wonderful times they had had together.

Occasionally she had stayed the night when Sir

Greville was away on one of his shooting weekends. She and Marcus had grown very close. One day while they had been enjoying a post orgasmic coffee together in the comfort of his luxurious bedroom, Marcus had said he was feeling dizzy. He got out of bed and holding his head, had cried out and fallen at her feet; dead of a brain hemorrhage. It was a huge shock. She had been devastated and had cried copiously at the loss of her generous friend and lover. What she didn't know was that even in death Marcus had thought of her welfare and had left her his capacious Chelsea Townhouse. She couldn't quite believe it when the solicitor had contacted her, but she realized that he had now given her the chance to leave Sir Greville and start again.

First of all she had decided to let the house for a large sum of money to some Arab people and even though, as she told the agency,

"Not my first choice, you understand. Isn't there a nice English family who could take it? Titled perhaps?"

The agency had informed her that as the rent was substantial not to say exorbitant, only wealthy Middle Eastern families would be able to afford to stay there. She reluctantly agreed but asked the agency to keep a strict eye, especially with regard to cleanliness. She had said,

"I hear their toilet habits are disgusting".

And so she put the Chelsea house to good use and was able to salt away many thousands of pounds for her new life away from Sir Greville. Just as she had everything organized to do this, he upped and died; accidently shot while out pheasant shooting. After his estate had been wound up and she had sold the Norfolk pile, she moved with her son Giles to Chelsea.

Giles, struggling with his sexuality in a repressed London circle with his mother breathing down his neck, had decided to up sticks and head for New York where he planned to pursue his theatre career. After a year or two, feeling lonely and yearning for new experiences, his mother went to visit him in New York. As it turned out, a fateful decision. She met an American steel magnate and his ardent wooing catapulted her into a rushed marriage. A short sharp lesson followed interwoven with poisonous input from his two spoilt teenage daughters. After 18 months of hell, she hightailed it back to London and the welcome security and peace of 32 Davenport Gardens.

Rattling around in the old house she had decided to become a landlady and take in a couple of young society girls, one of whom had fallen out with her parents. They were both working as lowly filing clerks in dusty offices but liked nothing more than to kick up their heels in bars and nightclubs when off duty. Lady Pamela, worrying about their safety, began to allow their boyfriends to stay over from time to time; not only did she think of herself as liberal but also kind and generous. She charged the girls minimal rent but as new boyfriends appeared she had made the men pay for the bedrooms on a nightly basis. From there it was a short slide toward running an escort agency and so Number 32 became Casa Blanca.

As it turned out Number 32 was a perfect place for clandestine activity. On one side an elderly German gentleman lived alone. Lady Pamela had discovered many years ago that he was profoundly deaf. They had nodded to each other politely in passing. He had made precisely two complaints and they were in regard to Dandelion fouling his doorstep. She had apologized profusely in a loud voice and always made sure from then on that she had plastic bags at the ready when walking Dandi. No comments were ever made about the number of visitors streaming through the doors and in the main he remained reclusively out of sight with all his curtains drawn. Occasionally he ventured out in his 'all weather' carpet slippers to buy provisions from the local grocery store. The Polish shop keeper regarded him with suspicion and had said to Lady Pamela that he thought 'old Fritz' could be a German spy hiding from the world. She had laughed.

"Well if he is, he's like a mouse next door, an excellent neighbor".

The house on the other side of Number 32 had been vacant for many years. She had no idea who it belonged to. It had been sold soon after she had moved in and had remained strangely quiet ever since. She had tried to peer in through the ground floor windows but all she could make out in the dim light was a lot of heavy furniture covered in sheets. So there she was in the middle, happily going about her illegal enterprise with no possibility of being shopped by the neighbors for running a house of ill-repute.

Later, while getting herself ready for bed and feeling the weight of the previous few days inhabit her bones, the old lady began to wonder if the time had come to ease back on her operation; of course there was no-one who could buy it as a going concern; the books of which there were none could not be laid bare. As she was dozing on her pillow she did wonder if Laura, her marriage in tatters, might need a new career, something completely different away from her connections in the country. A huge question mark hung over Lady Pamela as she fell into a deep sleep.

CHAPTER 16

Back at Pippin Cottage on Sunday around two o'clock, Laura heard David's car turn into the driveway. He jumped out and came whistling in through the front.

"Hi. I'm back".

Laura, clutching a tea cloth in the kitchen, steeled herself and waited for his entry. He came bounding in and tried to give her a kiss 'hello'. Seeing she had a face like thunder, he pulled back,

"What's happened?"

"The sky has fallen." Her voice shook slightly but she held her ground and then added,

"I know everything David or is it Mr. Darcy?"

He paled at this and took a step back,

"How did...?"

Laura put her hand up to stop him continuing and then began to reveal all the sordid details, starting with the porn site and moving on to Nefertiti and Casa Blanca. She really went to town on seeing him at the party and how humiliating it was for her to have to make an undignified escape. He kept on trying to interrupt but Laura was on a roll. At one point when he again tried to interject, she said loudly,

"YOU OWE IT TO ME TO LISTEN ".

At this point he had cowered and turned his back and put his hands over his face.

Having exposed him in his deceit, the old wound of not having another child had opened again and Laura began to berate him further about his rejection of her and how she had felt like shit and then she had found out about his porn habit and had sunk further into the depths of despair. She screamed and yelled at him until she was spent. The color drained from his face, he said not a word and took to his heels, grabbing the car keys and swinging the vehicle out of the driveway as though The Devil himself was on his heels. Running away again. He never was one to face up to the truth especially if the truth was ugly; confrontations, of any kind, terrified him.

Laura, took a deep breath and splashed some cold water on her face to help her simmer down. Her heart was pounding; she done it. She'd exposed him and survived. She sat stunned in an easy chair for what seemed like a few minutes but when she looked at the clock, two hours had passed. The phone in the kitchen rang and hesitating to answer it, she let it ring. She did not want to speak to David now under any circumstances. After a minute she listened to the message. It was from her father.

> *Hello...hello, Laura? It's Dad. Can you hear me? Are you alright? I haven't heard anything from you for ages. Please call me back...Oh yes. I wanted to ask if you would all like to come down to Woolacombe for a week by the sea when Juliet breaks up from school...It's this week I think... Call me...I hate these confounded answering things...*

He hung up.

The enormity of what had just happened came rushing into her head. It would mean an abrupt end to their marriage and their split would affect all the people around them. Juliet, Dad, Cindy and Peter. Her head was splitting but she had to think about the next move. She lifted the phone to call her father back but decided the person who needed to know as soon as possible was Juliet. She replaced the receiver.

Juliet was due home in a few days and Laura remembered that she had promised to go down to the end of term presentations with David and collect Juliet

234

and her school trunk. Grimly she realized that this would still have to be done but perhaps she could go alone.

As a last blast she sent a text to David which read.

> *This marriage is over. I have moved my stuff to the spare room. Re Juliet. I am going ALONE to fetch her.*

He immediately texted back.

> *Re marriage-yes. I AM COMING WITH YOU TO COLLECT JULIET. YOU CANNOT STOP ME.*

She was not surprised at his response. He wanted to give his side of the story and she knew he would underline the fact that Laura had also lied about her whereabouts.

Laura was right there, while driving to clear his head, David could not understand why Laura had not told him about the old lady. It was an innocent invitation. Did Laura know that Casa Blanca was a brothel? He began to wonder if there was more to her being at the party, a lover perhaps. He had noticed the odd strange phone call. He determined to challenge her on this before the journey to Juliet's school. He made a mental note to call his lawyer in the morning.

David had not returned that evening. Laura would normally have been worried but in light of the circumstances she realized that she didn't care either way.

Around 6 pm she poured herself a double gin and tonic and contemplated her next move. As she was staring unseeing at The News on TV, she received two texts in quick succession.

The first was from Lady Pamela.

> *Laur deAR Laura. So very sordid about last niggle.*

235

Laura threw back her head in annoyance. Why was it that old people were incapable of texting coherently? '*Sordid about last niggle*'. Yes. It was bloody sordid.

> *Need to talk to you. please calm me.*

She deleted the text and read the next one,

> *Darling Laura.. Are you alright? Please call me. Can we meet? Desperate to see u xxxx Capt NHook*

She was just about to text back when the phone rang. She hesitated; she didn't want to talk to anyone at present. She let it ring. A few moments later the phone trilled again. This time she answered. It was Cindy wanting a catch-up. There followed a stilted conversation from Laura while Cindy rattled on about how she was feeling, names for the baby, how she had been looking on line for baby stuff and then, when Laura had given monosyllabic replies, she said in a concerned voice,

"Is anything the matter? You don't sound yourself."

Laura not wanting to confide in Cindy and certainly not wanting to tell her about the horrendous experience the night before said,

"Fine…I'm fine. Just a bit tired…I'll call you tomorrow. Bye." And hung up.

She knew full well that the shit would hit the fan in the morning. With no sign of David, Laura took herself off to bed at nine pm. She had already taken her pillow and personal stuff into the spare room and had made up one of the single beds. Her Mum and Dad had used this room and thinking about them made her tearful. She would have to face the whole world in the morning. She just wished her mother could be nearby. Perhaps there really was a spirit world where all the loved ones who had passed on went to congregate, families-in-waiting for their next of kin and their dear friends to pass across the earth's divide and into the next life. She dozed off dreaming of her mother, not as a cancer patient but as she was when Laura was little, a vibrant, warm and loving presence. This image gave Laura some solace.

In the early hours of the morning she heard the front door bang shut. David; probably pissed as a newt. She could hear him crash up the stairs and then pause outside the spare room; she prayed that he would not come in and became panicky when she realized that she had forgotten to lock her bedroom door. He seemed to be out there for ages and she held her breath. At last he thundered into their room and shut the door with a bang; she heard two shoes being hurled at the wardrobe cupboard and then silence.

She took her phone from the bedside table and texted Captain No Hook.

> *It's done...feeling shattered...in spare room. David just came home drunk-Passed out in the marital bed. Give me 2 days then I'll call u promise....Miss U. Laura xxxx.*

Back at Casa Blanca, after all the hullabaloo at the party, the disaster that had befallen poor Laura was talked about endlessly and the news that Smooth Eddie had turned out to be a jewel thief made for some incredulous discussion. Pandora couldn't stand him and told them so.

"About time he was found out, smarmy creep. Hope Lady P presses charges".

Nefertiti was particularly appalled that Mr Darcy had turned out to be Laura's husband.

"Mind you, she made a spectacular escape under the table and then into The Butler's Pantry like a bullet from a gun."

Over a cuppa with the girls in the kitchen, Nefertiti

237

told them she had seen Laura twice before, once having tea with Lady P and then on the landing with Gentleman Jim.

"She went into the Chinese room with him".

Tanice was all ears as she sorted out the fridge. So the old lady had got up to one of her tricks after all, selling the pretty Laura to the American and no doubt billing him for the room to boot. She kept quiet as Pandora echoed Tanice's thoughts.

"Some fresh meat for gentleman Jim perhaps? He's a glutton for variety that one. Very pretty and obviously a favorite of Lady P's. Did you see that necklace she was wearing? Worth a fortune. She lent it to me once". And then she added wistfully, "Many moons ago".

Tanice did not tell them that she had managed to save the said necklace from the clutches of Edward. After Tony had confronted him, wrenched the pearl bracelet from his pocket and unmasked him as a common thief, she was pleased that The Colonel had taken control and marched him off to the police station; and MadamPam, Tanice had never seen her so angry. She thought the old lady was going to blow a gasket. It was about time people realized what a con artist Edward was. She then pictured poor Miss Laura stuck in that dungeon after her crazy escape and smiled to herself and vowed to keep silent about the events that followed. Nefertiti chimed in,

"When she was with Gentleman Jim and we bumped into each other on the landing she was dead embarrassed and shot into the bedroom like a scalded cat."

Pandora remarked. "Not one of our profession then. How did she meet Lady P?"

Tanice filled them all in on what happened the day MadamPam got entangled in Dandi's lead. Pandora laughed,

238

"That woman is a creative genius. Gets assisted by a pretty young stranger who should be rewarded for her kindness, but instead gets sold to Gentleman Jim for a substantial sum. Knowing Lady P, he would have had to put up a truckload of cash. Wily old bird!"

Cherry was listening intently to this exchange and as the story unfolded her eyes widened and her mouth began to drop. Tanice noticed.

"Careful Cherry. You catch a bee" And she mimed with her finger a bee flying between Cherry's rosebud lips. The girls all chortled and Pandora then said,

"Got keep that mouth free for tea soaked Cocka doodle dos Cherry". She mimed lewdly.

The loud laughter that followed alerted Lady Pamela in her study and she came through and poked her head around the kitchen door.

"Nice to see that everyone is enjoying themselves". Then looking at her watch and tapping obviously, "Time is marching on girls".

After she left the room the girls all burst out into further peals of laughter. Lady Pamela shook her head and wondered what the joke was about. Bustling back into the study, she took the old hard backed ledger with her accounting jottings and even though the party had turned out badly in some respects, financially she was well ahead. She smiled happily to herself while totting up the Caribbean Night's takings. The cash, in a sturdy leather pouch monogrammed with her initials, lay bulging on the desk beside her. Even though the guests thought themselves privileged to be asked to attend one of her soirees, Lady Pamela made sure the men all paid handsomely for the opportunity. Each male client was billed 1,500 pounds-cash in advance; all the ladies along with the Chelsea Pensioners came to the party for free. She had asked three or four ex-employees who were told to

"Spice up the Chelsea oldies but for God's sake don't give them a heart attack".

Tony now a good friend came for free along with Edward. It galled her to have 'Arry attend but she knew it would keep him quiet about the state of the electrics.

The Colonel chipped in by providing all the grog for the evening and judging by the amount consumed there were many guests who would take several days to recover. She had been appalled the following morning to see 'Arry, wearing those despicable velvet flairs, emerging from the Butler's Pantry like some creature from a Zombie film; and then to incense her further he had cleaned up all the breakfast left-overs. Even though he had helped Tony clear up, she decided that he would never again be invited to any of her soirees.

She hated to admit to herself but the evening had been an unmitigated disaster even though on the surface everything appeared to have gone very well. What with Laura almost coming face to face with her errant husband and Edward turning out to be a jewel thief. She could not quite believe that this young man, so charming and eligible, had got into fisticuffs with Tony and that Tony had knocked him down and then proceeded to wrench her favorite gold and pearl bracelet from Edward's pocket. She was still simmering over this betrayal of her friendship with him. The Colonel had recounted the details of the police interview. Edward too befuddled to know what was going on kept saying,

"I didn't do it officer. I wasn't there".

The police had asked if the owner of the bracelet wanted to press charges and in any case they would have to come and interview the owner and view the place where the theft had taken place.

At that point The Colonel had backed off and taken

240

Edward home. She did wonder if The Colonel could organize for Edward to be sent to The Colonies, a moniker she still employed for Australia and New Zealand. Perhaps a stint at a sheep farm with a tough boss and miles from civilization might sort him out. The Colonel had said he was going to teach Edward a hard lesson. She made a note to speak to The Colonel about the idea. Unbeknown to The Old Girl, The Colonel had devised a nasty surprise for Edward and this would hopefully place him back on the straight and narrow.

The business with Laura had distressed her more than she realized. She couldn't get the poor dear girl out of her mind. Perhaps in a few day she would ask her out to lunch; there would be a great deal to discuss and Lady Pamela knew that she was just the right person for Laura to use as a sounding board in regard to her disintegrating marriage. Perhaps Laura might like to come and stay for a week or two and they could put their heads together over the legal issues and what Laura would be doing next. At the back of Lady Pamela's mind was the audacious idea that Laura might consider learning the business and even become her partner in crime. The dear girl might even be willing to learn bridge and join their little group.

After everyone was back at work and MadamPam's home-made leek and chicken soup with two slices of crisp toast had been served in the study, Tanice made herself a pork and tomato sandwich and took out her exercise book from its hiding place behind the bread bin. Over the last week she had been so busy with MadamPam's demands that the book had stayed put. She had not had a moment to put pen to paper. She was looking forward to creating another lascivious episode for Rastus and Delphine but was concerned that sex between them had become rather mundane. Delphine

241

had now been tamed. Tanice smiled at the latest piece she had written for Rastus. He had put the paddle to good use and taught that crazy cow a lesson. But what next?

She opened the book and a familiar looping handwriting came up and smacked her in the eyeballs. She blinked rapidly and read.

> *Jean-Paul Pallisard, Le Conte de Charbonnarde, stood surveying his new Caribbean estate. Little did Jean-Paul know that, a few months back, a distant deceased uncle of the Pallisard clan in Martinique had willed his private estate of several hundred acres to his only nephew, living in Paris. So when this came to pass, Le Conte de Charbonnarde who lived impoverishly in a Parisian townhouse of faded magnificence had locked up and taken the first plane out to the West Indies to view this welcome and unexpected inheritance.*
>
> *His keen dark eyes swept down the lush tropical gardens that flowed effortlessly down to the shoreline and then gazed along the horizon of the Caribbean Sea. With pleasure he noted the gracious coconut palms waving in the warm breeze and the exquisite turquoise water lapping lazily along the pristine white sand. Unable to contain himself a moment longer, he removed his denim shirt to reveal a perfectly toned torso the color of nutmeg. Checking that no-one was looking, he removed his linen pants and strode down to the foreshore in glorious naked abandonment; a fine figure of a man at 6ft.2in with smooth dark hair, and the sort of muscled*

brown backside that could make a lady suffer a
serious case of the vapors. He had no idea that
the vapors were fast encompassing Delphine on
the second story veranda of her neighboring
estate while watching him closely through a pair
of binoculars held in her shaky hands. She had
trouble focusing on the distant figure as he
carved a powerful overarm in the waters of the
crystal sea.

Tanice looked up in horror at this point. Not only had someone hijacked her story but that someone had introduced another character and that someone was MadamPam. The jig was up. MadamPam had found the exercise book. Tanice had no idea what to do about this shocking revelation. Tanice began to simmer as she thought about the bloody cheek of the old bat taking over her masterpiece. She muttered.

"How dare she take liberties like dat."

She re-read MadamPam's words and reluctantly concurred that the idea of introducing another lover, as a rival for Delphine's sexual favors, could work to the plot advantage. A sudden thought struck her. What if this Conte Thingy turned out to be gay and became attracted to Rastus? Rastus a bi-sexual? Her mind turned cartwheels as she tried to decide what to do. Slamming the book shut, she resolved to take the story home and work through this knotty problem quietly in her own kitchen.

At that moment a bell tinkled in the distance. It was time to clear away MadamPam's lunch tray. Tanice decided to remain tight-lipped and bide her time with regard to the unexpected take-over of her masterpiece. She would wait for the right moment to confront the old bat. Still fuming during the retrieval of the tray, she clattered the plates together and then turned swiftly to leave the room, an obvious scowl on her face. MadamPam noticed something was amiss.

"Is everything alright Tanice?"

Tanice turned and glared at her employer. "Everyting jus'fine".

Then she snapped, "Thank You!"

She clumped out of the room and slammed the door behind her. Lady Pamela winced, shook her head and went back to writing her diary. She suddenly remembered that she needed to organize the girl's six monthly health check and warrant of fitness. She made a note. Due to the nature of their work she always sent them to Dr Ramsbottom, an ex-client of the business who could be trusted not only to be discreet but also to do a rigorous check in a sensitive manner. More to the point he did not charge like a wounded bull. It had not occurred to Lady P that it was somewhat insensitive of her to use Dr Ramsbottom's services bearing in mind the fact that he had viewed Pandora's anatomy from a completely different perspective. The other girls, in the dark over his connection with Lady P, all said how thorough he was and how gentle his examinations were, especially round the breast area. Pandora, wryly smiled and remembered his excitement at suckling her breast while she gave him a hand job.

Lady Pamela went back to detailing the last few extraordinary events in her diary. She felt that this memoir, the history of Casa Blanca, would make a wonderful novel one day. Raising her pen for a moment, she contemplated how Tanice would react when she found a new character striding through her amazing story. She'd probably be delighted.

Setting the spelling and grammar aside, Lady Pamela thought that Tanice had a tremendous flair for adventurous sex scenes. She had especially liked the paddle scenes and the taming of the shrew. She felt it best to allow Tanice to approach her with a view to working together on this wonderful bodice ripper. In her usual magnanimous way, she planned to give her all the credit for authorship. She felt the need to help Tanice from the kindness of her heart, as she did all God's creatures and her contribution would be in assisting Tanice to find a publisher. In fact she already had someone in mind; an old client of the business. Lady Pamela expected nothing in return; her name would not be on the cover as co-author and she would only require a small percentage of the sales.

In the kitchen storm clouds were gathering. Tanice while vigorously washing up was muttering to herself over the soap suds.

"Damn Cheek. She so high and mighty. Tink she can take my story and do what she want wid it. My story is MINE and she not gettin' it".

She banged a saucepan on the draining board so hard that all the cutlery jumped onto the floor.

CHAPTER 17

Monday morning passed in a blur for David back at Pippin Cottage. Laura got up early and went for a long run around the village. She knew David would be in no fit state even to talk things through before noon but she needed to be extra-sharp to deal with the aftermath and running helped her achieve this. When she returned and entered the kitchen, David was sitting over a large coffee pot and staring at his toast and marmalade. He looked up with such a distraught expression that she nearly caved in and gave him a hug but instead she stood her ground and waited.

He whispered in a croaky voice, "S...sorry…Oh Laura I'm so very sorry. That you should have been there....My God". And he raised his hands in supplication, "I've only seen her three times..."

He hesitated a moment hoping Laura would rescue the conversation but Laura stood and waited, staring at him intently. He tried to turn things around by asking,

"Why didn't you tell me you were going to the party? Surely there was no secret. Why did you say you were going to Putney when you obviously had other plans?"

Laura had thought about this question for most of the previous night and she decided to come clean and tell him about Blue Eyes, not the whole story but the part relating to the Caribbean evening. First of all she said she had no idea that Lady Pamela was a Brothel Madam. It was a huge shock to find that out. She then filled him on how she had met Lady Pamela and how the old lady had asked her to lunch and subsequently at the lunch she had met an American business man. As she was saying these words David visibly relaxed and eyed her carefully as she continued,

"I then had lunch..." Here she paused a moment,

"Only lunch you understand with the American and he told me about the Caribbean party at Lady Pamela's and then invited me to go".

David continued the story, "So you decided to go in the knowledge that the Yank would be there..." Laura interrupted, "Well he wasn't, was he?"

He then asked the obvious question, "And if he had been there were you planning to have sex with him?"

Laura held his stare and said heatedly, "Yes David. Our sex life is a dead duck and that quick fuck we had after Juliet's tennis victory does not count. It was nothing but a way of placating me after I confronted you."

Knowing she was telling the truth with regard to their sex life, he flinched slightly and turned away, all the while marshalling his thoughts for a counter attack. Before he could continue, Laura confronted him about the disgusting porn and said how appalled she was that he should be surfing the net so blatantly. She had been horrified at the images and again harped on about how betrayed she felt and how worthless she had become. David suddenly got up and faced her squarely. Taken aback she took a step backwards. He looked directly at her and said.

"Can you tell me in all truth that you have not slept with this American guy?"

With that, she floundered slightly and he pressed her again, "You have haven't you?"

She lifted her head and said clearly,

'Yes I have. Do you blame me? No sex from you for God knows how long. I was facing years of no sex love or intimacy 'til death us do part. You start an internet porn habit. I knew when I made that discovery that our marriage was over."

With that she turned on her heel and just as she was

247

leaving the room, she said,

"For your information, the American has been married twice and was off with someone else the night of the party". She added, "I'm sure that will make you feel so much better Mr. Darcy".

The Colonel had decided to allow Edward to cool his heels but he knew within a week or two Edward would be back for a hand-out regardless of the fact that he had blatantly taken jewelry from The Old Girl. No doubt there would be other items missing from Casa Blanca. The Colonel had rung his sister, Edward's mother, Amanda and they had had an in depth discussion over what should be done about the Bad Egg. The Colonel's sister felt sure, that with the right guidance, Edward would come right. It was only a matter of finding the right counsellor. The Colonel had told her in no uncertain terms that Edward was past being namby pambied and what he needed was a dozen whacks of the cane or something similar and did she not realize that her son was not only a thief, but snorted cocaine for kicks and owed money all over London?

Amanda had not wanted to continue their conversation. The Colonel knew then it was going to be up to him to sort his nephew out. He decided not to involve The Old Girl. He knew the party had exhausted her and what with their business to run he did not want to burden her further with discussions over what should be done about the Bad Egg.

The Colonel made a phone call late one evening and put his punishment plan into action.

Later that week Tanice asked to see Lady Pamela and as she brought in the tea tray a few days later, MadamPam asked Tanice to bring an extra cup and join her in the sitting room.

"Now what is it you'd like to talk to me about?"
Tanice, longing for a slug of something alcoholic to
steady her nerves, said,

"It ...is about...de story ...my writin'."

Before Tanice could voice her displeasure about
having her story high-jacked, MadamPam took over and
rattled on enthusiastically about how amazing the idea
was and how fantastic that Tanice was improving her
education by taking on such a daunting project and she,
Lady Pamela, would be only too delighted to aid
Tanice's inspirational bodice ripper. With proper
grammar and punctuation she felt sure that they had a
best seller on their hands.

During this lengthy rapturous monologue, Tanice sat
there, her eyes agog at the old lady's arrogant
assumption that together they would craft this story into
something that would go into the best seller list. As
MadamPam continued to bulldoze her way over any
objections Tanice might have had, she realized that the
wily old bat was deliberately out-talking any opposition.
At one point there was a slight pause, then,

"Oh My! Listen to me I've been going over-board.
But it's so exciting Tanice. I can't wait to get started.
Let's make some time each week to get together. I've
got a whole diary full of stuff'. And she chuckled and
lowered her voice. "Sex stuff...you know, that we could
use for our three main characters" .With that she leant
back and took a breath, "Please tell me you like the
idea?"

Tanice looked at her intently. "You should have asked
me...It private...someting I do for m'self......" And here
she paused and said quietly, "It rude you know....what
you did..."

MadamPam laid her hand on Tanice's arm, "Yes you
are quite right. I should not have assumed. For that I

apologize... but truly I am so excited about what we might achieve. Introducing a titled French lover for Delphine, I'm certain our readers will love that."

Tanice stood up and carefully replaced her cup on the tray and said,

"I tink about it…I let you know".

As she lifted the tray and walked out, Tanice experienced for the first time a triumphant feeling of having got the upper hand in her dealings with her employer. She could see that MadamPam was genuinely excited about the book but she would make her wait, something the old bat who always got her own way was not used to.

After Tanice left the room, Lady Pamela smiled to herself. She knew that Tanice would come round to her way of thinking; it was only a matter of time.

The more pressing question of apologizing to Laura and having a good heart-to-heart with her filled her thoughts. Lady Pamela had sent a couple of texts but no reply had been forthcoming. She wondered if she might ring Laura but had to admit that although thinking of herself as a strong confident woman unafraid of difficult or confrontational conversations, she felt decidedly weak over what Laura might throw at her. She should have told Laura about the business before the party. She did not like to admit to herself but she had come to the conclusion that Laura would have escaped through the Butler's Pantry and down the stairs and must have then let herself out through Pandora's dungeon of unmentionables. She had changed her clothes, so someone must have assisted her with the collection of her things from the bedroom. It must have been Tony. She knew there was an attraction there and they had obviously been in her bedroom to find something to add to Tony's outfit. The beads were a complete giveaway.

250

Dear Tony, he been an absolute brick over that bounder Edward. And there was another problem. By all rights Edward should go to jail. She decided to ring The Colonel and find out the latest development and upon what retribution Henry was deciding.

The Colonel said that he had everything in hand and she shouldn't worry over the Bad Egg. He would call her in a few days when the deed was done. She pressed him for further details but her plea did not elicit any more information. She then mentioned her idea about dispatching Edward to The Colonies and The Colonel laughed and said,

"Plonk Edward in the middle of a flock of sheep, now that's worth thinking about".

Then he assured he would call when Edward had been sorted and hung up.

Late on the Friday following the party The Colonel was well away from his usual haunts of his club and The Ritz Hotel and was sipping half a pint of Bitter at The Dog and Biscuit in Soho. He was seated in the Private Bar and tucked well out of sight although near a window looking out onto the narrow dimly lit alley way. From his position he had a clear view of the entrance.

At ten o'clock, two men approached the pub. The Colonel saw them enter the public bar and look around. The older was tall and swarthy with a buzz cut and leather jacket and the other man was short and muscular with arms full of gaudy tattoos. He was wearing a baseball cap. As they came through to the Private Bar the Colonel gave them the nod and they swaggered over and sat down. No word was spoken as they took their places opposite him. The Colonel ascertained what they wanted to drink and ordered two beers with whisky chasers, with a double whisky for himself. A quiet communication took place. There were general nods of agreement and The Colonel then took a large fat envelope from his inside jacket pocket and passed it across the table. Buzz cut had a quick look and with an expert eye deduced that the package contained the exact amount agreed upon. The Colonel then took a photo from his inside jacket pocket and handed it over. The Heavies looked at it and nodded. The Colonel downed his whisky, gave another nod and left the pub striding purposefully away to find the nearest taxi rank.

Back at The Manning Property Company the word was out that the marriage between Laura and David was over. They had both agreed that neither would divulge all the intimate details at least not until they had spoken to Juliet first. The last thing they wanted was for Juliet to find out all the sordid stuff from a third party. Laura knew for a fact that once Cindy knew everything she would not be able to keep her big mouth shut and the gory details would be all over Kingbridge and beyond. David had a long heart-to-heart with Peter who was surprised at first and said that he had no idea that they were unhappy in their relationship. He knew Laura had been upset about not being able to have another child but thought that she was over that and enjoyed being fully involved with the business. Peter mentioned counselling as an option but David flatly refused to even consider that idea.

The question of what would happen to Pippin Cottage was left hanging and they parted with the knowledge that their lawyer would have to be involved. Cindy consoled Laura and pressed her hard for details, even berating her a little for not sharing the pain she must have been experiencing. She then apologized to Laura for being so insensitive about the baby news and finished the conversation by throwing numerous questions at Laura,

"What are you going to do now? Will you have to sell Pippin Cottage? Where are you going to live? What about the business?"

Laura asked her not to pressure for answers and in any case Laura had no idea what she was going to do next except to consult a lawyer. Cindy then apologized again and backed off.

The journey down to Springcourt School to collect Juliet was excruciating for Laura. Hardly a word was spoken over the three hours. Juliet had asked them to be at The Assembly Hall no later than 11.30 am in order to get a good seat for the beginning of the end of term prize giving at midday. They had left Pippin Cottage at 8.30am. David had driven recklessly through the suburbs and had swept on to the Motorway and into the fast lane where he proceeded to break the speed limit for most of the way. She clung to the seat and gritted her teeth. Normally she would have said something but the tension was so palpable between them she thought he might spontaneously combust if she confronted him about his driving.

About halfway to Springcourt a question was asked. It came from David.

"Are you sure you didn't you know the party was taking place in an escort agency?"

"You mean a brothel. No I did not."

He turned and looked at her. She continued, "That genteel Lady Pamela turns out to be a Knocking Shop Madam comes as a shocking surprise".

In a clipped tone, Laura posed a question of her own.

"What about you? I suppose you found the contact for Casa Blanca through one of your porn sites?"

"I met her at Gupta's party".

Laura stared at him a moment and then burst out,

253

"Bloody bloody Gupta".

And with that she clamped her lips in a line and stared out of the window at the passing countryside. They continued their journey in silence.

Usually they would have stopped for coffee at the Cafe On The River but this time they swept right past and as a result got to the school with plenty of time to spare. Sitting in the school carpark David said,

"I would like to be the one to break the news to Juliet and I'll do it on the way home. We'll stop at the Cafe On The River."

"I suppose I don't get any say in the matter?"

"Laura, one of us has to do it".

"Oh I see. You get in first and put your side of the story and no doubt make it look like my fault."

"No. No blame will be apportioned to either party".

"It is actually your fault but you don't want her to know that do you?"

David did not answer and looked out at the other cars that were beginning to fill the carpark. Parents, dressed in their best, were making their way to The Assembly Hall.

"We have to go".

They both got out of the car and Laura slammed the door. She then marched ahead of David and went as far to the front of the room as she could finding one seat between two different sets of parents. She smiled at them as she sat down. David, seeing her sitting, went to the end of the row and tried to catch her attention. She ignored him and started to talk to one of the mothers alongside her. He sat two rows back on the end of a row.

There was a hush as the senior school filed into the hall in front of the parents. The Head Mistress and staff were already placed in a semi-circle on the stage in front of the junior school and were smiling benignly at their favorite parents. Laura saw Juliet, her height making her stand out, follow her class and sit down at the end of one of the rows. The girls all craned their necks to catch the eye of their parents. Juliet saw David first as his physique and distinctive hair stood out from those around him and he smiled at her. She looked puzzled as she searched for her mother and eventually had to turn back to face the stage when the proceedings began.

The Head Mistress gave a welcome speech and then the school orchestra, placed on a platform to one side of the main stage, started a ragged rendering of 'Welcome and Bienvenue' from the musical 'Cabaret'. Laura could see that Juliet was suppressing a giggle as various bum notes echoed across The Hall. After the orchestra had slid drunkenly to a halt, The Head Mistress then introduced a well-known journalist and an ex-pupil of Springcourt as the guest speaker. She addressed the leavers' class about the new horizons and opportunities that would open up for them. Laura was only half listening but she suddenly realized that this woman was actually referring specifically to her own situation in that she too was about to leave one part of her life and start another. Laura began to pay closer attention.

The woman talked about not being fearful of the future and to grab and assimilate new knowledge so that the girls could make the best of what lay ahead in their working lives. Laura, at one point, looked across at David and saw that he had his head bowed and he was not engaged in what the journalist was saying. He was obviously pre-occupied with Juliet's reaction to what he was about to tell her. Laura decided to let him have his say and at a later date she would fill Juliet in on everything. The child was no longer a child and she owed it to Juliet to reveal the truth, however heinous.

After the speeches, the prizes were given and the girls

255

trooped up on the stage and took their certificates and silverware on every subject from Applied Mathematics to the cross country winner. Juliet proudly picked up her tennis trophy and smiled broadly at David when she returned to her seat.

After the ceremonies were over the parents were asked to attend a finger-food lunch accompanied by tea and coffee in the main dining room and terraced area; an occasion were everyone could mingle and parents and staff could congratulate each other on the end of another successful school year.

David and Laura waited for Juliet a few feet apart. David helped himself to a mushroom vol-au-vent and munched disconsolately as Juliet's friend's mother came rushing over and saying how kind it was of Laura and David to ask Diana to stay down in Devon and that Diana was really looking forward to her week by the sea at Woolacombe. Laura, her mind elsewhere, had completely forgotten about this invitation to stay with Laura's father at his house by the sea and looked blankly at Diana's mother before collecting herself and saying that it would be lovely for Juliet to have a friend to stay during the holidays.

Suddenly all the seniors arrived on mass and the girls rushed up to their respective parents who voiced their approval for prizes and trophies won. A general feeling of excitement prevailed except for one corner where the only excited people where Juliet, Diana and her mother, while Laura and David, on either side of this group having hugged their daughter and given their congratulations, stood awkwardly watching the two teenagers. Juliet, full of bounce over the end of term and the prospect of a long fun-filled summer, did not notice their demeanor. She and Diana then dashed off to say goodbye to their class mates in between munching on sandwiches and cake. Diana's mother reiterated her thanks and melted into the crowd.

After lunch, the Mannings went over to Juliet's boarding house Leamington to collect her things and say goodbye to Juliet's house mistress, Miss Dixon, a formidable person who had played Hockey for England in her heyday. She was full of praise for Juliet and commented on her prowess on the tennis court and the fact that the house tennis cup had at long last been wrenched out of hands of Barratt Boarding house and now stood proudly on Leamington's trophy stand.

On the drive back to Kingbridge, Juliet nattered on about the holidays and what she would like to do; a shopping trip to Knightsbridge was mentioned and could they all go to a show in the West End, then she said,

"When are we all going to Grandpa's? I have to let Diana know".

Laura looked at David who, keeping his eyes on the road, made no response and left her to answer. "Not sure yet. We'll sort it soon."

As they were approaching The Cafe On The River, Juliet asked, "Dad, can we stop and get an ice cream?"

Without answering in the affirmative, David turned into the cafe carpark and turned off the engine. Juliet leapt out and said, "Aren't you both coming in?"

She gave a puzzled look at one and then the other.

Laura exited the passenger side and put her arm round Juliet's shoulder and they both went in to get their favorite flavor:-chocolate for Juliet and strawberry for Laura. After her mother had paid for two ice creams, Juliet said,

"What about Dad? He likes mocha".

Laura turned to her daughter, "Dad's not feeling well. I don't think an ice cream would agree with him at present".

Juliet turned a concerned face to Laura, "Is Dad alright? He seems strange somehow."

"Just pre-occupied darling. Don't worry. He has work issues mainly".

And so the journey continued back to Kingbridge mainly in silence, punctuated by the slurping consumption of ice creams.

Laura glanced at David furtively from time to time. He had said nothing to Juliet and for that she was relieved and she began to formulate a plan for them both to be there when they broke the news to their daughter. This would have to be almost immediately on their return to Pippin Cottage for once Juliet saw her parents' sleeping arrangements, the news would be half broken already.

As soon as they arrived back at Pippin Cottage and Juliet had run inside to see Percy and her beloved bedroom, Laura hissed at David urgently,

"We have to do it now".

They had called her into the sitting room and Laura patted the seat next to her on the sofa,

"Daddy and I have something to tell you".

By the tone of voice, Juliet knew it was serious.

"What is it?"

Laura looked at David and could see he was struck dumb at the thought of having to tell his darling daughter that her home, where she had been born, was about to break apart. He gulped and turned his face away so neither of them could see his tears. Laura put her arm round Juliet's shoulders and said,

"Daddy and I have decided to live apart. We…are separating. I'm so sorry darling".

Juliet's usual bright expression disappeared immediately.

She looked from one to the other with stricken eyes.

258

"Separating...you mean…"

Her voice faltered as the news sunk in, "But ....you can't..."

And before Laura could take her in a comforting hug, Juliet leapt up went straight to her father and flung her arms around him. They clung to each other as they both became engulfed in tears. Laura, distraught, turned towards them and as she went to put her arms round them both, Juliet pushed her away and rushed upstairs to her bedroom and slammed the door. Laura was left standing looking at David as he reached for his handkerchief to mop his tear-stained face. He too turned away and went out into the garden. She was alone. Alone in body and spirit; her marriage of 18 years broken in pieces and without a word being spoken she knew that Juliet had put the blame squarely on her. Sides had been taken; the messenger had been shot. On top of everything this was a serious blow, a compound fracture of the heart.

Laura stood, head bowed as the tears rolled down her face and the enormity of the consequence of what had just happened sank in. Her beloved daughter had sided with her father which meant that, however sordid or upsetting, Juliet would have to be told everything. The truth would have to be revealed including her own part in it. The moment was not now but at a time when she could persuade Juliet to listen to the whole sorry saga quietly just the two of them.

They all sat later that evening in silence consuming Juliet's favorite dinner of roast chicken and chocolate mousse. Both Laura and David were unable to finish their meals and as soon as Juliet had finished hers, she looked up at David and said,

"I want to go for a drive. Dad will you take me?"

He nodded, "Yes of course. Let's go". And without a

word to Laura they both left the room.

She was left staring at the dirty plates wondering what David was going to say. She guessed that any half-truth would be massaged in order to put him in a favorable light but then giving him the benefit of the doubt he might decide to tell Juliet everything. Laura shook her head. That was very unlikely. Never in a million years would David turn to his daughter and say,

"Well I haven't had sex with your mother for a long time and anyway I prefer black women and went to a brothel to find one. In retaliation she started an affair with an American so we decided to call it a day".

No, that was definitely not what he would say. She guessed he would say something nebulous; that they had drifted apart and now wanted to separate and that this was a joint decision. She hoped David would reassure his daughter that she was no less loved and that her parents' separate lives would not disrupt her life to any great degree.

The question mark over Pippin Cottage would have to be resolved and she knew that Juliet at aged 16 would have the choice of whom she lived with. Laura put these disturbing thoughts from her mind and got on with cleaning up the dinner plates. Just as she was stacking the last dish, her cell sent through a text. She looked, hoping it was Captain No Hook but it turned out to be Blue Eyes. He asked her to contact him and said he was missing her. She texted back.

FUCK OFF

And then deleted everything to do with him from her phone.

Two hours later father and daughter returned. Both looked flushed and David's speech was slurred. Uneasily Laura realized that he had taken her to the pub and alcohol had eased their pain. As Juliet approached her mother and kissed her on the cheek, Laura embraced her and caught a sweet smell of an alcoholic raspberry drink on her breath. Juliet gave her mother a lop-sided smile said a quick 'good night' and went straight up to bed.

Laura turned to David with a questioning look. He waved his hand,

"Told her we'd drifted apart. She wanted to know if we could get back together and then got upset that her summer holiday was going to be buggered. I reassured her that in the short term nothing was going to change. We could all live here until..."

He stopped and put his hand on his head and sucking in air through his teeth, continued,

"God I'm pissed...Sorry...in essence it's done".

Laura said quietly, "Perhaps giving her alcohol to dull the shock wasn't a very good idea".

David glared at his wife and snapped, "Oh shut up Laura. Stop being so bloody sanctimonious".

With that he turned on his heel and went into the study.

Laura, knowing that a difficult few days lay ahead and anyway 'if you can't beat'em join'em', decided to hit the gin bottle. She poured herself a slug and took the bottle upstairs to become her bed companion for the night. She hesitated outside her daughter's door, listened for a moment and hearing nothing, at least no tears, took herself off to the spare room.

While dozing after a quadruple dose of gin to take her to oblivion, her cell trilled with a message; it was No Hook checking on progress. He texted that he missed her terribly and was there anything he could do to help. He finished by begging her to contact him. She sent him a short reply.

Juliet knows re marriage. Feeling horrible. In spare room with the gin bottle. xxx

261

Then as an afterthought she wrote

> *Juliet is my 16 year old daughter in case I didn't*
> *tell you before...can't remember....anything. L x*

CHAPTER 18

Edward after the party had not been able to remember very much at all. He had a vague recollection of there being some sort of fight; was it with Tony? He had no idea why the fight had started. He remembered the early part of the evening when he had met the lovely Laura and now she was occupying his mind in between trying to work out how to pay off yet another round of debts that he had incurred over the last couple of weeks. He did at last have one lucrative modelling job during that time. The fact that he had purloined Aunty P's bracelet had completely slipped his mind and as it was no longer in his pocket to remind him of his misdemeanor, he was none the wiser.

The Colonel had rung and given him a bollocking about drinking too much; nothing unusual in that but then the old man had accused him of stealing the old girl's bracelet; of that he had no recollection and denied all knowledge. The Police Station was mentioned and Edward let the old boy ramble on about breaking the law and having to pay for his crimes. He almost laughed at one point but managed to suppress a chortle as the old boy rabbited on about sending him to Australia, like a common convict, to cool his heels in some God forsaken sheep station miles from anywhere. Edward surmised that it was best to be very contrite, even though he was unsure of what had come to pass, but by doing that he would very soon be back in the old people's good books. So, as he had done many times before, he apologized profusely and said it would never happen again.

The Colonel had gruffly finished their conversation by asking,

"S'pose you'll be down at that dreadful Devil hell hole as soon as you get off the phone?"

263

Edward said cheerily, "Going tomorrow actually. It's a good friend's birthday bash. Oh by the way. Do you have that beautiful Laura's contact number? The girl that disappeared under the table? Thought I'd ask her out".

The Colonel answered in the negative and made a mental note to tell Lady Pamela of Edward's intentions. They would have to think of some way to head him away from the vulnerable Laura.

A few nights later completely oblivious to what was coming next, Edward set off to his favorite haunt "The Devil's Domaine" in Soho. He would have liked to have asked Laura to come with him; what a pretty thing she was; all alone too with only that shambolic bookworm Tony as a rival for her affections. Edward considered him to be no contest, no contest at all. It was strange that she had suddenly disappeared like a rat down a sewer pipe. He had the feeling there was more to her sudden disappearance than a fainting spell.

He had partied hard that night at "The Devil's Domaine". It was run by a couple of old Etonians who were very particular about the caliber of guest and there were strict entry requirements to be adhered to. You had to be young, very well dressed and you didn't quite have to show your name as listed in Burke's peerage but the more blue bloodied you were the more The Bouncer liked you. Edward drank until he was legless and between drinks he managed to score a nose of cocaine. In this heightened state all his friends seemed funnier and larger than life. When it came time to leave in the early hours of the morning he kissed them all sloppily and said he loved them all before staggering off to find the taxi rank.

Buzz Cut and Side-Kick had received a phone call earlier in the evening and were waiting in their black Rover just out of sight in a side street. They could see the entry to the club opposite and it was very easy to spot the tipsy crowd come staggering out while shouting their goodbyes and weaving their way down the street. They had a photo of Edward in their possession and as the group approached the car, even though the street was dimly lit, Buzz Cut was easily able to distinguish the tallest man in the trio of revelers as their target. Edward lurched into the side of the car and then back into the middle of the street as his other two friends waved and turned into another side street. Edward yelled something to them and continued his zig-zag path toward the main road.

Buzz Cut inched the car forward and came almost alongside and before Edward could get his head round what was happening he was dragged inside the back seat by Side-Kick and punched hard on the ear. A smelly sack was placed over his head and tied tight round his neck. Edward terrified gave a muffled yell and tried to gulp for air. Buzz Cut roared away; and so it was that Edward found himself to be at the wrong end of a knife and bicycle chain not attached to a bicycle. His life would never be the same again.

Tony thought constantly about Laura. He wished he could do something to help her. After her text had come through about Juliet he had almost decided to take a train to Kingbridge and seek her out; common sense prevailed and he decided to bide his time. He knew that turning up out of the blue would probably freak her out as well as put suspicions in the mind of her husband and daughter. To calm his troubled heart, he closed the shop early and went over to Spa Hill to visit his allotment; a gentle tilling of the soil and checking his vegetables would calm his mind. The community of fellow gardeners of whom there were many on sunny evenings would be soothing to his soul.

When he hopped out of his car he was pleased to see there were one or two familiar cars belonging to gardeners, with whom he had become friends, parked close by. As he removed his gardening paraphernalia from the back of the car, he looked up and noticed at the far end of the allotment land three police cars and an ambulance. He cast his eyes across the rest of the vegetable plots and very close to where he tilled his own plot a large crowd were gathered. Tony hurried over, all the while thinking that one of his gardening mates had had a heart attack while digging. As he approached he saw old Will an avid gardener in his early 80's. Will waved and full of excitement said,

"There's a body…covered in blood…face cut to ribbons…in your shed".

"What? My shed?   God…A body…Dear Lord. What happened?"

"He's been beaten and left for dead at the back of your potting shed. Buggers broke your lock mind and chucked him under a potato sack… he's unconscious…they're just shifting him now".

Tony was horrified that the victim of a mugging could have ended up in his shed and to add insult to injury the perpetrators had broken the lock. The police were securing the site as Tony slid round the edge of the crowd and craned his neck to see the ambulance crew stretchering a man covered with a blanket into the ambulance. Tony could see he was a tall slim guy with coal black hair. As his body and almost all his face was obscured by the blanket, Tony could not discern what nationality he might be. As the man was lifted up, a policeman asked him to,

"Stand well back please. This is a crime scene."

Tony caught a glimpse of the victim's left arm as it

266

fell below the stretcher and he was just able to make out the man's expensive watch, possibly a gold Rolex; it was studded with tiny diamonds. Tony's mind did a mini jolt; he'd seen a watch like that very recently and then he remembered. He'd seen a watch just like that on the wrist of DE -Dickhead Edward. He turned to Will,

"Have they identified him?"

"Dunno…Didnt see any hidentification. Fancy 'im being dumped at the back of your shed. The rozzers'll want to interview you mate…Quite exciting. S'like Prime Suspect innit?"

And then before Tony could quietly melt away with the crowd in order to disengage himself from anyone knowing his connection with the victim, Will hailed a policeman,

"This is the bloke what owns the shed…you'll want to talk to 'im".

Tony's heart sank. This would mean a lengthy interview.

He made a split second decision not to reveal that he knew the victim's name.

Tony's visit to the local police station did not take all that long. They ascertained that he was the lease holder of the plot and it had been in his family for three generations. His father had put the shed up. When they came to asking about his movements over the last 24 hours, Tony was able to give a clear account of his whereabouts and the fact that he had been at the movies last evening with some married friends of his. He gave their names and phone number. He underlined the fact that he was horrified that something like this should have happened on his vegetable patch, and did the police know who the victim was and why the guy was beaten so badly?

The police said that no wallet or identification had

267

been found although there was a business card in his pocket with a South London phone number which they were following up on. They said he was free to go and much to his relief would be eliminated from their enquiries.

Later that evening with a strengthening beer in his hand at the local pub Tony tried to piece together what might have happened. Edward must have got himself into even more trouble, the fact that the watch had not been taken meant that it wasn't necessarily a mugging but must mean that the beating was inflicted for another reason. It was probably about money. Edward had no doubt owed a great deal all over London and someone, a very vicious someone, had got tired of waiting and decided to teach Edward, with his good looks, a grisly lesson. Tony mused that Edward's modelling career would probably go down the toilet. He sent a text to Laura giving her the whole story. He did not receive a reply.

Laura sat with Juliet in the studio the following day while Juliet cried her eyes out. Percy kept rubbing against her legs and mewing softly as he knew something was amiss. Juliet brushed his soft fur as she poured out her grief to her mother. Her main concerns were having to leave Pippin Cottage where she was born and brought up and the scary questions of where she was going to live and with whom were troubling her. She also was very upset that her precious summer holidays were about to go down the pan. Tearfully she asked,

"Are you absolutely certain that you want to break up with Daddy?"

Laura gently told her that it was a joint decision but Juliet did not seem convinced that her father was in agreement over the split. Laura realized that David must

268

have put a subtle doubt in their daughter's mind over who wanted out and had emphasized perhaps that he did not want the marriage to end.

Laura did not question Juliet further about this but tried to comfort her as best she could. She decided that to tell the whole story at this time would be far too shocking for her vulnerable daughter. Instead she said that the holiday in Devon would definitely go ahead with Juliet's friend Diana and that she would ring Juliet's grandfather and fix the date that evening. At that news Juliet leapt up and went to her room to call Diana.

David had gone into the office and faced a long day trying to placate the subbies on The Gupta job. Gupta, having paid with a flourish in cash in the early part of the job, was now on a 'go slow' or more to the point 'no go' with regard to his next payment. It looked like another visit to the bank was imminent. The atmosphere at The Manning Renovation Company was tense with all employees treading carefully round their two bosses. Laura was not mentioned although Cindy put in a quick call to enquire after her niece and had to leave an answer phone message. With regard to Gupta, there was one huge advantage for Cindy, his interest in her had waned since she had become pregnant and now he rarely came into the main office to brighten her day with a little sexual harassment.

Laura had cancelled her two interior design appointments and even though she had one art work to complete her mind was too full of her daughter's distress and her own worries over her next move. She had read the text from Tony about Edward but was too distracted to respond. She had turned her cell phone off. At some stage in the near future she knew she would have to make an appointment to see a lawyer but even that seemed unsurmountable.

269

Even though the news from The Hospital remained the same: - that the mugging victim was still unconscious and in intensive care, the police were beginning to unravel the mystery of the unknown man. They were piecing together an identity for the allotment victim. The business card they had found in the victim's pocket belonged to an outfit called Casa Blanca.

When the young Sergeant rang the number a very posh voice answered.

"This is Casa Blanca. How can I assist you? Your fantasy is our command".

When he said he was from the South London police making enquiries about a gentleman who had been viciously attacked and left for dead and one of their cards had been found in the victim's pocket, the posh voice went completely silent and the phone was quietly replaced. When the young sergeant tried the number again, he received a busy signal.

He relayed this information to his guvnor and as they took another look at the business card and re-read the words

"Your fantasy is our command",

The guvnor pressed a finger to his lips,

"Sounds like a knocking shop to me. I'll get Roger to check the number on the computer for an address and in the morning, you and I, lad, will pay them a visit"

As soon as Lady Pamela had put the phone down with a shaky hand she had picked it up again and dialed The Colonel's number. When she told him what the police had said to her he went very silent.

"Are you still there Henry?"

After a pause and without telling her in whose pocket the card would have been found, he began to instruct her, with a manic rush of words, on what she should do.

She listened as he listed all the actions to be taken and at the end of the instructions she said,

"Who on earth was it do you think? Obviously a client, but who?"

"Yes a stupid bloody client who had one of our incriminating cards in his pocket. Now get to it Old Girl and time is of the essence. You must have everything in place before that knock on the door".

"But Henry they've only got a land line number, there was no address".

The Colonel, shouted with exasperation,

"PAMELA. For fuck's sake don't you realize what computers can do. These days they can find the location of a person in the gents at a golf club on Mars."

"Alright… alright. No need to swear", and before she could ask him what he was going to do, he rang off.

She tried the number again but it went to voice message. As he was deeply involved with the business and her trusted advisor, she was somewhat peeved that he had hung up so abruptly. She would need his counsel in the days to come.

What she didn't know was that The Colonel was leaving town: - Hightailing it out of London into the country where he would hole up at his sister Amanda's house until the business with Edward had blown over.

After The Colonel had finished talking to Pamela he ranted in his head about the idiocy of his nephew and that bloody business card lying in wait to ruin him, Casa Blanca, the Old Girl and her employees. He prayed The Old Girl would get started right away and carry out all that he had instructed. The dismantling of everything was vital. No incriminating evidence must be found. He tried to calm his nerves with a double shot of whisky but he knew in his pounding heart that the business was, for all intents and purposes, totally buggered. He only hoped that no one would get hurt, or worse in the process. Pamela had always said she was invincible and sincerely believed that there was no possibility of being nicked. She used to say,

"I'm just a genteel lady of advancing years with my arthritic dog for company. I like to have the company of pretty girls around me to keep me youthful."

It hadn't occurred to her that this statement gave people the impression that she was a Lesbian. Ironically it was a perfect cover in light of what really went on in Casa Blanca.

Even though he was an army man, when it came to saving his honor and reputation, The Colonel would lie and lie and lie. Now, with the police breathing down his neck, he did a runner leaving The Old Girl to parry the Sword of Damocles.

Life as she had known it for the last 20 years was hanging by a horse hair.

Lady Pamela came flying out of her study and started shrieking for the girls to come downstairs IMMEDIATELY. Tanice, cleaning one of the upstairs rooms, came barreling down the stairs,

"MadamPam. What happened?"

Lady Pamela, her hands flapping, "It's what's going to happen Tanice"

Tanice then whispered "Police?" Her employer nodded.

All the girls came rushing into the sitting room as their clients, some half-dressed shot out of the front door like scalded ferrets.

"Girls, the time has come. The Police could make a visit at any time. Something has happened to alert them. We have no time to spare. Go to your rooms, remove all evidence, be very thorough, collect all your belongings and come to me in the study. Pandora, we have to clear the basement."

Pandora, her eyes wildly looking from Lady P to the front door, "But where are we going to put all the stuff? Storage units are almost impossible to find close by".

Lady Pamela clutched her head and swore, "Fuck. Shit. Think. Fuck. Think."

Tanice then said, "My Victor could take some tings… He have a van."

Lady Pamela whirled round and almost hugged her, "A man with a van...Tanice…You are brilliant. Can he come now?"

Tanice said she would call him and rushed off to the kitchen phone, only to come back to say, 'De truck at garage. It broken down".

Pandora could see Lady P was extremely distressed so she gently took hold of her arm, "I will support you Lady P -no matter what." And then as an afterthought, "What about Tony at the bookshop? He must have a storage area or a basement surely".

Lady Pamela looked at her trusty dominatrix and said, "Thank you Pandora...for everything".

She shot into the study to phone Tony. He answered the call on the second ring and without any preamble from Lady Pamela, it was ascertained that he did have a basement and although half full of books could accommodate the larger items such as the gym horse, the trunk, the stools and the wall rack. The truckle bed could be a problem and Lady Pamela made a decision to leave it in situ, after all a bed was for sleeping on wasn't it and if she prettied it up with a flowery bedcover no one would be the wiser. She made a mental note to remember to remove the restraints for the hands and feet.

Pandora then took charge of the basement and Casa Blanca, for the next couple of hours, was a whirl of activity. Tony had said he would hire a trailer and be

273

around as soon as possible. At one point Lady Pamela called Nefertiti and Cherry into her study and said how much she had enjoyed working with them but it was now time for a two week holiday after which she would let them know when and if they would be required to return to Casa Blanca. She thanked them both for their dedication to satisfying men's lust, not an easy task, and gave them several thousand pounds in cash. Tears and hugs followed and the two girls left Casa Blanca not knowing if and when they would return.

Pandora and Tanice flew round the house getting rid of every tiny scrap of incriminating evidence. Pandora's dungeon took the most time to sort out and clean up. All of the equipment was stacked ready to disappear on the arrival of Tony and his trailer. While the basement was being cleared Lady Pamela, instructed by The Colonel, packed her ledgers, cash, bills and black books and any other paperwork to do with the business into a suitcase which she firmly locked and took down to the basement. Dandelion was very confused and lolloped up and down the stairs in search of an answer. Lady Pamela cuddled him to her and gave him some treats while the jittery trio then waited for their knight with the trailer.

Pandora tried to text Tony but got nothing in return so they had no idea when he would arrive. Lady Pamela was longing for restorative whisky but knew she had to keep her wits about her. The business phone rang a few times but went unanswered. Lady Pamela decided not to contact any clients. It was decided that contact would cease completely with the outside world. Lady Pamela cut the wires to the intercom; if anyone came to the door it would not be answered. Tanice made some sandwiches in the kitchen all the while keeping a watchful eye through the front window. It was all quiet in Davenport Gardens. She took the food down to the basement and the trio munched in silence while Dandi panted hoarsely and looked from one to the other in hopeless confusion. Pandora felt they looked like a gang of jewel thieves, with their watch dog, waiting for darkness to fall.

Tanice suddenly jumped up in alarm,

"What about de finger prints...They goin' to find our prints. Lordy we have to clean dem".

And she made for the stairs. Pandora stopped her.

"Tanice, calm down. No one has committed a murder or laundered stolen money here. Illegal activity has taken place but the police will not be looking for dabs".

"Dabs what is dabs?" Asked Tanice, her brown eyes flickering in alarm.

She was told it was another words for finger prints.

Pandora was somewhat dismayed that her career was about to come to an abrupt halt. She would have to find some alternative income to support her family. Lady P had been very generous in her severance pay but that wouldn't last forever.

Around 7pm there was a soft tap on the basement door. The trio leapt to attention and Pandora went over and said,

"Who is it?"

Tony's welcome voice came through the woodwork.

"It's me. Got the trailer outside".

It took over an hour to heft everything into the trailer. It was fortuitous that Tanice and Pandora were strongly built so together with Tony they were able to lift the confounded gym horse and ghastly wall rack into the trailer. The trunk had been emptied as full of weapons it proved far too heavy to lift.

At one point Pandora told Lady Pamela to go upstairs and get a bottle of any type of alcohol and some water and some sustenance to aid the shifters; so for the first time ever Lady Pamela was transformed from titled upper class lady to lowly kitchen maid. She went about the task with gusto and brought down a veritable feast for the hungry crew. Symbolically Lady Pamela thought of it as the Last Supper but as she was not prepared to follow in Christ's simple culinary footsteps, she brought down a groaning tray of Fortnum's delicacies that she had been keeping for a rainy day, two bottles of Chateau bottled Cabernet Merlot and a full bottle of her best Cognac. Emergencies needed drinks that packed a punch.

Tanice could not quite believe that she was sitting in the dreaded dungeon sipping excellent Cognac and partaking of MadamPam's special supplies. Her world as she knew it had come to a spectacular end. Could one go to prison for aiding and abetting an illegal enterprise? She could hardly deny knowing what went on at 32 Davenport Gardens. She prayed that she would not have to answer that question.

As it was getting late, Pandora stated that she felt sure that no one from the police would call at this hour but Lady Pamela must be ready for a knock on the door in the morning and more to the point, have her story straight. Pandora now in charge, rehearsed her jittery employer. The script stated that she, a frail old lady, lived alone with only her dog for company. She employed a colored maid who had been with her for several years. The business card related to a business that had closed down 6 months before:-A costume and fancy dress hire company.

Thinking ahead Pandora had decided to leave her French maid's costume hanging in Nef's bedroom and she had asked Nef to leave a couple of Turkish belly dancer costumes behind.

"Don't you think we should clear all the clothes out?

276

Get rid of the evidence so to speak".

Asked Lady P.

Pandora pointed out that the Casa Blanca business card mentioned the word "fantasy" so to leave some fancy dress costumes hanging in a wardrobe cupboard would not alert The Fuzz to anything amiss at the heart of Casa Blanca.

Lady P congratulated the Dominatrix on her sensible head and poured them both another snifter of Cognac. She needed to sleep well that night in readiness for the grueling interview in the morning. It was agreed that Tanice, Pandora and Lady P would re-convene at 8 am sharp. The police were early risers.

When all the paraphernalia was packed away, Pandora said that she and Tanice would go round to Tony's shop and unload.

As Lady Pamela was shutting the basement door Pandora could see the utter relief on the old lady's face and the pallor of exhaustion setting in. She put an arm round her employer and having second thoughts about leaving the old lady alone in the house overnight, said,

"Leave the front door on the latch. I'm coming back to spend the night here. I don't think you should be left on your own"

The old lady nearly cried with relief and she hugged Pandora to her and whispered,

"Thank you…Oh thank you..." And as an afterthought, "I couldn't bear to go to jail. I'd rather kill myself."

CHAPTER 19

The following morning round about the same time the Detective Inspector and his Sergeant were driving towards the Chelsea address, Edward in hospital was beginning to surface. Still in pain from his cuts and bashed head, he was suffering horrendous withdrawal symptoms and was not a happy patient. His identity which he remembered on waking was now on his chart. The pretty nurse who came to check his dressings did perk him up a little but when he asked for a mirror to inspect the damage, she hesitated and said,

"Might be best to wait a few days Mr Hanbury'.

He gingerly touched his face and could feel 2 bumpy lines each side of his cheeks under the bandages and his nose felt like it had sprouted a Rhinoceros horn; he knew then that the damage was extensive and he remembered some chilling words spoken a few weeks before,

"We'll turn yer face into strawberry jam'.

He slumped back on the pillows in despair. He was meant to be doing some photographic work that week for a fashion catalogue and filming in Spain for a TV commercial in a week's time. He realized with complete loss of hope that with a bashed up face his modelling career was rapidly going down the toilet. He tried hard to recollect something about the night in question but came up with a fat zero. The only thing he could remember was a lot of laughing and fooling about at a club somewhere in London.

Tanice had started work as requested at 8am the following morning and had made MadamPam's favorite breakfast of a beetroot smoothie followed by a crisp piece of toast topped with thinly sliced tomato.

MadamPam enthused regularly over the curative properties of beetroot. Not only did it keep you regular, an ongoing problem for the old lady, but the vegetable helped to lower blood pressure, pep you up with iron and improve the condition of skin and nails. As she had told Tanice, you had to be aware that you pooped deep pink; rather alarming at first but you got used to it. Tanice was not impressed and made sure beetroot never passed her lips. She could not abide the vegetable.

Pandora had insisted that Lady P should stay in bed and rest after her breakfast tray had been cleared away. Tanice had made some scrambled eggs for them both and she and Pandora ate their breakfast in silence in the kitchen. Dandelion had been fed and watered and Pandora had let him out for his morning dump in the park. As she was collecting his little present and putting it into a plastic bag she looked furtively around for any unmarked police car. The street was very quiet.

The tension that pervaded Casa Blanca was almost unbearable. All of them were desperate to get the wretched police visit out of the way. When Lady Pamela appeared around 10am she was dressed for the part. She had found an old baggy tweed skirt that fell to mid-calf and was wearing an ancient dark grey twin set and pearls. To complete the picture she wore an old pair of sensible lace ups; her hair was flattened against a pallid face devoid of makeup. She had her reading glasses perched on the end of her nose. Even Dandi did a double-take when she entered the sitting room.

"What do you think?" She said in a quivery voice.

"Brilliant. Lady P".

Pandora then mentioned that Tony had texted her saying that all was stowed away safely and he had wished them all "Good Luck". The trio then sat around, for the next couple of hours in the sitting room, awaiting that knock on the door.

Just as the Police Inspector pressed the defunct intercom button at Casa Blanca, his cell trilled and a text came through to say that the mugging victim had regained consciousness and had given his identity as Edward Hanbury.

The Police Inspector gave a cursory glance at this information and pressed the intercom button for a second time. Answer came there none. The Sergeant then banged on the front door.

Tanice pouring tea for Pandora and MadamPam in the sitting room shook the teapot so much that some tea fell onto Dandi's head as he waited alongside for his treat. He yelped and pulled back. Pandora gripped Lady P's arm and enunciated clearly,

"Remember, keep calm. You are a dignified elderly lady, somewhat confused and a little put out that The Police have knocked on your door".

There came another thunderous knock.

As Lady P got to her feet, Tanice yanked Dandi with her into the kitchen and shut the door and Pandora went down to the basement through the Butler's Pantry with the promise she would re-emerge if needed. On her way down she realized that she had forgotten to invent a new identity for herself.

Pandora was born Tracy Crapper and was descended from the man, a plumber like her father, who had invented the ballcock.

A very fitting profession in light of what she got up to in Casa Blanca but the time had come to re-invent herself. She decided to become Pandora Lancaster, Lady Pamela's niece.

Lady Pamela made slow progress to the front door and opened it a fraction. She squinted into the light and in front of her stood two men; the elder in a business

280

suit, with thinning grey hair and a pot belly and the second man in the uniform of a police sergeant, with sandy hair and buck teeth.

Lady Pamela bent forward slightly and leaning heavily on her stick said in a soft quaver,

"Yes?"

An introduction followed as they ascertained her name and they both showed her their identity cards. They then asked if they could come in. Lady Pamela played the frailty card and with a shaky voice asked,

"Um...I'm...I'm not very well. Could you tell me what this is about?"

They persuaded her that as the matter was of a delicate nature it would be better to conduct their enquiry inside. She reluctantly acquiesced and they followed her bent frame into the sitting room. Lady Pamela played the role of confused geriatric to the hilt, even professing to be hard of hearing. She offered them tea which they refused. She explained that the business card in question was out of date. The Fancy Dress business had been closed down six months before. She finished up by saying,

"So sorry your visit has come to nothing. Poor young man ...Do hope you can find out who he is".

With that she rose stiffly to indicate that the interview was at an end. Inspector Pot Belly looked up at her and fished out his phone saying,

"We now have the victim's identity" And he read off the screen, "A Mr Edward Hanbury...Ring any bells Your Ladyship?"

A humungous peel of bells went off in her head and momentarily flummoxed over this dreadful news, she started to cough loudly and then she shouted between the false paroxysms,

"TANICE...My pills... TANICE."

Tanice came bounding out of the kitchen closely accompanied by Dandi who set up a loud barking defense. The two men pulled back and begged for the hound to be brought under control. At the same time Pandora came racing into the sitting room and in a very posh voice enunciated.

"Aunt Pamela. Are you alright? Who are you people? You have frightened my Aunt. I think you should leave now." And then turning to Tanice, "Take Dandelion and put him the kitchen. I've told you before about letting him out when my aunt has callers."

Tanice, her eyes out on stalks, did as she was told. Pandora approached Inspector Pot Belly, her magnificent boobs rose majestically in front of him, and said in her most confident manner,

"My aunt is not well and needs to rest. What is it you want from her? Can't you see she's over eighty and frightened out of her wits. "

Lady P took her cue and with hand on heart she sat down lurching slightly to one side in the process. The young sergeant genuinely concerned for her welfare asked if he could get her a drink of water. She shook her head and closed her eyes.

From then on Pandora took over. She firstly introduced herself as Pandora Lancaster, the daughter of Lady Pamela's sister. When told that the mugging victim's name was Edward Hanbury, she gave a snort,

"THE Edward Hanbury?" And then qualified her remark by saying, "He's a drunk. A party animal. Always coming by to dress up as a pirate or something. I think I read in the paper that he had been busted for drugs...I know him because I used to go out with him...but he was a loser....He owes money all over London...Not surprised he got beaten up. "

During this revelation Lady P kept her eyes firmly

shut although if you looked closely you could detect a mouth twitch from time to time. What a trooper Pandora was.

The young sergeant was busily jotting down all this information and even though Pandora knew that her false name could be a risk, all the stuff about Edward was true, in the main. He had been a client and she had serviced him from time to time. She knew he was a drunk and took cocaine. The hospital would verify this.

During a pause as Inspector Pot Belly took in her statement, she suddenly got up,

"My Aunt is very frail. I now have to make sure she can get up the stairs and into her bedroom without falling. If you will excuse me." And she took Lady Pamela by the arm gazing fiercely all the while at Inspector Pot Belly. He calmly waited until she was at the stairs and then said,

"We'll just wait here then." And as an afterthought, "Thank you Lady Pamela for your time. I'm sure you won't mind us taking a look around. Miss Pandora can show us the layout".

With no answer for this the two ladies made their way slowly up the stairs and knowing that the two Rozzers' ears would be flapping at the bottom of the stairs, Pandora looked directly at Lady P and put her finger to her lips. She gently put her employer into the bedroom. It was now up to the dominatrix to downplay any pointed questions and get Inspector Pot Belly and his sergeant off the premises as quickly as possible. The one unknown factor was Tanice. She might panic and blurt out the truth but Pandora had forgotten that there was one other person who could give the game away.

She ran down the stairs and entered the sitting room. The two men were in exactly the same position as before. She popped her head into the kitchen and said an inaudible something to Tanice who was gripping a chopping board and holding it in front of her like a shield as though waiting for a knife to pierce her heart. Tanice was told to 'keep mum' and hold her nerve. Dandi on his bed looked up and nodded.

The tour of Casa Blanca started in the study. Pandora suddenly realized that for a search of a premises to take place a Search Warrant should be obtained. She made a fuss about this and said she would lodge a complaint to the relevant authority. Inspector Pot Belly opened the desk drawers and finding nothing incriminating shut them again. He looked at her with cold grey eyes,

"So you do have something to hide?"

With no answer other than denial, Pandora showed them the hall and toilet area and then Inspector Pot Belly said,

"I'd like to see the upper floors please."

Pandora pretended firstly to be incensed at this intrusion and then followed that by saying that her aunt needed peace and quiet.

The Inspector parried, "We're quiet as brothel creepers, aren't we Sergeant?" And he laughed eerily.

Pandora took them upstairs and showed them all the bedrooms bar the one in which Lady Pamela was resting. Even though her room had been stripped of all its brothel tat and explicit pictures, it was done out in a pink Hollywood theme with Las Vegas overtones and the bloody give-away mirror on the ceiling elicited raised eyebrows and a chortle from The Sergeant. They both looked at her, waiting for an explanation.

"Alright. I hoped that I wouldn't need to tell you. In her heyday, Lady Pamela was a show girl."

Inspector Pot Belly stepped in close to her and giving her a sharp look, enunciated,

"You mean a Prost-tit-tute?"

284

"No. No. She was a dancer. She made her name in Las Vegas and this room was decorated in the style of Movie glamour to remind her of those heady days of show biz."

Inspector Pot Belly narrowed his eyes, "Well if I believe that, I'll believe anything".

He did not follow on with any other tricky questions and so Pandora led the way downstairs to the hall. Expecting them to leave, she went to the front door and opened it. Inspector Pot Belly turned to his Sergeant, gave him a knowing look and said,

"Stay here a moment. I'm going with Miss Pandora down to the basement...lead the way MISS PAN...DORA".

His emphasis of her name made the hairs stand up on the back of her neck.

She took him through the Butler's Pantry and down the stairs to the infamous dungeon all the while praying that the clean-up had been thorough. They entered the room and Pandora switched on the light.

"It used to be the old kitchen, but my Aunt, for convenience, moved everything up to the ground floor".

"Um...I see and what is it used for now?"

"Nothing much. It did house some old furniture. My aunt collected antiques on her travels and she stored them here".

Inspector Pot Belly went over to the dumb waiter and asked, "And this was used to ferry food and china up to the dining room?"

Pandora nodded.

He surveyed the room with an expert's eye and spied the truckle bed now adorned in a soft rose colored bedspread and 3 floral cushions. Giving her a keen look he asked, "Who sleeps here?"

Just as Pandora was about to answer there came a decisive tap on the basement door that led out onto the

285

street. She opened her mouth and then stopped mid breath, smiled sweetly and thought who the fuck is that? The Inspector pressed on.

"The door. Aren't you going to answer it then?"

As she was pulling the heavy bolts on the old door, a hideous realization struck her right between the eyes. It was Mr. Big. She had forgotten to alert him to a problem by leaving a banana skin on the dustbin lid outside. It had been agreed between them that this was to be their sign in times of danger. She opened the door wide and said confidently,

"Darling, come in and meet The Inspector".

It was best to confront the problem head-on.

Mr. Big rocked back slightly on his heels and then strode in smiling broadly. Pandora hung onto his arm and continued, "This is my fiancé, Inspector".

Fishing wildly for a suitable name, she found an unsuitable one and continued,

"Mikey…Meet the Inspector. He's here inspecting us...Actually I'm not sure why...something to do with some poor chap getting bashed up".

Inspector Pot Belly looked up at Mr. Big and even though their height difference was marked, Pot Belly showed no signs of being intimidated. He enunciated clearly,

"The....fiancé....of....MISS   PAN…DORA.   It's   a pleasure Sir". And he stuck out his hand. They shook hands forcefully. The Inspector took a step back and making an obvious sweep of this tall business man from head to foot, he addressed Mr. Big again,

"Extraordinary Sir, you look exactly like Patrick Partington Q.C. A very impressive character. I've seen him in court a few times and I can tell you he's like a dog with a bone. I've seen witnesses practically wet themselves under his cross examination".

286

He then paused and in true detective style waited for a confession. Pandora was first to jump in.

"Patrick darling, sorry I should have introduced you properly."

She turned to The Inspector and said in her most sincere voice, "I call him Mikey. Mikey Mouse. Of course he's not really...Yes...you're right. He's a tiger in the Court room".

Inspector Pot Belly could not resist. "And in the bedroom too perhaps?" He gave his eerie laugh. "Nothing to say Sir?"

They stared at each other like two pit bulls about to strike. Mr. Big, mustering the most authoritative voice he could,

"Nothing at all Inspector".

Tension broken, The Inspector gave a cursory glance at his surroundings allowing his gaze to land for a moment or two longer than necessary on the truckle bed. Then with a toothy grin at the guilty pair, for he was sure they were, he turned on his heel and exited the basement the way he came in. Pandora grabbed the arm of Mr. Big and pretending to canoodle, said clearly enough for The Inspector to hear,

"Aunt Pamela will be up from her rest soon. She's so looking forward to seeing you".

Inspector Pot Belly strode into the sitting room and The Sergeant joined him shaking his head in the process, indicating that nothing unusual had been found in the study. At that moment Tanice, assuming all was well, opened the kitchen door and Dandelion released from his confinement, came bounding in. He stopped dead in front of Mr. Big. Looking this way and that as The Policemen backed away, Dandi raced round the assembled gathering barking with excitement. Pandora tried to catch him but he skittered away into the dining

287

room.

"Tanice, catch that wretched dog will you. The gentleman are just leaving".

As they were all gathered in the hall, a weak voice was heard from the top of the stairs.

"Is everything alright?"

Dandi hearing his mistress' voice came racing from the dining room with a long pink object in his mouth. He skidded to a halt, dropped the object in front of Mr. Big and looked up with imploring brown eyes, his pink tongue slobbering on the hall floor. The Dildo had arrived. You could have heard the ping of a tart's pantie elastic.

Everything happened at once. Lady Pamela, on high, forgot her doddery persona and screeched,

"DANDI.COME UPSTAIRS IMMEDIATELY".

Pandora laughed uproariously. "My aunt thought it was a doggy toy. Her eyesight's not what it was", and she opened the front door.

The policemen looked first at the offending sex toy and then at Pandora. Breezily she said,

"I don't think it's an offence, Inspector, for a dildo to be in a dog's mouth... "And giving a fond gaze to Mr. Big out of her deep blue eyes, she continued, "Is it Darling?"

He smiled at her and shook his head.

The policemen stood on the top step and Pot Belly eyeballed Mr. Big and gave a parting shot. "Be very careful Sir. In your profession it would not be to your advantage to be caught out. Wouldn't like to see your face splashed all over the news of the screws."

And with that the policemen marched off down the road.

Later while driving back to base, Inspector Pot Belly, his eyes full of malice, snapped.

288

"If Pandora's not a prostitute, I'll eat my hat...fiancé. Huh. The bloke's married with 2 kids. He's a prominent QC. Bloody idiot." He snorted and added, "That Dildo... a dog's toy...My arse. Something's been going on in that house. I can smell it".

Back at Casa Blanca, the guilty quartet were roaring with laughter and congratulating each other on getting through the grueling visit with their facade still intact. Lady Pamela sent Tanice down to the wine storage area to bring back a couple of bottles of the best Krug. This called for a celebration. Pandora sent Tony a text saying that everything had gone according to plan, well almost everything and asked him to come round and join the celebrations.

Mr. Big, now unmasked as Patrick Partington QC, made a few phone calls in order to clear his schedule for the rest of the day. He then suggested that Casa Blanca should close down for good. In any event he would not be able to return. Pandora looked at him.

"I'll miss you Mr. Big".

"And I'll miss you my naughty little Mathilda".

He sat down close to her on the sofa and took her hand. "Now tell me your real name".

"Do I have to?"

"I insist".

Pandora then had to admit that she was christened Tracy and that her surname was Crapper. Patrick raised an eyebrow. "You're not serious".

"Yes. Indeed. Tracy Crapper. I'm descended from the man who invented the ballcock. It is thought that Thomas Crapper invented the flush toilet. He didn't, but he did improve it and it has become an essential item in every household round the world."

Lady Pamela piped up,

"And after all the crap we've managed to shovel at the

289

police, we all deserve a drink".

Tony arrived after closing the shop for the night to find Lady Pamela pissed as a newt alternately hiccupping and laughing. Tanice was dancing a Caribbean Jig with Dandi leaping alongside her and Patrick and Pandora were making out on the sofa. The remnants of a pizza feast were strewn all over the sitting room. Casa Blanca, already a den of iniquity, was now transformed into a drunken student squat. They all tried to tell Tony what had happened and Patrick having been introduced informed him gleefully that he was "an accessary after the fact" but as the police would never suspect a bookshop owner's basement to be full of BDSM paraphernalia, perhaps he could set up an alternative venue for Patrick and Pandora to conduct their practices. Tony looked horrified and then realized Patrick Partington QC had made a joke.

When Tanice disappeared quickly to The Butler's Pantry to throw up it was decided to conclude the party and take tipsy Lady Pamela up the stairs to her room to sober up. She protested,

"Nooo Noo. I'm fine. Lez havenother lickle drinkee..." Then swinging around her glass of champagne she watered the carpet and shouted, "Fuuuuck the fuuuuzz".

Tony and Pandora helped the giggling old girl up the stairs with Tony pulling gently on her arm and Pandora pushing her tweed backside. They laid her gently on the bed and by the time they had unlaced her shoes and removed them she was fast asleep, snoring slightly with her mouth open.

With Tanice now prostrate on the sofa and Dandi slumped beside her, Tony Patrick and Pandora cleared away the debris and washed the glasses. Tony, not wanting to play gooseberry, decided to leave the two

290

love birds to their unfinished business whatever form that might take. Just as he was leaving he said,

"Pandora, I wanted to ask you about Laura. I'm crazy about her but I might scare her off if I jump in now and tell her how I feel. Do you think I should allow her some space...after the business with Mr. Darcy? She's told him the marriage is over."

Pandora kissed him on the cheek. "You go for it Tony. Don't wait. Too many people wait and miss golden opportunities".

Patrick chipped in. "Carpe Diem. Seize the day. I'm going to". And he hugged Pandora to him.

What Pandora did not know was the fact that Patrick Partington QC was locked in a sex-less marriage and that his background, public school and The City had honed a very rigid upper lip. His father a fierce History teacher and a disciplinarian had caned any tears out of him and public school had forced him to grow an impenetrable shell to protect his feelings. His family also taught him the importance in their eyes of keeping a respectable exterior with all emotions under control; to show an acceptable face to the outside world. As a result his inner life was in turmoil and his fortnightly session with Pandora allowed him a safety valve. She had no idea he was falling hopelessly in love with her.

While Tony was walking back to his flat above the shop and trying to decide whether or not to throw caution to the winds and go down to Kingbridge in pursuit of his fair lady, another lady, versed in the art of dark seduction looked at the man standing next to her and realized their triumph in duping the police called for some clitoral stimulation. Pandora took Patrick's hand and led him upstairs to her Vegas love nest. In the privacy of the bedroom they could devour one another without fear of interruption. Now on equal terms, they stood together looking into each other's eyes. Mr. Big encircled Pandora's waist and whispered.

"Miss Crapper, may I take you to bed?"

Without answering she laid her arms around his neck and kissed him gently on the mouth. He pulled her closer and began to release his passion on her mouth, his tongue finding hers while his hands roamed over her backside. She undid the buttons on his shirt and started feeling his muscled torso. While their lips were still locked together, her hands moved down to undo his belt and caress his aroused penis; he was pulling up her skirt round her thighs with one hand and cupping her breast with the other. Laughing together and in no time at all, they were stripped and on the bed. Pandora's luxurious curls fell over his chest as she straddled him, teasing his cock as she rubbed her clitoris up and down over his shaft. He begged to enter her but she shook her head and grinned, saying softly,

"Look up".

He did, and saw their beautiful writhing bodies reflected in the mirror. He lifted himself to meet her golden breasts and as he took a nipple in his mouth and gently flicked and rolled it with his tongue, she moaned softly and placed him inside her.

With her powerful thighs alongside his hips she slowly rode his magnificence. Bending forward, she place her hands on his shoulders and as they looked into each other's eyes, they came together in one rolling shattering climax.

He said three words.

"I love you".

She took a quick intake of breath and lay full length on top of him, turning her face away to hide her tears. After all the tension of the day culminating in this passionate encounter, her body released a torrent of emotion. He said nothing but turned her sideways and held her close until her shuddering had stopped.

Tracy knew then she could not go back to being Pandora. Her old life was over. Mr. Big loved her. Patrick said he loved her and like a fool she had cried. For the first time they were on equal terms and this had resulted in her losing her mask; her mask of protection. This was not play-acting anymore this was real; scarily, wonderfully real and it frightened the living daylights out of her.

For what of life now? What could she do, now she was back to being a real person again?

They lay together quiet in each other's arms as the mirror reflected their intimacy.

The deep pink walls seemed to cocoon their love and as she reflected on all that had happened Tracy knew she loved Patrick and nothing would ever be the same again.

CHAPTER 20

Laura made the decision not to contact Tony until her life had some semblance of order. She had been to see a lawyer and had wisely determined that the Manning family lawyer, an old school friend of David's whom he was consulting, might not give advice in her best interests. She found someone through one of her design friends and he proved to be very helpful.

The biggest hurdle for her was Pippin Cottage. The lawyer had reassured her that as Juliet had two years left of her schooling and needed to be in a stable environment along with her mother, the sale of the property could be deferred for that time but Laura knew eventually the cottage would have to be sold. In light of the fact that she was unable to buy David out and he, having said as much, would refuse to buy her out, the cottage and her beloved garden would have to go on the market eventually. In any case if David decided to sit tight, stating that he had equal responsibilities where Juliet was concerned, Laura would have to bear two years of living with a cold shoulder alongside her. That would be intolerable.

The lawyer had put her mind at rest over the business. As she had contributed by organizing the interior design side for most of her married life she would be entitled to part of the value of the business and also its future revenue. She knew David would be most unhappy about this but needs must. She had to live on something. She planned to put the word out among her design contacts that she was looking for new opportunities.

To ease the domestic situation she told Juliet that they, just the two of them plus Juliet's friend Diana, would be off to Woolacombe the following week. Ten days by the sea at her father's retirement cottage near the beach in

Devon would replenish her energy and give her time to think. Juliet was disappointed that her father was not going to come with them.

Laura's father Joseph Redman, a retired printer known as Rusty, was looking forward to seeing his daughter and grand-daughter and was hoping to talk some sense into Laura. He was sure that after a break from one another, she and David would both see that patching up their relationship and getting back together for the sake of Juliet at least, would be the most sensible thing to do. When Laura told him of the split, he glossed over the news,

"We all have our tiffs Laura. Your mother and I had several but we always kissed and made up".

Laura knew this was patently untrue. Her mother had stoically endured his argumentative nature but eventually left the marriage after twenty five years and then had sadly succumbed to cancer. Laura wished she could confide in her mother now. She would understand. In childhood, if anything unpleasant came up, her father would ride rough-shod over everyone's sensibilities and loudly declare that he had no idea what all the fuss was about and say something like.

"What you need is a brisk hill walk my girl".

It was a standing joke in the Redman family and she and her brother Chris, who could mimic him mercilessly, would collapse in a fit of giggles when he said the inevitable.

Now in his late seventies, he had mellowed considerably. He enjoyed pottering about in his garden shed and still made wooden toys for the local children's charity. Dear Dad she loved him dearly and she knew how much Juliet meant to him. Reflecting on the holiday ahead she mused that perhaps a couple of hill walks might do them all good. Dear God she was turning into

295

her father.

Cindy, blooming beautifully with pregnancy, dropped in almost every day following the announcement and in her usual over-helpful manner brought home-made cakes, biscuits and on one occasion a beef casserole. Laura wondered what it was that made people press food on the emotionally troubled. Cindy wanted to comfort and it was her way of doing it. In times of trouble Cindy ate for solace and she assumed everyone else did the same. Juliet happily enjoyed the home-baking but Laura, her stomach tight with nerves, could not. She thanked Cindy and said gently that Cindy's company was all that was required.

Laura and David passed by each other like people on a station platform travelling to different destinations, each with their own baggage and preoccupied with appointments and cell phones to check. Meals were taken mainly in silence with a few frosty enquiries made from time to time. Juliet ate her dinner in front of the TV with the sound increased as if she couldn't bear to hear the silence that pervaded the space between her parents' thoughts. Their connection had been severed and soon Juliet's security and the assurance of their joint love for her would change from a tight triangle to the length of a piece of string with her caught in the middle. She would be pulled this way and that. She was scared; this domestic crisis was wounding her heart. In the process she would come of age and become a woman.

Edward now recovering back at his London flat and refusing to see anyone could not believe that someone could inflict such vicious wounds to his face. When he had been told by the doctors that he had twenty stitches in his cheeks and that he was lucky to be alive, he morosely answered that he wished he were dead.

The Hospital staff had gone into a huddle and he was persuaded by an attractive young drug and alcohol counsellor that he should go into Rehab and have some counselling for depression. He hated the idea but after a couple of phone calls to his most sensible friend from school days he was persuaded to go into the country, three hours from the bright lights of London for a two month stay at a private facility paid for by his long-suffering mother. She could not believe that her darling son had turned into an alcoholic drug user and had been beaten up as a result. Who on earth could have done such a terrible thing?

The Colonel kept very quiet during these negotiations and even though he had the odd guilty thought about what had happened to his nephew, he did nothing to assist other than being a listening ear for his sister, Amanda. His sole contribution was a terse phone call to Edward,

"Sorry about your predicament. Rehab will sort you out. Get that crap out of your system. Stiff upper lip and all that", and then rang off abruptly. As Edward's lip was still swollen from the beating, this comment was deemed as singularly unhelpful.

The Colonel chose to forget all about his instigation of the attack and in his mind he was stubbornly convinced that Edward would recover, dry out and become a fully-fledged contributing member of the human race. The matter of Casa Blanca had been playing on his mind and even though he knew he had perpetuated a cowardly act by throwing his cell phone into the river and severing ties with The Old Girl, he was terrified of being exposed in The Daily Express with the description under his photograph stating,

"Colonel Henry Dunwoodie, the business partner of Lady Pamela Spencer-Brown and co-owner of Casa

Blanca a high-class Chelsea escort agency, on his way to court".

More to the point he was terrified of having to share a cell with the equivalent of Buzz Cut.

After the party Lady Pamela had awoken in the middle of the night and thought she was dead in her coffin dressed in some hideously baggy tweed skirt and an ancient grey woolly thing. Who had put her in these ugly clothes? As she raised her head from the pillow a sharp knife appeared to pierce her head and she yelled out. She raised herself slowly from the bed and holding her pounding head staggered to the bathroom where she peed and skulled down 3 glasses of water. She looked around for Dandi but his bed was empty. That was odd, where was he and what on earth had happened to give her such a terrible hangover? The fog of incomprehension slowly lifted and she began to remember the events of the night before. The police, Patrick Partington QC, Dandi and the dildo and then Pandora saving the day. She stripped off the offending costume and lay back and fell almost immediately into a restorative stupor. It would all become crystal clear in the morning.

Tanice awoke at the sound of a bark. In her dream the noise turned itself into the bark of a vicious Alsatian dog on the end of a policeman. She sat up with a start and wished she hadn't. She thought her head was about to explode. Dandi was desperate to go out and had jumped on the end of the sofa and was alerting her to the fact that a dump was imminent. She rocked into a sitting position and then levering herself onto her feet she staggered across the sitting room to the hall and let him out into the back garden by way of MadamPam's study.

Listening at the bottom of stairs for any sign of life,

298

she could hear nothing. She wondered if Pandora and her lover were still here and if MadamPam had expired in her drunken excess during the night. Dandi came back in looking mightily relieved and stood in the kitchen with his mouth ajar waiting for breakfast. She made herself a strong cup of coffee and fed him his biscuits. Reviewing the previous day, she marveled at Pandora's ability to avert disaster and chuckled as she remembered the look on The Inspector's face when Dandi had bounded in, a dildo between his teeth. Pandora had saved the day and that Mr. Big was a bit of alright. She just wished she hadn't drunk so much. Two large brandies on top of Champagne had finished her off. MadamPam would be in a shocking state and she was not relishing being on the end of her bad temper. Tanice began to prepare breakfast.

Upstairs Lady Pamela was stirring. After a refreshing shower she inspected her face in the mirror and was alarmed to see a ghostly apparition with flat damp hair staring back. The dark circles under her eyes gave her the appearance of an aged alcoholic. Being normally a light drinker she had spectacularly overdone it. She made her way gingerly to the kitchen and beheld Tanice slumped at the table with two hands round a cup of black coffee. Tanice began to get up.

"No need. You look as bad as I feel" And she asked, "Do we have any bacon and eggs?"

Tanice nodded glumly.

They sat together in silence at the kitchen table and ascertaining that they were alone, both consumed a large greasy breakfast with Dandi hoping that a piece of bacon might fall from a careless fork for his delectation. He was unlucky.

Tanice was just placing more toast on the kitchen table when there was a loud knocking at the front door.

Lady Pamela nearly choked on her last piece of bacon and giving Tanice a terrified look, said quietly,

"Don't answer".

Tanice was already backed against the pantry door, her eyes wide with fright. Had Inspector Pot Belly returned?

After a moment MadamPam got up and peeked cautiously through the kitchen window. She could see no-one. The reason no-one was visible was because 'Arry was kneeling on the front step and pushing open the letter box flap. He shouted through the aperture,

"Anyone 'ome? Yer Ladyship are you awright? Hintercom's on the blink". It's 'Arry Yer Ladyship".

Lady Pamela had completely forgotten she had asked Harry to call round to assess the wiring. His comments about her plugs being 'feather plucked' and therefore a 'fire 'azard' had played on her mind and now here he was frightening she and Tanice to death by banging on the front door and having them believe that The Old Bill was making a second visit.

"Tanice please let him in and put him in the study".
Lady Pamela drank the last of her coffee gave a gentle burp and went through to deal with Harry.

After Harry's inspection it was determined that 32 Davenport Gardens needed to be completely re-wired.

As he trouped behind Her Ladyship through the Butler's Pantry and down to the basement to inspect the ancient switch board and the defunct bell system, he remarked,

"Corker party Yer Ladyship, got rat arsed and don't remember a bleedin' fing,… scuse my French...'aving anuver party any time soon?"

They entered the basement and gazing round the empty space he jokingly said, "'Oo's 'ad a tidy up then?" And continued in a sly tone, "Visit from The Old

300

Bill was it?"

She looked at him keenly. "What do you think?" And turned on her heel.

'Arry did not need wizardry skills to work out that the business had gone tits up and in an 'urry too. He was disappointed not to see the lovely Pandora. He did so admire big knockers. On his return upstairs he popped his head into the kitchen, sniffed and said to Tanice who was washing up,

"Any chance of a bacon sarnie?"

"Chance'd be a fine ting" came the reply.

He tipped Tanice a wink and went back into the study to work out the cost of sorting out her ladyship's electricity. Lady Pamela knew it would be extremely expensive and Harry told her that she would also have to redecorate completely as the whole house needed extensive upgrading and this would mean damage to the walls and ceilings. She silently cursed that The Colonel, that bastard, was not around to consult. She knew she could afford it but the intrusion of workmen possibly for weeks would send not only Dandi demented but she and Tanice as well. She decided to delay a little in order to give her some breathing space; so much had happened. She needed to sober up and take stock of her life and decide where to from here.

'Arry did not have good news.

"Its 'orrible Yer Ladyship.'uge job. Don't fink I can do it by misself."

Lady Pamela's face fell. "What am I to do?

"I'll ask about and get back to you," then he asked cheerily, "No chance of a brew then?"

When the answer was not forthcoming he said as an afterthought,

"I could take that mirror down if yer like". And he pointed his finger up the stairs.

Lady Pamela let him out and yes perhaps the mirror could come down. He whistled his way to his van, all the while thinking that it was a rotten shame that the old lady had been forced to shut up shop sharpish-like. She'd been good to 'im and he wanted to see her awright. He'd done lots of work for her over the years and she'd always treated him fairly and paid up pronto too. It took balls to run a Hescort Hagency among all them Chelsea toffs. She'd fooled 'em all and that took guts. The old dear had looked done in this mornin'. He resolved to help her get the house back in good condition.

After Harry left, Lady Pamela went into the study and tried yet again to get hold of The Colonel. She was extremely annoyed that his number had become unobtainable. Where was he? She deduced from his silence that he had gone to ground or in the vernacular,

"Done a runner and left her holding the dildo".

She had been badly let down by his cowardly behavior. And what of poor Edward? That this once dear boy had led to their downfall and in the process had almost got himself killed, filled her with alarm. She had no idea where he was or in what state he was in. The Colonel should have kept her informed. He was a man with no regard for anyone but himself and now he had disappeared. She was almost certain that Henry would have run back to his sister Amanda and holed up in her country house. When her strength returned she would have it out with him.

Her second call was to Tony to say thank you for being on the spot with regard to storing the grisly evidence and would he mind hanging onto it for the time being until she could organize to have it removed. He was happy to oblige and then said.

"I'd like to be in touch with Laura. I've tried texting

302

but no response. She's in the middle of a hideous marriage split and I'm very worried about her. Do you have an address?"

Lady Pamela informed him that she lived in Kingbridge and her husband ran a renovation business near Twickenham but she didn't have an address. She wished him good luck and rang off. His enquiry about Laura put her in mind that she too would like to contact Laura and apologize for that appalling evening. Her third call, a nervous one, was to Laura.

A young voice answered. "Hi, this is Mum's phone".

Lady Pamela paused a moment and tried to remember Laura's daughter's name. She failed.

"Oh ...May I speak to Laura please?

"Just get her" and a distant shout was heard. "Muuum...Phone."

Laura then spoke and not recognizing the number said, "Laura Manning speaking."

"Hello Laura .It's Pamela. Please don't hang up. Just hear me out...please".

Lady Pamela could hear deep breathing at the other end of the line. She continued,

"Firstly I am so sorry that Mr. Darcy turned out to be your husband and also that you found out in such an appalling way what goes on ...or what did go on in Casa Blanca".

At that point Laura interrupted,

"Stop. I can't talk to you now, it's not convenient and in any case I'm going away next week".

She was about to hang up when something Lady Pamela said made her stay on the line.

"Please please accept my apologies."

Lady Pamela then implored her to come to lunch the following day to which Laura said she was unable. The old lady pressed her further and asked if they could meet

303

for a cup of tea. Reluctantly Laura agreed to come for a brief visit in two days' time. Lady Pamela rang off and began to plan a special something for Laura to make amends. While she was planning she thought of Tony and how desperate he was to see Laura. She knew it would improve the atmosphere for everyone if he was present. She called him back.

CHAPTER 21

Back at The Manning Renovation Company, Mr. Gupta was proving to be even more elusive than usual; yet again behind with his payments. Cindy tried to charm him into parting with his money by phoning almost every day, but even the voluptuous Cindy, who even resorted against her better judgement to asking him to come and have a drink with Peter and herself after work, could not persuade him to drop by. After a while her calls went straight to voice mail until she hit the telephone brick wall - the unobtainable signal. Peter was beside himself with worry and David pre-occupied with his breakdown with Laura was no help at all.

Mr. Gupta's domestic situation was in turmoil. He had shifted his second wife Meena and their daughter Promila into a penthouse apartment in Knightsbridge while his mansion was being restored by David's company.

The trouble started when Meena's mother Hansa had arrived from Mumbai and insisted on staying and staying. She was a fat cantankerous character who looked more like an ugly duckling than the swan her name denoted. She was rude and demanding and one day after a flaming row with Mr. Gupta which culminated in her insulting his manhood, he gave her a bunch of fives and knocked out one of her front teeth.

Screeching, she grabbed the rolling pin and tried to beat him until Meena intervened and wrenched the instrument from her mother's hands. Her mother cried,

"Assault! He assaulted me".

Before they could stop her she locked herself in the bedroom and called the police.

A visit from the police was the last thing Mr. Gupta

wanted as his business interests would not stand up to close scrutiny. He threw two pairs of underpants and 3 shirts into a holdall and grabbing fistfuls of cash from the safe and scarpered before the police could get there. Along with a now toothless mother-in-law and a distraught wife, his troubles had magnified to include being followed by a couple of plain clothes policemen from the drug squad who had been investigating him for some time as the 'go-between' for drugs coming in from Pakistan and China. On the night of the rolling pin incident, knowing he was being shadowed, he donned one of Meena's saris, carefully secreted away in case of trouble, a coat and headscarf and by resembling his mother-in-law, he was able to elude the eyes of the agent lying in wait. He slipped away into the darkness and holed up in a seedy hotel in Soho.

His distribution network had been earning him hundreds of thousands of pounds and even though his Indian nature made him typically tight-fisted, he was busily laundering cash through the casino and into extensive building work on his mansion. The Manning Renovation Company had no idea they were being paid with dirty money and another rude shock awaited: - David and Peter were about to discover that Mr. Gupta had disappeared and was now on the run. Their most lucrative contract was heading for the toilet.

Laura was determined to get the Casa Blanca episode out of her life and the embarrassing incident of meeting up with David banished from her mind, so why she agreed to meet with Lady Pamela came as a troubling mystery. She nearly sent a text to cancel, but something, a niggling curiosity around this extraordinary woman and how she as someone of note had started this illegal enterprise, made her want to discover more. Laura accepted that it wasn't the old lady's fault that she,

Laura, had come face to face with her errant husband. That Lady Pamela had deceived her over the true reason behind Casa Blanca rankled like an insect bite. She blatantly threw this Caribbean party where all the guests, bar Laura, knew what lay behind the facade of 32 Davenport Gardens and were therefore complicit in its operation. She felt humiliated at having had to crawl away under the table. Ending up in the dungeon of sadistic doom had added insult to injury.

She made the mistake of telling Juliet that she was planning a trip to London, ostensibly to check on some interior design materials. Juliet insisted on coming with her. Laura tried to dissuade her but Juliet was adamant. She wanted to go to Knightsbridge and check out sale items at H and M and Zara department stores. It was agreed that Juliet would accompany Laura and be left for a couple of hours to browse the sales. Two days later they drove to Twickenham and took the train into London.

They parted at Earl's Court and made an arrangement to meet again two hours hence. Juliet was bubbling with excitement and keen to spend her holiday allowance on some new clothes for the Woolacombe holiday.

"Don't spend it all at once darling "said Laura as the tube doors were shutting.

Juliet waved and was gone.

Laura arrived at 32 Davenport gardens with a fluttering stomach. She pressed the intercom buzzer and nothing happened.

She tapped on the front door and Lady Pamela, looking less robust, her complexion pale, opened the door. Almost tearful at the sight of Laura, the old lady threw her arms around her astonished guest and drew her into the elegant sitting room .A tea tray was waiting on the coffee table.

Alarmed Laura counted three cups. Was The Colonel, a man now not to be trusted, going to be joining them? Her heart sank. There was no way she could endure sharing anything, especially any intimate secrets with a man whom she was sure was complicit in setting her up with Blue Eyes. She resolved to stay as short a time as politely possible. Lady Pamela called to Tanice who brought in a pot of tea and some ginger oat cakes. She smiled at Laura,

"Nice to see you again Miss".

Dandi followed her and plopped down at Laura's feet. She shifted slightly away from his dribble and commented,

"Dandi looks well".

"He's been through a lot...Haven't you my lovely boy".

Her hostess served the tea and before Laura could ask a question, Lady Pamela proceeded to pour out all her woes with regard to what had happened after the party. There was no stopping her. She started by apologizing profusely for the faux pas, for that is what she called it, and how horrified she was that Laura's evening had been ruined with the appearance of Mr. Darcy. She berated herself for allowing something like that to happen.

Laura tried to interrupt but the old lady was on a confessional role. She then apologized again for not telling Laura what went on behind closed doors at Casa Blanca. She followed on with the news of Edward's attack culminating in the Casa Blanca business card being found in his pocket and the visit from the police. Laura's eyes flew open when she heard this. There were so many questions she wanted answered but she let the old lady continue. Lady Pamela relayed how Pandora had saved the day and that Tony, "What a brick that man is", had collected all Pandora's paraphernalia and stored it in his basement. Laura felt she was turning into Alice in Wonderland and that the whole episode was becoming-

"Curiouser and curiouser".

The Colonel then came in for a tongue lashing.

"Disappeared. He was integral to the business but he's done a runner. What a coward. I have been betrayed, my dear", and then clutching her heart dramatically, "Betrayal. Such pain. It's a sword in my heart".

Laura nodded sympathetically and for the first time began to see the funny side of the situation. Envisaging The Colonel, with his pants down running for his life with the cops in hot pursuit, she hid a smile. Lady Pamela continued,

"You'll be wondering about the third party". She nodded at the tray.

"Tony will be dropping by. He doesn't know you're going to be here".

Slyly she gauged Laura's reaction. The dear girl visibly relaxed and gave her first full smile. A good decision had been made.

Lady Pamela badly wanted to make amends and this was one way to do so. She also planned to give Laura the sapphire and diamond necklace as a conciliatory gift.

Laura then asked the old lady about the history of Casa Blanca. Lady Pamela, keen to get off that subject asked,

"First of all, how are you dear?"

While Laura, now completely relaxed, was confiding in her hostess, Tanice let Tony in and he was standing at the door quietly observing and listening to his beloved Laura.

She suddenly realized he was there and got up suddenly. Lady Pamela looked from one to the other and she knew there and then that that these two had met their

309

match. She excused herself and taking the teapot, murmured that she would get some more hot water.

Tony approached slowly and held out his arms. She went straight to him and throwing her arms around his neck, they embraced. She touched his thick unruly curls and murmured,

"Captain No Hook. It's so good to see you".

He whispered her name. They kissed; a long lingering kiss. They sat together on the sofa and Tony took Laura's hand. Lady Pamela returned after a few minutes and smiling broadly said,

"Well I can see you two are pleased to see each other".

After that time rushed by. Laura realized it must be time to meet up with Juliet. In fact glancing worriedly at the mantle clock she was going to be late. Tony said he would accompany her to Sloane Square and as they were gathering themselves to leave, Lady Pamela suddenly said,

"Wait…Wait. I have forgotten something. I wanted to give you something Laura".

Laura, desperate to leave with Tony, was at the front door.

"I must go Lady Pamela. Thank you for the tea".

She smiled and kissed the old lady on the cheek. Before their hostess could stop them, Laura and her pirate were walking hand in hand down the street. Lady Pamela called out to their retreating backs.

"Please come back....Please. "

They turned and waved. She waved back and with a saddened countenance she softly closed the door.

The poignancy of seeing them together made her feel strangely alone. She had been looking forward to their visit and now it was over she wondered if she would ever see them again. After all that had happened, she had become fond of Laura and Tony and with no family nearby other than the employees of Casa Blanca now scattered by the winds of fate and her son so far away, she started to look upon them as surrogate children.

Her relationship with Tanice also underwent a subtle change. What with all the explosive events of the last week, nothing more had been mentioned by Tanice with regard to MadamPam taking over the plot of the Bodice Ripper. Tanice decided that having her employer assist with the book, assist and not takeover, could work to her advantage. She knew her spelling was atrocious and her grammar was not much better so having a well-educated turn of phrase would definitely improve her chances of publication.

Lady Pamela noted how loyal Tanice had been over many years of the operation. That she was still willing to come and work at Casa Blanca after all that had happened impressed the old lady; she did admire spunk and Tanice had a barrel-full.

Tanice was quite happy to work reduced hours; the lighter workload suited her aching back and legs. She was pleased too that her employer had begun to treat her with some respect, even sitting and sharing their lunchtimes together. MadamPam had stopped trying to impress as 'Lady of The House'; she took Tanice into her confidence; how could she not after what had occurred and now wanted to share her worries and fears. They were almost on an equal footing; at least when they were alone together. When people called - there were few since the demise of the business - Lady P and Tanice again became mistress and servant. One must keep up appearances.

Juliet had been waiting 25 minutes at Earl's Court tube station and was beginning to worry something had happened to her mother. Her texts had gone unanswered.

She was never late and would always send a text if she had been delayed. Just as Juliet started to phone she saw Laura come running down the stairs, her face flushed and her hair flying.

"Sorry darling. So sorry. I met someone I haven't seen for ages and we got talking."

She gave Juliet a hug and they clambered on the next train out to Waterloo. Juliet, carrying three bags, was full of what she had purchased:-Two bikinis, a short black and white summer shift dress, new sandals, T shirts and some jeans as well as a load of makeup. Laura normally one to discourage Juliet from buying too much enthused about the shopping haul. Filled with thoughts of Tony and what he was beginning to mean to her, she smiled lovingly at her daughter and knew that they would somehow get through the next difficult period of their lives. Seeing Tony had lifted her spirits and made her believe that perhaps there was a future for her after all.

After they left 32 Davenport Gardens, Tony and Laura walked hand in hand to the tube. He kept grinning at her and at one point pulled her into a clinch and kissed her. She tried to pull away.

"Tony. People will see."

"So? Let them". He kissed her again.

Breathless, she felt slightly giddy and having his strong presence alongside her made her heart beat a little faster. He was only half a head taller than her and they paced together in a comfortable stride as a light breeze fanned their faces. While walking they made plans to meet again and when Laura mentioned Woolacombe, Tony pressed her to allow him to visit her down in Devon. She resisted,

"Too soon Tony. My daughter is very fragile and my father…"She broke off for a moment and shook her head. "No I certainly don't want you to meet him...yet".

312

Tony backed off but knew he would be counting the days until they could meet again.

Lady Pamela was mentioned and Laura was still having trouble coming to grips with the whole Casa Blanca business; it seemed like a dream to her. Tony made the comment.

"Sly old bird. Blatantly flouting the law for years and under the noses of The Chelsea Set. For months when I was playing bridge there, I had no idea what was going on".

He then mentioned the odd phone calls. "Someone asked about coming in by the back door. In my innocence I thought it was because they wanted a private entry. Turns out they wanted anal sex".

Laura looked appalled and then burst out laughing. He hugged her to him.

"I am such an innocent Laura. Would you like to corrupt me?"

"Captain No Hook. You wicked pirate you."

And on the corner of Sloane Square in front of all the shoppers, they kissed passionately until a gentleman with an umbrella poked Tony in the thigh and said,

"Get a room. You're causing an obstruction".

Laughing they broke away and headed for Sloane Square tube. There was so much more to talk about but that would have to wait until their next meeting.

Encasing Laura in a bear hug Tony said, "I miss you already, my love. You must text me every day and call me when you can".

She took his dear face in her hands and looking into his soft brown eyes, kissed him.

"Goodbye my darling pirate".

She turned quickly and ran down the tube steps and was gone.

313

CHAPTER 22

The Colonel's conscience eventually got the better of him and he slipped back to his Chelsea flat under cover of darkness. The fact that Casa Blanca had blown up so dramatically, along with him possibly being implicated, made his worried mind play tricks. He had a horror of being followed; every black car or marked police car appeared to be shadowing him on the street in London and his nerves played havoc with his perception, turning every dark-suited man into a plain clothes police officer.

The fact that he had engineered the attack on Edward did not trouble his conscience to any extent. In his mind, what he did was for the good of the boy but being splashed all over The News of the Screws made his sphincter curl up like a baby hedgehog.

He decided to try and meet up with the Old Girl on one of her walks with Dandi. He knew her regular route and roughly what time she would pass by so one overcast afternoon he waited furtively around the corner from Casa Blanca. He was unlucky to start with as Tanice passed him by without noticing his presence although Dandi, smelling The Colonel's familiar musty Old Spice, pulled strongly towards where he was concealed. Tanice yanked the dog away and they lumbered off down the road. Eventually realizing that Tanice was taking over the afternoon dog walks, The Colonel bought a new cell phone and rang The Old Girl. A familiar screech greeted his name.

"Where the fuck have you been?"

There then followed a long aggressive scolding which at one point made him hold the phone away from his ear as a torrent of abuse came out of the other end. When the

314

screecher drew breath, he said quickly,

"Let me buy you a medicinal brandy. Taxi will be there in half and hour". And before The Old Girl could continue the bollocking, he hung up.

Lady Pamela crashed the phone down and stumped upstairs to change. Tanice had left for the day after preparing MadamPam's supper tray of home-made fish pie and mixed salad.

"No cream Tanice and no cheese in the sauce thank you".

Tanice had been told many times that her employer's stomach could not take dairy and that cheese sauce wreaked havoc on her insides. This made no sense to Tanice who knew that MadamPam was quite happy to pile cream onto her scone and jam. Perhaps that sort of cream was different; maybe cream in a sweet context was acceptable; it was Cornish clotted cream so perhaps that made it alright. In any case one did not argue or even discuss the merits of diet with the old lady. She had her ideas and she stuck to them. Tanice did as she was told where diet was concerned. The book was another matter and Tanice now resolved over her worry about a takeover was looking forward to turning it into a best seller with the help of her employer.

Lady Pamela was sitting in her favorite chair when the taxi arrived. She was dressed in her second best gold-braided beige Chanel suit with matching chain link handbag and low heeled cream pumps. She knew The Colonel would try hard to placate her to compensate for his shocking behavior, first with a cocktail at The Ritz Bar and then he would buy her a gourmet dinner at the hotel accompanied by the best champagne. After venting her spleen on the phone, she was looking forward to seeing him and her view of him had mellowed a little. She would allow him to cosset her but she would underline the fact that she had almost died from the stress of the situation. She planned her attack on his conscience,

"You nearly killed me Henry, my heart practically gave out with the stress".

She would make him feel guilty and then enthuse about how marvelous both Pandora and Tony had been in helping her out of the mire. Tanice too would come in for praise and the fact that he, The Colonel, had let her down, would be down-played but with a nasty barb in the tail, using such words as,

"I was betrayed Henry. I thought we were old friends. One does stand by one's friends, don't you think?"

She knew that this type of barbed approach would hit home far more deeply than telling him he was a "fucking loser". In any case The Ritz Manager would probably have them thrown out for bad language if she laid into him again.

After a prickly start their evening went well. After relaying the aftermath of the party - Henry was particularly amused at Inspector Pot Belly and the dildo incident - they had talked endlessly about Edward. The Colonel kept stressing that he felt that the attack was the best thing that could have happened to his nephew, the result being a spell in hospital where the doctors could assess him.

"Rehab for two months. Bit like a boot camp for addicts apparently. It'll make a man of him."

The Old Girl was particularly upset to hear that Edward's face would be permanently disfigured and asked what he would do, now his modelling career had gone down the gurgler.

"Lots of men were disfigured or worse, fighting for our country Old Girl, they all went back to honest work. Leave it to me. I'll sort him something. Out of London".

316

The Colonel still had the idea of persuading Edward that a spell in Australia out in the sun and fresh air would turn his life around. What The Old Boy did not know was that Edward had struck up a relationship with a buxom Australian nurse who was employed by the Rehab center. She was called Charlene and hailed from Perth on the West Coast. They were enjoying a vigorous love life in various locked rooms throughout the center including the linen closet. Clearing himself of booze and drugs was a hideous experience in the beginning but Charlene had stood by him and now she was lying on top of him quite frequently. Cleaning himself up had improved Edward's sex life no end, and his end was having a rip-roaring time.

At one point during dinner Henry asked,

"What on earth shall we do now Pamela?"

"Retire. That's what I'm going to do".

Then she added, "I'm writing a book".

He raised an eyebrow.

"Well it's not mine 'per se'. Tanice has written a fairly dreadful attempt at a Bonk Buster".

"A what?" Laughed The Colonel.

"A Bodice Ripper set in the Caribbean. It's ghastly but believe you me by the time I've finished with it, it'll be a best seller".

The Old Boy chortled. "I don't doubt it and knowing your expertise where bonking is concerned, it can't fail, my dear". He raised his glass to The Old Girl's new venture.

By the time the taxi dropped Lady Pamela home - they had been laughing together in the back- they were back to their old comradeship. She bid him goodbye at the door of Casa Blanca and kissed him on the cheek.

"Bridge next Sunday?"

He answered in the affirmative and then said, "I've

asked a couple of the Chelseas to make up a four".

They parted company. After kissing Dandi goodnight, she dropped her shoes at the bottom of the stairs and made her way wearily to bed.

Back at Kingbridge the weather forecast was ominous. Storm clouds were gathering in the heat of the early morning as Laura and Juliet prepared to leave for Devon.

David was home and was quite emotional in saying goodbye to his daughter as if he was not going to see her again.

He ignored Laura and even though he watched her heft their heavy cases into the car he did nothing to help. They had hardly spoken the day before and now on the morning of departure all he did was give Juliet a big hug and ask her to text or call regularly. Laura watched him from the driver's seat and knew she would have to find an answer to the unbearable tension pervading Pippin Cottage.

She knew David well and chillingly realized that he saw himself as the one to remain at the cottage and in so doing retain his daughter in her rightful place. For him moving out was not going to be an option. Despite what the lawyer had told her, she would have to be the first to make a physical break. Her nerves, stretched to the limit, could not withstand any more tightening.

Just as she was leaving she remembered with horror the computer and what their daughter might find while researching one of her school projects. She jumped out of the car saying to Juliet that she had forgotten something. David was looking at them through the study window when he saw Laura approach. That Laura had not mentioned the Indian porn sites with regard to Juliet had surprised him, so when he saw her approaching purposefully he guessed what was coming. He sat

318

behind the desk and pretended to sort papers.

Laura flung open the study door and giving him a cold hard stare said,

"David" He looked up but said nothing.

"Get that filth off the computer. NOW. Think of Juliet for once".

He raised his hand, "It's done." And started shuffling papers.

She glared at his impassive features and strode back to the car. Juliet had plugged in her music so was unaware of what had transpired. Laura resolved not to think about David and his disgusting habit and she turned to Juliet, saying

"Darling, let's work out a plan for Woolacombe."

Juliet nodded happily and they set off.

They drove South West in heavy cloud and sticky traffic laden conditions. When they got to Exeter, they met up with Diana and continued their slow journey to Woolacombe. Just as they passed the Woolacombe town sign the heavens opened.

August thunderstorms had been predicted and the weatherman highlighted that North Devon and Cornwall would be badly hit. On this occasion the forecast was accurate so Laura and the two girls were in for three days of torrential rain. Laura did not relish being cooped up with two bored teenagers and a father who would harangue her constantly either about the state of her marriage or the state of the nation. She gritted her teeth and prayed she could endure without cracking.

Rusty Redman greeted them effusively and presented them with a roast chicken with all the trimmings followed by a chocolate mousse made from Laura's mother's recipe. She was touched that he had remembered that it was his granddaughter's favorite meal. They ate heartily and crawled into bed. Dear Dad, he'd outdone himself in the kitchen; it was so good to see him despite what poor weather might bring.

In the following days, the four of them played endless card games while the girls checked their phones constantly which brought some sharp comments from Rusty. He dragged out a couple of 1,000 piece jigsaws which the girls initially reared away from in mock horror but once they all got started on them, the girls settled into a few hours of amusement.

Although Juliet's grandfather disapproved of daytime television, he relented on the third wet day and allowed the girls to watch their favorite shows. He had no computer in the house and Laura had forgotten the charger for her lap top.

Rusty held forth about technology. "Computers and stuff. Don't hold with the things...no use for'em".

Laura tried to escape his 'getting to the bottom of your marriage problem' talks by reading and resting in her room.

At least they could not go on one of her father's famous uphill tramps where he would extol the virtues of exercise to all and sundry passing by.

She did have a burst of creative cooking to fill the time and made a Victoria sponge cake which she filled with home-made plum jam from her pantry at Kingbridge. She also made some gingerbread biscuits getting the girls to cut out different shapes. They were amused at how babyish this was but enjoyed themselves trying to outdo one another with bizarre designs; a flying saucer made by Diana complete with a domed top windows and decorated with smarties for lights took the top prize. Everyone sighed with relief when the sun came out on the third day and the girls shot off to the beach at the first opportunity.

Tony sent numerous texts to Laura. She rang him late

at night when the house was asleep and filled a happy half hour on Face Time. They arranged to meet for lunch on her return. He suggested "Le Petit Jardin" but she, not wanting to be reminded of the knicker-less incident, said she would prefer a casual pub meal. They agreed to meet the following week at The Chelsea Potter in King's Road.

After she had spoken to Tony, she lay in the little attic bedroom at the top of the cottage and stared at the mottled ceiling and ancient flowery chintz curtains that her mother had made many moons ago. She could hear the rain softly pattering on the roof and the gurgle of the ancient guttering.

She thought of Tony; his eyes and warm smile and imagined them on the beach together, not windy Devon where one had to wear two jerseys in summer and run a mile to get to the sea at low tide, but a tropical island somewhere, with soft sand and a turquoise sea. This idyll was dispelled as she thought of what lay ahead, the enormity of disentangling an 18 year marriage.

The last few days passed happily with the sun shining. The girls disappeared and spent most of the time on the beach and enjoyed being ogled by the local Devon boys who showed off playing football in front of them. On the last full day Rusty commandeered everyone after breakfast and said they were all going on a walk.

"Good healthy walk to Croyde. It's not far."

The girls were aghast and protested but Rusty was adamant. Laura was ruefully resigned to the inevitable. Her father's belief in a stiff walk to clear all troubles. With the girls grumbling behind her, she went to put on her trainers. They set off in bright sunshine and the girls quickly forgot their complaints and set off to Baggy Point and from there to Croyde. There was a distinct increase in their enjoyment when two young men in their twenties ran past and nearly cannoned into each other as they turned round to take a gander at the shapely long legs they had just passed.

Rusty tried again to reassure Laura that all would be well on her return, she acquiesced quietly. She knew there was no use discussing the situation. Assuming she had agreed with him he smiled and nodded at her and then strode ahead to the girls.

"Treat you all to a Cream Tea at the Sandleigh Tea Rooms".

That idea was greeted enthusiastically and the trio strode ahead of Laura in anticipation of a good feed the other end. Laura watched them and despite the rainy week she was pleased that Juliet was chatting and laughing with her grandfather and that they were enjoying some quality time together. She put from her mind what might happen in the next few weeks.

When Laura piled everything back into the car on the morning of their departure, her father took her aside and said how much he'd enjoyed seeing Juliet and her too and could they please not leave it too long before coming back down to the coast. Dear dad, he was lonely; what he needed was a new woman in his life. His parting words were,

"Don't worry Laura. It'll blow over. David will have had a rest from you and vice versa. Just kiss and make up."

As Laura waved goodbye she knew that making up with David was the last thing she wanted.

To pass the time while Laura was away, Tony busied himself with clearing out the grisly paraphernalia in the basement. As Lady Pamela had not been forthcoming on what she wanted done with the stuff and the landlord, a retired banker, was due to make his yearly visit, time

322

again was of the essence. Something had to be done.

While flicking through a gardening magazine one evening and thinking how lovely Laura would look wearing nothing but peonies, he came upon the idea of re-cycling the BDSM gear at his allotment. The ghastly torture rack would make an excellent climbing frame for the new variety of beans he was planning. He had a brainwave with regard to the old gym horse. He would give it to the children's play area. They could paint a dinosaur on the side. Pandora's Box with its tin interior and lid would turn itself into a two compartment compost bin. He would make a few aeration holes in the bottom and place it on some old bricks. It would look quite splendid with its carved wooden dragon design and be practical too.

The rest of the weaponry he would dispose of discreetly at the rubbish tip although the paddles might come in useful for a children's boating game on the allotment pond. He had a sudden thought about the handcuffs. They would come in very useful when that insufferable bore Lenny followed him round the garden with his drone-like monologue on the merits of differing soil types. He would take him down to the children's play area and handcuff him to the climbing frame.

Tony rang the garage and booked himself a trailer for the morning.

Meanwhile back in Chelsea, Pandora made a surprise visit to 32 Davenport Gardens. She had meant to phone first but finding herself in the vicinity decided to call by instead. It was nearing lunchtime. Tanice and her employer were sitting with heads together at the kitchen table, pouring over the Bonk Buster and trying to decide how and where the Frenchman would have his first encounter with the sex-crazed Delphine.

There was a knock on the door. Tanice as usual

jumped to attention fearful of who it might be. Lady Pamela went to the hall and said imperiously through the door,

"Who is it? If you're selling something we don't want it".

When Pandora announced her name, the door was flung open and Lady P greeted her favorite filly with great enthusiasm.

"We've been wondering how you are, haven't we Tanice?"

Tanice came rushing over and gave Pandora a big hug. Lady P then invited their guest to stay for lunch and the three of them sat at the kitchen table. They plied Pandora with questions while enjoying a piece of Tanice's leek and tomato flan. Lady P remarked at how well Pandora looked; retirement must be suiting her. Pandora laughed,

"Retirement? I'm working harder than ever",

She then proceeded to tell them that Patrick Partington QC had set her up her with her mother Dot in a fancy lingerie shop catering for more kinky tastes. They had a backroom full of Dominatrix gear and had never been busier. On top of running the shop, Pandora was giving lessons to fledgling BDSM artists. Patrick dropped by regularly and they were able to continue their titillating sessions, in private, after hours.

"Never a dull moment Lady P".

Lady P filled Pandora in on what had come to pass since the demise of Casa Blanca, noting especially her displeasure at The Colonel's disappearance during their hour of need.

"Turned up eventually, like a bad penny. The bastard."

Pandora gleefully announced that Mr. Big had not only set her up in a business but moved the whole family to a lovely three bedroom maisonette in Pimlico. Due to their elevated status, Dot Crapper had started elocution lessons and her grandson Ethan was already talking about wanting to be a lawyer when he grew up.

"Wonderful news Pandora. I'm so pleased for you".

Pandora then asked after Tanice's welfare and they both began to talk about their new project:-The book. Pandora suppressed a smile as she thought of the change of circumstances for both of them. Writing a book together? What an extraordinary enterprise for these two people from opposite ends of the social spectrum, especially in light of their relationship.

It looked now as though they were good friends and Tanice appeared to have the upper hand for a change, saying proudly,

"It my book. MadamPam is assisting ME now."

Lady P smiled indulgently and parried, "It is indeed Tanice. You're in charge of the plot and I am in charge of the spelling and grammar. We have a masterpiece on her hands".

They grinned at each other.

Pandora marveled that the closing of Lady P's illicit enterprise had brought them closer together and started a new project for them both. Tanice asked about Nefertiti and Pandora filled them both in with regard to Nef's new life. As old habits die hard, Nef had joined another escort business and worked part-time there while trying to kick-start a modelling career. She had asked Mr. Gupta to help her by introducing her to some of his contacts but after talking initially to him, it now became apparent that he had disappeared. Lady Pamela commented,

"Always was a bit sleazy wasn't he? Probably on the run from the law".

Then she laughed and said, "There but for the grace of

God".

She asked Pandora for Nef's contact phone number as she was sure there was some favor she could do the dear girl. She reiterated how helping people was something she was very good at. One thing Lady Pamela had maintained over the years was an impressive list of people of influence and there would be someone on that list from whom a favor could be extracted.

They chatted on for another hour until Pandora got up to leave.

"Wait Pandora, I have something to give you".

The old lady went up the stairs and into her bedroom while Pandora waited in the hall.

She removed the sapphire and diamond necklace from the jewelry box and inspecting it closely put it on the dressing table while she searched for a container. Not finding something suitable she took one of her brightly colored scarves and laying it out on the bed, she placed the necklace in the middle. She hesitated a moment thinking of Laura but then decided that Pandora had done so much for her that she deserved to have something special to thank her for all the help she had given over the last few weeks. She wrapped the necklace carefully and went downstairs. Pandora was overwhelmed to see the gift and gave Lady P a big hug.

"Oh-it's lovely...Thank you so much".

Pandora felt quite tearful saying goodbye to Lady P. How sweet of the old girl to part with such a beautiful necklace and for her to be the recipient of it too. She took her leave, again enthusing over the lovely gift and promised to keep in touch.

CHAPTER 23

Laura was expecting a frosty reception back at Pippin Cottage. Driving back to Kingbridge she had a text from Cindy saying that Mr. Gupta had disappeared. They had tried in vain to get hold of him. The business was looking distinctly wobbly. She knew that David and Peter had a few small jobs on the go but The Gupta job had been their big coup and now it looked as if the whole contract was about to go down the toilet. The Manning Renovation Company would be left owing thousands to sub-contractors and suppliers. She did not relish the atmosphere at home with David now struggling to sort out this business disaster as well as avoiding contact with her whenever possible.

After she and Juliet unpacked the car they went inside to find David nowhere to be found. His car was not in the drive. She tried texting and got no reply. Juliet then tried on her cell and he did answer saying he was just leaving Chelsea and would be home within the hour.

What Laura did not know was that David, not being able to contact Casa Blanca by phone, had driven into Chelsea and had knocked on the door of 32 Davenport Gardens in the hope of contacting Nefertiti. He received no reply. Lady Pamela was having her afternoon nap, something she had started after the business folded and Tanice had taken Dandi out for his afternoon constitutional. He hung around outside for a while and then decided to put a note through the letter box. It read,

> *Darling Star,*
> *I am missing you so terribly. Please call me on this number.*
> *Your Mr Darcy.*

Then rashly he wrote.

Your caramel breasts are haunting my dreams.

He scribbled his cell number down and searched for an envelope. Finding none, he folded the paper in half and stuffed it through the letterbox.

When Lady Pamela awoke from her nap, she went downstairs to make a cup of tea. Tanice had left for the day and Dandi was sitting expectantly on his bed in the kitchen.

On the kitchen table a piece of paper fluttered. She inspected it and read David's words. Harrumphing to herself, she called the number. It went to voice mail. Speaking clearly she said,

"Mr. Darcy. Do not ever call again at my premises. If you do I shall call the police. What you did to Laura was unspeakable and if I had my way I'd have you horse-whipped."

David in a South London pub picked up the message later that evening after a tense phone call with his lawyer. Everything was collapsing around his ears. He chucked the phone onto the pub table and clasped his head in his hands. Not being able to contact Nefertiti was the final blow.

Juliet, wanting to tell her father all about the holiday, waited up 'til 11 o'clock but in the end fell asleep on the sofa. She awoke when David arrived back smelling of booze in the early hours and crashed through the front door. He saw her raised head and said a perfunctory,

"Sorry", and staggered up to bed.

Overnight Laura, in the spare room, made plans to move out. It was now the only thing she could do. Being away made her see on returning that her current situation was untenable.

There had been no obvious moment to talk to Juliet while they were both in Woolacombe and in any case Laura did not want to ruin Juliet's holiday.

328

The big question of where she should move to was a taxing one. She had to get away from Kingbridge. Cindy, being her usual kind self, had begged Laura to come and stay for a while to allow things to cool but Laura knew a clean break was required. Being anywhere near David was not an option even though it wrenched her heart to leave her daughter at Pippin Cottage. She also felt certain that Juliet would want to stay with David; their bond was very strong. Once she told Tony of her plans he would insist she move in with him; that would be the easiest option but Laura was not ready for another full-blown relationship. She needed breathing space. In any case she was sure David and Juliet would think she had started an affair with Tony well before the marriage split. She contemplated calling some married friends in Fulham but they had a house full of children and couldn't fit her in.

She resolved first of all to sit Juliet down and explain to her that the move Laura was about to make was a temporary one and in the long term Juliet, if she chose, could come and live with her; but where? That was the question.

Although she already knew the reply, She sent Tony a text.

> *Darling Pirate. I'm all alone in the spare room. Unbearable here. Have decided to move out. Any ideas?*

Immediately a text shot back.

> *My Love, my bed (clean!) awaits you darling. Please come to me...please please.*

She sighed and replied

> *Tony sweet Tony.I can't .Too soon. Must find somewhere where my daughter can visit.*

There was a pause after this and then Tony sent another message.

329

What about Casa Blanca? Plenty of empty rooms. The beds may be well used! Lady P would love to look after you and I can visit. Shall I call her?

Casa Blanca. How ironic thought Laura but turning the idea over in her mind, a definite possibility. She had been adamant about not setting foot in that place but having the conciliatory meeting with the old lady had changed her view.

She could have her own room and there would be plenty of other bedrooms to accommodate Juliet when she came to stay. Would Lady Pamela be happy for them both to be there? She had no idea for how long. She laughed to herself at the thought of ending up in a defunct knocking shop.

She sent through a text to Tony asking him to sound out Lady P. He replied saying he would text her in the morning, finishing the message with lots of hugs and kisses.

Lady Pamela couldn't be more pleased to welcome dear Laura into her home and Juliet could be accommodated at any time.

When she told Tanice the news, she was fluttering with excitement and gave instructions for the bed in the Chinese room to be made up with the best linen. The old lady did not think that Laura would appreciate being put up in the Egyptian room where her husband had been pussy-whipped by Nefertiti.

She ordered some flowers and made sure the pantry was well-stocked with delicacies from Fortnum's. She then sent Tanice out with a shopping list to Harrods' Food Hall and asked her to buy the best fillet steak.

"The child needs iron. She's too pale. We need to fortify her for the weeks ahead".

Tanice thought to herself that fortify was a bit over the

330

top; it wasn't a battle. She kept her own counsel and set off to buy provisions to nourish Miss Laura.

Juliet was very quiet when Laura sat her down and told her what was going to happen. David hovered in the kitchen but did not interrupt their conversation. Juliet burst into tears and ran upstairs to her room. David poked his head round the sitting room door and said,

"Now look what you've done."

What followed was a raging torrent of abuse on both sides. David accused her of causing their daughter even more grief by leaving Pippin Cottage as well as telling her how selfish she was and didn't she know how stressed they all were over the disastrous business of Gupta's disappearance.

He underlined that the business could go under at any time and that she would get nothing from it. He began to say she was a failure as a mother but Laura overtook him and started up on the porn, his visits to Nefertiti and how he had betrayed her. Before he could parry she then returned to the nub of the problem. His unwillingness to keep trying for a child culminating in the death of their sex life.

What they didn't appreciate was that Juliet had crept half way down the stairs and heard the tail end.

Laura then said, "For your information David, Casa Blanca has closed down so you won't be able to fuck your whore there anymore."

There was a gasp from the stairs and a scuffle as Juliet raced out of the front door and ran into the lane. David rushed after her but her long legs had taken her well away from the house. Laura shaking went into her art studio and shut the door. The truth was out now on all fronts; the ugly truth.

After that it was only a matter of speed; how quickly she could extract herself from the marital home. During

331

the time Juliet was running away from the discovery of her parents' indiscretions, Laura ran upstairs and dragged out two suitcases. With adrenaline fueled urgency she got ready to quit Pippin Cottage that day and bugger the consequences.

She threw as many clothes and shoes as she could into the cases. She took a favorite photo of Juliet from her dressing table and from the bedroom wall a small watercolor of the cottage and the garden that she had painted.

Tipping all her toiletries and makeup into a plastic bag she chucked the bag into one of the cases and then spying her ancient heated roller set, grabbed that and stuffed it into the other case. Rummaging in the bedside drawer she took her passport, just in case. The rest of her personal papers, in a file in David's study, would have to wait. Mentally she assessed her financial status and was relieved to remember that she had a healthy bank balance in her savings account. Their joint account she would have to leave to chance and hope that David would act honorably. She didn't hold out much hope.

While she was hefting the cases downstairs her cell pinged. She dragged it out of her jeans pocket and noted four messages from the pirate and one from a number she didn't recognize. She scrolled down and read,

> *Dear Laura so pleased u r coming. Ball me 2 day. Execute fingers. P*

She smiled; dear Lady Pamela, her extraordinary Savior; a place of refuge was found.   Casa Blanca with all its outrageous connotations was going to be her new home.

David spied Laura through the study window. He watched her lift the cases into the back of the SUV; she was abandoning them. He and Juliet would be left to pick up the pieces. He shook his head and thought how

332

selfish women could be. Was she really going to leave without saying goodbye to her daughter?

Laura came inside and went directly to her art studio shutting the door behind her. She set to work packing up all her paints and canvases. The week before she had finished a canvas for a client and it stood packed and waiting to be delivered. She left a note on it for David. She went systematically through all her sketches and scraps and threw out half a sack full. Her large canvases she stacked neatly against the wall. Most of the paints fitted into the large cupboard that David had built for storage. She closed the door and locked it putting the key in her bag all the while wondering whether or not she would ever open the cupboard again. Her work for The Manning Renovation Company was completely up in the air. She had no desire to talk to David about it before leaving.

With a quick look around the studio, she glanced out of the window onto her beloved summer garden. The beans were dripping off the trellis, the tomatoes needed watering and she could see that the apples, on the old Pippin tree, were ripening nicely.

This would all have to be left behind. She thought of Lady Pamela and decided to cut as many roses as she could to give to the old lady. Taking the secateurs she collected a huge bunch of pink roses in different shades also white and yellow roses. Wrapping them in damp newspaper she placed them in the front seat of the car.

David did not appear during these preparations. She knew he was watching her. She went about her business as though he wasn't around.

She planned to leave and then look for Juliet who she knew was probably either down by the locks on the river, a favorite haunt, or up on Rook's Hill.

Laura took a last look around the house, pausing

outside the closed study door and grabbing her coat from the hook by the door, she collected her handbag and strode across the drive. Before she got in the car, she turned back for a last look at Pippin Cottage; so many happy years; all the time and effort spent developing the garden and redesigning the interiors; All gone at a stroke and there was Percy without a care in the world sunning himself as usual in his spot by the front step. She couldn't even say goodbye to him. Tears began to well up as she climbed into the driver's seat and buckled her seat belt.

As she started the car David came racing out from the front door and strode quickly toward her. She looked at him and as he approached alongside her and through the open window said two words,

"Too late".

She started to drive away.

He shouted after her, "When will.......?

The rest of the sentence was lost on the breeze.

She turned left out of the drive and headed purposefully away. She wended her way through the heart of the village, passed the pub, the hairdresser and the village newsagent.

The vicar walking his golden Labrador was just coming alongside her as she slowed for a delivery truck and she waved, he waved back happily, unaware that this would be the last time they would greet each other.

Travelling along the narrow road to the river she passed water meadows covered in cow parsley and buttercup. There was no sign of Juliet. She turned the corner to reveal the lock gates and the river, again there was no sign of her daughter. She turned the car in the small car park and headed to Rook's Hill on the other side of the village. Driving passed the village sign she made a right turn and followed the winding road for nearly a mile, climbing slowly. She passed the field where Juliet as a child had loved to come and see the ponies belonging to a local farmer. The road twisted sharply and as she drove into Rook's Hill parking area she could see Juliet in the distance sitting high up on the bench by the copse of Beech trees. Her head was bent over her phone.

As Laura opened the car door the wind from the west made her hair blow around her face. She pulled her coat around her and as she walked up the incline, Juliet saw her and got up, her body hunched and turned away.

As they came together Juliet bowed her head and stood stiff as a rod, her arms tense by her sides. Laura took her daughter in her arms and Juliet began to sob uncontrollably. Laura fought to control her own tears and then gently sat Juliet down.

On the bench overlooking the village with the church spire in the distance, Laura tried to comfort her daughter and apologize to her for all the hurt both she and David had caused and that there was only one solution for the marriage rift and that was to go their separate ways. Juliet looked at her mother out of stricken eyes, tears welling anew as she said,

"But what about me?"

"Could you stay with Daddy for a little while until I get settled?"

"What do you mean?"   Fear was palpable in her daughter's voice.

"Darling, I have to leave. I can't stay with Daddy anymore. I'm going to Chelsea to stay at a friend's place."

Juliet's voice choked a little. "Are you coming back again?"

Laura knew in her heart that this was the most difficult question to answer and the fact that her daughter was asking it, made it doubly hard.

She said softly, "I'm not sure darling. I have my stuff in the car and I am leaving now".

There was a broken cry from Juliet "Now? Mummy! You can't ...You can't just go!"

Before Laura could answer Juliet jumped up and ran down to the car. Laura followed, caught up with her and grabbed her arm. Juliet tried to pull away but Laura pinned her fast to the car.

"I hate you" hissed Juliet.

Laura desperate to temper the devastating news tried a consoling tone.

"Juliet please...You will be coming to stay with me as soon as I am organized. The house is large and roomy and you can have all your things in your own room. The lady I'm staying with knows all about you and is looking forward to meeting you."

Juliet yanked her arm away and snarled, "Well I don't want to meet her".

Then pulling back from her mother, and swinging her arm dramatically in the direction of the exit. "GO...GO on...then GO. I'm staying to look after Daddy".

As Laura started to move towards her again, Juliet put her hand up,

"Don't touch me".

They stared at one another, one defiant and the other stricken with remorse.

There was only one thing for it. Laura got into the car and giving her daughter a wide berth turned the car and drove slowly out of the car park. She glanced in the rear view mirror and saw her beloved Juliet, chin held high, face impassive and her arms wrapped around herself for protection.

While Laura's mind went into a disassociated state, the car appeared to drive itself until she eventually

336

realized she was well clear of Kingbridge and heading for London. She stopped at a coffee shop on the main road to take stock of what had just happened. Ordering a Cappuccino, she sat at a corner table in a state of disbelief.

That it had ended like this, her marriage, her relationship with Juliet so dramatically chopped into pieces made her feel weak with shock. Should she turn the car round and go home? No, she had passed the point of returning and picking up the pieces. Would Juliet ever forgive her for abandoning them? Wracked with guilt she sipped her coffee with trembling hands. As she relaxed a little, another emotion arose within her and that was one of a burden lifted.

Despite feeling guilty at what she had just done, a strange lightness of being began to take over her troubled mind. Was she really free, as in emotionally liberated after 18 years of marriage? Her cell phone pinged and she read the fifth text from the Pirate.

> *"Laura, my love. What is happening? I'm going crazy here. Please please reply. Darling I am so worried."*

How odd, she thought, to be experiencing freedom from her relationship with David, only to experience the pressure to commit from her pirate rescuer.

She resolved to keep the pirate at arms' length, at least until she was settled at Casa Blanca. She sent him a text to say she was on her way to Casa Blanca and feeling wrung out like a wet dishcloth. She then confirmed lunch as planned at The Chelsea Potter and to please give her some space for a few days.

To her benefactor she wrote,

> *On the road. See u around 6. You are my Savior. Thank you from the bottom of my heart.*

As she was entering the South London suburbs she

suddenly wondered what she could do with the car. Parking in the street in Chelsea without a permit would garner a huge fine. She could abandon it in a side street but would then have to lug all her stuff on The Tube.

She pulled over and phoned Lady Pamela who said she was so relieved to hear Laura's voice and was she alright? Laura explained about the car and the old lady resolved the problem immediately by saying that her old Jag had long gone but she still kept the parking permit current for trades' men.

"The car hit a bollard all by itself. I was in the driver's seat and it just took off on its own…nearly collecting a meter maid in the process. Quite extraordinary".

Laura laughed to herself. The old lady added.

"We're having fillet steak for dinner. You're not a vegetarian are you?"

Laura reassured she was not.

"Darling girl, we are going to have such fun you and me".

Laura rang off thinking that perhaps "fun" wasn't really what she was up for in her present state.

As Laura drove the final distance she thought of Cindy. She decided not to call or text her as she knew full well that her dear sister-in-law would insist they talk and then try and persuade Laura to return to David and Juliet. Cindy hated conflict and strife and she also loved happy endings. Laura knew in her heart that her situation was not going to end prettily. Lawyers' letters would flow between she and David and that could increase the acrimony if she allowed the wrangling to go on for too long. In any case she had to think of Juliet.

The sooner a settlement, in her mind a 'fait accompli', was reached, the better for everyone's piece of mind. She did not relish having to fight for what was rightfully hers but hoped her lawyer would see that the settlement

338

was fair. She had to trust him. She resolved to call him in the morning after a good night's sleep.

A little while later Lady Pamela opened the door to a huge bunch of roses and a person standing behind it. Dear Laura had arrived. Lady Pamela enthused over the flowers and then gave her guest a warm hug. She said she would get them both a double brandy and soda to ease the nerves. She bustled off to the kitchen to put the bouquet in water while Laura carried her things up to the Chinese bedroom. She couldn't help remembering her liaison with Blue Eyes in that very room but she didn't like to mention this to Lady Pamela. Her hostess, of a different mind, did not think it would be seemly for Laura to be accommodated in the bedroom where her husband had fucked Nefertiti. She quietly congratulated herself on her sensitivity.

Laura entered the infamous bedroom and put her cases down just inside the door. She glanced at the lavish gold and red room and then washed her face in the adjoining bathroom. As she inspected the opulent silk coverlet on the King size bed, she banished any thought of the number of men who had lain there. At least the sheets would be clean.

Tanice had prepared some smoked salmon pate on little toasts to have before dinner. Laura came downstairs and sank into the comfortable sofa. Her hostess had placed a large brandy with ice on a side table and exhorted her to relax and have something to eat and drink. Laura realized she had not had anything since the Cappuccino and was ravenous. Lady Pamela started to reassure her that she would be safe at 32 Davenport Gardens and she could come and go as she pleased and for as long as she wanted.

As Laura unwound from the day's stresses and sipped her brandy, she listened to Lady Pamela talk about all

339

the events that had taken place since they had last met. How The Colonel was now back in her good books after taking her for a slap-up dinner at The Ritz and that Edward appeared to be holding his own with regard to drying out at the Rehab place in the country. What Lady Pamela did not know was that Edward was not only holding his own but holding his buxom Aussie nurse in all sorts of places and falling in love.

Laura munched on the salmon toasts as Lady Pamela's voice washed over her and then lying back on the sofa cocooned by cushions, she began to drift off to sleep.

She awoke at midnight to find the place in darkness, her shoes had been removed and someone had laid a blanket over her sleeping form. Beside her on the coffee table was a plate of sliced fillet steak, some mixed salad and a fresh roll and butter along with some Brie cheese. Dear Lady Pamela; what a sweet thing to leave Laura resting and then place her dinner beside her to be eaten later in the night. The old lady was truly Laura's Savior.

CHAPTER 24

Tony, honoring Laura's request for space, busied himself in the shop. Now with a cleared basement he could re-design the layout of the shop by re-organizing the sections and putting some of the slow sellers into storage. As sales of second hand books were on the up - kindle having taken very little of this market- he decided to increase the size of this section and at the same time make more room for browsers. He re-cycled Pandora's low-seated punishment stools for this very purpose. It had crossed his mind to have a coffee machine in one corner but he determined that he wanted customers to buy and not sit around on their arses all day cluttering up the shop. There were already one or two customers who were outstaying their welcome and using his shop as a shelter from the cold. He had found one of them asleep on the floor last winter near the radiator in the Biography section.

On the long summer evenings, he went to the allotment to check on his new layout. The Playground Committee were delighted to receive the gym horse and one curious mother asked him where he had acquired it. He gave a nebulous answer and changed the subject. The children had already decided on a design for both sides. A large dolphin leaping in a wave adorned one side while the other was covered with star fish and an octopus curling round a treasure chest. The committee organized thick rubber mats underneath to cushion a child's fall.

The rectangular torture rack, now transformed into a plant climbing frame, was much admired and two people asked where they could acquire one. Lenny commented,

"Those leather straps'd hold an oak tree in a high

wind. Very sturdy".

Tony held back a smile and said he had been given the rack by a defunct antique shop. The new compost bin also came in for comment. Old Will inspected it thoroughly and said,

"Bit fancy for a compost bin with them dragons. Chinese design is it?"

Tony gave no real answer but did say the tin interior would heat up the decomposition.

Old Will nodded sagely and continued, "I reckon some poor Chink, probably a druggie, got trussed up and stuffed in there. He'd decompose pretty damn quick".

Tony was amused at how Old Will turned everything into a crime drama, glanced at the old man and they nodded sagely at one another. He couldn't wait to show Laura his handiwork.

Tony also decided that his one bedroom flat above the shop needed a spring clean so he set to scrubbing the bathroom until it gleamed and dusted and vacuumed the rest of the tiny flat.

When he inspected his double bed with its stained army blanket he knew this was not going to enhance any kind of bedroom liaison with the lovely Laura. His sheets also were in a lamentable state. He went out and bought some new ones from Peter Jones. He dithered over the choice of color and design but eventually decided on pristine white. Then, with a rush of blood to the head, he bought a brand new navy and beige duvet with matching pillow slips along with some large white fluffy towels for a possible tryst in the shower.

Not done there he browsed through the kitchen department and bought some bright new mugs, better than the chipped stained ones he normally used, to have a cozy coffee before 'the event' or even after for that matter. 'The event', in typical male fashion, was looming large in his mind and even though it would be a huge mistake to rush things he couldn't wait to take a naked Laura in his arms and make love to her.

He suddenly noticed his clothes and was alarmed to see how threadbare and battered they all were. Never one to be sartorially elegant- one mean friend had commented -

'Why do you always look like a jumble sale reject?'- He came to the conclusion that a complete wardrobe overhaul was imperative.

Having not bought any clothes for some time he had no idea that his bank balance, already smarting from the sheets and duvet, was going to take another punishing hit from his clothes purchases. He bought three long sleeved cotton shirts from an outfit called 'Rip Cord' and realized on bringing them home that, as they were a designer brand, he had been royally ripped off. He needed new jeans - his holey ones were not going to cut the mustard - and some smarter pants for a couple of posh restaurants he was planning to visit with Laura. He suddenly remembered what went underneath jeans and rifling through his undies draw was horrified to find all his socks and undies were either in holes or grey from use. He binned the lot and made yet another visit to Marks and Spencer to re-stock.

After all these preparations, he was ready. He couldn't wait for their lunch date the following Tuesday. He itched to text Laura but having been told to give her space, he kept his fingers well away from her cell number.

 Having partaken of her midnight feast, Laura crept upstairs praying that Dandi would not awake and start barking. She paused outside Lady Pamela's room and noise came there none.

She awoke the following day in the Chinese bedroom feeling refreshed and ready to face the day. She showered and dressed and went downstairs to be greeted by Dandi wagging his stump and standing guard near the kitchen door. Tanice was busy preparing Laura's breakfast. Lady Pamela came bustling in from the study and asked after Laura's welfare.

"Couldn't bear to wake you. You looked so peaceful lying on the sofa".

Laura thanked her for leaving the dinner and they sat down together in the kitchen. Laura tucked into bacon and eggs. She felt a little piggy eating again so heartily while Lady Pamela daintily spooned away at her fruit and yoghurt and sipped her beetroot smoothie. She was told,

"I love bacon and eggs but can't over-tax my stomach at my age." Then she went on to say, "Did I tell you that Tanice and I are writing a book together?"

She smiled conspiratorially at Tanice who spoke up.

"It MY book actually. MadamPam helpin' me wid it."

"Wow. That's wonderful. What's it about?"

"It about sex in de Caribbean. It a bonk buster".

Laura hid her surprise. "Really?"

Lady Pamela chimed in, "As you know my dear, being the proprietor of Casa Blanca, I have a lot of interesting liaisons to draw on and not just my own, you understand".

They went on to tell her all about Rastus and Delphine and their sexploits all set in the lush tropics. Laura nodded as they rattled on and it felt surreal that these two from opposite sides of society had come together to scribe this extraordinary project-A bonk buster indeed.

After they finished telling her the outline, she said,

"Well Tony might be able to edit it for you. Perhaps get it before a publisher".

344

Lady Pamela pronounced that to be a brilliant idea and then she said,

"Now Laura dear, I want you to treat this house as your own. I'll give you a set of keys and please help yourself to anything you would like from the kitchen. Tanice now comes in for four days normally from ten 'til 4. There is much less workload for her now Casa Blanca has ceased to be."

Tanice joined in, "Me legs says tank you for dat".

Lady Pamela continued, "We usually write together in the afternoons but it depends on how the whim takes us. Tanice takes Dandi for his afternoon constitutional around 3..."

Laura interrupted, "Would you like me to do that? I'd like to contribute something to my keep".

Lady Pamela thanked her and said that would be a very welcome idea especially as the creative spark, inherent in both she and Tanice, was particularly strong in the afternoons and it had been a pity to interrupt this when Dandi needed his constitutional. Laura was pleased to be of help.

Laura then excused herself and went to send a text to Juliet. She prayed her daughter would reply but answer came there none. It would take a while for Juliet to forgive her mother for abandoning them and Laura knew that Juliet would withhold contact as a punishment. She hoped this treatment would not go on for too long.

Unable to get anything from her daughter, she then called Cindy. Cindy sounded frantic.

"Laura! Where the bloody hell are you? Everything's frantic here. We've been worried sick".

Laura then explained that because of the bloody awful row with David she had left Kingbridge in a hurry. Things had been said which could never be taken back.

"At least tell me where you are Laura?" Then another

345

question, "Are you coming back to work? Clients are asking for you".

Laura hesitated but she knew she owed Cindy her contact details and what she planned to do for the next week or so.

She gave Cindy Lady Pamela's address which would immediately be sent on to David and Peter. She imagined David's face as this news hit him. He would be mystified. She would not elaborate further.

She told Cindy that she was going to be in London for the unforeseeable future and any client wanting her design services should be passed on to another firm in the locality. Cindy's voice took on a sharp edge,

"Are you telling me you are not coming back...at all? Bloody hell. We are in the shit here already with bloody Gupta".

Laura interrupted, "What do you mean?"

"He's disappeared. No sign. Just fucked off. The contract's stuffed....and now you bugger off."

"Gupta? On No. I'm sorry Cindy...I'm sorry to have dropped you in it but if you knew what David has been doing then you would understand".

"To do with the business? Tell me."

Laura paused and said, "No not the business. Personal stuff. It's too raw .I can't. I had to leave".

Laura finished her conversation with her sister-in-law promising to be in touch and asking her to keep an eye on Juliet. She also said she hoped Juliet would, in time, come and stay with her in Chelsea.

After breakfast Lady Pamela sat Laura down and asked her if she had a good reliable lawyer from whom to seek advice.

"Even though you've left your family home Laura, you mustn't allow your husband to sit tight and hold onto what is partly yours."

346

Laura and her hostess discussed the ramifications of the marriage split. Laura voiced her concerns about her daughter and the effect on Juliet's lifestyle to which the old lady responded,

"Children are very resilient my dear. As long as there can be an amicable agreement. She will be smarting at present and feel you've abandoned her but in time she will return to you. As I said to you earlier she is very welcome to come and stay here at any time for as long as she wants".

Laura felt quite tearful talking to her benefactor but her sensible approach helped Laura formulate her plans for the future. She then told Lady Pamela everything, re-stating her grief at not being able to conceive for the second time and the discovery of David's porn habit. Her hostess remained quietly sympathetic as Laura poured out her heart. When the dear girl told her about the disgusting revelations on the computer, she raised her eyes to the ceiling.

"How frightful…such a nasty surprise…of course men have looked at dirty pictures ever since photography was invented. Men my dear are driven by the sexual urge; it's in their DNA-To think sex, look at sex, and do sex and we the fairer sex are unable to stop that".

Then she leaned forward and patted Laura on the arm, "What we can do, with proper legal advice, is take them to the cleaners", and she laughed in that way that made one look around for the stable door.

They continued discussing strategy with Laura underlining the fact that even though David would probably dig his toes in about selling Pippin Cottage she did not want to fight him in court.

Later in the day as Laura was reviewing the chat with her benefactor, she began to feel a little less stressed. Talking to Lady Pamela was like confiding in a friendly

347

aunt or Godmother. That she was the purveyor of vice slipped conveniently into the back of Laura's mind. It was wonderful to take this friendly soul into her confidence, a person who neither criticized nor tried to take control of the situation. She realized that in Casa Blanca despite its murky past she had found a safe haven.

Tanice and MadamPam closeted themselves away in the kitchen in the afternoon and worked on the bonk buster. They decided to introduce Le Conte Jean-Paul Pallisard to Delphine and her sister Tamara, a new character to add spice, at a little soiree on the terrace of Delphine's beach house. Rastus furious at Delphine's interest in her new neighbor peers at them through the bushes.

"He not invited?"

"Oh No Tanice. He's just the garden boy, Delphine's plaything, but we will make sure he gets his revenge".

MadamPam then suggested they should pit the sisters against each other for Jean-Paul's attention.

"Dey have a treesome then?"

"Not straight away. That would be unseemly. We want to draw the reader in. Let's write an erotic beginning to titillate the reader".

And so Delphine and her sister Tamara prepare for their meeting with The Frenchman.

> *Tamara, Delphine's half-sister was, in contrast to Delphine with her dark-eyed smoldering looks and impressive curves, a petite honey haired beauty with green eyes and the dainty gracefulness of a dancer. For the soiree with their exciting new neighbor she chose a cream and gold diaphanous....*

Tanice interrupted "Di..aphan...us? How you spell dat? I thought it was Di..fani..ous."

Her fellow scribe laughed uproariously, "It will be Tanice. It will be."

And so they spent a fruitful afternoon on the next erotic instalment of "Copulation Capers in the Caribbean".

During this time Laura took Dandi on his first walk or more to the point Dandi took Laura. As she was leaving Lady Pamela called out to her to take two plastic bags for any possible pavement dump.

"One inside the other dear in case of holes. Leakage is not very pleasant".

She was slightly nervous of the dog who in her eyes could only be described as ugly and she laughed inwardly at his totally inappropriate name.

As they paced the locality he kept glancing back at her to check on his new acquaintance and after a while settled happily at her side. She hadn't meant to enter the street where "Le Petit Jardin" was situated but Dandi in his surreptitious way pulled her gently along in that direction. When she saw where they were headed she hesitated and wondered whether she wanted to be reminded of Blue Eyes, but Dandi kept pulling determinedly and so she relented not knowing what was coming next.

As soon as they came to the restaurant entrance Dandi sat down firmly on the pavement at the bottom step and would not budge. All was quiet inside the restaurant and Laura could see that the tables had been laid for dinner that evening. She was relieved that no-one could see her trying to prize the dog off his arse and even the treats that she had stuffed in her pockets at the last minute did not tempt him to budge.

She tried pulling and even pushing his backside. He remained immobile and knowing he would be impossible to lift and carry the distance to Casa Blanca, she was stumped.

Dandi, glancing slyly at her worried face as she beseeched him to move gave a loud bark and then another. Before Laura could stop him making a scene, an upstairs window flew open and Monsieur Georges' head appeared. He saw them and shouted,

"Dande...leon ...Quelle surprise... J'arrive. Tout de suite"

The head disappeared.

A few moments later Monsieur Georges in his designer tracksuit came running down the steps his hands flapping like fish. He was delighted to see them and greeted Dandi effusively.

"Il a soif peut-etre? Thirstee?"

He shot back up the steps to collect a bowl of water from the kitchen and as Dandi licked his chops in anticipation of what else might appear, Laura stood in awkward embarrassment at this unforeseen event. Not only did Monsieur Georges bring water but also six chunks of the choicest steak on a stainless steel platter. The dog wagged his stump and promptly wolfed the lot. Laura couldn't believe how she had been duped by the wily Dandi and she laughed with Monsieur Georges over the incident. He exhorted her to bring Lady Pamela for lunch.

"She iz well, j'espere?"

Laura said she was very well and they would come by next week. Dandelion would be left at home.

Thanking him profusely for his help she collected the dog's lead and he trotted alongside her quite happily as they made their way back home. Laura silently vowed never to repeat the experience.

When Laura relayed what happened on her walk with Dandi, Lady Pamela roared with laughter,

"Oh dear! I should have told you about his love of a

free meal. What a sly one he is. Monsieur Georges adores him" and then to Dandi, "Such a clever ickle doggy, aren't you?"

Laura didn't think 'clever' came into it but she did not belabor the point at how embarrassed she had been. She then mentioned that Monsieur Georges would love to see Lady Pamela and it was agreed they would pay a lunch visit in the near future.

While Laura was settling into Chelsea, the news that Mrs. Manning had left her husband and daughter was all around the village. Not having the full facts did not deter the gossips from criticizing Laura's escape.

"Fancy leaving her daughter and husband like that. How could anyone be so selfish".

"I've heard he's got business problems too. Poor man and now his wife's bolted".

After the initial shock Juliet, a strong practical girl, took Daddy in hand and made sure he had clean shirts and a full stomach at the end of the day. He became an invalid for a few days and was unable to even get out of bed.

Cindy rang him and said she had spoken to Laura and that she was staying at a house in Chelsea and then she gave the address. David hesitated and said

"Are you certain that is the address?"

Cindy assured him that the address was correct. He did not inform her of his connection with that address and rang off saying,

"I'm not calling. She can stew".

Peter and Cindy held the fort at work and managed to keep the company afloat, at least in the short term; of Mr. Gupta there was no sign. His home phone had been disconnected and his cell no longer rang at all. Peter visited a lawyer to discuss what could be done.

No-one had any idea that Mr. Gupta was being sought

351

by the drug squad as "Mr. Go-Between". Having been holed up in Soho, he eluded his shadowy followers and then dressing as his mother-in-law had organized himself a false passport and escaped to the South of France. He had managed to contact his wife through a friend and had exhorted her to leave London as soon as possible. She had refused stating that their daughter Promila was well settled at University and there was no way Meena would uproot the family yet again. She told him that Hansa her mother had gone back to India to have her tooth fixed saying that British dentists could not be trusted and anyway they all charged liked wounded buffalo. For that the runaway thanked his Hindu God.

When the police called at Mr. Gupta's mansion they were greeted by an angry carpenter who was collecting his tools and materials. He had not been paid.

"Owner's done a runner. A bloody Indian bloke. Peter Manning owes me a few grand."

Eventually Peter got a call from a drug squad agent looking for Mr. Gupta.

"Aren't we all?"

The man proceeded to tell him the whole sorry saga.

The Manning Renovation Company now had a half-renovated mansion on their hands and by the look of it no possibility of ever re-cooping their costs. As David was in no fit state to make decisions, Peter decided to close the site down until further notice and pay off, where he could, money owing to his subcontractors. He said to Cindy that evening.

"We've built up such good relationships with our contractors and suppliers. We have to maintain those connections at any cost even if it means re-mortgaging our own property".

They then discussed the break-up of David and

352

Laura's marriage and Cindy mentioned that Laura had eluded to something in David's private life.

"Do you know anything Pete?"

He said he didn't and that David had always been a guy to play things close to his chest. He then wondered if there was another woman on the scene. Both of them agreed there had been no sign of anyone else. With regard to their own plight, it was decided to concentrate on re-organizing their liabilities as best they could on Mr. Gupta's contract and as soon as everyone had been paid off they would have to draw a line under that job.

Laura would be left to her own devices and hopefully would come to her senses sooner rather than later and return home.

CHAPTER 25

Tony woke early on the morning of his lunch date and took a long hard look in the mirror. His faded pajama bottoms did not impress and his hair looked as though it had been struck by lightning. His nails, grubby from the allotment, needed a good clean and trim and a visit to the barber was in order. He had arranged to meet Laura at 12-30pm at The Chelsea Potter, a popular pub in the Kings Road. It was a favorite watering hole of Tony's. When his relationship with his French girlfriend Francine was in the Honeymoon period, he had taken her there many times for lunches. As he thought about the lunch date with the gorgeous Laura his stomach did a flip and he wondered if he would be able to eat anything at all. He shaved, showered and dressed and deciding on just a coffee for breakfast, he set off to visit the barber's.

Over breakfast at Casa Blanca Lady Pamela hearing about Laura's date asked if she would like to borrow anything to wear.

"I have some very pretty silk blouses dear"

Laura tactfully declined knowing that these blouses would probably be vintage and circa 1980. Vintage was not her style. She decided to wear jeans, a tailored white shirt and heeled boots. When she inspected the boots she realized that the high heels would add centimeters to her height and make her taller than the pirate. She was not sure whether or not he was sensitive about this. As this was their first real date she decided to play safe and wear flat boots instead.

She was looking forward to seeing dear Captain No Hook but decided to try and keep his attentions at bay. She knew he was already smitten and would press her to move in with him. He was so kind and she knew in her vulnerable state that it would be so easy to slip into bed with him. She resolved to maintain her distance and tell him that Lady Pamela was helping to sort out her marital mess especially with regard to her daughter. She hoped she would not have to tell him that it was far too soon to start a new relationship although in essence she mused they had already started....something.

After a rainy start to the morning, the sun appeared and started to dry the pavements until they steamed gently. The Kings Road was full of tourists and shoppers all clogging the pavements as they gawked in shop windows and took photographs of the famous London street. Laura strode happily along, pushing her way through the crowd, the sun on her face.

Laura could see The Chelsea Potter, a pub once famous for its rock and roll, across the street. It had an attractive black and white exterior with old fashioned arched small pane windows. The main attraction was a mass of summer bedding plants all rammed into boxes along the lintels of the windows giving a bright and welcoming look.

She was a little early for her date so she decided to sit down at one of the outside tables. A few people approached and went inside and then she noticed a familiar figure coming towards her. Was that really the pirate beautifully groomed wearing a smart striped open neck shirt and with immaculately tidy hair? She couldn't believe how well he had scrubbed up. She rose to greet him and he took her in his arms and gave her a bear hug.

As the weather had improved, the sun now warming the outdoor tables, they decided to sit on a table on the pavement and watch the world go by, although Tony had eyes for only Laura. They ordered a couple of glasses of Chardonnay and Laura spent the best part of an hour filling Tony in on what had happened since the infamous party. At one point he asked,

"So you've really left David? For good?"

She affirmed she had, but then said how stressed she was over Juliet and the fact that David could dig his toes in over the sale of Pippin Cottage. They discussed lawyers, Tony emphasizing that she should fight for what was rightfully hers and that he would support her whole-heartedly throughout. She then told him about Lady Pamela and they both agreed what a brilliant old bird she was. After their meals arrived - they both ordered fish and chips - Tony took her hand,

"You are the best thing that's happened to me. Whatever happens I will never let you down".

Laura felt tearful on hearing these words as she was reminded not only of her husband but that bastard James Jefferson KirkPatrick 3rd. She determined that Tony did not need to know anything about her sexploits with Blue Eyes. Tony noticed Laura's distress,

"Are you alright? Do you want to leave?"

She reassured him that she was fine and that the difficulties she was facing had momentarily caused her to choke up.

"It's so good to see you and I want to thank you for supporting me."

Over coffee he told her about the allotment and how he had found a use for practically all the grisly equipment in Pandora's dungeon by recycling them at the allotment. She laughed on hearing about the ghastly gym horse and said how amazingly creative of him to hand it over to the children's play area. They discussed a possible time for to visit the garden and he also pressed her to visit the bookshop.

"I live in a shoe box above it".

He was longing to ask her back to the flat after lunch, especially as he had laid upon his bed the new sheets and duvet but he knew this could be a bit premature and turn into a horrible blunder especially in light of the fragility of Laura's emotional state.

After Tony paid the bill, Laura wanted to split it but he insisted, they stood together on the pavement for some time. Tony was reluctant to let her go and held her hand as he chatted on about the shop and its re-organization.

As he paused for a moment, Laura said softly, "Thank you Tony. It was lovely to see you. I'd better be getting back".

She put her hand on his shoulder and kissed him on the cheek. He pulled her to him and kissed her on the mouth. Eventually she pulled away and they said goodbye, with Tony adding,

"What about coming to see the allotment this coming weekend. We could take a picnic. Sunday?"

Laura smiled and nodded and told him to call her and then she turned and walked back towards Casa Blanca. As he watched her walk away his heart sank slightly and he knew he would be counting the hours 'til he could see her again.

As Laura walked back, her mind was in turmoil. She knew distancing herself for the dear pirate was going to be almost impossible. How solicitous he was over lunch, so sensitive to what she was going through and she had to admit to herself how attractive he looked. From a hilariously shambolic failed Captain No Hook to a suave book shop owner. He was full of surprises. She couldn't stop thinking about his dark wavy hair and how nice he looked in his brand new open-necked striped shirt. She also noticed that he had beautiful tanned hands, broad and strong with sensitive fingers and well-kept nails.

She admonished herself for beginning to find him seriously attractive. She realized she knew nothing about

357

his past - shades of Blue Eyes - and resolved to find out if he had been married and from what sort of background he came. She thought about the party and how he had taken her by surprise; their mad roll around on Lady Pamela's bed at the time seemed just a crazy caper. It seemed now to take on more significance. She had said perhaps rashly that she missed him when she was down in Woolacombe. Was she falling for him? Far too soon she thought. She had so much to sort out; any new relationship would get in the way of sorting her future, or would it?

On arriving back at Casa Blanca all was quiet. Dandi looked up from his bed and then slumped back asleep. Lady Pamela was having her afternoon rest and Tanice had gone home. Laura sent a text to Juliet and prayed she would reply. She waited and then kept checking her phone for the next hour. Answer came there none. Later on a text did come through. Laura checked hopefully. It was from Cindy giving a progress report.

> *Hi Are u alright? Thinking of you. Juliet seems very together about everything. Asked one question "is Mum OK?' told her yes. She is now coming into the office and relieving me at reception. She's a quick learner. Baby fine but I'm a bit tired in the afternoons.*
>
> *David not said a word and getting on with sorting Gupta's mess. Think we will pull through. Clients are asking after you. Call me when you can.*
>
> *Cindy xxxx*

Laura sent a quick response in essence thanking Cindy for keeping an eye on Juliet and hoping the pregnancy was not taking too much of a toll. She did feel guilty over Cindy's condition but it sounded as though Juliet was now assisting her father and as a result was helping

358

Cindy in the office. It was a relief to hear that her daughter was rising to the challenge and she felt tearfully proud of her.

She was about to call David but half way through her call she lost her nerve and stuffed the cell phone in her bag. She needed to get hold of Juliet first before talking to David.

She had instructed her lawyer to start divorce proceedings and she knew this would make David more angrily taciturn than he already was. She was not prepared to wait for something, anything from him. She decided to instigate proccedings and wait for his response; it would be an uncomfortable wait. With Juliet in the mix anything could happen.

Later around the kitchen table as Laura and Lady Pamela ate chicken portions stuffed with olives and prunes wrapped in bacon that Tanice had prepared, her hostess wanted to know all about the lunch with Tony. Laura told her where they had had lunch and how supportive the pirate had been. Lady Pamela commented,

"Salt of the earth that one. He managed to remove all the evidence from Pandora's domain. Thank God someone had a sane head that day...I felt mine was going to explode with stress."

Then she asked, "Do you think the police will make another visit?"

"Well if they do, they won't find anything...except perhaps Dandi's dildo under the sofa".

And they both laughed at the memory.

Laura looked fondly at her benefactor and realized she had completely forgiven the old lady for withholding the truth about Casa Blanca. She felt at peace in her company. As her hostess rattled on with what they could do together including having Juliet to stay and supporting Laura on her visit to her lawyer, the old lady suddenly said,

"Let's all go to Le Petit Jardin for lunch next week. I'd like to treat Tony properly for his kindness...and I'll ask The Colonel too…he owes me for covering his backside. He can pay for all of us".

She clapped her hands in excitement. She loved a party.

Laura, in light of her introduction to Blue Eyes as a new sexual plaything instigated partly by The Colonel, was not particularly keen to renew his acquaintance. At least having Tony there would lighten the atmosphere; and so it was arranged that they would all meet up at "Le Petit Jardin" in a few days hence and Dandi would spend the time in the kitchen hoping for a treat from Tanice.

The following day Laura received a call from Juliet. Her voice was hesitant.

> *Mum?*
>
> *Juliet darling. How are you? I hadn't heard anything. Are you alright?*
>
> *Yes I'm OK.*
>
> *And Dad?*
>
> *Um...He's pretty upset...but I'm helping him...cooking and that…*

Laura felt a lump form in her throat. Her voice caught slightly.

> *Sweetheart I'm so proud of you. Cindy told me you're helping in the office?*

They continued their stilted conversation with Juliet telling her about answering the Manning Company phones and getting experience on the computer system in between caring for Daddy at home. As she mentioned that they had gone out to dinner a couple of times at the local pub. She mentioned that the son of a client had asked her out to the movies. Her voice became bright and full of energy. Laura was silent but nodding dumbly as tears began to stream down her face. She took a breath,

Are you crying Mummy?

Laura's voice caught slightly,

I'm so proud of you darling. Would you like to come up and stay with me for a few days…That is if Daddy can spare you?

There was a pause as Juliet mulled this over then she said softly,

Yes. I'd like that. What's your address?

Laura told her and then said she would be in touch after she had spoken to Lady Pamela. She finished the call by saying how much she loved Juliet, there was a little gasp the other end and both were fighting back the tears as Laura ended the conversation with,

See you very soon darling. It will be alright…I promise.

After she hung up, she almost crowed with relief and went to tell Lady Pamela of Juliet's news. Her hostess said she would be delighted to welcome Juliet to Casa Blanca then adding

"She must come out to lunch with us too".

Laura voiced her concerns. The last thing she wanted was for her daughter to be introduced to the lascivious Colonel and she pointed out that her relationship with Juliet was still fragile. It might be better to have Juliet to stay after the lunch. There were fences that needed to be mended. The old lady concurred reluctantly.

Laura refrained from saying that she did not want The Colonel eyeing her daughter up and down as possible new meat. Even though Casa Blanca was no more, the lusty old leopard would never change his spots.

"Perhaps we could delay the lunch 'til she gets here?"

Laura was adamant in her negative response.

Lady Pamela backed down and then added,

"Didn't I say your daughter would return and now she's coming to stay? Wonderful news. We must get the Egyptian room ready for her."

Laura knew that the choice between the room where Juliet's father had fucked his dusky maiden and a Las Vegas bordello with a mirror on the ceiling meant the option was between a rock and a hard place. Her hostess, having forgotten completely about Mr. Darcy, chose the Egyptian room and made a note for Tanice to clean the bathroom and make up the bed for her new visitor. She enthused,

"I'm so looking forward to meeting her. I'm going to make sure that her time in London is fun and informative. Let's factor in some visits to the sights and we must do a show too".

Full of ideas she bustled away to her study to make a list.

And so it was organized that Juliet would come up in a week's time to stay at Casa Blanca and get to know Lady Pamela, Tanice and Dandelion in between things cultural and entertaining. Laura was amused that she did not have a say in any of this and in a way she was relieved that the old lady had taken charge of the arrangements. Having to patch things up with Juliet would take all her emotional strength along with trying to keep Tony at bay. Dear pirate, he would be meeting her daughter eventually. She was excited but also for some reason apprehensive about the forthcoming lunch at Le Petit Jardin.

On Sunday the weather was overcast and cool. Tony, normally at the shop on Sundays until 3pm, was to pick Laura up at around 10 o'clock for brunch at his local cafe and then they were going to drive out to his allotment at Spa Hill. He said there was a thriving community and on Sunday it turned into a meeting place for everyone to share gardening tips and get the latest gossip. This Sunday was the monthly market day where people could trade cuttings, home baking, preserves, crafts, gardening paraphernalia and more gossip.

He knew the arrival of Laura among the gardening fraternity would ignite a fire of interest and Lenny would come bounding over and try and stick by them all day as he peered at Laura's chest. Tony had to think of a way to lose the limpet Lenny. Perhaps this was the day to use the handcuffs.

He was a little nervous about his mode of transport and hoped she wouldn't take a negative view of his ancient, open-topped MGB. It still looked amazing in racing green but the roof did not close properly and there was a hole in the floor by the passenger side. In wet weather not only did puddles slosh up the ankle of the unsuspecting passenger but if left in the rain for any length of time, the car would sulk and refuse to start.

Noting grey skies before he left, he kept the car roof shut, prayed that it wouldn't rain and made sure his trusty tarpaulin was stowed in the boot.

He was hoping to take a picnic lunch and had put aside a nice bottle of champagne to accompany but the weather made him dither over this arrangement.

On the way to Casa Blanca he dropped into The Chelsea Deli and purchased a variety of fancy salads and some bread rolls along with a wedge of French Brie and some home-made chocolates to finish. Praying for the sun, he did not relish cramming the lovely Laura onto the broken garden chair in his potting shed while he sat alongside her next to a load of muddy old pots, forks and spades on one of Pandora's punishment stools.

When he called to collect Laura, Lady Pamela asked him to come in and have a cup of coffee but keen to be alone with his lady love he declined and whisked Laura out of the door. When Laura saw the car she grinned and said,

"Cool car. It's vintage isn't it?"

"More than vintage pretty much stone age".

He felt relieved that the transport hurdle had been overcome.

They drove over The Thames to a local riverside cafe for brunch and he laid out the plans for the day. As Laura nodded enthusiastically and smiled happily, he had difficulty keeping his eyes on the road. Her golden hair swung round her face as she laughed and her perfume was intoxicating. As he gazed at her profile, the car drifted into the middle of the road. She shouted,

"Look out. There's a bus".

He swerved alarmingly across to the left, narrowly missing a parked car.

He over-apologized, "Sorry, Oh dear so sorry. Stupid of me."

Laura touched his arm, "Don't want to end up under a bus before the day's even begun, do we?"

She looked up at him sweetly from behind a curtain of hair. His heart melted.

Tony forced himself to concentrate on the road and managed to find a park within easy distance of the cafe. Laura ordered poached eggs on toast and coffee and Tony decided on the pancakes and bacon with maple syrup on the side. When their meals arrived Laura tucked in and chatted away about Casa Blanca and how pleased she was that her daughter Juliet had phoned while Tony, his throat constricted with lust, picked at his breakfast and tried to concentrate on what she was saying while watching her stunning blue eyes and beautiful hands move as she expressed herself.

After their meal – Tony insisted on paying – they

364

went back to the car. Overhead the sky looked ominous. On the way to Spa Hill he mentioned the picnic and then said,

"We might have to sit in my potting shed".

She laughed. "Well that'll be cozy".

He then went on to tell her about the vagaries of the car and was pleased to note she was wearing low heeled boots and he hoped the puddles, if it rained, would not reach her knees. He had already attached some extra plastic over the passenger corner of the car roof to catch the drips and he was relieved knowing that the drips would not be sliding down her neck. He loved the old duck but it may be time to sell and get himself something more in keeping with his new found hopeful status of 'The Boyfriend". Laura was unaware of all of this as they trundled along heading for the South Circular. The South side of the river was very down at heel compared to the posh haunts of Chelsea and they passed terraced houses with scruffy gardens and rubbish piled at intervals along the edges of the driveways. Grubby corner shops and garages, apartment blocks with no architectural merit only idly registered in Laura's mind as she mused at how happy she was, sitting here with The Pirate, listening to him tell of Spa Hill Gardens and watching the tanned backs of his hands on the steering wheel.

Even though it was a Sunday morning, traffic held them up from time to time, but both agreed they were in no hurry.

Laura began to ask Tony about his background something she had failed to do with Blue Eyes. He told her about his parents, his father, a Science teacher at St Edward's School Oxford and his mother a librarian,

"Surrounded by books at an early age so running a bookshop seemed an obvious career path".

365

He took an English degree at Durham and then worked as a publisher's assistant for a while before his parents helped to fund him into the bookshop.

"What's it called?" Asked Laura.

"Fredericks. My surname."

He then told her about recycling the BDSM gear at the allotment and she asked,

"How?"

"Wait and see". And he grinned.

Laura laughed when Tony said this and he looked at her keenly, his eyes bright with anticipation of the day ahead.

Just as they were turning into Northwood Road and the entry to the allotments the skies opened and the rain belted down, thundering on the old car's roof. Tony drove into the car park and they sat looking out at the bleak scene.

"Better stay here until it passes over."

As it was market day and despite the rain, the car park was almost full. The outside stalls in the distance constructed of canvas and poles were getting a hammering. People were huddled together in boots and raincoats, either under the canvases with children hiding under the tables or scurrying towards the Community Hall. Some were trying desperately to dismantle their stalls and getting drenched.

"There is a coffee place inside... so if you like..."

Laura turned to him and smiled. "I'm quite happy...here...with you".

He took her hand and kissed the inside of her wrist as they stared out at the grey skies and listened to the rain drumming on the car roof. Tony longed to take her in his arms and kiss her there and then, feeling her lovely breasts against him but he knew that if he did that, someone, likely to be Limpet Lenny, would tap on the

366

steamy window and leer in.

They sat in silence for a while. Laura felt warm and relaxed. Here with the pirate in their own private world and even though the weather had packed it in, she realized that being with Tony anywhere was utterly the right place to be.

"Tell me more about your family? Not from the Caribbean are they?" And she giggled.

"Nothing so exotic. Brought up in Oxfordshire, near Witney where the blankets used to come from and went to St Edward's school where my Dad taught Science. Difficult to make friends with my Dad breathing down my neck."

"What about brothers and sisters?"

"Two ghastly sisters. Just kidding. I'm the youngest, the baby of the family. Belinda lives in Hampshire with her husband and three kids and Rosalind, the brainy one, is a professor of Medieval European History based at present in Boston. She's big on witches and torture".

Laura quipped, "Might have been a good consultant for Pandora then."

They continued their conversation and Laura learnt that he was 36, a little younger than her. He told her about the bi-polar Norwegian girl that he had fallen for and foolishly married at 22.

"I didn't know she was bi-polar at the time..."

He trailed off and she noticed how guarded his eyes became as he remembered. Lots of hurt there. He mentioned one or two other relationships and brought this information up-to-date by saying he had just broken up with his French girlfriend Francine. She had gone back to Avignon, her home town.

Laura then told him about her brother Chris in New Zealand and married with two children. She was about to fill him in on her family background and tell him about

Juliet and David. She was about to tell him the truth about their problems over conceiving a second child when the rain began to ease and a glimmer of sun sneaked out between the clouds.

Tony gingerly opened the car door and said quickly,

"Don't step out. There's huge puddle under the car".

Laura looked at her feet and lifting the rubber mat she noticed a jagged rip in the floor near the side door. The water was so deep it began to seep in under her foot. Tony hopped about changing into his gum boots. He cursed inwardly at parking over the deep indentation which everyone new caused a problem in wet weather and sloshed around to Laura's side of the car.

He opened her door, "Fireman's lift Madam?"

"Oh God I see...marooned".

She gazed out at the small pond that surrounded them.

"Thank you pirate fireman".

Tony leant forward and lifted her easily onto his shoulder as her golden hair cascaded over her head. She giggled uncontrollably at yet again making an undignified exit from a situation. He strode to The Hall and just stopped himself, in full view of numerous spectators, from stroking her pert backside. She was shaking with laughter and at one point he too, seeing the funny side, staggered slightly and she screamed,

"Don't drop me!" Her words muffled into his back.

They collapsed in a heap just inside the entrance to The Hall. All head swiveled to see the commotion and a hush ran round the room.

Tony Fredericks had brought a girl, a very pretty girl, to Market Day.

The rest of the morning passed in a blur with Laura being introduced to all of Tony's veggie friends for that's what they called each other. She tried to keep track of the names. Jasmine and Luke, Steve and Tilly, or was

368

it Dilly, Old Will, the two sisters whose names she forgot immediately and of course Lenny. As Laura smiled and turned to be introduced she kept noticing a long thin shadow which seemed to swerve from one side of her to the other. She turned quickly, smelt stale sweat and caught Lenny leaning over her chest from behind and peering down her top. His pointed nose twitched as he sniffed her aroma while his lank mouse-colored hair hung down to his jaw-line.

Tony took Laura quickly away to another part of The Hall where he managed to block her from Lenny's spooky attentions.

"He's a nightmare. Lenny the Limpet. He's taken a shine to me and will not leave me alone. Sorry. He's dreadful and now he's seen you...a vision of loveliness. This could be my day for using the handcuffs".

Laura looked startled, "Handcuffs?"

"Yes Pandora's. I kept them. I've been planning to use them on Lenny for some time. When the time is right and when the rain stops I'll lure him into our camp, the potting shed and show them to him. You will be my lure... well actually he's going to follow us right back to my patch when the weather clears.

"Then what..?"

"I'll show them to him and how they work. He'll ask all sorts of questions while leering furtively at you and at that point we will lead him over to the children's play area to give a demonstration."

Laura clapped her hands. "And you will place one cuff on his wrist and pretend to put the other on mine and then quickly cuff him to...the gym horse?"

"The climbing frame".

"Pirate you are wicked but I do like you".

He pulled her to him and not in any way concerned about the gossip that would follow and kissed her neck.

369

What followed was exactly how Tony described. The pair strolled round the indoor stalls and Laura bought a pot of strawberry jam for Lady Pamela and a couple of home baked cupcakes for the picnic. She admired the hand-made glass jewelry, wood work, scarves and baby clothes. Lenny stood in a corner and watched from afar.

People stopped and chatted. There was much talk about the weather and after a while, seeing the rain had ceased, the crowd began to disperse to the outside stalls and their own allotments. Tony took Laura's hand and started to walk across the car park towards his patch. Laura's boots were soaked but she didn't seem to mind. They edged their way along the muddy paths and came to rest outside Tony's shed. He took a key and opened it up. A musty smell rose up to meet them. Laura sniffed,

"Heaven".

He turned to her in wonder and she added, "Soil. How I love the smell".

Tony in that moment knew he must never let this girl go.

As predicted ten minutes later Lenny appeared looming in his stooped way round the side of the shed, his long hair greasy from the rain.

He croaked, "Don't mind do you?" And then to Laura, "Sorry forgotten your name".

She told him what it was and he began a long irrelevant monologue on climate change and how the glaciers were melting and we would all be under water before going into our graves and he droned on about all graves being under water eventually. Tony interrupted him at one point and said,

"Got something to show you mate".

He lifted the hand cuffs from the hook on the wall, quickly hiding the key in his pocket.

Lenny took them and lifted them to the light.

"Hand Cuffs. Where d'you get them then?"

"Antique shop".

He turned deliberately to Laura and gave a conspiratorial leer.

Lenny's mind immediately jumped to the wrong conclusion and he grinned weirdly exposing his missing teeth. Laura gave a false grin back and shuddered inwardly. What a creepy guy.

Tony took the initiative, "Come on Lenny I want to show you something".

He took Laura's hand and led her in front of Lenny who followed them out with a loping stride.

They all walked over to the playground. Tony quickly ascertained there were no children around and he positioned Laura next to the climbing frame. Lenny looked puzzled but was pleased to be placed next to Laura. She cringed but stayed silent. Tony took the cuffs and placed one of them on Lenny's willing wrist and clipped it shut and then taking Laura's wrist as she looked at him in mock alarm, he paused a moment for effect. Lenny started to give a croaky laugh.

"I know what you're going to do now you dirty devil".

Tony swiftly cuffed Lenny to the climbing frame and taking Laura's hand they started to run away.

Lenny asked, "Oi. What's the trick then? You a magician or somefing?" Then realizing he'd been duped, roared out ,"Get me outta here. You bloody little creep. I'm fuckin' cuffed to the bleedin' climbin' frame".

Back at the shed Laura and Tony fell into each other's arms laughing and laughing at Lenny's plight. They could hear him roaring in the distance and that set them off again.

After their mirth subsided, they discuss how long to leave him and decided a good 20 minutes would deter

371

him from coming near them. Tony was desperate to have an enjoyable picnic alone with Laura, albeit in a dilapidated garden shed and he was already searching for the garden chair with the torn canvas. Laura was so slight that he was sure it would not give way under her weight.

After five minutes they could hear large drops plop down on the tin roof and Tony looked at Laura with mock horror.

"Oh dear. Someone's going to get wet" And as they cocked an ear they could hear faint swearing coming from the children's play area.

This set Laura off on another paroxysm of giggles. Tony grabbed her and planted a big kiss on her willing mouth and he held her tightly as she returned his ardor. They swayed with laughter, clunking against the garden tools as the heavens opened again for a second time.

"We better unlock him" said a concerned Laura.

"Give him 5 minutes. He should be sodden by then".

They stood together in an embrace listening to the torrent on the roof. There was a tap on the half-open door and releasing each other they beheld The Ancient Mariner dressed in yellow oilskins with a matching hat. His gumboots were covered in mud. The water poured off his hat. The Mariner spoke. It was Old Will.

"Lenny's got hisself 'andcuffed to the children's frame. Says you done it. He's effing and blindin' like a navee...and wet...looks like a drowned ferret".

Laura chortled anew and Tony, unable to give a sensible answer, fished in his pocket for the key. Old Will took it and giving Tony a flinty look.

"You court trouble you do...first the body on the floor" and he pointed to where Edward had been dumped, "and now the 'andcuffs. S'like an episode of Prime Suspect innit?"

372

He touched his hat to Laura and stumped away to free the drowned ferret.

Eventually when they calmed down from the entertainment Laura asked,

"What did he mean -'the body on the floor'?"

Tony decided that the moment to tell her about Edward was not on this first date so he glossed over Will's remark and said he was prone to exaggeration.

He invited her sit on his one canvas chair.

"I'm sure it will hold you. It's only a little torn".

While Laura was perching gingerly on the dodgy chair and Tony was trying to look as if he was a natural sitter on one of Pandora's punishment stools, a perfect height for weeding but not for looking casually elegant, they talked about their families, their childhood dreams and everything in between.

As the rain eased Tony remembered two things-the picnic in the car and the fact that he had forgotten to cover the car with his tarpaulin. The consequence could be dire; they could be marooned overnight if the old duck refused to start.

As he poked his head out of the shed he noticed that most people had packed up for the day. There was no sign of Lenny or the handcuffs. He sprinted to the car and waded through the giant puddle to the door. He reached for the picnic basket behind Laura's seat and noticed that the floor was an half an inch deep with water. At this rate they would be floating home. Placing the picnic down, he grabbed the tarpaulin and threw it over the bonnet and part of the roof that leaked, tying it down as best he could all the while praying the old duck would start. He tossed up between a picnic in the shed and a picnic in the car. The shed seemed the lesser of two inhospitable places.

He raced back and placed the basket between them on

the dirty floor. Laura seemed quite relaxed and accepting of this arrangement and started opening up the salad containers. Tony popped the Champagne cork into the garden and looking out onto the sodden landscape they began to eat. At one point he raised his glass,

"To you Laura and to new beginnings".

Gazing into each other's eyes, they toasted.

Tony, in his lowly position on the stool, had a fine view of Laura's profile as she munched on her salad and bread and cheese and he marveled at how slim she was, her neat backside lightly molding into the chair.

As she leant toward him and talked about her past he couldn't help observing her small soft rounded breasts exposing a peak of themselves between the buttons of her sky blue shirt. He listened intently as she chatted and at one point tried to cross his legs, not an easy feat on a low stool, to hide his mounting erection. He nodded away and prayed she wouldn't notice. He then made the fatal mistake of leaning sideways to grab the Champagne bottle, lost his balance and landed on his backside. Laura leapt up and hauled him to his feet. A look passed between them. Tony held her tightly and they kissed longingly and lovingly.

Their eyes alighted on the canvas chair and they both started laughing. Throwing caution to the winds Tony promptly sat down and pulled Laura onto his lap. They kissed and with trembling fingers he began to undo the buttons of her shirt. Laura pulled away.

"Someone might come in....Lenny?"

Tony picked up a handy stake and pushed the door too and it wedged itself firmly shut. Now with only dim light coming from the dirty little window on the side wall he began to devour her.

She removed her shirt and reaching behind her back he unhooked her bra. Her perfect breasts fell in front of

374

his eyes. He sighed and touched them gently, cupping them with his hands and leaning forward caressed the nipples with his tongue. She squirmed beneath him and throwing her head back and moaned softly.

Lifting her silken hair he exposed her neck and ran his tongue from inside her ear to her collar bone. She shivered with desire. She helped him strip off his shirt and touched the dark hair on his chest. Running her hands all over his torso, along his shoulders and across his back, her fingers trailed his waist and came to rest on the button of his jeans.

"Wait" he said and they moved as one out of the chair to standing position as he gently peeled off her jeans.

She stood before him in pants and boots, a vision of erotic beauty. He quickly removed his jeans and she, feeling emboldened, immediately put her hand on his straining cock and began to rub gently up and down.

"Oh my God ...Laura. Stop…Stop. You'll make me come".

She peeled off her lace pants and he swiftly shed the rest of his clothes, tossing them into the depths of the shed. He sat down and pulled her on top of him. The chair gave a little squeak.

They grinned at each other. Laura moved her hips as she rubbed her pudenda against his cock and then looking directly at him guided him inside her.

His voice caught as he said thickly, "Oh ...So good".

The chair gave an ominous creak but they were lost in one another and didn't hear it.

Laura leant back slightly and exposed her clitoris, with her hand, to his shaft. She began to rock slowly up and down.

He groaned and whispered, "Oh Wow... stop a moment...too quick".

She sat motionless looking down at his soft brown

eyes and taking his dear face between her hands she kissed him gently. He teased her nipples with his tongue and rocking her back slightly, touched her exposed clitoris. She cried with pleasure. Laura grabbed his hair and pulled him toward her, rocking him back and forth more fiercely as they shouted out climaxing together.

At that precise moment the chair gave up the unequal struggle. The canvas screeched dramatically, shredded and deposited them in a heap on the muddy floor.

Hysterical, they rolled together and cannoned into a stack of bamboo poles which then dispersed all over them like a surreal game of Pick-Up-Sticks.

So much for pristine new sheets and immaculate flat.

At that moment there was a knock on the door. Laura threw a horrified look at Tony and then looked around frantically for her clothes. Old Will's gruff voice came through the door,

"Yew awright in there? Heard a funny noise."

Tony strangled a "yes" as Laura clapped her hand over her mouth. He cleared his throat while grabbing a piece of black plastic to cover his privates.

"Fine Will. Thanks. Yes. All good here. Just leaving Will"

"Ok then. Motor awright? Need 'elp starting her?"

"No. Thanks. All good".

"Righto".

They could hear his boots stump off toward the car park.

Tony hugged Laura to him and into her hair he said, in Will's Cockney accent,

"She started very nicely fank you".

She play punched him on the arm.

Laura was covered with grey dust and bits of mud and her face was striped like a tiger. Her hair having collected some leaves from the floor tumbled about her

376

dirty face. Tony said she looked like some exotic wood nymph. He carefully wiped away the excess with his handkerchief and kissed her eyelids and nose, sliding his mouth down to hers.

Gathering their clothes they dressed hurriedly and taking the remnants of the picnic went back to the car they sloshed through the puddles. The car stood alone in the middle of its small private lake.

Thankfully the rain had stopped. Tony sent up a little prayer for it to start. He removed and stowed the tarpaulin and apologizing to Laura for the damp floor on her side, he jumped in and pressed the starter button. There was a chug chug noise and then nothing. He tried again twice and on the fourth try the old duck fired, stuttering slightly and then holding her own. He reversed carefully and they drove slowly out of the car park leaving a pall of smoke in their wake.

Old Will watching from The Hall entrance smiled and shook his head.

Later that evening after Laura had been safely returned to Casa Blanca, she was having a glass of wine with Lady Pamela and reviewing the events of the day. She omitted to tell her benefactor about her carnal encounter on a canvas chair and its subsequent collapse and instead talked about Spa Hill, the people and the weather. The handcuff story was amusingly received and it was only when Laura was drifting off to sleep after dinner while the old lady was telling her some salacious story of her showgirl past that Laura realized with a jolt that she had had unprotected sex with the dear pirate; the heat of the moment overcame her; how delicious that heat was.

She frantically calculated her cycle and with a mixture of rueful relief she deduced she was not in any danger. Mulling over the events of the day, she laughed to herself over their hilarious tryst on the canvas chair and began to experience mixed emotions over what had happened. How crazy of them but how deliciously naughty and possibly dangerous. That chair could have ended up injuring one of them and what if they had been discovered?

Old Will would have enjoyed a thrill and news of the copulating couple would have been all over the allotments. On one hand she was relieved that pregnancy would not be an issue but she was unable to put from her mind a strange feeling a tiny spark of excitement of what the future might hold.

She called the pirate to say thank you for a wonderfully surprising day and they whispered sweet nothings to each other for half an hour, neither wanting to hang up the phone.

She lay in the Chinese bedroom looking at the dancing dragons all around her and the deep red lanterns that hung from the ceiling, replaying in her mind the hilarious but erotic afternoon until sleep overcame her and she fell into a deep dreamless stupor.

In the morning she received a text from Juliet saying she was looking forward to coming up to London on the following Monday and as she only had a couple of weeks of holidays left could they please go and see a show. She mentioned a musical, set on a cruise boat that she was keen to see. Laura replied to the affirmative and they texted back and forth about time of arrival and what she should bring to wear. Laura did not ask about David and Juliet, full of her impending visit, did not proffer more than just news about the business.

Daddy's OK. Mr. Gupta's job has closed down. All subbies paid up to date. Jonathan took me to the movies. We saw the new Jason Bourne movie. Cool and then had Mexican. Yum and J is

378

too!!

Laura laughed and wondered if she meant Jason or Jonothan. She was pleased that her daughter was getting a thorough grounding in the office by learning on the job. It was also keeping her busy and hopefully was stopping her brooding about her parents split up. And this Jonathan? Cindy would fill her in.

After the potting shed incident the pirate called by daily to see her usually after closing the bookshop for the day. Lady Pamela got Laura to open a nice bottle of crisp French Chardonnay and they sat around the sitting room while the old lady nattered on about brothel stories.

The two love birds were longing to be alone but Lady Pamela was intent on leading the conversation and did not take the hint to leave them together. To combat this and to give them some time alone, Laura went to Tony's bookshop and up to the flat for a home-cooked dinner a few days later.

It was not worth cooking anything up for one so Tony lived on warm-up meals from the supermarket with an occasional takeaway. He wanted to impress Laura and even though his culinary skills were limited, he had mastered a few dishes. He couldn't decide between Thai chicken curry that his sister had taught him, or the old favorite of pork roast with crackling and apple sauce. Unsure of her taste for spicy foods he picked roast shoulder of pork and went about gathering the ingredients along with a good bottle of French Merlot.

Before she arrived he made sure everything in the bedroom was in place, including new lemon-scented candles in the bathroom and next to his clean-sheeted bed. He placed fresh flowers, neatly arranged, on his tiny dining room table. For obvious reasons, he went overboard with the flowers and noted that there would be no place for plates, let alone vegetable dishes. The flowers were removed and placed on the old side board.

Everything went smoothly and she enjoyed looking around the shop and hearing about the business and as he followed her up the stairs to the flat he softly stroked her swaying backside. She stopped and turned suddenly. Standing one step above him she leant down and took his face in her hands and kissed him.

He pressed her to him and they staggered on the stairs while he drank in her perfume and marveled at her pert peeping breasts. Laura had chosen to wear a low-cut pink silk top and a black and cream figured straight skirt under which she had on sheer black stockings and a lacy suspender belt.

As he showed her round the flat he commented, "It's a glorified shoe box really".

She acknowledged the table settings and the beautiful bunch of deep blue delphiniums and white phlox. She sniffed the cooking aroma.

"Pork? I love pork" and began opening the dark blue curtain that screened off the freshly made Queen bed.

Laura touched the new duvet cover and took in the glowing lemon scented candles, their light flickering softly over the cream walls. She turned and beamed him a warm smile. He turned off the center light and without a word and certainly no thought of dinner, he came towards her and placed his hands around her waist and drew her to him. She laughed as they sank down on the bed and her shoes fell to the floor with a soft thud.

He rolled her over and back until she lay spread-eagled under him with her arms thrown back over her head.

"Pirate. Are you trying to roll me into submission...like the crocodile in Peter Pan?

He nuzzled her. "Didn't he swallow the alarm clock?"

380

Before she could answer he said softly,

"Tick Tock". He started to nibble her with tiny bites all over her neck and along the top of her breasts until she squealed. He suddenly released her,

"Now Miss Laura, I'm going to take off your top, skirt and bra and you're going to lie down while I warm my hands".

She giggled at this.

"...And cream you, in the nicest possible way, all over".

"What about my stockings?"

His eyes widened in excitement, "And suspender belt?"

"Well I've got to keep them up somehow".

"Oh Miss Laura, let me take a look".

As he was undressing her she shivered slightly. She stood in front of him in only pink panties, black sheer stockings and a suspender belt. He swept his eyes from toes to top and then took her hand and twirled her round.

"Stunning...!"

He laid her gently down on her stomach and stroked her smooth stockinged legs from ankle to thigh and nibbled the flesh just above the stocking tops ending with his face buried in her backside. She squeaked with pleasure. He carefully drew off her pink panties and threw them with abandon over a table lamp. The room took on a rosy hue.

He then removed his clothes, straddled her waist and lifted her hair over her head until it fanned out in golden threads on the pillow. He took some rose scented massage oil and started a gently pressure with his palms over her neck, golden shoulders and back. Laura started to purr. When he completed her back and arms he turned her over and seeing her perfectly rounded breasts and neat landing strip he groaned with pleasure.

381

With his erection getting in the way he straddled her hips and started to massage her breasts gently cupping them and tickling the nipples until they hardened with pleasure. As his hands moved to her stomach and the area around her waist Laura began to breathe deeply and whispered,

"Oh Pirate ...you're spoiling me."

She gripped his cock and started a downward stroke.

He whispered "can't concentrate" He moved out of reach.

As he massaged the tops of her thighs, softly rubbing the creases either side of her landing strip, she could feel her wetness; aching for him to enter her she lifted her hips to him. He lay full length upon her and kissed her fully, their tongues caressed one another and then moving slowly downwards his mouth found her clitoris and he began to suck on it gently with his tongue. With that exquisite increasing pulse of an approaching climax she let go and cried out with pleasure.

He entered her smoothly and they rocked together, their hips in alignment, her hands stroking his back and buttocks. As their movements became more frenzied she lifted her legs higher and wrapped them around his back. They moaned together and he shot his seed deep inside making a deep growl as he did so. Clasping her to him, his head buried in her neck, he lay inside her. They did not speak.

In the kitchen the pork roast crackled merrily away becoming smaller and browner.

He then pulled away from her and looking into her flushed face said,

"Will you marry me?"

"Tony!" She laughed.

He grinned but his eyes beseeched her. "I'm serious".

"Darling pirate. I'm married to someone else".

382

"Then Miss Laura may I have first refusal when your divorce comes through?"

This was totally unexpected and she had to think fast. Was he really serious?

"Tony darling. I'm so honored but I've so much baggage to sort out".

"You're not saying 'no' then?"

"I'm...I...I don't know".

He lifted her chin and kissed her gently, "I love you Miss Laura".

They put their arms around each other in a warm embrace.

He knew not to pressure her further. With a light heart, his love declared and a question mark over their future, he got up and dressed and went into the kitchen to rescue what was left of the dinner. The joint resembled a burnt offering and the roast potatoes had turned into shriveled artefacts from some obscure African tribe.

Laura laughed when she saw the cooking wreck and it was decided to go down the road to the local Italian restaurant.

Much later that evening Laura turned her key in the lock at 32 Davenport gardens and shoes in hand, tiptoed across the hall and up the stairs. Lady Pamela heard Laura's bedroom door shut with a soft click and she smiled to herself, turned over and went back to sleep.

CHAPTER 26

On the morning of the lunch Lady Pamela was examining her wardrobe and choosing something appropriate to wear. It was important for the old lady to look her best for their outing to Le Petit Jardin especially as they were celebrating the arrival of Laura and strangely in contrast the demise of Casa Blanca as a business. On reflection she was pleased it had come to an end, albeit suddenly, as she knew she had been getting to the point of giving up entirely. It was all becoming too much of a chore.

In the old days it had been fun. She had enjoyed the illicit nature of the operation; the famous names who had passed through her door and the laughter of all "her girls".

She was still laughing about the elderly judge who liked his anus being cleaned with a tooth brush. One of the girls had been a little too enthusiastic and the brush had got stuck up his back passage. Of course they had to call an ambulance. The girls all hid in their rooms, smothering their laughter and she had to pretend that the gentleman was her elderly cousin who liked to indulge in unusual practices. She told the two young ambulance men that she had no idea he would do something like cleaning his back passage with a toothbrush. He'd been hauled off on his stomach to the Emergency Department. They had all laughed about that episode for weeks.

Now with age upon her and energy waning she felt relieved that Edward's attack, appalling though it was, had resulted in shutting up the shop. She made a mental note to ask Henry how Edward was getting on.

The Colonel had amused her with regard to Edward's progress at the Rehab Centre, especially in relation to a certain buxom Australian nurse called Charlene. The

384

Colonel, with his usual pithy turn of phrase had said,

"Cleansing his body using his cock my dear. Fucking himself to health".

She picked a classic light-weight navy wool sleeveless dress with matching curved hem bolero jacket from her Christian Dior collection. She added her best pearls and seeing the 18 carat gold pearl and leaf bracelet that Edward has almost purloined, she decided not to put it on but to give it to Laura as a celebration present.

Laura, knowing the lunch would be a dress-up affair, hoped her pink silk shirt and black skirt would pass muster and remembering uncomfortably the knicker-less episode on her last visit to the restaurant, she made sure her black lace panties were securely in place.

The bracelet, given to her as they were leaving, was very beautiful and she was quite taken aback by her benefactor's generosity. Laura touched the large exquisite pearls and little gold leaves between them.

"I've never had anything so beautiful. Thank you so much".

Lady Pamela, looking at her fondly, commented, "It was given to me in the seventies by a member of the underworld. Actually, I think it was stolen...but that adds to its allure...don't you think?"

Laura grinned and kissed the old lady on the cheek all the while thinking how ironic that Edward had tried to steal it and it had already been stolen by a mobster to give to his showgirl.

Lady Pamela admired it, adding, "Time for it to pass on my dear."

Dandi looked a little forlorn as they climbed into the taxi. Tanice reassured MadamPam that she would take him for his constitutional later that afternoon. She also planned to write another episode of "Copulation Capers in The Caribbean", this time a threesome with Jean Paul

385

Pallisard wedged seductively between Delphine and her pretty sister Tamara. Poor Rastus was about to miss out again and rivalry was going to spark a fight between the two men in the nude on the beach. Tanice licked her lips in anticipation.

The lunch guests arrived to an effusive greeting from Monsieur Georges who ushered them to Lady Pamela's favorite table near the window and reassured them that the special seafood was readily available should anyone want to have the choice of lobster or fresh salmon.

A few minutes later Tony arrived looking dapper in his new dark pants and striped shirt. He had added a bright blue tie for good measure. He came straight over, greeted them and kissed Laura on the cheek. Lady Pamela was delighted to note the fond looks passed between them. She strongly wished for the dear girl's happiness and Tony seemed besotted. Perhaps it was only a matter of time.

She ordered her special Champagne and they were happily chatting together so engrossed in each other's conversation that they did not see The Colonel arrive. Alongside him was a silver-haired gentleman in an impeccable dark suit. As the two newcomers approached the table Laura looked up and beheld James Jefferson KirkPatrick the 3rd smiling down at her.

Tony was quick to observe the expression of shock on her face. Lady Pamela, slapped her napkin down and narrowing her eyes at The Colonel, said in steely tones, "Henry, you could have told me we were going to be five. Our table seating will have to be re-arranged". She tutted audibly and waved to a waiter.

The Colonel gave a sly smile and said affably, "I thought it would be a nice surprise and for Laura too". He gave her a wolfish grin.

Laura, trying to collect herself, smiled tightly and

thought that the surprise could only be described as a fucking nightmare. She was aware that Tony had already registered her reaction so she would have to play it cool and keep her composure. Unfortunately the waiter laid a place right next to her and it became impossible to move to another seat.

Blue Eyes sat down and gave her a penetrating look, smiling with his mouth while his eyes looked glacial. More introductions were made and The Colonel said,

"Ran into this Yankee fella at The Club...he's been asking after you Pamela and was especially interested in Laura's news". He leered at Laura as he said this.

Laura was determined to ignore the American and say as little as possible while Lady Pamela was kicking herself for telling The Colonel that Laura had left her husband and had come to stay at Casa Blanca. She glanced at Laura and could see the dear girl was uneasy.

As lunch progressed Tony filled in any conversational gaps while Laura kept her own counsel, picked at her salmon and longed for the ordeal to be over.

At one point Blue Eyes asked her a direct question.

"And how's the little artist then?".

She coldly told him she was fine and turned away, smarting at his belittling question. What a complete bastard. To ease her nerves she gulped down three glasses of Champagne but didn't seem to notice that Blue Eyes was quick to refill her glass and she was unknowingly on her fourth drink. At intervals Tony turned his worried brown eyes toward her and she held his gaze, willing the lunch to end.

The Colonel and James discussed the lamentable state of American politics and then The Colonel insisted loudly on telling them what L B J called his old fella.

"Jumbo. The old dog. He whipped it on many occasions in front of his secretaries and-"

387

Lady Pamela laid a claw on his arm and dug her nails into his arm while Tony caught Laura's eye and grinned.

"-Henry.. Desist. We do not want to hear any more about the lewd goings-on of former presidents".

"I was just getting started." He guffawed loudly.

Lady Pamela asked Blue Eyes what he had been up to since their last meeting. The American droned on about his properties on the East Coast, explaining tediously about each one in detail and then he suddenly said,

"So sorry I couldn't make the Caribbean evening. My daughter Mindy was over from Connecticut and we took in a show that night".

Laura, now with little food taken but a skin-full of Champagne under her belt, turned to him and said in a slurred angry voice,

"Your daughter? That is a blatant lie. I saw you coming out of The Little Chelsea Hotel on the evening of the party and you were squeezing her backside and then you put your tongue down her throat. If that was your daughter then I'm a Chinaman".

Tony stifled a snort while the others looked incredulous. All conversation stopped after this outburst and Blue Eyes looked at her with cold eyes.

"Mindy is my step-daughter".

Laura ploughed on.

"So you go to bed with your step-daughter do you? Well you're a fucking pervert".

The American had no answer for this and knowing he had been caught out, rose slowly from the table.

Ignoring Laura he said a quiet 'thank you' to his hostess and turned on his heel as the others stared at his retreating back.

After he had gone everyone started talking at once. Laura was apologizing profusely and said she wasn't feeling well. The Colonel was laughing his head off and saying "Atta girl" and Lady Pamela was trying to keep the party from completely disintegrating.

Tony moved to the empty seat and said quietly to Laura.

"Would you like to go home? I can drive you". Laura nodded.

Feeling her stomach churn alarmingly and aware of that awful metallic taste from her salivary glands that signaled an imminent upchuck, she said,

"Sorry everyone, I'm going to be sick".

She clapped her hand to her mouth and leaning sideways, she grabbed the ice bucket and threw up spectacularly into the watery dregs.

As heads turned and people started whispering, Tony helped her out of her seat and they limped away making their apologies while Lady Pamela and The Colonel were left to pick up the pieces.

Lady Pamela snapped, "Why the fuck did you have to bring him?"

People began to titter as they relished the oncoming storm. The drama of a row in public.

"Thought it might be fun…best laid plans of mice and men and all that. No idea The Yank would have that sort of effect on her…" and he guffawed loudly.

The Old Girl then laid into him and berated him for not letting her know he was bringing the American and in any case his presence would not have been at all welcome. They bickered together for another ten minutes and when the bill arrived and The Old Girl informed Henry that he was taking care of the damage, another rumbling row ensued.

While this was going on, an unsuspecting waiter cleared the table. He gagged audibly at the sight of ice bucket, to the delight of the other diners, and whisked it away at arm's length.

Monsieur Georges fluttered about trying to be consoling but they took no notice of him and were still growling at each other as their taxi arrived.

As Tony was helping Laura into the front seat of his MG and gently putting on her seat belt, he noticed she was white as a sheet and shaking slightly. He looked at her and said quietly "Is there another load coming up?" She shook her head.

As they were driving back to 32 Davenport Gardens he glanced across at her,

"Well that went well...let's get you home and into bed" and then he quipped,

"Mine or yours?" She looked at him dolefully. "Sorry, that was crass".

She put her head in her hands and then looked up stricken.

"Oh Sorry...I'm so sorry. What a dreadful thing to be sick in an ice bucket in front of the whole restaurant". She wailed slightly.

Tony grinned and squeezed her hand, "At least it wasn't into the old girl's lap".

She gave him a watery smile. "I feel so embarrassed".

"Don't be. You were spectacular and calling that boring Yankee fart a fucking pervert...it was brilliant."

Laura took a breath. "I think I owe you an explanation".

"Sweetheart, you don't owe me anything. Any history with him does not concern me. Now I'm going to get you back to Casa Blanca. You're going to have a hot bath and climb into bed".

They drove sedately home.

Tony deposited her in the hallway and asked her if she was going to be alright. She affirmed she was and touching his cheek she said a soft 'thank you' and climbed the stairs to her room. She did not look forward to facing her benefactor and hoped she could swallow enough pills to combat a raging headache and get some much needed sleep before facing the consequences of ruining Lady Pamela's celebratory lunch.

That evening Laura opened her eyes and sat up in bed. She felt fragile but at least her headache had dissipated to a dull ache around the temples. She knew she must make amends for the shocking faux pas as soon as possible so she gingerly lifted the bed covers and put one foot in front of the other, climbed out of bed and went into the shower. She washed her hair and freshened her aching body. Her teeth felt as though they were covered in wall paper paste. She gave them a good scrub.

After sculling back two glasses of water she looked in the mirror; two bleary eyes under-hung by black circles looked back. It was not a pretty sight. She dressed carefully and after drying her hair put on a lick of lipstick, took a deep breath and went down to face her hostess. In fact she need not have been concerned. Lady Pamela greeted her warmly.

"How are you dear? Do you feel like a little soup? It's minestrone".

Laura faltered slightly and said, "I'm…um…Oh dear…I'm so sorry-"

Lady Pamela interrupted, "-Don't be. It was all The Colonel's fault. He just loves to meddle…did it on purpose….he knew you'd be uneasy. In typical fashion he wanted to see how you would cope".

She went on to tell Laura that Henry had been strongly chastised and when she forced him to pay the bill, he grumped and growled like an injured tiger.

As her benefactor was reassuring her, Laura realized that she had yet again managed to bugger up another of Lady Pamela's social engagements and yet the old dear seemed totally unfazed by Laura's dreadful mishap. She nattered on about The Colonel's misdemeanor and then applauded Laura for taking James to task. She gave a familiar braying laugh when recalling the way Laura had attacked him.

"You're well shot of him Laura. He may be rich but he's addicted to sex my dear and used our services regularly. He had you, discarded you and moved on to new meat and to put you further in the picture. Married twice, four children none of whom are called Mindy."

Laura's face portrayed shock and disbelief at Lady Pamela's crude portrayal of Blue Eyes and the added sting that she and The Colonel knew this all along made Laura feel a stab of anger at the pair's collusion.

Had they used her for their own amusement?

Laura's mind stewed with feelings of disgust and embarrassment. She felt badly hurt and was about to challenge the old lady when she was pre-empted,

"Don't be angry Laura dear. Even though you may not believe this, I have always wanted what is best for you. I introduced you to James because I knew he could give you what you needed...and he did, didn't he?"

Laura said nothing but smiled and looked down at her hands.

"See I'm right".

The old lady continued, "And now you've left your husband. A very wise decision by the way and already you've met someone who I am sure will make you very happy."

Laura rested her weary head on the plush cream cushion and sank down into the depths of the comforting sofa.

She did not tell her benefactor that she'd had a proposal of marriage. Her mind had to prioritize the next couple of weeks and she was already feeling over-burdened with problems to sort through.

"It's all so much to take in ...so much to process."

"Don't...You are quite safe here. Now let's have some soup and scrambled eggs and toast".

She got up and went into the kitchen to prepare their supper.

For Laura, setting aside Tony's amorous intentions, there was one ray of light. Her daughter Juliet was coming to stay.

CHAPTER 27

Juliet arrived around lunchtime on the following Monday. She had caught the train from Kingbridge, picked up the tube from Waterloo and walked from Sloane Square tube station bringing a backpack and small wheelie suitcase.

When Laura opened the door she was struck at how grown up Juliet looked. Had she grown another inch? It did appear so. Her ash-colored hair, normally in unruly tangle round her shoulders, was swept up in a neat pony tail. She was wearing new jeans and a smart black denim jacket. For a split second mother and daughter stared at each other and then Laura threw her arms around Juliet and drew her inside.

Juliet was introduced to Lady Pamela who gave her warm kiss and she then said 'hello' to Tanice in the kitchen. When she saw Dandelion she bent down and let him sniff her hand before touching him behind his ears. From then on he stuck by her side and both Laura and her benefactor were amused to notice him sit by her at all times looking up at her longingly.

"Made a friend there Jules."

"He's sweet".

'Sweet' was perhaps not the adjective to use on a British bull dog but beauty was in the eye of the beholder and in any case Juliet's immediate bond with Dandi would stand her in good stead with Lady Pamela.

Laura took Juliet up to the Egyptian room and this brought forth "oos and "aahs" from her amazed daughter.

"It's so cool Mum. I love the Sphinx thing". She jumped on it and rode it like a horse.

She gazed around the room, at the opulent peach

furnishings, camel and pyramid murals and the golden light fittings. She crashed down on the bed while Laura tried not to picture her father humping Nefertiti on the same.

"Amazing. I'm going to love it here".

Then a bit more cautiously, "What is she like Lady Pamela? Is she really a lady as in ..Lord?"

"Yes. She does have a title."

Laura smiled wryly. If Juliet knew what her hostess truly was, with all the associations of the various rooms in the house, she'd be totally shocked and probably would refuse to stay.

"And where's your room Mum?"

"Oh I'm in the Chinese room…Just down the landing".

She pointed airily in that direction.

She asked Juliet to wash up and come down to lunch. Tanice had made a spinach and bacon pie to be accompanied by a salad.

Juliet sat at the dining table, for it was decided to use the more formal setting for Juliet's first lunch, and minded her table manners.

Laura noted that she carefully wiped the corner of her mouth from time to time with the white linen napkin and she sat straight as a ramrod listening respectfully to her hostess. Inside her head Laura envisioned a bent back, elbows out and head down over her trough in the kitchen at Kingbridge. Dear Juliet she'd risen to the occasion.

Lady Pamela was asking Juliet all about school and what she liked and Juliet was talking fluently on her favored subjects.

Her hostess suddenly asked "and the teachers, are they all Lesbians dear?"

Juliet faltered slightly but to her mother's delight did not miss a beat.

"Some are. At least I think so. The games mistress, Miss Bone."

Lady Pamela threw back her head and brayed loudly.

"God. What a name. Did she throw you one?"

Juliet took a split second to click and then started to giggle. Laura looked from one to the other in disbelief. Lesbian teachers? It was unthinkable.

"No...but she certainly looks like one...She's very thin...like a skeleton actually".

Lady Pamela chuckled and prodded some more." And her friend?"

She raised an eyebrow as she emphasized 'friend'.

"Oh that's Miss Godfrey, the piano teacher. She's got a big bosom".

Lady Pamela was getting into her stride and asked,

"Does Miss Bone play the bosom or does Miss Godrey play the bone, do you think?"

Juliet cackled loudly. Her mother, alarmed things were getting out of hand, tried to change the subject to Juliet's tennis trophy but the two were bent on boarding school gossip and would not be interrupted.

As the plates were cleaned, Laura took them out to Tanice in the kitchen and complimented her on the pie.

Tanice asked, "Your daughter? How's it goin?"

"Seems they are bosom buddies after five minutes. I feel the odd girl out".

"She lovely, your daughter. But how are you Miss?"

"Thanks for asking. Lots to sort out but I'll get there".

And remembering the bodice ripper she asked, "And the book?"

Tanice's eyes gleamed.

"Very excitin'. I just writing a threesome and next I got two naked men fightin' on de beach".

"Lovely".

Leaving Tanice slavering over her oeuvre she backed

out all the while thinking that the walls of Casa Blanca were so steeped in sexual shenanigans that they seemed to exude an almost pornographic atmosphere which was obviously affecting the inmates.

It went without saying that Juliet and Lady Pamela were getting on like a house on fire.

When Juliet excused herself to go up to her room, Lady Pamela turned to Laura,

"A stunner. What a wonderful girl...so mature and a huge credit to you my dear".

Laura was somewhat taken aback but felt utterly relieved that their meeting had gone smoothly.

"And now we must discuss events for her week with us. She has asked to go to the new musical in the West End…something about a cruise ship".

"Yes, I think it's called 'Blue Wave' but getting tickets at short notice may be-"

"—Leave it to me. I have a contact...he'll help us out".

She bustled away to her study to make some phone calls.

Laura went up to her daughter's room and tapped on the door. Normally she would have gone straight in but seeing Juliet's interaction with her benefactor and her marked maturity, made Laura treat her with renewed respect. There had been no talk of David but perhaps now might be a good place to start.

"Come in".

As Laura came through the door, Juliet rushed to her and gave her a big hug and words began to spill out.

"She's brilliant Mum. What a super lady…so funny and not stuffy at all. I thought she was going to be like our Headmistress. Funnily enough she looks like her but she's not, she's great…and when she asked me about the Lesbian teachers...hilarious…and Dandelion…he's so sweet but what a funny name".

Laura then filled Juliet in on how she had rescued her benefactor after a fall and that Dandi had caused it. They had become friends over the summer months.

She continued, "And when I left Daddy…."

Laura paused a moment to see Juliet's reaction; it was focused and calm.

"She said I could stay as long as I wanted and that you could come and stay too."

Juliet looked at her gravely. "Are you coming back Mum?"

Laura put an arm round her.

"No darling. Daddy and I are getting a divorce".

Her daughter looked down at the floor and then said softly, "He wants to stay at Pippin Cottage and Mummy, so do I".

So there it was. David had made a stand with regard to their joint family home and Juliet, understandably, had sided with him. The decision was made. Father and daughter would be staying at Kingbridge until further notice. Laura took a breath.

"Of course darling. You and Daddy will be staying at the cottage until you leave school".

Juliet's eyes brightened. "Dad will be so pleased. He was worried you'd want to kick us out".

As Laura listened, the word 'manipulation' came to mind and the emotive word 'kicked' rankled.

"I'd never do that Sweetheart. I love you." And they embraced.

Juliet pulled away and suddenly realizing the enormity of this, asked, "But Mum …what about you?"

"I'll be fine darling. I'll stay here for a little while and then I'll find a flat".

Her mind flew to a small flat above a bookshop. Was it really coming to this so soon?

She'd only just left Kingbridge and already events

were moving far faster than anticipated.

Juliet gave her a furtive look. "Dad said this house, the address I mean, has a reputation. He wouldn't say anymore. What did he mean?"

Well. Well. Sneaky old Daddy. That was below the belt.

Laura had to find a speedy answer. She decided to pass the buck.

"I'm not sure Jules. Perhaps you could ask Lady Pamela. She's been here many years".

With that they closed the conversation and Laura went back to her Chinese boudoir to mull over the day's events.

As she lay dozing on her bed, she smiled over what elaborate concocted story her benefactor would come up with when asked that loaded question.

It was asked at dinner. Laura knew Juliet was bursting to discover the secrets of Casa Blanca.

Lady Pamela did not let her down and said brightly, "Reputation? Well my dear, I did hear tell that it was a brothel-" She noted Juliet's startled reaction, "-But that was way back in the forties and fifties before my time. I heard also that it was raided by the police and The Madam, for that's what she was called, part Spanish I think was meant to be incarcerated for a month or two but according to the gossip of the day the Judge took a shine to her and released her almost immediately…"

By this time her young listener's eyes were on stalks and Laura was inwardly applauding this tangled web of lies and intrigue.

The following day while Lady Pamela took her nap, Juliet and Laura took Dandi for his afternoon walk. He looked on Juliet as his new best friend and trotted happily beside the two women, his eyes mainly on the tall blonde girl.

After they returned and were enjoying a coffee in the kitchen, Juliet was still full of questions as to the 'goings on' at Casa Blanca.

"So you think my room was used for…you know…" And she giggled.

"I do and all the other bedrooms too. It would have been like Paddington station with all the comings and goings". Juliet cackled and then she asked,

"But why is my room done up in such an exotic style? Pyramids and all that?"

"Perhaps Lady Pamela thinks she is Nefertiti re-incarnated or maybe she fell in love with a camel". They both burst into giggles.

Tony was texting Laura regularly asking when he could see her again and meet her daughter. He was also sending her naughty asides as well as a questionable limerick.

> *There once was a lady called Laura*
> *Whose pirate caressed and adored her.*
> *He put in his hook*
> *Tickled cranny and nook*
> *'Til she bloomed like a beautiful flora.*

She called him to acknowledge his poetical genius and told him that she felt it was too early to introduce him to Juliet.

"I've got to take it slowly. She's only just accepted the separation. She's very bright and will see immediately what's going on between us…not sure how you will be received-"

"-Well I haven't got a hook for an arm, Laura"

"Tony, I'm sorry I didn't mean-"

"-It's alright you kissable person, I quite understand".

It was left that she would call him should a meeting be

possible. Laura knew that Juliet would click to the nature of her relationship with Tony Fredericks as soon as they met and the news would go straight to David and could prejudice her dealings with him. In any case how would Juliet react to the news that her mother had a lover?

When she discussed this matter with Lady Pamela it was met with a 'to the point' response.

"Don't fret about what everyone thinks Laura. I never do. Just do it! They've got to meet sometime. Sooner the better."

Laura could see that her benefactor was hatching something. There was a gleam in her eye.

"On Saturday Juliet's last night we'll have a nice dinner here at Casa Blanca. She can meet Tony and to add some spice I'll ask Pandora and her QC friend. She rang and told me that he had separated recently from his wife... The Colonel might be free and it would be so nice to meet Edward's new lady friend Charlene. The Colonel said Edward was back in town. I hear Charlene has been Edward's savior. A girl from Australia. Who'd have thought it?"

Laura's heart sank. She had hoped to take Juliet out to a quiet dinner just the two of them but as usual the old lady had other plans. Feeling weakened by Lady Pamela's typical 'ride roughshod' attitude, she acquiesced and went to tell Juliet.

Lady Pamela called Tanice in to discuss a menu. They decided on fillet of beef en croute which Lady Pamela would finish preparing and to accompany, potatoes Lyonnaise and some fresh green beans and a tomato salad. For dessert Tanice said she would make a Lemon Meringue Pie. MadamPam clapped her hands.

"Wonderful Tanice. Oh yes. Can you make sure we have some horse-radish sauce in the cupboard?"

Tanice was told she would not be needed to serve and

for that she was extremely grateful.

With her release from the work load of the old Casa Blanca she often went to the movies with her husband and to the pub for dinner on Saturday nights.

As Tanice was leaving for the day, MadamPam stated, "Next week we'll have time for a complete overview of the book. We're nearly there aren't we? So exciting and I already have someone who is interested in taking a look at it".

Tanice smiled. With a happy heart and dreaming of fame, she took her weary legs along to the bus stop.

After that, Juliet's week in London seemed to fly past. Laura took her shopping to Selfridges in Oxford Street and they battled the tourist crowds. Her daughter could not believe the number of people. They queued for Madame Tussauds and spent a happy couple of hours looking at The waxy Royals, George Clooney and Colin Firth around whom a gaggle of Japanese girls were clustering for pictures. Juliet thought Jennifer Lawrence looked amazing as Katniss and Daniel Craig was a knock-out.

In the evening Lady Pamela, dressed in a black velvet trouser suit one from her Ralph Lauren collection, took her two guests to see the new musical 'Blue Wave', a cruise ship love story; one woman caught between two men, with a big storm thrown in. Juliet adored it and couldn't stop talking about the songs and dancing. She especially liked the slick production which included a simulated storm at sea with the enormous cruise ship being rolled and tossed on an invisible motorized platform.

On Saturday Laura and Juliet helped their hostess prepare for the evening. Flowers arrived from Lady Pamela's regular supplier and Laura organized them around the main sitting room. Juliet was happy to make

402

sure the bathrooms were clean and she arranged fresh towels as requested. She also ran a duster over the antique furniture and plumped the cushions.

Laura laid up the place settings, polishing up the silver as she went and even though she was nervous about Tony's attendance she was looking forward to seeing him.

There had been discussions over clothes and Juliet had wanted to wear her black denim jacket over a short black chiffon mini dress under which she planned some black leggings and heeled ankle boots. Lady Pamela had muscled in on the discussion with Laura, and on seeing the outfit, she put up her hand dramatically,

"STOP. Juliet dear, you are not attending a funeral. I have one or two things that would be far more suitable". And then as an order, "You will come into my bedroom and take a look at my collection. There we will find something dressier and much more appropriate for my little dinner".

Juliet started to protest but was hushed and she looked at her mother pleadingly. Laura lifted her palms a little as if to say 'there is nothing I can do about this' and the decision was made.

The first guests arrived at 7pm. Pandora and her QC both beautifully attired and looking radiantly happy gave their hostess a warm kiss and were ushered toward the drinks table laid ready in the sitting room. Pandora, remembering Laura from the infamous Caribbean evening, raised her eyebrow,

"Laura? How lovely to see you again".

Patrick was introduced to Laura and it was ascertained that Laura was a house-guest along with her daughter. Laura asked Pandora not to mention to her daughter the undignified exit of last time. Laura made it clear that her daughter knew nothing of the nature of Casa Blanca.

403

Pandora whispered, "Make sure Edward and The Colonel know. They're coming aren't they? Or they'll have fun at your expense. By the way my real name is Tracy."

The Colonel, Edward and his Australian lady friend Charlene, turned up next. Charlene with deep auburn hair was dressed in the tightest low-cut shiny black evening dress that seemed to be stuck to her like glue. Laura greeted Edward who she remembered from the party and he gave her a kiss on each cheek and introduced his girlfriend who put a protective arm round his waist. Laura got the distinct impression she was laying claim to her property.

The Colonel smiled and shook Laura's hand saying, "I'm still laughing about the way you dispatched the Yank with a flea in his ear". And he guffawed loudly.

Edward looked at her inquiringly and giving a tight smile she quickly pulled away from the group and made busy making sure everyone had something to drink while Lady Pamela was preparing the first course in the kitchen. There wasn't an appropriate moment to inform the new guests of her daughter's innocence. At one point Laura went into the hall and looked up the stairs. Was Juliet alright or had she got an attack of nerves?

Tony arrived at that point and took her in a warm embrace but she pulled away immediately and drew him into the sitting room.

Juliet, upstairs, felt very nervous. She was tweaking her dress and tidying her hair in the bathroom. She shakily put on some lippy and then making sure yet again that her backside was well-covered she left her room and started to descend the stairs.

She could hear a low chatter coming from the living room. She entered and everyone turned to look at this vision with ash blonde hair partly swept up on top, the rest curling round her shoulders. Embarrassed at the attention, she smiled and dropped her head as she made for her mother standing by the entrance to the kitchen. Lady Pamela swept over and introduced her to everyone,

"You look sensational Juliet dear. I knew that dress would be a knock-out on you".

Eventually Juliet was persuaded to wear the black lace and white ribboned sleeveless mini dress from her hostess' collection. It was a vintage number and even though the label had been removed, the old lady said it was probably Mary Quant circa 1968. Lady Pamela had given Juliet a pair of diamond and black pearl earrings to wear along with a chunky solid silver Mexican bangle studded with Turquoise which she said Juliet could keep.

"Are you sure? It's beautiful. Thank you so much".

The old lady assured her and another piece of jewelry was successfully handed on.

Edward and The Colonel marveled at the new filly's length of leg and Edward particularly liked the high heeled ankle boot that gave a modern zing to the dress. Charlene kept a very tight hold on his arm and made quite sure he was nowhere near Juliet or the drinks table. Edward's face was completely healed and now with his cheeks neatly divided in half from obvious knife marks and his Aquiline nose slightly bumped in the middle, he strangely resembled a true pirate. In essence his injuries had enhanced his pretty boy looks making him even more employable as the rugged man about town and country much to the chagrin of The Colonel. At least the boy was clean, and by the look of the strong auburn-haired bombshell and her hold on his arm, would remain so.

Laura, noticing the admiring looks thrown toward her daughter, kept protectively close to her during the pre-dinner drinks as people came up to chat. Tony caught her eye and she ushered Juliet over to meet him.

"Tony, may I introduce my daughter Juliet?"

Tony grinned and said 'Hello" and they shook hands. She could see he was appraising her and then he asked her how long she was staying. In her breezy style she started chatting easily to him, telling him unbidden about what she had been doing in London. She raved about the show and starting all her sentences with 'Mum and I' he deduced quickly how strong their bond was.

The hostess, wearing a short white frilly apron which would have been more appropriate on a hooker than a cook, went in and out of the kitchen looking a little flustered. With no Tanice to back her up she insisted on getting the dinner ready on her own and had shooed Laura out of the kitchen earlier in the evening. She had allowed Laura to lay the table and prepare the prawn cocktail entree. Lady Pamela was now carefully placing the prawn-filled cut glass goblets on the dining room table. At one point, Dandi, not wishing to be forgotten, got under foot and she swore loudly,

"Bloody dog. Bugger off".

He looked up at her sadly and she relented saying,

"Soree darling. Mumeee busy sweetee".

Realizing he was not wanted he snuffled off and climbed the stairs to his owner's bedroom where he planned to climb onto her bed - a forbidden place - and roll around there in plush beige luxury.

The Colonel was in conversation with Edward and Charlene. They were telling him their plans. Charlene with a strong Aussie drawl was describing the beauties of Perth and the West Australian coast line.

"It's bonzer fer serfing y'know".

The Colonel nodded vaguely but was only half listening as his eyes were clamped to her ample front and he was imagining what it would be like to pitch

406

himself between the two rounded hills that stood in front of him.

"So yew see, Eeddie and I are leaving nixt weeek".

The Colonel sprung to attention. "Leaving?"

"Yees. I just sid" And she touched his arm gently and said as if to someone mentally challenged, "Xcuse me but I theenk yew need a visit to the audeeology peeple...yew can't hear can yew?"

Edward suppressed a smile as The Colonel retorted,

"I'll have you know I can hear a badger's fart two fields away", and he stomped off to get another whisky.

At that moment a familiar bray was heard. "To the table. Tout le monde. Dinner is ready".

The group, barring The Colonel who realized a substantial toilet visit was essential before dinner, came in and sat in their marked places. Juliet with her calligraphic skills had carefully written the guests names on white cards.

Tracy and her QC, so obviously besotted with one another, sat together and held hands under the table. He had moved out of the family home and had set himself up in a flat two streets away from his beloved Tracy. They happily engaged in bondage sessions regularly and in between, Tracy and her mother worked hard in the specialist lingerie business. The demand for B and D training was on the increase too. There was never a dull moment.

When everyone was seated with Lady Pamela at the head of the table, their hostess welcomed them all.

"You are all my most favorite people".

She then noticed that Henry was not present and that she had sat down still wearing the hooker's apron. Laughing she stood up and removed it. She continued. "Colonel's in the lavatory I presume?" And then sniffing a little, she went on "God is that the pastry? I think I

407

may have-"

"-It's smoke and it's coming from the hall" Tony interrupted.

The guests all leapt up and went into the hall where they could see that smoke was pouring down the stairs. At that point the fire alarm shrieked into life. Something was alight upstairs. Had The Colonel set fire to himself?

Patrick Partington shouted, "Everyone out".

He quickly ushered everyone outside while calling the fire brigade on his cell phone.

Lady Pamela screeched, "Where's Dandi? Oh my God DANDI..."

She tried to go back in to rescue her beloved dog but Tony stopped her.

"I'll get him" and he dashed inside before anyone could stop him and raced up the stairs.

As mayhem followed the fire sirens could be heard approaching. At that point someone noticed that The Colonel was missing. Patrick rushed back and was half way up the stairs only to be almost bowled over by a figure looming out of the smoke. It was The Colonel with one hand on the bannister and the other on his half-mast trousers, bent double and coughing his heart out. He was helped outside. Everyone started talking at once.

Edward helped the old boy to safety and sat him down on the pavement. Where had the fire started? Lady Pamela was inconsolable at the thought of a barbecued Dandi and Laura, frantic that Tony could die up there, rushed to the bottom of the stairs and shouted.

"Tony...Tony..Come away...O please, get out of there".

Meanwhile Tony had grabbed the startled Dandi and with a towel over his mouth and nose, he was on his knees half pushing the dog in front of him on the landing toward the stairs. Disorientated, the dog started to bark

408

and as they passed flames leaping from the Egyptian room, Dandi tried to turn back. It took all Tony's strength to keep hold of the squirming animal. He pushed the dog down the stairs and Dandi tumbled over landing in a heap by the front door. He skittered out, down the steps and into the waiting arms of his mistress.

Tony followed and staggering out into the street and lay prostrate coughing and gasping. Laura leaving Juliet's side flew to him and kissed him deeply between coughs and then she whispered in his ear.

"I love you pirate".

Even though Juliet did not hear what her mother said, she was in no doubt as to the nature of their relationship.

Three fire engines arrived and blocked the street and a dozen beefy firemen got to work. Straightway it was ascertained that no-one was inside and the people were all herded across the street where they waited in shock, watching the flames and smoke pour from an upstairs window.

Just at that moment Lady Pamela remembered the Beef En Croute and yelled, "The oven. I've burnt the pastry". A fireman was dispatched to turn the oven off.

It was lucky that the fire was localized and did not spread further than the bedroom bathroom and landing outside. It was determined very quickly where the fire had started - The Egyptian room. When this was announced Juliet gave Laura a horrified look. The fire chief told everyone that an appliance for curling hair was the culprit. Juliet went to her mother and burst into tears.

She had borrowed Laura's ancient hot roller set to curl her hair before the party and had forgotten to turn it off.

The combination of the old wiring and an electric appliance accidently left on caused a short and the old wall plug ignited. Lady Pamela was immediately reminded of 'Arry's words…

'Yer plugs, feather plucked, Yer Ladyship'.

How right he'd been. She went over to console Juliet and Laura.

"At least no-one was killed".

Hearing this Juliet started another round of tears.

The Fire Chief then took Lady Pamela aside and gave her a lecture on the state of her wiring and said he would be running a check on her to make sure she re-wired the whole place, now red flagged, immediately. In fact he suggested she move elsewhere while this was being completed. She took it well and thanked him for saving the rest of the house from destruction. She didn't tell him but she had no intention of going anywhere else.

When the coast was clear and The Colonel and Tony had been checked out by medics, the bedraggled party trouped back inside. The main course, now ruined, was under water in the sink where a zealous fireman had dowsed it. Smoke still pervaded the air and black boot marks made a disordered pattern all over the cream carpet on the stairs and landing. Water damage was extensive. The landing carpet was sodden and the walls dripped, pictures askew.

Lady Pamela decided that everyone deserved a medicinal Cognac which was well received. She was able to salvage the Lemon Meringue Pie which was gratefully consumed by the smoked out guests.

After the guests had said how sorry they were and disappeared out into the night, Lady Pamela and Laura peered gingerly into the Egyptian room. They were shocked to see the destruction. The wall paper blackened and peeling and the bed half burnt with water saturated covers. The flames had licked the ceiling and the sphinx was a charred lump. An antique table now with three legs lay drunkenly on its side. Lady Pamela gasped and Laura held onto her as she sobbed.

Laura strangely felt cleansed. The room where David had betrayed her was no more.

Juliet still in shock was made comfortable in Laura's room and given a sleeping pill. She was concerned about her clothes and personal effects and Laura had to tell her that they had managed to rescue her black denim jacket but all the rest of her stuff was either water damaged or infested with smoke. Her little case was charred. She looked up tearfully from the double bed.

"Oh No…I'm so sorry…it was all my fault too".

Laura comforted her and it was decided that she should stay at least another night although Juliet said emphatically that she wanted to go home. Her mother persuaded her that they would go and shop for a whole new wardrobe before her return to Kingbridge. Juliet then relayed another worry.

"Mum…Term starts in a week. I've got to buy a whole lot of new stuff including uniform."

Her mother reassured her that she would accompany her to Kingbridge in two days' time and help equip Juliet with what was needed for the new school term.

Laura also owed a visit to Peter and Cindy whom she knew were guiding and supporting Juliet through this difficult time and in any case her responsibilities and interest in the company needed to be addressed. There had been lawyers' letters and Laura had signed a legal separation agreement.

She was battling with her feelings for the pirate. He had become more to her, she realized, since his rescue of Dandi. It had taken this heroic act to put her feelings for him in perspective and she knew, as she lay next to her sleeping daughter that she was falling in love with him.

An agreement over Pippin Cottage and its contents needed to be drawn up. She was resigned to David and Juliet living there for another two years but she planned to remove half the contents and all her painting gear. Where this stuff would all go she had no idea.

With these thoughts tumbling about her mind, she fell into a fitful sleep.

CHAPTER 28

And so the clean-up began. Juliet awoke refreshed and even though she still felt terrible about setting Casa Blanca on fire, she was reassured about the immediate future. She went down to make everyone breakfast.

Lady Pamela had put a call into 'Arry who turned up at ten to assist. He went straight into the kitchen expecting to see Tanice but instead beheld a pretty blonde leggy girl in T shirt and shorts, cooking pancakes.

"Mornin'".

Juliet turned quickly, "Oh. You gave me a shock".

"How do…Name's 'Arry. Bin a fire then. Not surprised. Told her Ladyship those plugs were feather-plucked".

Juliet looked at him questioningly. He continued. "Any chance of a brew?"

"There's coffee" And without hesitation he helped himself. "What's your name then?"

She told him and giving her a grin, he quipped, "I bet you gotta Romeo".

He left before Juliet could answer and ran upstairs to survey the damage.

Laura and Lady Pamela were standing in the middle of the Egyptian room undecided as to where to start. 'Arry came bounding in and immediately told them both that he would sort the lot and assess the damage.

"'Ave to bin it all Yer Ladyship". Then he wagged a finger at the old lady.

"Told you....them plugs…huffed… puffed and ...stuffed. Lucky you weren't burnt in yer beds."

Then he shooed them out making a quick aside,

413

"I'll take three pancakes and some of that Maple syrup".

Lady Pamela raised an eyebrow at Laura and they went back downstairs to the kitchen leaving Cockney 'Arry to sort out the mess.

Tony turned up around eleven. Even though he had showered, he still had a smell of smoke about him. With complete abandon and no thought of her daughter's reaction, Laura gave him a huge hug and kissed him. He held her to him and returned the kiss.

Juliet's usual bright expression closed down and she pulled away. She bent her head and went to sit with Dandi who luxuriated in her attentions. Thankfully he was none the worse for wear after inhaling smoke and tumbling down the stairs although Lady Pamela was factoring in a visit to the vet that week to check for any after-effects.

Laura glanced at her daughter's bent head and knew that yet another difficult conversation would have to be conducted later in the day. Wasn't it about time that Juliet knew the whole dirty truth about David, his porn habit which led to him visiting a prostitute? Her mother's affair with Blue Eyes. Juliet knew for sure about Tony; of that there was no doubt. For Laura, it was time to come clean.

Lady Pamela astutely noted all that had just happened. She knew what was coming next and resolved to be there for both Juliet and Laura when the truth came out. She hoped Laura would be brave and tell Juliet everything. She also wanted to underline to Laura that financially she need not worry and the dear girl was very welcome to stay as long as she liked at Casa Blanca. Her benefactor was going to insist that any costs incurred, Juliet's expenses, lawyers' fees or living expenses would be met from her income. She intended to give her

414

considerable fortune a severe dent before kicking the bucket.

Tony then set to helping 'Arry carry the old half-burned bed down the stairs and into the street. Various curious onlookers were enjoying the spectacle and the old German recluse next door had his face pressed against the window.

An old lady asked her young companion. "Is it a jumble sale?"

Lady Pamela in her usual controlling manner was buzzing about like a bee visiting flowers and she spent her time either exhorting the onlookers to check their wiring, or getting under foot as 'Arry was clearing the bedroom.

At one point he got annoyed. "I'll be on me arse in a mo with a table on me 'ead."

"That antique table, could it be saved? It's Sheraton you know?"

"Don't care if it's the bleedin' Queen's. S'only got free legs...get out of it Yer Ladyship".

She got the message and stood aside, eventually sitting down with Laura comforting her as she started gasping for breath from all the stress of seeing her prize possessions chucked out on the street. Laura had to put her benefactor's head in a paper bag and get her to breathe in carbon dioxide to combat hyper-ventilation.

The most important conversation that Laura was to have with her daughter came later that evening after dinner. She knew the timing was off but truth telling had to be done.

Lady Pamela had stressed to Laura to be brave and tell Juliet everything from woe to go. With a faltering start she sat Juliet down next to her on the sofa and began at the beginning. Before the start of their talk Laura asked Juliet to remain silent and at the end she could ask questions. Juliet was puzzled by this but did as she was bid. Lady Pamela asked Juliet if she could stay in the room during the mother and daughter talk and Juliet nodded.

And so began the story of Laura and David's relationship; how they were very much in love at the start and when Juliet was on the way how pleased they were and how her arrival had deepened their love for one another.

Laura talked fondly of Pippin Cottage and became a little tearful when telling Juliet how much the cottage meant to her as a mother bringing up her lovely baby girl in the country. Juliet blinked her eyes a few times but stayed focused.

Laura then moved on to the fact that she and David had tried over many years for another child a brother or sister for Juliet and that ultimately they had been unsuccessful. She mentioned that David would not consider the option of fertility treatment, saying if they could not conceive naturally then another baby was not meant to be.

Many years passed and Laura said she had kept busy in the business helping to build up her interior design clients and painting commissioned works. In the beginning this seemed to fulfil her but still at the back of her mind having another baby would nag at her regularly.

She then went on to tell Juliet about her parents' love life. Juliet pulled away a little and looked at her hands as Laura told her, without preamble, that she and David had stopped sleeping together the year before and that David was not interested in her sexually. Did Juliet understand what this meant for her parents' relationship? Juliet nodded glumly.

Laura took a deep breath and glancing at her

benefactor for support she continued,

"What I didn't know darling was that Daddy was looking at pornographic material on the computer. Horrible images. Women that were completely the opposite of me".

Juliet clapped her hand over her mouth and let out an audible "OH...No..."

"And then Daddy turned for sex to an Indian prostitute".

Lady Pamela turned her head away and Juliet said croakily, "I don't believe you. He wouldn't".

Laura then back-tracked to what her daughter had overheard on the stairs, the day that Laura had left Pippin Cottage.

"Darling I'm sorry you heard that bit about Daddy".

Juliet said quietly. "You said something about your sex life being dead and then I think you mentioned his whore and not being able to..."

She trailed off too upset to continue.

"I did and it was to do with the Indian prostitute"

"Did he really...?"

"Yes he did. There's more darling and this time it concerns me. Can I tell you?"

Juliet, stricken, kept her eyes on her mother and nodded.

Laura said how she had found the porn stuff on David's computer and had been extremely upset. "I was angry Jules and I decided, probably foolishly, to have an affair".

She then unfolded the story of her meeting with the American through a friend and their subsequent affair, now ended.

"And now I've got to tell you about Tony".

By this time Juliet had tears pouring down her face. Lady Pamela gave her a hanky and she blew her nose.

417

Poor Juliet it was a lot to process especially after the recent fire disaster. She started to tremble slightly.

Lady Pamela moved to sit next to her and the old lady held her hand.

"I met Tony through Lady Pamela. She asked me to have tea one afternoon after the accident with Dandi and I went along not knowing that she had asked Tony too. He owns a book shop nearby. Anyway we hit it off and I thought he was a nice guy. We had nature and gardening in common and we seemed to chat easily together about all sorts of things."

Laura then omitted the dinner party fiasco where she and David had crashed into one another and went on to say that after she left David she called Lady Pamela who said that there was a bed available here at her home. She said that before Juliet arrived Laura had been out with Tony a few times and they had become close.

"But you kissed him Mummy...as in a proper kiss".

"Yes I did darling and he kissed me back".

At that point the whole episode became too much for Juliet and she flung herself out of the room and up into the Chinese bedroom. Lady Pamela took a tearful Laura in an embrace and said,

"Leave her for a while. Let her process what's just happened. And by the way. Well done."

Juliet was half asleep when Laura came up to bed. She had sat over a Cognac with her benefactor for an hour or two feeling too wired for sleep. When she did eventually climb into bed beside her daughter, she lay flat out staring at the ceiling until Juliet turned on her side toward her mother and whispered,

"Mum?"

Laura turned her head, smiled and whispered, "I love you darling" And took her in an embrace.

After a moment, Juliet looked at her and said, "And I

418

love you too Mum. Can I tell you about Jonothan?"

There followed a whispered conversation with giggles from both sides. As the gossip subsided and Juliet turned over to sleep, Laura smiled to herself and thanked her stars that Juliet had reverted to a teenage preoccupation – The self.

The following day was 'shopping' day for Juliet and Laura. They took off early in the morning and went over to Knightsbridge and Sloane Street to hit the shops. Lady Pamela insisted on giving Laura her Harvey Nichols store account card and account pin number and said she would be very cross if Laura did not use it.

Juliet was keen to visit Harrods and they planned a nice lunch somewhere 'cool'. No more was said about the previous evening's confession.

On leaving Casa Blanca, much to Juliet's astonishment, Lady Pamela pressed a hundred pounds into her hand.

"Buy yourself something pretty dear".

Tanice arrived mid-morning and was shattered to see the fire devastation that had wreaked havoc on the Egyptian room.

"You lucky to be sittin' here with me MadamPam. You coulda got burnt to a crisp. Is de dog alright?"

Lady Pamela told her all about Dandi's rescue from the fire and embroidered the drama a little more than was necessary,

"He was black as soot poor darling with a singed backside and he coughed all night from the smoke".

Lady Pamela related the whole story to an astonished Tanice and then remembered she had to start seriously thinking about having the whole of Casa Blanca re-wired as soon as possible. It was ironic that the London Fire Department had ear-marked the property with a red sticker. It felt as though Casa Blanca was marked as a

419

brothel after all. It all seemed over-whelming and she considered not doing anything until Laura returned.

She went into her study and rang 'Arry. He called back late morning and said that he felt his small group of electricians would find the job too complicated.

"Fink you need one of them big boys yer ladyship. When you get someone I'd be happy to help...sorta consultant. Let me know when you need me" He rang off.

Flustered, the old lady decided to ring The Colonel to see if he had any bright ideas.

His one comment was, "Ask Laura. Her husband runs that renovation company doesn't he?" Then he added, chuckling "By the by, how's it going with the daughter?"

She omitted to tell him about the confession. It was none of his business anyway and even if, in the old days they had shared everything, all the gossip and goings on at Casa Blanca, she did not feel inclined to air Laura's dirty washing and have him ask her pointed questions about Laura's beautiful daughter, so obviously a virgin. The man could not stop himself where the subject of sex was concerned.

They finished their conversation with him asking if she would like a quiet dinner the following week. It was agreed he would pick her up in the taxi at 7pm and they would go to Le Petit Jardin for a meal.

When the shopping pair returned laden with parcels, Lady Pamela was excited to see what they had bought. She could see many Harvey Nicholls labels and was pleased Laura had used the shop card to very good advantage. Laura also bought some new luggage for Juliet and they opened the smaller case out of which shoes, a coat and jeans fell out. Juliet, in buoyant mood, shot upstairs to try on her new clothes.

420

Over a cup of tea Lady Pamela mentioned her worries over finding a suitable company with a good reputation to re-wire Casa Blanca. She told Laura that 'Arry was unable to do it.

"I know you've split from your husband but do you think your husband's company might be able to do the job?"

Laura knew David and Peter would jump at the chance especially in light of Gupta's disappearance. It would be a lucrative contract for them. Thinking quickly that she and her team could be involved with the re-decoration as well, she said,

"Yes…yes I think they would be very interested. Have you thought about re-decorating?"

"There's so much to sort out, isn't there?

"I could help you. Be your project manager so to speak"

"Would you really?"

"We could take it slowly. I have carpenters, painters and interior design people that I use and I can help you choose a completely new decor".

They looked at each other in excitement. For Lady Pamela it would mean she could keep in touch with Laura constantly and be able to leave a supervised renovation in the dear girl's capable hands. For Laura the job would act as a boost for The Manning Renovation Company and directly help her finances. It would certainly make dealing with David a little easier.

The old lady took Laura in her arms and said,

"Thank you. Thank you. It takes a weight off my mind".

Then she looked at her closely and said, "You mean so much to me dear."

Her benefactor was musing on the fact that for ease of supervising the contract Laura could stay at Casa Blanca for as long as she was needed. The old lady smiled and silently congratulated herself on this excellent plan.

The following morning Laura and Juliet were preparing to leave Casa Blanca. Juliet humming to herself was placing her new wardrobe carefully into the bright blue cases. Lady Pamela still feeling tired from the events of the last few days and their consequences was having a quiet morning in bed.

Mother and daughter carried their cases to the front hall and Laura went into the kitchen to make a cup of coffee. She looked out onto the street to see if Tony was in evidence. He had said he would come by to say goodbye. As she was wondering whether or not to disturb Lady Pamela, there was a knock on the front door. It was Tony. Laura made some more coffee and the three of them sat round the table. Laura looked at the two people who were dearest to her heart, took their hands in hers and said,

"I love you both...so much".

Both Juliet and Tony were not prepared for this and Juliet, confused that Tony had been included in this intimate declaration, looked at her mother and almost like staking a claim on her mother's love, half stood and put her arms around Laura and pressed her cheek to Laura's. She then stood erect and with focused poise gave Tony a long appraising look.

Even though she would be shuttling back and forth between her Mum and Dad, Juliet realized that Tony was not taking her mother from her but that he was possibly about to join them in their future life together. She smiled at them and looked at their joined hands. She said maturely,

"I think you have some unfinished business".

She left the room almost bumping into Lady Pamela who was hovering just out of sight. The old lady smiled

422

at her and put a finger to her lips.

Laura and Tony looked into each other's eyes and the pirate said quietly,

"I love you".

Lady Pamela in her dressing gown, standing unseen just outside the kitchen, almost crowed with delight. As the couple turned towards each other to kiss, a sudden wave of nausea hit Laura and she leapt up quickly and vomited neatly in the sink. Startled he put his arm around her as she rinsed and wiped her mouth on a tea towel. Tanice was about to bustle through to continue her cleaning duties when a thin arm barred her path. Giving her employer a quizzical look she stepped nimbly out of view.

"What is it about me that makes you vomit? That's the second time it's happened".

As Lady Pamela grinned at Tanice and mouthed the word "pregnant", Laura was looking at Tony. With a beaming smile she held his hand.

"I'm pregnant".

Tony looked at her in amazement; his eyes like saucers.

"You mean…you and I…are having a baby?"

Laura nodded madly.

For a split second nobody moved and then everything happened at once. Tony grabbed Laura and hugged her as Lady Pamela came racing in, quickly followed by Tanice and Dandelion.

"Wonderful news Laura. So exciting for you both".

Dandi barked in agreement.

As the couple were receiving congratulations, Juliet dragged her new cases across the hall and popped her head round the kitchen door. All eyes turned to Laura and the assembled group held their breath and waited.

"What is it Mum?"

423

"I was just saying a big 'thank you' to Pamela…and everyone".

She gave Tony a soft look and then turned to her daughter, "Are you ready darling?"

Juliet nodded and said a quiet 'thank you'. They all gave her warm hug and said to come back soon. She stroked Dandelion's head and he looked up at her adoringly.

The cases were loaded into the car and Juliet climbed into the passenger seat. Laura caressed Tony's cheek. He took her hand and placed it on his heart. She smiled, all the while thinking life is messy and always will be. She had a lot disentangling ahead of her and how would Juliet react to the news of a baby brother or sister?

But she had found love again and a new life was quickening within her. Her needs were met and she rejoiced.

LOOSE ENDS

As in life this story has loose ends.
Here to the best of my ability are a few tied up.

I can tell you that Laura and Tony had a beautiful
brown-eyed baby son called Marco Joseph Fredericks
and Juliet his half-sister became his Godmother.
Cindy and Peter had a baby girl named Lucinda.

Dandelion yet again was almost the death of Lady
Pamela.She fell over him half way down the stairs and
broke her hip. Laura was not there to pick up the pieces
and the old lady ended up in hospital where she
contracted pneumonia from which she took some time to
recover. Soon after, Dandelion contracted a stomach
complaint and had to be put to sleep.

Tanice retired and lived off the proceeds of her best
seller "Copulation Capers in The Caribbean"-Now a
major motion picture. She became a celebrity in the
media and enjoyed her 15 minutes of fame.

The Colonel made sure the Old Girl was looked after but
one day he went to his club in his pajamas and never
returned home.

Of Edward, no-one knows. He was last spotted in Perth,
Western Australia, pushing a double baby buggy along
the waterfront.

Casa Blanca still stands in the borough of Chelsea, now
re-wired and re-decorated and with new owners:-A
young couple with a baby son called Marco and his
adopted grandmother GrannyPam.

THE HOUSE OF TRYSTS.

MadamPam's Recipes.

MadamPam's favourite soups "No cream Tanice. Thank You!"

MadamPam liked all her soups made with home-made stock. She abhorred bought soups or stock as she reckoned the additives ruined her kidneys.

Home-Made Ham or Chicken Stock (freeze some for use later)
Carcass of a large chicken, or Ham Hock joint.
An onion, 2 carrots, 2 celery sticks and tops, 5 cloves, 1 tablspn of mixed herbs, 2 tspns of ground cumin, 1 whole head of garlic(unpeeled). Italian parsley.

In a deep iron casserole dish put a splash of olive oil and rice bran oil. Fry the roughly chopped onion, carrots, celery and garlic. Add in herbs and cloves and sauté the mixture until onion is soft. Add the ham hock or chicken carcass, turn in the mixture, fry and then add enough water to fill the casserole almost to the top. Heat everything on the stove and then put into the oven at 150 degrees for 3 hours. Remove from the oven and cool. Strip the meat from the bones and discard bones. Pass the vegetables through a sieve.

- Ham Hock can be very salty so initially best to bring the hock to boil in deep saucepan and simmer for 5 minutes. Throw away the water and then commence the recipe.

Chicken and Leek Soup

426

Finely chopped cooked chicken thigh and drumstick.
2 leeks
1 cooked potato (diced)
2 tspns of Tarragon (dried or fresh)
1 tspn of Thyme.
Knob of butter
Seasoning.
Home-made stock

In a deep fry pan, sauté the finely chopped leeks in a little butter and olive oil. Add herbs and sauté gently for 5 minutes. Into the pan put 4 cups of stock. Bring up to simmer. Add the potato and chicken pieces. Season. Simmer for 2 minutes and serve with a garnish of chopped Italian parsley.

Even though Tanice was told many times NOT to put cream into the soups, MadamPam always kept a little pot of cream at the back of the fridge and would a add a teaspoon of the illicit substance just before serving. She disguised this indulgence by putting the cream in one of Dandy's old treat containers. Of course Tanice was fully aware of this nonsensical habit but knew it would do her no good to comment.

Casa Blanca Minestrone
A variety of summer vegetables to include red onion and red capsicum and 2/3 tomatoes.
2 tablespoons of cooked couscous.
Home-made Stock
Fresh Chives and Basil
Seasoning

Dice onion and capsicum finely and sauté in olive oil. Place tomatoes in boiling water until they split and remove their skins.

Dice all other vegetables finely.

Tanice uses courgettes, green beans, a celery stick and spinach.

Add to onion mix together with pulped tomatoes and chopped chives. Season. Sauté vegetables for 5 minutes. Add 3 cups of stock and 1 cup of water and simmer for 5 minutes. Season to taste.

Before serving add in a half cup of cooked couscous, bring up to heat and sprinkle with chopped basil.

MadamPam's Beetroot Smoothie

MadamPam would bore people to tears- Tanice was one of them- with her rapturous extolling of the humble beetroot.

"Marvelous for cleansing the blood, the bowels and lowering blood pressure. Popeye ate spinach for energy but beetroot is so much more fortifying and look at my skin Tanice" ...and so on.

4/5 large Beetroot.

Chop off the ends of the beets and chop them into chunks. Place them in a large saucepan and cover with cold water almost to the top of the pan. Boil without seasoning for 20 minutes or until soft through. Leave to cool and then place in the kitchen blender and puree with the beetroot water.

Keeps in the fridge for a week and freeze some for later use.

Whole almonds and walnuts can be added to the smoothie if desired

To make into a tasty beetroot soup. Fry 2 spring onions, add in a cup beetroot pulp, and a cup of stock, season. Serve with a dollop of sour cream (*Alright to use*

428

in MadamPam's book) and a sprinkle of chives and some French bread.

Watercress and Tomato Gazpacho
15 large tomatoes
3 sprigs of watercress
2 mugs of stock
1 mug of water
2 garlic cloves
3 tablespoons of olive oil
1 red capsicum finely diced.
Bunch of fresh basil.
Seasoning.
Toasted Pita bread.
Sour cream (*a small dollop thank you Tanice!)*

  Pour boiling water over tomatoes and ease the skin off. Put chopped tomatoes and watercress into kitchen blender. Add stock, water, garlic, chopped basil and seasoning. Add olive oil and more stock if needed. Puree. Refrigerate for a few hours and serve chilled with a garnish of chopped red capsicum and Pita bread oiled and crisped in the oven.

For some strange reason MadamPam openly allows herself a dollop of sour cream on the top of the Gazpacho before serving.

MadamPam's Starters and Entrees

Smoked Salmon Pate
3 slices of smoked salmon
2 tablspns of spreadable cream cheese

429

Juice of half a lemon
Pinch of dill or 2 finely diced fresh fennel slices
Seasoning

Mash salmon with the cream cheese. Add lemon juice herbs and seasoning Mix well.
Serve with very thin toasts or crackers of your choice.
You can substitute smoked mackerel for salmon if desired.

Prawn Cocktail (8 people)
500 gm of cooked prawns (shells removed) or bag of cooked prawns.
1 jar of Mayonnaise (Praise is best)
½ cup of milk
Juice of a lemon
1 tspn Tomato Ketchup.
Handful of crushed unsalted cashews.
3 or 4 chopped radishes.
Cos or iceberg lettuce to line the goblets.
Seasoning.

In a large bowl combine prawns with thinned mayonnaise. Add ketchup and lemon juice. Season. Mix carefully. Spoon prawns into glass goblets or coupe dishes lined with Cos lettuce. Sprinkle with cashews and chopped radishes. Serve chilled.

Prawn, Avocado and Spinach Salad
4/5 shelled cooked prawns
Half an avocado
Crisp bacon pieces
1 skinned and diced peach
Handful of spinach leaves

430

Handful of baby kale leaves.
Chopped parsley and mint

Assemble prettily on a salad plate. Season. Dress with a home-made French dressing.

MadamPam's favorite dressing

Combine virgin olive oil (3 parts) with Balsamic vinegar (1 part) Season. Add 2 crushed garlic cloves, 1 tspn American mustard, 2 tspns maple syrup, 2 tspns unsweetened berry puree (Any berry is fine).

Lentil, Orange and Carrot Salad

1 tin of cooked lentils (red or green) or a cup of fresh cooked lentils.
1 orange
2 carrots
1 parsnip
6 chopped dates
MadamPam's favorite dressing
1 tablspn fresh chopped coriander (cilantro)
Ground cumin
2 tspn sweet chilli sauce
Olive oil.
Seasoning.

Rinse tinned lentils well in cold water. Drain. Slice carrots and parsnip thinly into sticks, sprinkle with olive oil, seasoning ground cumin and sweet chili sauce. Roast in a hot oven for 15 minutes. Peel and chop the orange into pieces. Combine orange pieces, dates and lentils. Add roasted carrots and parsnip. In a bowl mix coriander, the dressing, and season. Add this mixture to the lentils and mix well. Check seasoning. The salad is served warm.

Sweet Potato, Peach, Raspberry and Coriander Salad (8 people)
4 sweet potato
3 peaches peeled and sliced
1 diced red onion
Punnet of fresh raspberries (or blueberries)
2 tablspns of coriander or mint
MadamPam's dressing
Seasoning.

Peel and cook the sweet potato. Combine chopped potato, peaches, onion and coriander or mint. Season. Add the dressing and mix well. Sprinkle raspberries on top of the salad.

Green Banana Salad (8 people)
This is the cooked banana salad from the Caribbean Soiree.
4 large green bananas
(These are a special type of banana sold in the tropics but ordinary unripe bananas are suitable)
1 punnet Cherry Tomatoes
A cucumber (peeled and cubed)
2 chopped capsicum
2 avocados
1 red onion (diced)
8 chunks of water melon
Bunch of chopped fresh basil
1 tablspn of fresh mint
Seasoning
MadamPam's dressing
2 packets of pine nuts.

Peel bananas, halve and boil until soft-about 10

minutes. Drain and refresh with cold water. Combine halved tomatoes, capsicum, water melon and red onion. Add basil and mint and chopped bananas. Peel and slice the avocados and add to bananas. Season. Pour the dressing over the salad and mix up well. Chill. Just before serving sprinkle pine nuts over the salad.

*Note that bananas and avocados do discolor so make salad just before eating.

Egg and Caviar Igloo
10 hardboiled eggs
Jar of Mayonnaise
A little milk
Juice of ½ lemon
1 jar of pink caviar
2 tspns of black caviar
1 tablspn chopped chives
2/3 finely chopped radishes for garnish
Seasoning
Watercress or spinach leaves

Combine the mashed eggs and lemon juice with the mayonnaise. Make a thick mix. Milk may be needed. Add the pink caviar, seasoning and chives. Combine. Place mixture in a bowl and press down to mold. Chill for a few hours or overnight. Turn the igloo out onto a platter. Spread the top with black caviar. Surround with watercress or spinach and sprinkle with radish.

Lady Pamela used to eat a great deal of black caviar in her youth but when she had to pay for it herself she baulked at the expense. The pink caviar "somewhat inferior to black but passable" adds a delicious flavor. This dish is easy to prepare and spectacular to present. Lady Pamela serves it with top quality crackers.

Stuffed crab backs (8 people)
Served at the Caribbean Soiree.
8 large crab shells or 8 scallop shells
Fresh crab meat or 2 tins of crab meat-well drained.
2 fillets of white fish
6 cooked prawns finely chopped
Approx half a liter of béchamel (white) sauce.
Fresh dill and Italian parsley
1 beaten egg
Parmesan
Grated zest and juice of a lemon

In a little olive oil fry finely chopped fish and crab meat with the lemon zest. Season. Add the béchamel sauce and lemon juice. Mash mixture and Simmer for 5 minutes. Reduce heat. Add finely chopped prawns and beaten egg. Place mixture in the shells, dust with parmesan and bake at 180 degrees until browned on the top. Sprinkle with chopped dill and parsley and serve piping hot.

Carrot pudding

A favorite of MadamPam's as she believes that the carrots are good for maintaining eye health.
3 carrots
1 potato
2 beaten eggs
3 tablspns of cream cheese
Grated zest of ½ orange and juice of the orange
2 tspns of ground cumin
1 chopped spring onion
Seasoning
1 tspn of 5 spice

Mash cooked carrots and potato with a little milk. Season. Add onion, cream cheese, eggs, zest and orange juice, cumin and all spice. Combine well. Place mixture in oven dish and bake at 170deg for 25 minutes or until golden brown.
Serve with a green salad and your favorite chutney.

Smoked Fish French bread Pie (6 People)
2 sides of smoked fish or approx 500 grams of a mixture of fish-smoked and plain

MadamPam likes to use kippers (smoked herring) but Tanice prefers smoked boneless fillets as kippers are "a bugger to prepare as dey are full of de bones". Tanice has adjusted this recipe for her family to include cream and cheese. MadamPam would not approve.
2 hardboiled eggs
1 onion
Zest and juice of a lemon
1 small carton of light cream
1 celery stick and green top
1 red capsicum
1 mug of cooked lentils
2 tablspns of grated cheddar cheese
1 small carton of fish stock
Seasoning
French bread stick
Olive oil

In a deep pan fry diced onion, capsicum, lemon zest and chopped celery for 5 minutes in some olive oil. Add lemon juice and fish stock. Remove skin and bones from fish and cut into bite size pieces. Add fish to stock mixture and heat through. Season and simmer for a few

435

minutes. Add chopped eggs, cooked lentils and light cream. Mix and set aside.

Cut bread stick into thin rounds and oil on both sides. Place in hot oven 220 degrees and brown on both sides. When browned remove from the oven and turn oven down to 180 deg.

Grease a baking dish with olive oil, put fish mixture into dish and line the top with browned bread slices .Sprinkle cheese over the top and bake for 20 minutes or until golden brown.

Macaroni Pie (8 People)
Served at the Caribbean Soiree and very popular with men who were nannied as children!
1 and 1/2 packets of Macaroni
Approx 1 liter of cheese sauce
4 rashers of streaky bacon
2 onions
Seasoning
1 tablspn of pesto
Parmesan

Boil Macaroni in salted water until just cooked. Make a béchamel (white) sauce and add a handful of grated cheddar cheese or your favorite cheese.

In a deep pan fry diced onion and chopped bacon in a little olive oil. Bacon should be cooked until crisp. Season and add pesto. Mix and fry. Add cheese sauce and simmer for a few minutes.

Combine Macaroni and the sauce and place in a baking dish. Top with parmesan and bake at 170 degrees for 20 minutes until golden brown. Sprinkle parsley and serve.

Leek and Tomato Flan

Frozen short crust pastry.
2 leeks
6 large tomatoes
1 tspn pesto
Panko (Japanese) bread crumbs
Grated parmesan
1 tspn Thyme
Olive oil
Chopped fresh basil
Seasoning
8 stone less olives (black or green)

Line a greased flan dish with the unfrozen pastry. Prick with a fork and bake blind for 15 minutes at 180 deg. In a frying pan fry chopped leeks, thyme and pesto in olive oil until leeks are soft.

Place mixture into pastry case and add finely sliced tomatoes in rings on top. Season well. Top tomatoes with half olives and dribble virgin olive oil over the filling. Sprinkle Panko crumbs and dot with butter. Bake for approx 20 minutes at 180 degrees or until golden brown on top. Garnish with fresh basil.

Spinach and Bacon Pie
Frozen Short crust pastry
Bunch of spinach
4 rashers of smoked bacon.
1 tablspn ground almonds
2 beaten eggs
2 tablspn of soft cream cheese
Squeeze of lemon juice
Seasoning

Line a greased flan dish with unfrozen pastry. Prick with a fork and bake blind for 15 minutes at 180 deg.

Boil the spinach for 5 minutes and drain well. In a fry pan fry chopped bacon until crisp. In a bowl add spinach to the cream cheese, lemon juice and ground almonds. Add beaten eggs. Season and mix well. Place bacon on the bottom of the flan, add spinach mix and bake at 180 degrees for approx 25 minutes or until mixture is set.

Rice and Black-eyed beans (8 people)
Served at the Caribbean Soiree.
In the West Indies Pigeon peas (beans) are used and this dish is called 'Rice 'n peas' or 'Peas 'n Rice'.
Tanice likes to add in some herbs and spices.

   Soak 1 1/2 mugs of black-eyed beans in cold water for a few hours.
Cook your favorite rice-enough for 6 people. Rinse well.
Boil beans until tender-approx 20 minutes. They will swell a little. Drain and rinse.
Sauté a diced red onion in a little olive oil, add a tablspn of chopped fresh mint, 1 handful of crushed unsalted cashews, and a handful of cranberries. Mix and fry for 5 minutes.
Add beans and rice and heat through.
For some extra heat add a sprinkle of chili oil or some hot pepper sauce.

MadamPam has to be fed this dish without any extra heat or there will be hell to pay!

Two Meat Layered Meatloaf
300 grams of chicken mince
300 grams of lean pork mince
2 flat mushrooms
3 garlic cloves
I red capsicum

438

Olive oil
1 tablspn of chopped coriander
1 tablspn of fish sauce
1 tspn ginger puree
Seasoning

Combine ingredients in 2 bowls as follows –
Bowl 1 – Chicken mince, very finely chopped mushrooms, minced garlic and seasoning.
Bowl 2 - Pork mince, chopped coriander, fish sauce, ginger and seasoning.

Oil a deep oven proof dish and place thin capsicum rings on the base. Place the pork mixture as the first layer then add the chicken mince on top and press down well. Cover with foil and place in a Bain Marie in the oven at 160deg for an hour and 15 minutes or until the juices run clear. Test with a knife. Remove from the oven and let stand for 20 minutes. The meat will have shrunk away from the sides and exuded juice. Pour off some of the juice and keep for soup mixes. Turn the meatloaf out onto a platter and serve with relish or chutney and a crisp green salad.

MadamPam had to teach Tanice how to use the Bain Marie. Tanice was not at all sure about this water bath but meekly took instruction as her employer extolled the virtues of French cooking and how she had learned about this method at the Finishing School in Switzerland. Tanice needed a strong cuppa at the end of that boring discourse.

Stuffed Chilli Paw Paw (4 People)
Tanice adds in extra heat for her family using chili oil to fry the beef and a whole chopped chili with seeds.

439

2 Paw Paws
500 grams prime beef mince
1 diced onion
2 diced rashers of streaky bacon
1 tablspn chopped garlic
5 drops Tabasco sauce
2 tablspns tomato puree
1 tablspn oregano
1 carton of beef stock or use homemade
2 tablspns plain flour
Breadcrumbs
Grated cheddar cheese
1 green capsicum cut in rings for garnish
Olive oil
Seasoning
2 or 3 knobs of butter.
Chili oil (optional)

Cut the paw paws in half and remove seeds. Hollow out each half taking some of the flesh.
In a casserole dish fry the onion, bacon, oregano and garlic. Set aside mixture on a plate. Fry seasoned mince in the casserole, breaking up well. Add the flour and brown the meat. Add onion mix, paw paw flesh, beef stock and tomato puree. Cover dish and simmer for 40 minutes. Grease a baking dish, fill each halved paw paw with the mince, sprinkle breadcrumbs and cheese over the meat and dot with butter. Brown in the oven at 180 degrees for 20 minutes. Garnish with rings of green capsicum.

Slow Roast Lamb
This is a popular dish with the girls on Saturday nights at Casa Blanca.

Tanice has to stab the lamb to insert the garlic cloves.
When she has had a particularly trying day at the coal
face she imagines the lamb is… guess who……
This dish improves in flavor if done the day before,
refrigerated and then re-heated in the sauce. Add half a
cup of boiling water if sauce has coagulated.
1 large oven bag
Large leg of Lamb (bone in)
8 cloves of garlic
2 sprigs of rosemary
Olive oil
Sweet chili sauce
1 tablspn ground cumin
Seasoning
1 cup of cranberries
10 stone less black olives
Approx 1 liter of stock
2 glasses of red wine (French of course!)
2 tablspns plain flour.

Trim the lamb of any extra fat. Make deep knife cuts
in the lamb and insert halved garlic cloves.

Season the meat with salt pepper and cumin and pour
over a little olive oil. Place the lamb in the oven bag
with the rosemary sprigs. Tie the bag. Bake in the oven
for 3 ½ hours at 150 degrees. Remove lamb from the
oven and rest for 15 minutes. Keep the juices. Take the
meat away from the bone and slice. Place in a deep
baking dish. To make the gravy add the flour to the
juices in the roasting pan and mix well. Slowly add the
stock to avoid lumps. Add the red wine, a dollop of
sweet chilli sauce, the olives and the cranberries. Check
seasoning and Simmer for 5 minutes. Pour gravy over
the lamb and serve.

Roast Chicken with Orange, Tarragon and Fresh Fennel
(6 People)
1 Large chicken
1 orange
Juice of half a lemon
1 tablspn fresh or dried tarragon
1 Fennel bulb
2 rashers bacon
1 sachet Miso soup dissolved in ½ liter boiling water
1 Large oven bag
Seasoning
Toothpicks

Trim off extra fat and skin from the bird. Make small cuts in an orange and place inside the chicken. Prick the chicken with a sharp knife. Season and rub the tarragon over the breast. Pour lemon juice over the breast .Cover the chicken with the bacon strips securing each end with half tooth picks. Place the chicken in the oven bag. Chop the fennel bulb in half and put one each side of the chicken and then secure the end of the bag. Roast at 170deg for 1 hour and 15 minutes then remove from the oven and rest for 10 minutes. Discard bag and place bird on hot serving dish. Retain juices. In the roasting pan squeeze juice from the orange into the pan, Season and mix up bacon pieces and chopped fennel bulb, add Miso soup to the gravy and mix well.

Chicken Breasts stuffed with Olives and Prunes (6 People)
6 chicken breasts
4/5 Bacon rashers
Chopped Tarragon
8 stuffed olives

4/5 Prunes finely chopped
Butter
Seasoning
2 tspns paprika
1 beaten egg.
Breadcrumbs
Cooking String or twine

Flatten out the breasts and beat until thinned out. Season. Fry two finely chopped bacon rashers and chopped Tarragon until crisp in a little olive oil. In a bowl combine finely chopped olives, prunes, paprika and bacon mix, add 2 tablspns fresh breadcrumbs, the beaten egg and approx. 50 grams of softened butter. Mix well. Season. Spread mixture into the center of the chicken breasts and roll up and wrap the other bacon rashers around the meat. Secure each breast with string. Place the breasts, seam side down, in a baking dish and sprinkle olive oil and seasoned breadcrumbs over the top. Bake for 50 minutes at 175 degrees or until juices run clear. Decorate with Italian parsley and enjoy with a crisp salad.

MadamPam enjoys this dish with a crisp glass of New Zealand Sauvignon Blanc.

Tanice's Coconut Chicken Curry with Okra (8 People)
This was served at the Caribbean Soiree.
10/12 assorted chicken pieces-legs and breasts.
3 onions
2 celery sticks and tops
2 liters homemade stock
2 cans of coconut cream
1 Large jar of Chicken Tikka Marsala Sauce
2 handfuls fresh Okra (Obtainable from an Afro-

Caribbean store)
Bunch of fresh coriander
Seasoning
Juice and zest of 2 limes
Chili oil or vegetable oil for less heat.
Asian greens.
Crushed unsalted cashews

Trim chicken pieces of all extra fat. In a deep casserole dish fry diced onion, grated lime zest and celery in oil. Add chopped Okra and lime juice. Season and fry until okra are soft. The okra will exude a milky substance Place on a plate. In the casserole fry the chicken in oil in batches until well browned and season. Add onion and celery mix, coconut cream, stock, Tikka Marsala sauce and the stalks of coriander. Mix well. Bring up to simmer. Cover and place in the oven for 2 hours at 160 deg. Remove from heat and mix in chopped Asian greens. Serve and garnish each plate with fresh chopped coriander and cashews.

Garlic Pork with Sage and Hot Pepper Sauce (8 People)

This was served at the Caribbean Soiree
Hot Pepper Sauce is served on the side as per MadamPam's instructions.
"Don't want my stomach lining bursting into flames Tanice".
1 fresh half leg of pork – Bone in.
5/6 twigs of fresh sage
10 cloves of garlic
1 large oven bag
1 ½ mugs of Hoisin Sauce or Chinese marinade
Half a mug of sweet chill sauce.
Half a mug of lime juice

1 glass of red wine
Half a mug of olive oil
Approx 1 liter of chicken or ham stock
1 tablspn of smoky sauce /marinade
Seasoning – 3 tspns salt and pepper.
Corn flour

With a sharp knife remove the pig skin and reserve for crackling. Cut round the central bone and loosen flesh. Stuff space with some of the sage leaves. Make deep cuts through the meat and insert halved garlic cloves. In a bowl place Hoisin sauce, oil, lime juice and sweet chill sauce. Add salt and pepper and mix well. Place joint into a bowl and slather with marinade. Leave for a few hours in the fridge. Turn from time to time. To roast – Place joint on a bed of sage in a large oven bag and slow roast at 160 degrees for 3 ½ hours. Remove from oven and rest for 10 minutes. Remove the bag, sage twigs and bone and reserve the juice. Slice the meat and place in hot baking dish. Cover and keep warm

For crackling-Score the pig skin with a sharp knife and roast at 240 degrees until crisp through. Break into chunks.

For gravy – In a bowl, dissolve 2 tablspns of corn flour in cold water and make a thin cream. Add to warmed juices in the roasting pan. Add stock, smoky marinade and wine. Stir well to avoid lumps. Check seasoning and pour over meat. Serve with crackling on the side and hot pepper sauce to your taste.

Fillet of Beef En Croute. (8 People)

Sadly the fireman threw this dish into the sink and consigned it to a watery grave.

445

MadamPam keeps the thin piece at the end of the fillet for Dandi - much to Tanice's disapproval.
Fillet of best beef in the piece.
2 rashers of bacon
Flaky Puff pastry
3 flat mushrooms
2 spring onions finely chopped
1 tablspn tarragon
1 tablspn rum
Seasoning
1 beaten egg
Olive oil

In a little olive oil fry the finely chopped mushrooms, tarragon and chopped onions. Season. Add a tablspn of rum and simmer for a few minutes to reduce. Set aside. Trim the fillet of any fat, season and quick fry on high heat until browned all over. Roll the rashers of bacon round the fillet. Prepare pastry into a rectangular shape making sure that there are 2 ends to fold in around the meat. Place the mushroom mix in a line in the middle of the pastry. Place the fillet on top, check seasoning and roll the pastry round the fillet tucking in the ends. Secure the center seam with a little cold water. Brush pastry with beaten egg. Place seam side down on a greased baking tray and cook for approx. 30 minutes on 180 degrees or until pastry is risen and golden.

MadamPam's Desserts and Baking
As MadamPam does not approve of dessert "but I do like a creamy homemade ice cream with fresh strawberries while watching Wimbledon tennis on the television", the dessert section of this chapter is somewhat meagre.

446

Apple and Blackcurrant Crumble

Popular with the girls on Saturday nights. Lovely with ice cream.

Any sharp-flavored berry is good or substitute berry for rhubarb.

3 Apples-Peeled and sliced
1 pack of frozen blackcurrants or similar.
2 tablspns white sugar
1 cup of water

  Place mixed apples and berries in a baking dish. Add water. Sprinkle sugar over fruit

Crumble Mix

200 grams of plain flour
200 grams of brown sugar
150 grams of butter

  In a bowl place the flour and cut up pieces of butter. Rub the butter into the flour until crumbs are formed. Add the sugar and mix well.

Pour the crumble mixture over the fruit and place in the oven at 180 degrees for 35 minutes or until crumble is golden.

Lemon Meringue Pie (8 People)

Sweet Short crust pastry

  Line a greased flan tin – medium size- with the pastry and prick with a fork. Bake blind at 180 degrees for 15 minutes or until pastry begins to color.

Filling

1 ½ tablspns of corn flour
1 cup of white sugar
Rind of 1 lemon
Half a cup of lemon juice
1 tablspn of lemon curd

447

3 eggs – separated.
1 tablspn butter
4 tablspn cold water

In a saucepan blend corn flour with cold water and make a smooth cream. Add rind, lemon juice, sugar and bring slowly to boil. Simmer until mixture thickens and stir constantly to avoid lumps. Remove from the heat, allow to cool a little and add yolks, lemon curd and butter. Beat and set aside.

Meringue

Beat the egg whites until they peak and hold their shape. Beat in 2 tablspns of icing sugar, one at a time. Mixture should be thick and glossy.

Pour lemon mixture into flan and top with meringue. Bake at 170 degrees for approx. 15 minutes or until meringue browns on top.

MadamPam's home-made Ice Cream with Tanice's additions

Mango and Coconut ice cream was served at the Caribbean Soiree.

5 eggs – separated
1 large bottle of cream *(MadamPam's secret indulgence)*
1 Mug of icing sugar
2 tspns vanilla essence

Bowl 1.   Separate the eggs
Beat the egg whites until stiff and add half the sugar in small amounts until well mixed and glossy.
Bowl 2.   Beat yolks and the rest of the sugar until mixture is a pale cream in color.
Add the vanilla essence. Beat again.
Bowl 3.   Whip the cream until peaked.

Gently fold yolk mixture into white mixture and then fold in whipped cream.
Freeze until almost frozen. Remove from freezer and churn adding your favorite flavor of berry puree, chocolate or nuts. Re-freeze.

MadamPam enjoys this with fresh strawberries.
Tanice adds in 1 tin of coconut cream, diced fresh mango or paw paw puree and a little mango juice.

Rich Dark Chocolate Mousse (8 People)
MadamPam allows herself this dessert only once a year...or so Tanice is told.
2 large bars of dark chocolate (400grams)
6 eggs
2 tablspns brandy
1 cup of water
Half a cup of sugar
Whipped cream

Place broken chocolate into a basin over a saucepan of boiling water. Add   water to the chocolate. Melt on low heat.

Separate the eggs and when chocolate is fully melted and taken off the heat, add the yolks, sugar and bring the mixture up to heat, stirring constantly.   Remove immediately from heat, add the brandy and beat.

In a clean bowl beat the egg whites until stiff and then add the whites to the cooled chocolate mix, slowly folding them in, a little at a time.
Place the mixture into 8 large glasses or ramekin dishes. Refrigerate. Serve with a dollop of whipped cream and grated chocolate and fresh berries.

Orange Cup Cakes
125 grams of plain flour
125 grams caster sugar
125 grams of butter
2 eggs
Grated rind and juice of half orange
2 drops of orange essence
2 tspns baking powder.
A little milk.
Topping
75 grams of butter
100 grams icing sugar
1 tspn grated orange rind
2 tspns of orange juice.
Whole almonds

Cream the butter and sugar until pale and creamy. Separate the eggs and beat yolks into the butter mixture. Add orange rind, essence and juice .Beat until well mixed. Add baking powder to the flour and sift in small amounts into the cream mixture. Fold the flour in carefully. Beat egg whites until peaking and fold into the mixture. Add a little milk if needed to make a thick dropping consistency.

Fill paper cup cases to just over half and bake in the oven at 180 degrees for approx. 20 mins or until the cakes are well risen. Allow to cool and top with creamed butter and sugar to which rind and orange juice has been added. Dot an almond on the top.

Scones
MadamPam likes these with jam and cream. Apparently cream, especially Cornish clotted cream, when served on top of a homemade scone is perfectly fine. Tanice

450

doesn't dare question this dietary anomaly.
300 grams of plain flour
75 grams butter
4 tspns of baking powder
½ tspn salt
1 tspn cream of tartar
Approx 1 cup of buttermilk
Beaten egg and milk mix

Add baking powder, salt and cream of tartar to flour and sift into a bowl. Cut butter into small pieces and rub through flour to make crumbs. Add buttermilk and make into a soft dough. Turn out onto floured board and lightly shape. Over shaping or kneading makes the flour elastic and tough. Roll out gently into a thick layer. Use a scone cutter to make shapes or slice with a knife into triangles. Brush with beaten egg and milk mix.

Place on greased baking tray and put in the oven at 220 degrees for approx. 15 minutes or until golden. Remove from oven and test the scone center with a thin knife. If still sticky return to the oven for another 10 minutes at 170 deg. Cool
To serve; split, spread with strawberry jam and whipped cream.

Ginger Oat Cakes
1 mug porridge oats
½ mug plain flour
80 grams of butter
200 ml water
1 tspn salt
1 tspn bicarbonate of soda
2 tspns ground ginger
1 tspn cinnamon
1 tspn ginger puree

3 tablspns maple syrup
Lemon curd topping

Combine flour, bicarbonate of soda, salt, ground ginger and cinnamon and put through a sieve into a bowl. Add the porridge oats and mix well.
In a saucepan heat the butter in the water and when melted add the maple syrup and puree of ginger.
Make a well in the dry ingredients and pour in the butter mixture. Mix up.
Place medium spoonfuls on a greased baking tray or into a muffin tray and bake at 170 degrees for 15 minutes or until golden.
Cool and top with lemon curd or berry jam.

Gingerbread Shapes
Laura persuaded the girls to get involved with this at Woolacombe when the rain was teaming down.
350 grams plain flour
1 tablespoon of ground ginger
250 grams of brown sugar
170 grams of butter
2 cups of black treacle or Molasses
1 tablspn of lemon juice
1 tspn of bicarb of soda
2 tspn baking powder
½ tspn of salt

Sift the flour into a bowl and add all the other dry ingredients. In a saucepan melt the butter and sugar and treacle and bring up to simmer. Add this to the dry ingredients and stir well making into a dough. It will be sticky. Cover and leave in the fridge for a few hours or overnight.
Flour a board liberally and roll out the dough making

452

the shapes of your choice.

Bake at 200 degrees for approx. 15 minutes or until golden brown. Put on a rack to cool and then sugar ice to your design.

Roti Bread (Makes approx. 12 rotis)

Served at the Caribbean Soiree to accompany Curried Chicken

400 grams of plain flour

2 tspns of baking powder

½ tspn salt

2 tablspns Sunflower oil

¾ mug of boiling water

2 tablspns of melted clarified butter

Vegetable oil for frying

Optional- ½ cup of cumin seeds or 3 mashed cloves of garlic.

Sift the flour and baking powder into a bowl. Add the cumin seeds or garlic. Add the sunflower oil and the boiling water. Mix up with a spoon into a dough ball. On a floured board knead the dough for about 5 minutes. Cover with a damp cloth and allow to rest for 30 minutes.

Take a piece of dough and roll into a large circle of about 3 cm thickness. Brush the circle with clarified butter. Roll up like a Swiss Roll and slice into approximately forefinger length sections. Form these sections into circles and press down into a circle shape with the heel of the hand. Dust with flour and roll thinly into a larger circle. Repeat with the rest of the dough.

Use a little oil and clarified butter in the pan and bring up to almost smoking temperature. Fry rotis individually. Cook for about 15 seconds and then turn over. The roti should rise a little and bubble. Turn again until parts of it are well browned.

Place on plate with kitchen paper between each one and cover.

Rotis are best made on the day of eating but will keep in aluminum foil and an airtight plastic bag for 24 hours if needed. Allow to cool before storing.

Reheat individually in a hot pan or leave in foil and reheat at 220 degrees for approx. 15 minutes.

Tanice's Desert Island Pineapple Cake (10 People)
Tanice made 3 of these for the Caribbean soiree.
225 grams of self-rising flour
2 tspns baking powder
3 eggs – separated
225 gram caster sugar
225 grams butter
Zest and juice of a lemon
2 tablspns Rum
2 tablspns ground almonds
Whipped cream
Fresh chopped pineapple /berries.

Cream butter and sugar until creamy white. Add the beaten yolks, brandy, zest and lemon juice. Beat well. Add the ground almonds and mix well. Sift the flour and baking powder and fold into yolk mixture a little at a time. Add a little milk if the mixture is too thick.

Beat the egg whites until peaked and fold into flour mixture.

Pour mixture into 2 greased 20 cm cake tins and bake at 180 degrees for approx. 30 minutes or until firm to touch. Test middle with a knife. If still sticky cook for an extra few minutes.

Remove and cool on a wire rack.

For the filling, whip some cream and fold in small pieces of fresh pineapple or berries. Sandwich the 2 halves together.

Sides and Topping

To make the desert island. For the effect of sand -
Make enough rich butter cream icing flavored with
vanilla essence and colored with orange essence and
cover the sides of the cake. Keep enough for the desert
island on the top. Mix up some icing sugar and water
with some drops of blue coloring for the sea. On the top,
run a band of blue icing in a ring around the edge of the
cake leaving the center circle. Fill the center island with
the orange butter icing.

To decorate, place little palm trees on the island and
round chocolate sweets as coconuts. Cut small banana
boat shapes out of fresh melon and dot on the sea. Add
colored cocktail parasols round the sides of the cake.

Bon Appetit!

44851613R00254

Made in the USA
Middletown, DE
18 June 2017